BLOO

Every assassin had a Midnight Marauder. Ev Towne, the Little Luthien killer, *he* had a name. So what sounded good? He needed a real kick-ass name because he was going to be famous.

Thinking, he trailed his fingers absently over the contours of a small caliber handgun. A plinker. Do the job, sure, but it wasn't BIG. He wanted BIG. He wanted POWER. He wanted a cannon, something blocky and loud, with a blinding muzzle flash and enough recoil to break his wrist. Something like the Northwind Star 720 tucked in a quick-draw holster on his left hip.

His ears pricked at a far-off rumble, a little like thunder. A car: a ground vehicle, not a hover. He edged his head around. Saw a glint of fading sunlight off chrome, and then heard the crackle, pop, and squeal of rock as the car pulled into the cemetery's gravel drive.

Peeling away from the monument, he knelt before the stone angel. The earth nipped his knees through his trousers. He placed his walking stick within reach of his left hand, shoved the handgun into his left coat pocket, and bowed his head: just an old man praying at the forgotten grave of a fallen comrade. He smelled dust kicked up by the car's tires, and then cool blue-white halogen light from the car's headlamps broke over his back, throwing his shadow into crisp, bold relief. Then he caught the pop of a car door and the crunch of a boot against gravel.

At that moment, for a reason he couldn't explain, his eyes again drifted to the stone angel. The angel's left wing was gone and its face tear-streaked with age. The angel clutched a sword in its left hand and the Scales of Justice in its right.

Then, like a revelation, he knew his name, and soon, very soon, *this* man would know his wrath: that of the Angel of Death, the Avatar of Judgment. Because *he* was Gabriel.

...shed by New American Library, a division of
...nguin Group (USA) Inc., 375 Hudson Street,
... York, New York 10014, USA

...nguin Group (Canada), 90 Eglinton Avenue East, Suite 700, Toronto,
...ario M4P 2Y3, Canada (a division of Pearson Penguin Canada Inc.)
...nguin Books Ltd., 80 Strand, London WC2R 0RL, England
...nguin Ireland, 25 St. Stephen's Green, Dublin 2,
...land (a division of Penguin Books Ltd.)
...nguin Group (Australia), 250 Camberwell Road, Camberwell, Victoria 3124,
...ustralia (a division of Pearson Australia Group Pty. Ltd.)
...enguin Books India Pvt. Ltd., 11 Community Centre, Panchsheel Park,
...ew Delhi - 110 017, India
...nguin Group (NZ), cnr Airborne and Rosedale Roads, Albany,
...uckland 1310, New Zealand (a division of Pearson New Zealand Ltd.)
...enguin Books (South Africa) (Pty.) Ltd., 24 Sturdee Avenue,
...osebank, Johannesburg 2196, South Africa

Penguin Books Ltd., Registered Offices:
80 Strand, London WC2R 0RL, England

First published by Roc, an imprint of New American Library,
a division of Penguin Group (USA) Inc.

First Printing, December 2005
10 9 8 7 6 5 4 3 2 1

PUBLISHER'S NOTE

This is a work of fiction. Names, characters, places, and incidents either are
the product of the author's imagination or are used fictitiously, and any resemblance to actual persons, living or dead, business establishments, events, or
locales is entirely coincidental.

The publisher does not have any control over and does not assume any
responsibility for author or third-party Web sites or their content.

MECHWARRIOR
DARK AGE

BLOOD
AVATAR

A BATTLETECH™ NOVEL

Ilsa J. Bick

A ROC BOOK

For Dean, who showed me the way

Acknowledgments

Anyone trolling some of the message boards devoted to *BattleTech* and *MechWarrior* this past summmer has doubtless heard that this book is a bit of a departure. That's probably right and I'm as interested as anyone in how this is going to shake out. I'm sure everyone will let me know.

Yet no writer does anything in someone else's sandbox without the say-so of the people, charged with ensuring the integrity of that sandbox—or universe. In that, I have been blessed with two of the most flexible editors any writer could ask for, both of whom gave me an opportunity to try something just a little different. And so, my profound thanks and gratitude go to:

Sharon Turner Mulvihill, for her patience, enthusiasm, and willingness to stand back a bit and let me push the envelope while making sure I didn't bust anything. Thanks for thinking of me.

Randall Bills (whose sigh of relief—when he realized that he wouldn't get nearly as many panicky e-mails this time around—I heard *waaayyy* over here), for his great good humor and lack of ego; and for being the kind of guy who didn't get his knickers in a twist even when I interrupted for about the thousandth time. Next time, buddy, I clean up the coffee.

Last, my love goes to my husband, David, and our daughters, Carolyn and Sarah. Thanks, guys, for soldiering on, foraging for nuts and twigs when I forgot about little things like, oh, groceries—and, most especially, for not making good on that threat to eat one of the cats.

The Messiah will come only when he is no longer necessary, he will come only one day after his arrival, he will not come on the last day, but on the last day of all.

—Franz Kafka

Prologue

New Bonn, Denebola
Prefecture VIII, Republic of the Sphere
9 December 3135

All Jack Ramsey needed was one scream. Then he'd kill the son of a bitch.

What Ramsey got instead was snow hissing over brick and wind roaring through ferrocrete and titanium canyons like a hundred DropShips. He stood at the lip of an alley, pressed against the ice-slicked brick of a condemned tenement. Snow sheeted in frigid gusts, stinging his face and neck, like getting slapped with broken glass.

Ramsey was a big man, with muscular shoulders and forearms, and large, scarred hands. His eyes were a startling blue-green framed by angular cheekbones and a broad forehead. He wore police-issue cold weather gear: thick-soled black boots, a black parka with a gold police insignia, insulated pants, gloves lined with olefin-polyester insulation and gel heat crystals, and a black, militia-standard watch cap.

Where was *McFaine*? This had to be the place because Ramsey felt the monster like a malevolent force. They had this weird . . . *connection.* Or maybe Ramsey was just obsessed. Bad enough to be out in a blizzard, tracking a maniac, and probably suicidal to do it with no backup. But McFaine's message was explicit: *Come alone. Tell no one.* Or, well, McFaine would kill the five boys, and wouldn't Ramsey feel terrible about that?

McFaine wasn't bluffing. Last time, Ramsey went in with a micro-SatNav and a backup team. Oh, he found the killing floor—strewn with body parts, not all from the same child, like McFaine had taken a snip here, a slice there. And scrawled with blood on brick: *Naughty boy.*

Another gale tore through the alley. Feeling the cold. His face was wet where it wasn't half-frozen and melt-water trickled down his chin and neck. Even with the gloves, his fingers were numb, and his toes didn't feel like much of anything. He transferred his personal carry, a blocky Skye Raptor 50-Mag semi-auto, to his left hand and flexed the fingers of his right. Running out of time . . .

"Goddamn it," he said. He talked to the storm. "Where is he? I've done everything he's wanted. Now where *is* he?"

Later, Ramsey thought all McFaine wanted was for Ramsey to beg. Because then it came: the thin, quavering wail of a child's scream.

From the left, *left*! And there, a sliver of yellow light where there had been nothing an instant before. *Basement window.* The dark rectangle of an alley door.

Go, go! A swift cop-kick and Ramsey burst through the door, out of the storm and into near-total darkness. He spun a full circle, Raptor at the ready. A sense of a short hallway to his left and ahead, the black-on-black of a stairwell going down. The air smelled of char, old urine, and dead rats. *Basement, basement, go!* Moving, heavy boots clapping ferrocrete, nothing to be done about the noise, his gun out. At the bottom of the stairs now, where it was no longer dark but grainy with a fan of weak, yellow light coming from Ramsey's left, and then Ramsey heard a child sob.

No, no, no*!* He kicked—short, hard. The basement

door snapped back, rebounded against its jamb, and Ramsey muscled through—and then he stopped, cold.

The basement reeked of fear, sweat, rotting flesh and wet copper. The cinderblock walls and poured concrete floor were smeary with old blood cracked into a rust-colored jigsaw pattern like a crackle glaze. The blood was old because four of the boys were in pieces, disarticulated limbs heaped like clearance items at a sidewalk sale. A pegged wallboard held McFaine's toys: pliers, wire cutters. A handsaw clogged with gore. But the reason Ramsey knew that *only* four boys were dead were the heads floating in specimen jars: eyes open, mouths agape in silent screams.

The last child, the fifth, was still alive. The boy was naked, roped to a chair with barbed wire. Crimson rivulets oozed down the boy's bare chest and legs, and there were quills of stitches where the boy had lost two fingers at the second joint and the entire length of his right big toe. An odd metallic torque hung around the boy's neck.

And there, crouched behind the boy, was Quentin McFaine.

"Dad." The boy's lips twisted with terror. *"Dad?"*

"I'm right here, son." Ramsey fought to stay calm. *Just get McFaine to move his head a few centimeters to the right and then* . . . "I'll get you out of here."

"Oh, Jack, so anxious to leave?" McFaine's voice was husky, sensual, sibilant as a snake, and just a little pouty. His shoulder-length honey-blond hair was pulled into a ponytail that shone like spun gold. His cobalt blue eyes were fringed by luxuriant lashes and set above an aquiline nose and generous lips sculpted into a perfect cupid's bow. "God, I thought you'd *never* get here. I waited as long as I could with the others, but then you didn't come and what's a mother to do?"

Ramsey put some steel in his voice. "Step away from the boy, McFaine. Then stand up, slowly, hands behind your head. You don't do what I say, I *will* kill you."

"And blow your boy's head off? Because you will, either way."

"What are you talking about?" But Ramsey already knew. *That collar . . .*

McFaine pointed at a nest of pipes hugging exposed ceiling joists. "A sensor net: programmed to register little things like gunshots or burnt cordite. I knew you'd bring your slugthrower because you hate the smell of burned meat, don't you, Jack? And I'm not bluffing." McFaine tapped his wrist, and the room filled with the sound of the raging storm and Ramsey's voice: *Goddamn it. Where is he, where . . . ?* McFaine tapped his wrist again, and Ramsey's voice cut out. "I'm pretty good with sensor webs. Shoot me, and your boy loses his head."

God, no . . . "What do you want, McFaine?"

McFaine laughed silently, like a dog. "You *know*," he drawled, his fingers skimming the boy's bloody chest, his pointed pink snake's tongue darting to taste his index finger. "Ah, Jack, *you* know what I want. I want *you*, and I won't make a trade."

Ramsey was silent.

"Cat got your tongue, Jack? I hope not. I was looking forward to that item myself. Admit it, you want me. You want to get your hands on me, *all* over me . . ."

"Shut up, McFaine."

"Because you *want* me." McFaine gave a low, throaty laugh. "I'm in your dreams, aren't I, Jack, your cop wet dreams?"

"Shut *up!*" Ramsey's voice was hoarse with rage and desperation. "Just shut the fuck up!"

"Temper, temper, Jack," McFaine said, and then, suddenly, he stood: a smooth, seamless unfolding of his legs and hips. He wore jeans and a black turtleneck, and now McFaine's long fingers worked, gathering folds, peeling the sweater from his hairless, sculpted chest and abdomen. "Come on, Jack. Show me what you've got."

Ramsey hesitated, his heart booming in his chest. He sighted down the Raptor's barrel. *Do it, kill him, kill him!*

Instead, he broke at the elbow and thumbed on the safety.

"Ah, Jack." McFaine gave a languid lizard's grin, his teeth stained orange with blood. "Mano a mano, like gladiators. Skin to skin and winner take all. Now why don't you get out of those hot things," McFaine said, as he tugged at his belt, "and down to business?"

1

Noah Schroeder huddled in an ancient tree house just up the hill from the old, haunted Roman Catholic graveyard and figured that, another couple minutes, these cigarettes were gonna kill him for sure.

And just a couple of hours ago, he'd felt pretty good. Friday, end of another school week, zip homework. He'd biked eight klicks out of town, working up a sweat and going so fast the scenery was a blur of brown and gray, of fields chunky with stubble and stands of craggy, denuded trees. The west wind blowing in from the distant snow-covered peaks of the Kendrakes was cold enough to make his ears hurt, and the tip of his nose felt like a brass button. But the sky was bright turquoise and cloudless, so when Noah looked up, he spied a pair of thin white lines drawn on the dome of the sky. DropShips, freighters probably, outbound from New Bonn spaceport to the system's jump point five days away. (Not that he'd ever seen a DropShip, or the spaceport, for that matter. New Bonn was seven, eight hours south, but the city might as well be on another planet. Farway was, well, far away.)

Joey handed over the cigarette. Noah said, "Wow, thanks," wondered what the heck was wrong with him, and sucked. Smoke blasted his mouth, and he felt his head expand to the size of a *Mule*-class DropShip from the nicotine buzz. He thought he might pass out, or vomit, or just roll over, arms and legs in the air like an Amaris dung beetle and die, or maybe all three.

Instead, he said in a thin, strangled voice, "Yeah, wow, Joey, man, this is *great*." Then Noah doubled over and hacked out smoke and what felt like half a lung.

Well, *that* made Joey Ketchum and Troy Underhill nearly bust a gut. Joey said, "Whoa, whoa, Jesus, don't drop it!" He grabbed Noah's arm and tweezed the cigarette free as Noah retched. "You know how hard it was to lift that pack?"

"How hard?" Troy asked.

"Hard." Joey screwed the cigarette into the side of his mouth then swept up a pack of greasy, dog-eared cards and started a Solitaire game of Kerensky's Run. At thirteen and change, Joey had three months on Noah and seven on Troy. Joey was also a budding sociopath: ironic, considering that Joey's father was the local sheriff.

"I thought Bert was gonna PPC my ass, he gave me the evil eye," he said, the cigarette marking time. Joey slapped down a Black Knight Six, squinted through a curl of cigarette smoke, made a horsey sound. "Piece a crap deck," he said, sweeping the cards up and butting them together. "Can't win Kerensky's Run, you don't got but three Binaries." Tossing the pack into a corner, Joey knocked a tube of ash from the cigarette, settled his back against a rotting slab of plywood and blew a streamer of gray smoke. "Man, I'm so cold my dick's gonna fall off."

"You got to inhale," Troy Underhill said, with the sage air of experience. Troy's mom smoked, a lot, and Troy usually reeked like an ashtray. "Smoke's gotta come out your nose."

"Yeah? You gonna to show us, big shot?"

"I *would*, only I *can't*," Troy said, puffing up. He was a scrawny kid with thick glasses, oversized ears and a small pointy chin that made him look like a myopic elf. Troy also had diabetes. At first, Troy's mom chased after Troy with orange juice and snacks. That stopped when Troy's dad walked out three years ago, and Troy got an insulin pump. Since then, Troy's mom just refilled Troy's prescriptions and worked as a waitress down at Ida's combo bakery and diner. She also made money another way, but no one liked to talk about that.

Troy said, "Doc Summers says if I smoke, my toes'll fall off on account of my capillaries getting all constricted."

"No shit," Noah said, his mouth still clogged with saliva. Noah liked saying *shit* and said it pretty often when his mom wasn't around. (But not *fuck*: that you saved up for when you wanted to make an impression.) He spat and said, "No shit, really?"

"I shit you not. Doc says if I'm not careful, I could end up in a *comma*."

Snorting, Joey dropped the smoldering butt and ground it out with the toe of his sneaker. "It's *coma*, you dope on a rope."

"How come your toes might fall off?" Noah asked Troy.

"Doc says it's because diabetics don't get good blood flow to their distal extremities on account of capillary constriction," Troy said, like he'd memorized a textbook.

"Yeah, problem like that, and your dick's gonna die," Joey said. "You ain't never gonna get it up. Everyone knows you got to have capillary constriction to get it up."

A shadow of worry flitted across Troy's face. "I *know* that. But *everybody* knows that the capillaries in your dick ain't the same as the capillaries in your toes."

"Naw, man, the capillaries in your dick . . . they're really delicate. I bet your dick's gonna fall off, maybe right in the middle of the cafeteria."

"Will *not*!" Troy spluttered, his pale cheeks flaming with sudden color.

"Joey," Noah said.

"Yessir, there'll be this little glassy tinkle." Joey shook his head, mournfully. "Troy's dick going to ground."

Troy was the color of a prune. "Whuh . . . whuh . . . !" He lunged for Joey, but Noah planted a hand on Troy's chest. "Hey, at least I *got* a dick to fall off, dickweed!" Troy shouted.

"Troy." Noah shoved again. "*Quit* it."

"So sad," Joey said. "A tragedy."

"Yeah, *yeah?*" Troy lunged again and Noah shoved him back. "Well, *up* yours, Joey." Troy threw Joey the finger. "Man, you can just sit on it and spin."

"Can't do that," said Joey, calmly. "A finger's a distal extremity. So I sit on that finger and that finger's gonna . . ."

Noah cut in. "Joey?"

"Yeah?"

"Shut the fuck up."

Twilight turned the air grainy, washing out color until everything was gray. From the west came the low wail of a landtrain.

"Six o'clock," Joey said. "Silver Star out of Clovis. Gonna get dark as tar in another forty-five minutes, an hour. We got to go."

"Yeah," Noah said, but he didn't want to leave. The tree house—a ramshackle construction fifteen meters up and shoehorned tight against the main stem of a Neurasian maple—felt peaceful. The maple was part of a grove and very old, its trunk scarred by generations of jack-knives and mini-lasers.

But Joey was right. So they climbed down: Joey first, then Troy and, finally, Noah making his way down flat, half-meter boards nailed to the trunk. The steps were even more fragile than the house, and Noah took it slow. This summer, they'd better nail up some new boards. Otherwise, someone was liable to slip and break his neck.

At the bottom, the boys fanned out for their bikes. When they were still little kids, they'd taken to hiding their bikes in a stand of high grass about seventy meters right of the grove. Why they started hiding the bikes in the first place, no one remembered and now it was just habit. Noah had reached down for his bike when he straightened again and cocked his head.

"What?" Joey asked.

Noah looked back to the lip of a hill that led down

to the graveyard and the road just beyond, and took a few steps in that direction. "You hear something?"

The killer heard the wail of the Silver Star, splitting the air like a clarion call. He was hunkered out of sight, a gnarled walking stick along his left leg, his back against the broad pedestal of an ancient grave. The grave canted left, top-heavy with an angel carved from veined gray marble. The icy stone leeched through his old man's rumpled overcoat and dusky blue wool sweater, walking chills up and down the ladder of his spine. The wind didn't help either: a light westerly breeze that riffled his white hair and made his eyes water.

He'd set the meet for six-thirty: not quite full dark around these parts but close. Nothing to do but wait. And think.

Every assassin had a name like Jackal, Scorpion, Midnight Marauder. Even whack-jobs like that one on Towne, the Little Luthien killer, *he* had a name. So what sounded good? He needed a real kick-ass name because he was going to be famous.

Thinking, he trailed his fingers absently over the contours of a small caliber handgun. A plinker. Do the job, sure, but it wasn't BIG. He wanted BIG. He wanted POWER. He wanted a cannon, something blocky and loud, with a blinding muzzle flash and enough recoil to break his wrist. Something like the Northwind Star 720 tucked in a quick-draw holster on his left hip. (So okay, fine, he cheated. The Handler hadn't said not to *bring* the cannon. He just wasn't supposed to *use* it because of the mess.)

His ears pricked at a far-off rumble, a little like thunder. A car: a ground vehicle, not a hover. He edged his head around. Saw a glint of fading sunlight off chrome, and then heard the crackle, pop, and squeal of rock as the car pulled into the cemetery's gravel drive. The graveyard drive meandered right and then left before angling right again. He knew he wouldn't be visible until that final right turn.

Peeling away from the monument, he knelt before the stone angel. The earth nipped his knees through his trousers. He placed his walking stick within reach of his left hand, shoved the handgun into his left coat pocket, and bowed his head: just an old man praying at the forgotten grave of a fallen comrade. He smelled dust kicked up by the car's tires, and then cool blue-white halogen light from the car's headlamps broke over his back, throwing his shadow into crisp, bold relief. Then the car's engine sputtered and died. In the sudden silence, the killer heard nothing but the tick-tick-tick of the car's muffler. But he didn't move. His skin prickled as his heart banged in his chest, and his mouth went a little dry. Then he caught the pop of a car door and the crunch of a boot against gravel.

At that moment, for a reason he couldn't explain, his eyes again drifted to the stone angel. The angel's left wing was gone and its face tear-streaked with age. The angel clutched a sword in its left hand and the Scales of Justice in its right.

Then, like a revelation, he knew his name, and soon, very soon, *this* man would know his wrath: that of the Angel of Death, the Avatar of Judgment.

Because *he* was Gabriel.

Frederic Limyanovich was mad enough to spit. A time warp, that is what Farway was, and this cell a product of a bygone era. Farway was so strange. No hovers, no 'Mechs; guns instead of lasers. Bicycles! He had landed in some kind of prehistoric backwater, surrounded by the moral and political equivalent of Neanderthals. The problem was there were more of these kinds of cells— quite probably, many more than his superiors suspected—scattered through the Inner Sphere. Oh, the initial principle had been sound. Insert small, cohesive cells to work behind the scenes, root out the enemy. The longer these operatives were in place, the more they infiltrated all levels of local government and social structure.

Only one drawback: When The Republic was born, everyone forgot about the cells. But the cells had not forgotten. Some still thought they were at war.

And another thing bothered him. How had they tracked him down in Slovakia? How could they have *known* about him? And the coded request they used was so old, he had to look it up. The instructions were quite specific, though, and he had brought the requested . . . materials. But he would not be the first to offer them up.

As it happened, they wanted to talk. Brother to brother, they said. To be brought up to speed, they said. To better understand how we are to finish what we began during the Jihad and so much easier now because the various factions—the Houses and upstarts—were turning on one another, gobbling up territory, consuming themselves like snakes eating their tails.

So he came, they met, he talked. The Jihad was finished, he said. Make your peace and be done with it, he said. Ah, but he knew which of them was not convinced. That old one, the one who sat and smoked until a cloud of blue veiled the old one like a shawl—but Limyanovich saw unspoken thoughts behind those glittering black eyes.

Well, talking once again would do no good, even if with another representative who, he already knew, would be as intransigent as the old one with the black eyes and blue smoke. And to talk about what? More revolution? Perhaps soon, but not now. This was not yet their time.

Limyanovich was so boiling mad, he nearly missed his turn in the fading light. The turnoff for the cemetery was on his left, and poorly marked. A streaked, dingy verdigris monument plaque, probably bronze in another life, announced its religious affiliation as Old Roman Catholic, and the cemetery's name: Our Mother of Sorrows. A crumbling stone pieta of the Virgin Mary and the dead Jesus perched above the plaque. Mary's nose was gone, as was her left arm, broken off at the elbow. Jesus had fared little better and looked as if someone had taken a sledgehammer and smashed the head and amputated both legs at the knees.

As he eased the car onto a pocked gravel drive, he flicked on the car's halogens against the waning sunlight. Glowing, ash-colored dust clouds boiled in the beams like smoke. The chassis swayed, bouncing as the tires found every single rut and depression. He drove slowly, his eyes ticking over headstones and degraded monuments that canted at bizarre angles like broken teeth. A right, then a left, and then as he eased the car right again, the halogens swung onto the back of a man kneeling before a grave.

Limyanovich rolled the car to within fifty meters then braked but kept the engine running as he weighed the threat. A shock of white hair and a walking stick . . . an old man. Limyanovich's gaze raked over gravestones then cut right to scrutinize the rise of a drumlin. The hill was covered in a nearly solid carpet of dead leaves but had no convenient depressions in which to hide. Certainly, a sharpshooter could take him from the hill but, somehow, he didn't think these people were that sophisticated.

But they are stubborn enough to be dangerous. Extermination is the only option. Space the executions far enough apart, and no one will look twice.

He cut the engine. Through the dusty windscreen, he watched as the old man stirred, groped for . . . Was that a cane? No, a gnarled walking stick as knobby as an arthritic finger, and Limyanovich watched as the old man hauled himself up like a winded mountain climber. Another ancient: soft in the mind and stubborn as a Marik goat. *Look at him, tottering over with his too-baggy trousers and shabby coat!*

Still . . . Reaching over, Limyanovich opened the glove compartment and withdrew a slender needler. These people might be bumpkins, but he was no fool.

Popping the door, he swung his legs around, unfolded his bulk and stood, all his senses alert. He was a big, physically imposing man, with a barrel chest and coarse features, and used his bulk to his advantage. He heard nothing but the sigh of a slight breeze and the hard crack of rock grinding beneath his shoes as he shifted his weight. Colder now that the sun was nearly gone. His breath steamed. He eyed the old man, the way the ancient walked. It had been Limyanovich's experience that imposters often forgot that it was one thing to put on a disguise, but quite another to inhabit the part. Uneven rock here, and the truly old—well, one that looked as ancient as this fossil, with his hunched back and wild hair and his right hand in his coat pocket, *very* interesting—frequently lost their footing.

As if on cue, the old man skidded and came down on

one knee with a startled yelp. Limyanovich didn't move. Instead, he watched, coolly, as the ancient clambered upright, swaying like a survivor on a raft lost at sea. But then, yes, that right hand sneaking back to his pocket . . .

Limyanovich waited until the old man was three meters away. Then he said, "Stop where you are, and do exactly as I say, or I will kill you and let the rats eat your eyes."

"No, no, not rats," the old man said. His voice quavered with age. "Out here, we got crows." But he stopped, his oversized coat flapping about his legs like a JumpShip's sun-sail half-ripped from its moorings. The old man squinted against the harsh halogen glare. "But why so hostile, Comrade?"

"Comrade." Limyanovich wanted to scream with frustration. "Listen to yourself. You sound like a peasant. You want to talk, eh? Then take your right hand out of your pocket. Slowly, and turn out the pocket at the same time."

The old man complied, though with a Herculean effort worthy of an Elemental. Limyanovich waited, his eyes flicking between the old man's face and the hand. Finally, the old man managed and the white liner drooped like a limp tongue. "There," the ancient said. "You see?"

"I see that your pocket is as empty as your head." Still, Limyanovich relaxed a fraction. "I have said all I have to say, old man. I should not have to repeat myself. We are done talking."

"But we would ask you to reconsider." The old man shuffled a little two-step, moving slightly to his left. "There are those of us more than willing to do the work."

"Your ideas belong to another century." Limyanovich's accent was heavy, guttural with rolling *r*s and long vowels. "It is time for new thinking and bold plans."

The old man nodded mournfully. "We thought you might say that. And that is most unfortunate for, you see, we *do* know."

That made Limyanovich pause. The old man's eyes sparkled with intelligence, but surely that was an illusion, a trick of the light. "Know what, old man?"

"That you have certain *items*." The old man paused, sidled closer. "We believe that it is best for all concerned if you entrust them to us."

"Items? What are you talking about?" But now a dark premonition touched Limyanovich. How could the old man know? How could *any* of them?

A small voice in his head, the one he associated with his first and best Handler: *Kill him. Kill the old man and get out* now.

Limyanovich listened to that voice. "Bah," he said, edging back. "We are done talking." His hand tightened around his needler, and his eyes ticked from side to side, searching for confederates.

His Handler, again, chiding: *No, no, there is no one else; they would have killed you already, you fool. Kill him, do it now, do it* now!

Now! Limyanovich was already pivoting, readying the needler as he said, "There is nothing to discuss, old man, nothing . . ." And that was as far as he got.

The old man moved, impossibly fast, whipping the walking stick around, the air parting with the whistle of its passage. With a wild battle cry, the old man jammed the stick into Limyanovich's chest, hard. Then, a loud *bang*, a flash of orange.

Limyanovich screamed. Pain rocketed into his lungs, roared up his throat. He tried pulling in a breath to scream again, and couldn't. No air, no *air*! Clawing now at his chest. Aware that his hands were wet with blood. Couldn't breathe, no air! Rock bit his knees as he buckled, his lungs pulling, pulling. . . . And then he was drowning as hot, fresh blood boiled in the back of his throat.

From the moment his chest exploded and his lungs shredded, Frederic Limyanovich was already dead in all but a technical sense. He would have died later rather than sooner, though not by much. As it was, he died flat on his back, still clutching the needler, his mouth gawping like a beached fish, and his vision constricting to a single point that he realized, at the very last second, was not a halo, or a ball of white light but the black circle of a gun barrel aiming for the naked space above his nose.

Limyanovich had time for one last thought so finely

edged and sharp the letters might have been cut out of black diamonds: *NO . . . !*

The scene was like a bad holodrama done in slow motion. First, out of the west and the dying sun, the car rocked down the gravel path, the headlamps of its high beams bouncing off broken headstones and toppled statues—the statues there and gone in an instant, like the briefly illuminated contents of a dark attic. And then as the lights swung right, Noah saw a man, haloed in white light, kneeling at the grave. The man was old; his hair was wild, and Noah realized, with a start: *I know him.*

But then the driver's side door popped, and then a much larger man emerged. The man was a giant: broad at the shoulders and as tall as an Elemental, with swarthy skin, a coal black mustache and a mane of long hair blacker than obsidian. The men began to argue, the large one shouting now, his accent hard—and then, in the blink of an eye, the old man whipped his walking stick round. So fast! A loud *bang* and a spray of orange flame, and Noah thought: *Shotgun.*

And then the big man was down, the white light sheeting over his body like glare ice. It had happened so fast, Noah was stunned. He couldn't move, couldn't think. He could only watch as the old man—upright now, not shuffling along but *moving*—stuck out his left arm, the pistol in his hand as clear as if scissored out of black paper. Another spray of orange, much smaller, arcing to the large man's forehead—*not a laser, or a needler, that's a* gun—and then the report, not sharp like the whip crack of a rifle shot but a flat, broken sound: *bap!*

Then Troy screamed.

Straightening, the old man spun round, saw them, then started up the hill, moving fast.

So fast, I didn't know he could run that fast! Noah was up, hauling back on Troy's arm. "Come on," Noah shouted. "Come on! We got to run, *run!*"

They wheeled and ran, Troy stumbling, gasping, "Oh, oh, oh, oh!" The hill was in near-complete darkness now and the boys veered left, heading for the high grass. Joey was further ahead, running flat-out. They had to get to the grass, grab their bikes, get out of there. Run, run, run, *run*! In the space of less than half a minute, Noah waded into grass that dragged around his chest and legs. He couldn't see anything, and for the first time, he realized just how dark darkness was. He could still make out gradations of blackness—the grasses were like a filmy gray sea—but the bikes . . .

Suddenly, Troy lurched forward, taking Noah down with him. Yelping in surprise, Noah twisted, smacked earth with his left shoulder, and felt the breath go whooshing out of his lungs in a sudden *huh!* The darkness spun, and he wanted to vomit. Moaning, he rolled, pushed up on all fours like a dog, and concentrated on dragging in a breath.

"My glasses!" Troy said, his thin whisper a bright line of panic etched in darkness. "I lost my *glasses!*"

"No time!" Noah wheezed. He pushed up on his thighs, sucked in air. His lungs were on fire. "We got to go. We got . . ." Something black rearing up next to his right elbow, and he spun around, terror jumpstarting his heart.

It was Joey. "I can't find the bikes!" Joey was panting, maybe crying. "I think we ran past them!"

"Oh, no, oh no no no no," Troy moaned. He crumpled into a tight ball, wrapping his arms over his head, tucking his chin into his chest. "Oh, no no no . . . !"

"Shut up!" Noah hissed, fury overcoming his fear. "Get up, get up! We got to go back. We just got to *do* it!"

"But we could hide," Joey whispered. "We can just hide, can't we?"

Noah opened his mouth, but his voice died in his throat. There was a heavy, thrashing noise, the kind of sound a man made rushing through meadow grass. Not directly behind, but close and in the cold, the sounds were much crisper, sharper as if chipped out of ice.

Jesus, he's fast*!*

Noah took one extra second to think. Open field, tall grass, but the trees, they were behind and right, and the bikes were on a straight line with the tree house. "Come on!" he whispered. He clutched Troy's hand with his left hand; Joey flanked his right. "This way!"

Troy balked. "You're going back. He'll get us, he'll get us. . . ."

"He'll get us if we *don't*, so just quit it, quit it, come on!" Noah said.

They went. Later, Noah would remember that it was like some horrible nightmare, the kind where you ran in slow-motion even though the monster just kept coming and coming. His heart battered his ribs; his lungs burned and his throat was raw. Time slowed down. He knew they were close to their bikes, but the monster had topped the rise and if he caught them, he would kill them.

Then, Noah's right foot whopped something hard, and he nearly fell. The bikes! Noah dropped Troy's hand and wrestled up his bike. Swinging his leg over the seat, his sneakers slipping off then finding the pedals, starting to pump. Joey, the faster and stronger of the three, was there and then gone, swallowed up in the darkness as he took off. "Come on, Troy, let's go!" Noah whispered.

"But I can't see!" Troy said, panicked. "I can't find my bike!"

Noah didn't even hesitate. Wheeling around, he leapt off his bike, let it fall, lunged for his friend. "Leave it, leave it, you can ride with me, we'll run and then you can—!"

He felt the bullet before he heard the shot: something humming a groove in the air just above his head followed by a *boom!* He ducked. Thought: *Big gun, more speed!* No time for the bikes, they had to run, go, go, go! Grabbing Troy's hand, dragging him up, legs churning now, free hand clawing air, running, running, run, run, they had to—!

The second shot missed. But the third one didn't.

2

After the cartridge exploded and that orange fire erupted like a volcano, Gabriel felt the power. The power was an organic thing blooming in his chest, as if some kind of god had slipped into the shell of his skin. The power was in him, and he *was* the power: stronger, better, more *alive* than he'd ever felt before.

And then, when things couldn't get any better, they did. When he drew the gun and put the muzzle a bare centimeter from Limyanovich's forehead and saw the look of naked terror in Limyanovich's eyes, Gabriel's pulse ramped up and his mouth tasted of the metallic edge of adrenalin.

That's right, look at it because I'm Death and your life is mine.

The gun kicked in his hand. There was flame, and Limyanovich's head twitched back. And then a ringing silence Gabriel wanted to fill with a howl but that, instead, someone else filled with a scream.

Behind. Up the hill! He wheeled round, looked up, and there! A twinkle of light against glass . . . no, *eyeglasses*. Somebody there!

Get him. His concentration focused to a point, laser bright. *Kill him before it's too late.*

Then he'd dropped the plinker, pulled out his 720 and pounded across the bowl of the graveyard, leaping for the hill. The hill was slick with leaves, and he slipped, coming down hard on the point of his left elbow and, suddenly, there was the barrel a centimeter from his left eye, so close he smelled steel and gun oil. *Careful. Jesus Christ, be careful.* Jamming the gun into the waistband of his old man's pants, floundering for traction, and then he was pulling himself up the hill, bent nearly double, his breath knifing his throat. And then he was on level ground, scanning the gray gloom of a field of meadow grasses spreading away to his left and, ahead and right, the denser blackness of trees. Nearly full dark now, stars in the sky and no moon because Denebola didn't have one.

He clamped his lips together, slowed his breathing so he could listen. Whoever was here couldn't have gone far. Then he heard a dry rustling, like crinkly dry paper. His eyes jerked left. Someone there. He squinted, slid forward, stepping carefully, wincing at the crackle of dry grasses underfoot. His overcoat caught and dragged, slowing him down. *Making too much noise.* But he didn't dare leave the coat behind. He might not find it again in the dark.

So, instead, he stopped moving. Cocked his head, listened. His calves tensed, ready to spring. Thought: *We're at the same disadvantage, only* I've *got the gun.*

For a few seconds—they seemed to last an age—he heard nothing more except the wild thrumming of blood in his ears. His elation was gone. In its place was dread laced with an almost preternatural calm. The calculus was simple. If he didn't catch whoever was here, the police would know where to look first. His plan depended on them looking elsewhere. Plus, he had to get rid of the body, the car. Worse, he had to make sure the police stayed away from the graveyard because . . .

A flurry of sudden movement and sound, and he thought, fleetingly, of grouse, flushed out of hiding. Now, he can see something . . . no, no, some*one*, a washed-out ash gray blur smeared against the dark. No, not one. His chest seized. *More* than one, at least two people, maybe three, scurrying like rats trying to stay ahead of water flooding a sinking ship, only these two were moving in erratic spurts, stopping, bending, fumbling for something on the ground . . .

Take them.

Gabriel reared up, gun drawn. Banged out a shot. Heard the *boom*, felt his wrist jerk with the recoil. Banged another, then another—and heard a scream.

Yes. He leapt forward, high-stepping, running . . . *Got you, I got you . . .*

Suddenly, as his right foot came down, he registered that he'd stepped on something hard. Then he was hurtling forward, sprawling over something metallic that ripped his right leg. He went down, crashing awkwardly to the ground, twisting left to absorb the impact, but he wasn't fast enough. His gun hand bammed against the ground, and the gun exploded next to his face, and he felt the hot gases dragged by a bullet whizzing past his left ear.

He lay there a moment, stunned, the gun still clutched in his left hand. His ears were still ringing, and the muzzle flash so intense he was blinking away bright afterimages. Jesus, that was *close*. He smelled the musty odor of cold dirt and dry grass. Sharp blades stabbed his cheeks. His right foot was still mired in something, but he was afraid to move. What if he'd broken something? His leg, his *leg* . . . He let go of the gun. Then, cautiously, he inched up a bit at a time, propped himself on his forearms, held himself there a few seconds, then pushed up to an awkward sit. Supporting his weight with his left hand, he felt down his pant leg. Just below the knee, his trousers were damp. A few centimeters further on, the fabric was ripped, and he touched something wet, tacky. He brought his fingers to his nose, smelled wet rust. He was bleeding. How bad? And what the hell was he tangled in? He patted around, felt rough rubber and then the thin metallic spokes of a bicycle wheel.

Using both hands, he eased his right foot free. His ankle hurt. Probably nothing more serious than a sprain, but the gash was bad. The large metal sprocket had chunked out flesh, but he couldn't tell how deep. Now that the first shock had passed, he could feel blood sludging down his shin.

He couldn't stay here. Had to get moving, get rid of the body. But what about the ones who'd seen him? He listened. Heard nothing.

But I hit one. I heard him scream. He might be hiding. He might be dead.

If not for his leg, he'd have searched until he was satisfied that whoever had been there was gone, or he found a body. But his leg . . . He couldn't afford to screw around.

There was one bright spot, though. Assuming that the one he hit hadn't died, that someone would have to go to the hospital.

And when he does, I'll know—and then I can take care of him once and for all.

He used his belt as a tourniquet, and then, somehow, he made it down the hill. His leg was screaming by the end, and despite the belt, blood pooled in his shoe. He squelched when he walked.

Gabriel ignored Limyanovich's body. Instead, he picked up his walking stick—glad now that he had it to lean on—and limped to a blocky granite mausoleum twenty meters from the stone angel. Patting along stone, his fingers tapped a large metal panel. The panel hadn't always been there, and legend had it that it had been used as a weapons cache during the Jihad. Gabriel hadn't found weapons: just dirt and mummified baby mice in a nest of leaves so desiccated they crumbled to dust.

Now he pried up the panel and withdrew a pryolene packet of powder, a glass vial containing a clear liquid, and then a separate egg-shaped blasting cap and a length of det cord. These he slid into a leather pouch and carefully placed in the right pocket of his overcoat. The hidden compartment was long enough to handle a laser rifle, and he slid in the murder weapon and his 720. He debated a long moment about the walking stick. With his bum leg, he could certainly put the stick to good use, but . . . Reluctantly he pushed in the stick to lie alongside his gun. Better not to be found with the stick. All someone had to do was look at the end to know something was wrong.

Limyanovich stank of runny feces and sharp urine. If Gabriel hadn't practiced on animals, he'd have been surprised, maybe a little disgusted. What *did* surprise him was how stiff Limyanovich was. Rigor mortis, already? That wasn't right. Rigor mortis didn't set in until hours after death. But Limyanovich's arms were stiff as the frozen joints of an AgroMech, his right hand clamped tight around a needler. No matter how much Gabriel pried, the fingers wouldn't budge. In the end, he had to break them to get at the needler.

A thorough pat down turned up a wallet, a sat-link and earbud. In the glare of the car's headlamps, Gabriel flipped open the wallet. A sheaf of bills. Identification. He stuffed the money into his back pocket but left the ID then pushed up and tossed the wallet and earbud onto the front seat, passenger's side. The sat-link might be useful. Maybe there were numbers there, other contacts.

But there was nothing else. No crystal on the body, and when he hobbled to the car and searched it, no crystal there either. He pulled up mats, stirred papers in the glove compartment, opened the trunk, felt along the wheel wells and undercarriage.

Nothing, not here; where's the crystal, where is *it?*

He thought a minute, then two, aware of the seconds ticking away. Finally, leg complaining, he pulled the body around to the back passenger's door on the right, grateful that Limyanovich had chosen a sedan. He opened the door then hooked his hands in the dead man's armpits and hauled Limyanovich's body along, humping it into the backseat like a rug. Gabriel left a nice wide blood smear from his leg on the vinyl backs of the front seats, but that wouldn't matter when he was done. Limyanovich's body was too long for the backseat, and Gabriel compromised, angling the dead man's head down into the right passenger's side foot well and wedging his feet into the upper left-hand corner of the rear windscreen.

He drove due west, away from Emerald Lake and Farway. Limyanovich stank. Gabriel drove, window down, cold air slapping his face, his leg throbbing in time with his pulse. The night sky was milky with stars. The headlights punched bright holes in the darkness. The tires hummed, and his was the only car on the road.

Emerald River ran northwest to southeast, and the

route he took brought the river in on his right as it cut through a steep, high gorge a hundred and fifty meters below. He couldn't see the water, but he could smell it: wet and a bit like iron.

The landtrain trestle bridging the gorge appeared first as white lights seemingly suspended in midair. As he got closer, he could make out the dark angles of girders and beams. The tracks, marked by warning beacons, ran across the road. Gabriel eased the car to a gravel shoulder. There was no guardrail. Then he killed the engine. Sat for a moment listening to the muted roar of water gushing over rocks far below.

Limyanovich was stiff as a titanium beam, and there was no graceful way to get the man into the driver's seat. In the end, he settled for a variation of the same option: angling Limyanovich left to right, head and shoulders sticking out the driver's side window.

Then he pulled the leather pouch from his pocket and tweezed out the pryolene bag, glass vials, cap and cord from his pocket. Carefully, he shook the powder into a separate glass container, sealed the vial and container together, attached the blasting cap and det cord, then fixed the homemade explosive to the right passenger's side in back, immediately in front of where he thought the fuel tank was. Then he gently shut the door, limped around front, reached past Limyanovich and released the emergency brake.

His leg ached and he couldn't put a lot of weight on his foot. Gritting his teeth, he heaved, pushing the car along a half meter, a meter—and then as the car picked up speed, he hopped back as the car bounced over the edge. He heard a window break, the squall of metal against rock—and then he thumbed the remote detonator.

The car went up with a hollow *whump!* The explosion was much bigger than he expected: a ball of orange-yellow flame pillowed into the night, and the ground shimmied under his feet. There were decrescendo whistles and then a series of pops and pings as shrapnel sprayed like the streamers from a fireworks display. In a few seconds, the car was burning hot and furious.

Time to go. Limping up the road a few dozen meters,

he crossed to the left side, away from the gorge. Stands of Hanson's woody briars grew thick and wild, and in a few moments, he'd uncovered a turbocycle he'd hidden earlier in the day. A crank of his left hand, and the turbo roared to life. Without thinking, he reached for the headlights then stopped himself. Smiled. Almost screwed up. But he hadn't.

He took one last look at the fire. He'd done well. Not finding the crystal was a problem. But there was nothing to tie him to this fire, and certainly no evidence remained to connect him with Limyanovich.

But he *had* been seen. Maybe he should go back to the graveyard and search for another body.

No. Follow the plan. Get home. Report in. Then decide. There's nothing to tie you to the graveyard, nothing. Even if someone finds a body, they still won't know it's you.

Turning east, Gabriel left the still-roaring fire and sped away in a spray of gravel and briars. In five seconds, the darkness closed around and then he was gone.

3

New Bonn, Denebola
Saturday, 14 April 3136
0430 hours

Phil Pearl hadn't been this happy in five months. A squat, blocky man, Pearl was built like a first-generation *Mackie,* with a wide, fleshy face pocked with acne scars, a steely bristle-brush mustache, and a shiny bald pate that sweated whenever he was pissed off. That was pretty often. Pearl had been with the Denebola militia, chewing up recruits for breakfast and picking his teeth with their bones at lunch. As a police captain, he still scared the crap out of most people except Jack Ramsey. They were friends, only Ramsey exasperated the hell out of him, so Ramsey figured they were even.

This time, Pearl was downright euphoric, showing all his teeth, square as pegs, in a broad, satisfied grin. "What the hell you waiting for? This is *exactly* what the doctor ordered."

"Yeah, but for who?" After a long workout and three pickup matches, Ramsey had finally managed sleep at one-thirty, only for the shrill of his link to claw him awake at three. He'd stood in the shower for ten minutes, dragged a razor over his face (wincing at the fresh purple-blue bruise along his left cheekbone), washed his teeth and then stumbled into Pearl's office downtown. He still felt like crap. His head pounded so hard his brain seemed to leak out of his ears, his eyes were gritty with sleep, and his mouth tasted like a Hel swamprat had crawled in, peed and died.

He said, "I'm supposed to be on admin leave pending the outcome of the review board. Remember?"

"Well, the mayor and the chief and the deputy chief are unadministrating you," Pearl said.

"I'll bet it was your idea."

"Of course. Bad enough we got to look at you in the papers and holos every morning. What, you got something better to do?"

"Not really. But what if the Internal Affairs guys want . . . ?"

"Screw IA. You know we're behind you. There isn't one cop in this city doesn't feel you did the right thing." When Ramsey gave an irritable shrug, Pearl paused, then asked, "You taken a good look at yourself lately, Jack?"

"Only when I can't avoid it. Why?"

"Because I notice you got a few new trophies there. That thing under your left eye looks like a piece of liver, and *you* look like crap, like you got hoverjacked. You been drinking?"

Ramsey shook his head. "Booze makes you stupid then kills you."

"Fighting?"

"A little," Ramsey lied. The truth was, most days he put in twelve, fourteen punishing hours at the gym: shadow-boxing, beating the crap out of the bag, jumping rope, sparring. Then an hour in the steam room, trying to sweat himself into exhaustion. He'd dropped kilos, a combination of the hard work and no appetite, forcing down food only because he knew he needed to. He was in the best shape he'd been since the military and about ten times more depressed. "Mostly pickup stuff. I didn't move fast enough, that's all."

"Uh-huh." Pearl looked unconvinced. "You sure you aren't begging to get the stuffing beat out of you? Maybe . . . I dunno . . . maybe, you know, one of those head games getting everyone else to punish you for what happened?"

"No," Ramsey lied again. "Nothing like that."

They fell silent, listening to the tick of an antique brass clock on Pearl's desk. Then Pearl said, "I could make you see the shrink again."

"Brannigan?" After McFaine—after his son—Ramsey had seen the department psychologist for debriefing. The debriefing was standard procedure whenever there was an "incident." "I don't need to see her again. She's the one cut me loose. Send me back, and she'll have a nervous breakdown."

"I don't doubt that. But can I ask why you're fighting this? I figured you'd snap this up like a Parthinkin large-mouthed bass."

Ramsey sighed, shrugged. "I don't know. I think . . . I think I'm worried that I'll start to feel good. That the job's the only thing left that means anything."

"I don't see the problem." Pearl looked befuddled. "I like my job."

"Yeah, but when you go home, you've got a wife. You've got two daughters. I come home, and . . ." He left the rest unsaid.

Pearl looked at him for a long moment. "Yeah. Jesus, Jack. This is a hell of a thing." He shook his head. "Hell of a thing."

There was nothing for Ramsey to say, so he didn't. Finally, Pearl said, "Okay, listen. This is not a request. You did your bit. No reason you hanging around. Sheriff from Farway calls for help, he gets help. Best thing for you is to get out of town, get back to work. Anyone wants you, it'll be easy enough to park your butt in a tilt-wing."

"A tilt-wing? No, thanks. I'll take my hover up."

"No, they want you there in"—he checked his clock—"two hours, not seven. There's a tilt-wing waiting at the spaceport get you there in forty-five minutes."

"Yeah, and then what? I'll need a vehicle."

"You got an expense account. Just don't go nuts up there and rent, like, a Bannson Cavalier, or something."

"When have I ever gone nuts?" When he saw Pearl's face, he added, "Right. What about my badge?"

Wordlessly, Pearl pulled out his top desk drawer, rummaged around and then pulled out a badge case and dealt it to Ramsey like a playing card. Ramsey flipped open the case, saw his number on the gold shield, and felt a queer tightness in his chest that was almost like joy. He looked up at Pearl. "Infernal Affairs has my service weapon."

Pearl shook his head. "Can't give that back to you, Jack. Only so far I can go."

"Okay. I understand." He did. Pearl was a friend, but he was a captain and a pragmatist. If this blew up— if, God forbid, Ramsey pulled another McFaine—Pearl would take enough heat as it was. "I've got a personal carry."

"I did not hear that. So"—Pearl scraped up papers and butted them together—"get out of town. I don't want to see you. I don't want to know you. Go do your civic duty and stay out of sight until all this blows over and, for heaven's sake, stay out of trouble. And, Jack? Godspeed."

Ramsey pushed up out of his slouch and stood. He was conscious of the weight of his badge case in his hip pocket. "I thought you were an atheist."

"Go." Pearl waved him out the door. "Get outta here before I do something and then my old lady'll drag me to confession."

Dawn, and three cups of coffee later. A squad hover, flashers going but no siren, took him back to his apartment and a uniform Ramsey didn't know waited downstairs while Ramsey threw together a travel bag: the clothes he wore plus more jeans, three shirts, underwear, socks, toothbrush and toothpaste, a razor. A leather bomber's jacket from his militia days. And his Raptor, snugged in a quick-draw on his right hip.

The tilt-wing was a cop blue, modified Cardinal transport with forward laser turrets instead of autocannons. The pilot was waiting, his hand on the throttle and headset jammed over his ears. Ramsey clambered up then dropped into the copilot's seat directly behind the pilot, and less than ten seconds later, they were airborne, the tilt-wing pulling a straight vertical and then leveling out as they streaked northwest out of the city. The sky directly overhead was black and crowded with stars, but east of the city and Lake Diamond, the horizon was smudged with orange: sunrise coming.

By the time they made Farway, the sky had brightened to a gray glow and the stars had winked out. Ahead, a misty expanse of water glittered and was dotted with the black humps of a dozen islands. Farway hugged the western shore: a jumble of dark buildings, empty streets, and a lonely street light changing from green to red at the center of town. Tidy squares of tilled farmland checkered the countryside further out.

Then Ramsey saw the sparkle of light bars from the county sheriff's cars, then the red and white flashers of fire trucks. Police and firemen scurried between the vehicles and lines of fire hoses, like oversized ants converging around plump worms. Bright, white light from generator-powered, high-intensity halogens bathed the black pavement and rocks in silver. Halfway down a rocky gorge was a twisted heap of blackened metal speckled with foamy fire-retardant. A thinning gray-black haze hung over the crime scene like a gauzy veil.

The pilot rotored past a line of landtrain tracks then spun a one-eighty and touched down. Ramsey unbuckled, took off the headset, twisted around for his bag. Then he popped his canopy, scrambled down the ladder and swung clear of the tilt-wing's saucerlike turbines. With a roar of turbo-wash, the tilt-wing lifted off in a swirl of grit and vectored away for New Bonn.

With the tilt-wing gone, Ramsey could hear the basso rumble of generators, the murmur of voices, and the hiss and pop of cooling metal. The air was heavy with the stink of gasoline, scorched metal and molten plastic—and something else that reminded him of black char and overcooked meat.

Deep in his chest, Ramsey felt his heart jump-start with a kick of adrenaline mingled with anticipation. He loved this. Probably that shrink, Brannigan, would say he was nuts. Or maybe just kind of twisted.

She was probably right.

4

Saturday, 14 April 3136
0730 hours

Something was up with Joey, no doubt about that. Sheriff Hank Ketchum stood on the gravel shoulder, arms crossed and thick eyebrows drawn together in a scowl, worrying about his son and wondering what the heck was what.

Ketchum was wiry and field-hand tough. He wore khaki pants, brown boots, his sheriff's hat firmly screwed in place, and a khaki parka with an embroidered gold sheriff's star. His thatch of straw-colored hair, still without a lick of gray, was cut regulation short. He had thick, horny calluses on each palm and the leathery skin of a farmer, ruddy and creased from years in the prairie wind and sun. His drawl was slow and a little hick-country, something he'd cultivated. Add a little good ol' boy, and people either warmed up right quick, or immediately subtracted about twenty IQ points. But Ketchum's eyes were quick and as blue as old ice. Didn't miss much.

When dispatch called about the fire, he had just returned home from cruising around town, looking for his boy. Stomped into the house, sick with worry, and Joey was standing there, leaves in his hair and sweat on his neck, like a blown horse running the Northwind Derby. His wife Lottie was standing behind Joey, one protective hand on the boy's shoulder and fire in her eyes: *Don't start.*

And now this. Ketchum's jaw bunched. *Doesn't rain but it pours.*

He watched as the county mobile crime scene people, dressed in neon orange coveralls that glowed unnaturally bright as the sun came on, picked their way down to the wreckage. The car was about fifty meters down, smashed up against a sturdy outcropping of granite that, thank the Lord, leveled out enough for a person to work. Getting there was the problem. The slope was near thirty degrees before it cut to sixty, and treacherous, slick with fire retardant foam and crumbly scree. Mountain rescue had jury-rigged a rope-belay system so the crime scene people could get up and down.

Ketchum was out of his league, and knew it. That was no ordinary fire, no sir: flared fast, burned hot as a blowtorch. The frame was still steaming, and a thick streamer of black, oily smoke was only now starting to dissipate. And there was that smell of charred meat. Have to be brain-dead not to figure there was at least one roasted body in there. Question was accident, or homicide?

He heard someone call, and turned. Two men, dressed in the same khaki outfit he wore but with an embroidered deputy star instead, trudged up with a very tall, muscled man dressed in faded denim jeans, broken-in black leather jacket, heavy boots that showed a fair amount of wear. No hat. In the growing light from the sun, Ketchum recognized the man immediately. Have to be a hermit not to have seen Ramsey's face splashed all over the vids and papers. But when they shook hands, Ketchum wasn't prepared for how violent Ramsey felt, an impression bolstered by a roadmap of scars: a slashing, white scimitar arcing along the angle of Ramsey's left jaw; another shaped, vaguely, like a half-moon turned upside down beneath his right eye, and more scars across Ramsey's calloused knuckles. Ramsey's nose was a little off-kilter, like he'd smashed it more than once, and there was a fleshy, two-centimeter gash embedded in a fresh, liver-colored bruise under Ramsey's left eye.

They went through the introductions. Ramsey was dancing the cold-man two-step and Ketchum eyed the leather jacket. "That the only cold-weather gear you got?"

"It's all I brought with me." Ramsey shrugged. "Didn't think it would still be this cold."

"Warms up during the day. We can maybe fix you up with something back at the courthouse. There's a pretty good outdoors place in town, maybe find you a parka."

"Thanks. Might do that, depending on how long I'm here." Ramsey jerked his head toward the wreck. "Arson guy here yet? What about the ME?"

"ME's already down there. Wanted to do the body first then holo the scene and move the body out of the way. Arson guy's in the air."

"How many bodies?"

"One that we know of. But the way that car blew apart, might have been more."

"Okay. You got any idea who it is? Friday night, people go out."

"You mean a guy on a drunk? I can think of three, four guys right off the top of my head, maybe cracked up. But they're all married. Wife would've called by now." Ketchum scratched at his chin, his nails rasping over stubble. "Probably not a local."

"You find where he went off the road?"

Ketchum shook his head. "No skid marks coming or going. Unless the fool was so drunk he passed out, ought to be skid marks, maybe fluid from a busted line. Something. There's nothing."

"Hunh." Ramsey stuck his hands into his pockets and looked back toward Farway and then glanced up the road heading out west. "What's out there?"

"A whole lot of nothing. A few farms, coupla bars, a gas'n hover station or two. But that's it for almost two-hundred-fifty klicks." Ketchum palmed off his hat, gave his head a good scratch, then clamped the hat back in place. "Flat no one."

*   *   *

The way down was treacherous, even with the ropes. Ramsey was strong but not experienced. Halfway down, he skidded and would've ended up slaloming down rocks if not for the rope. Closer to the wreck, the smell was worse: an eye-watering stink of gasoline, oil, oxidized synthetics, and roast human. Up close, Ramsey saw that the exploding gas tank had blown the rear of the car and taken most of the roof. The upholstery was burned down to the springs; the synthetic elastomer of the tires had melted, leaving congealing puddles under the axles and wheel rims. The engine block was a blackened relic that looked like something in a coal shaft a thousand years back.

A crime scene tech was holoviding the scene while another stood to one side as a woman backed out of what was left of the car's front seat. She was very tall and outdoors-lean. Her orange coverall was smeared with grime and char, and she wore a pair of scuffed work boots. Her sable-colored hair was plaited into a French braid that accentuated the graceful curve of her neck. Her face was oval, and a widow's peak surmounted a high forehead. Her jaw was nearly perfect, but a small scar curled along the left side of her chin. Her eyes were an exotic jade-green and canted, a little feline.

"Amanda Slade," she said when Ketchum introduced Ramsey. She wore smeary gloves and didn't offer to shake hands. Her hands were large for a woman but slender and her fingers were long. Her nails, visible through the latex, were a no-nonsense square cut. No rings. She hooked a thumb over her shoulder toward the wrecked front seat. "The guy's a mess, Hank. Looks like the front seat absorbed a lot of the initial blast, though. As it is, crime scene's going to be looking for a lot of little pieces."

"Can we take a look?" Ramsey asked.

"Okay by me," the tech with the holovid said. "I'm done until you move the body."

They shrugged into coveralls as Amanda hunkered down next to an oversized doctor's bag, rooted around, and came up with an open box of latex gloves. "He's in a pretty weird position. Be easier if one of you came in from the driver's side and the other into the backseat," she said as they gloved up.

The body *was* a mess: charred tissue, flash-cooked organs and scorched bare bone. The shins stuck up like tent poles and a litter of small bones from the feet mingled with charred shoe leather and blackened shoe shanks in the passenger's side foot well. The arms were clipped at the elbows. Small hand and finger bones dusted the front seat.

"Jesus," Ramsey said. He'd levered himself in the driver's side. "How do you know it's a guy?"

"Pelvis." Amanda was directly opposite, on the passenger's side. "A guy's pelvis is narrower than a woman's. Women need room to push out babies."

"Okay," Ramsey said. The victim's chest looked like a bomb had gone off and taken most of the sternum. He pointed at a black, fist-sized lump. "Is that the heart?"

"Uh-huh. He's been cooked. Depending on long the body burned, the interior of his organs might not be as bad. We'll just have to see."

Ramsey gave the chest a closer look. There was something there that didn't look like burned tissue, or fabric. He looked over at Amanda. "You got one of those little lights you guys use?"

"Yeah." Amanda dug in her coverall pocket, came up with a penlight, handed it to Ramsey.

"What you got?" Ketchum was in the backseat. He'd taken his hat off. A thin rim of red crossed his forehead where the hatband squeezed.

Ramsey thumbed on the penlight. "Around his collarbone. I think it's wire, or maybe a necklace. We'll need to get a picture before I take it off." When the tech was done, Ramsey used forceps to gently lift a loop of chain. Black char flecked off, revealing a glint of gold chain. A medallion the size of a small pecan dangled from the chain.

Amanda said, "It looks like the kind of religious medal, you know, that Old Roman Catholics wear." She palmed the medal in one gloved hand and lightly ran a finger over the surface. "Some kind of design. You can feel the ridges. Have to clean it up, but I could maybe scan it, see if my computer can come up with a design."

Ramsey's eyes were searching the front seat. If the victim was wearing a necklace, then maybe . . . "You got a ring here," he said. "At least that's what it looks like." They had to wait for the crime scene guy to take his shots and then Ramsey threaded a metal probe Amanda handed him through the metal circlet and backed out. The ring was chunky and a dull silver beneath a layer of soot and grime. But they could all see the stone: a red teardrop diamond.

"Looks like silver," Ketchum said.

Amanda shook her head. "Probably platinum. That gold chain's starting to fuse, so that means the fire was at least a thousand degrees C. Silver melts at seven-sixty and a person will burn up at about nine-hundred-and-thirty C, but platinum doesn't melt until the temperature's nearly double that. Once the crime people clean it up, they might be able to read an inscription, or maybe figure out where it was made. Red diamonds, they're rarer than hens' teeth."

"So it's probably safe to say that this was one rich guy," Ramsey said.

"Making it kind of weird he ends up out here," Ketchum said. "Farway's tourist trade died down over twenty years ago, what with everyone going to New Bonn and Lake Diamond. There just isn't much here."

"Same with the body," Amanda said, without irony. "If he had an ID microchip, it's probably fried. But the skull's intact. I might be able to match dental records. If he banked DNA, I might be able to rehydrate the bone and extract enough for a match. But I can tell you right now, Hank. This guy was dead when the car blew."

"How do you know?" Ketchum asked.

"The skull's intact," Ramsey said. He looked at Amanda, who nodded. "When a fire gets good and hot, the brain boils and the pressure's got nowhere to go, and the skull explodes. But *this* skull's in one piece. So this guy had a vent." Ramsey stabbed a spear of penlight at a neat hole drilled above the skull's left brow ridge. "And I'll bet you money that our guy wasn't a Cyclops."

5

His orange and white tom was asleep on a pile of laundry in a wedge of butter-yellow sunlight. But Gabriel hadn't slept at all. Too pumped up, and his leg hurt. The wound wasn't deep but very wide and a good half meter long. He'd irrigated the wound with sterile saline then sluiced the wound with peroxide. The peroxide foamed and hissed, and the wound hurt so bad he wanted to scream. Then he rooted around in his medical bag and came up with lidocaine, a Kelly clamp, prethreaded dissolvable suture. Then he injected himself with lidocaine, waited for his flesh to numb, then stitched himself up. When he was done, he applied a dermal spray to protect the wound, then chewed down a couple of painkillers that helped only a little.

He'd tested the leg, limped around the kitchen. He made a point of walking every half hour to keep the leg from seizing up. Had to remember to filch a tetanus shot from supplies once he made it to the hospital.

Gabriel brewed coffee, sat at the table, ruffled the cat's ears and waited for sunrise. He lived in the finished basement of a split-level. The apartment—an in-law's apartment, really—had a separate entrance and gravel walkway. The apartment was spare and functional, and that suited Gabriel fine. He spent his money on computer equipment and gadgetry, and one very fine prize: a black-market police scanner. So he heard when the sheriff's dispatcher relayed the alarm, knew which units were called to the scene, and even when Ketchum put in a call to New Bonn for help. He had police lingo down cold.

At half past seven, he heard the crunch of tires on the gravel drive, then the slam of a front door followed by footsteps thudding overhead, the flush of a toilet.

Oh, joy. Gabriel's mouth turned down. *Daddy's home.*

His father clomped around, showered, clomped some more. When the front door slammed again, Gabriel tensed. The last thing he needed was to deal with Dear Old *Dad.* But, a few moments later, he heard the *whomp* of a car door, then an engine revving, and tires crunching as his father pulled away.

At eight on the dot, he retrieved his sat-link from his nightstand and hobbled back out to sit with the cat. Gabriel screwed in an earbud, told the link which number he wanted and waited while the link connected.

The other end punched in. "Yes?" The Handler's voice—older, smoky, with the slight burr of an accent—against a background of tinny music.

"It's done," he said.

A pause. "Is this line secure?"

"The link's scrambled." Gabriel had downloaded the program and prepped the link himself. He stroked the cat's head, and the cat responded with a throaty rumble.

"Good." Another pause. "A very flamboyant exercise in pyrotechnics that will not go unnoticed. But why the trestle? You could not burn the car in the cemetery?"

This was the part he'd been dreading. "There were complications."

"What kind of complications?"

"I'd rather explain in person. Can I come over now?"

"No, no. Too many people might see you, and I cannot break away. Tonight, when you are through at the hospital. Did you get the crystal?"

"No. I couldn't find it. It wasn't on him and it wasn't in the car."

"I see." Silence. Then the Handler said, "Nothing should be out of the ordinary. You need to stick to your routine. Do not return to the cemetery. I know you are tempted, but do not. The task now is to *draw* in another operative, perhaps this Limyanovich's shadow agent. You left identification with the body, yes?"

He told the Handler about the wallet, omitting the part about the money. "What if another agent doesn't show? We need that crystal to expose the operation."

"All in good time. Perhaps it was destroyed in the fire."

"I don't believe that," Gabriel said. "That code we used worked the last time. So if he came here, he brought the data crystal because that's what the code told him to do."

"Then we wait and see. If no one else comes, we still might be able to lure other conspirators here through his sat-link, and barter. Limyanovich cannot be the only one with this information." The Handler paused. "I presume no one saw you."

"Of course not," he lied.

6

Troy saved his life.

Noah heard the *boom* of the second shot, ducked, and took three more running steps when something smacked his right shoulder, and he went down. A wave of nausea made his stomach buck, and he groaned, rolled to his right and screamed when hot pain lanced the middle of his back. He groped for his shoulder, felt something sticky and more pain.

I'm shot, I've been shot, I'm shot . . .

Run, he had to run! But he was dizzy, sick, and he panted, sobbed, "Troy, Troy, Troy . . ."

A hand clapped over his mouth. He tasted grit and sweat, and then Troy was hissing in his ear: Shut up, Noah, shut up. He's coming, he's . . . !"

Over the thrum of his blood, Noah heard the tall grass crackle and snap. His chest squeezed with terror. His senses went laser-bright, and he smelled everything, heard everything: his sweat, the copper scent of blood, the thud of his heart, the liquid pain in his shoulder. Troy lay, hand clamped over Noah's mouth and never let up, never let go.

Then the killer went down. Noah didn't see it happen,

but he heard it. A clatter of metal, and then a shout of surprise and pain, the heavy sound of a body hitting the ground, and then *bam* as the gun went off.

Tripped over Troy's bike . . .

Eventually, the killer got to his feet and shuffled away, his steps slow and uneven because he was hurt. After they heard the distant roar of a car fade away, Troy helped Noah sit up. "Thanks," Noah said, but it came out as a moan.

"You're not going to die, are you, Noah?" Troy's voice came out little-kid scared. "You going to be okay?"

"I'm okay." Nothing was further from the truth, but Troy sounded bad, worse than *he* felt. "But we got to get out of here. We . . ." His stomach bottomed out when he heard a dry rustle. *Oh, no . . .*

A harsh whisper: "Guys?" Pause. *"Guys?"*

They couldn't tell how bad Noah was, and after Joey's tentative forays—pokes and prods that felt like red-hot daggers—Noah decided he wasn't too keen on finding out any more. As long as his arm worked well enough, that was all that mattered.

"We got to tell somebody," said Joey, his face a white blur. "You got to go to the hospital."

"No way." Noah's head felt woolly. "If we tell, he'll know it was us. We just go home. We just make like this never happened."

Joey said, "Oh, yeah? So what are you going to say about your arm?"

"I can move it and it doesn't hurt much," Noah fibbed. "Probably not too bad."

"Yeah," Joey said, "but there's a *dead* guy."

"You ever seen him before?"

"No. But just because we don't know him . . ."

They were still arguing when Troy said, his words a little slurry, "Guys . . . we . . . I don't feel so good. I think I . . . I think I need to eat."

"Oh, heck." Noah groped for Troy's face and came away with sweat. "Joey, you got any food?"

Joey had half a smashed candy bar. They made Troy

eat the candy and then Noah said, "He can't go home alone. Even if we find his bike, he—"

"I can ride," Troy said, weakly. "I'll be okay."

"Like hell," Joey said. "I'll take you home and then I'll double back. Besides, what happens if you pass out or something? No one will find you until morning, maybe."

"But . . . but what about my bike?"

In the end, they decided to worry about Troy's bike later. No one really wanted to stick around in the dark. They walked Joey's and Noah's bikes out, Joey guiding both bikes and Noah coming up behind with Troy. Once they hit asphalt, Joey boosted Troy onto the handlebars of his bike, waited until Noah had mounted his own and then they took off.

The ten klicks home were the longest of Noah's life. Noah was wobbly, and his right forearm was wet clear through his parka.

Probably shock, just like in the holomovies, and I'm still bleeding . . .

The houses thinned, giving way to farmland and old two- and three-story houses, ringed with islands of trees, set far back from the road. Once he hit the Tanner place, which was the first farm north out of town, he started counting. Noah's place was the seventh out: a centuries-old homestead that Noah's father inherited. Not a working farm anymore, though the barns in summer still smelled of hay, warm oats, and horse manure. Noah spotted his house from the road because the trees were still bare, and his heart sank. Every light in the place was blazing: square and rectangular yellow lozenges suspended against an inky black sky stippled with stars.

As luck had it, his mother wasn't home, but his younger sister Sarah was. "Oh, boy, are you in trouble. Mom is going to—" Sarah stopped when she got a good look. Then she went wide-eyed: all ocean blue ringed by sandy blond curls. "Holy cow, Noah. Is that *blood*?"

In the upstairs bathroom, Sarah helped Noah peel out of his jacket. His jacket was a light blue, but the right arm was stained dark purple from blood. There were holes, too, front and back and holes in his shirt which was saturated with blood. The bullet hadn't tagged his shoulder at all but the fleshy part of his upper arm. In the yellow light of the medicine chest, Noah saw a long stripe of raw, angry-looking flesh slashing just above his biceps as if a little kid had drawn a horizontal line in bright red crayon. The wound was more of a trough: ripped skin, red meat, yellow fat, and crusted blood.

"Just a flesh wound," Sarah pronounced. Sarah already knew that she wanted to be a doctor and volunteered at the hospital. She made him scoot his butt around until he straddled the toilet and his right arm hung over the edge of the bathtub. Then Sarah washed off his shoulder with soap and lots of hot water. That hurt pretty bad and made the wound ooze bright red blood.

"That's good blood. Gets the poison out." She waited a few minutes, then dabbed away blood, unscrewed the cap from a brown glass bottle, said, "This is going to hurt," and poured peroxide over the wound.

Pain detonated in his shoulder, and he felt queasy again. The peroxide foamed pink with an audible fizz, like soda. Sarah sponged the foam off, doused the wound again, and Noah jerked his arm away. "Will you *quit* it?" he demanded.

Sarah gave him a hard look. "You want Mom to do this?"

That shut him up. Sarah rummaged then came up with a tube of antibiotic ointment, a coag gauze, and clear tape. With brisk efficiency, she smeared ointment then flattened and taped the gauze around the wound on all four sides. "That should be okay. But you need a tetanus shot."

"Nuh-unh." Noah leaned back against the toilet's tank. He'd broken into a sweat again, and his stomach rolled like he was in a tiny dinghy in the middle of the ocean. "But . . . thanks. You did really good."

"You're my brother," Sarah said simply. She gathered up the soiled sponges and his shirt and wadded them together. "I'll put these all in the trash outside before Mom sees them." She cast a doubtful eye at Noah's jacket. "I don't know if that blood's going to come out.

Maybe if I soak it in cold water first . . ." She looked at Noah and said, "What happened?"

Noah just shook his head. Sarah waited a beat, said, "Mmmm," then scooped up his jacket and marched out of the bathroom. He heard her tromp downstairs and then the bang of a door.

He'd dozed off, leaning against the edge of the sink, his forehead propped on his left forearm, when she came back. She woke him up, helped him get to his room at the end of the hall, and fussed with his sheets and blanket while he dragged on a sweatshirt, being careful of his arm. When he was in bed, she pulled his shades, clicked off the overhead lights, came over, turned on a black reading lamp on his nightstand, and then handed him a glass of water and two aspirin. When he'd taken the aspirin, she retrieved the empty glass and said, "You're going to have to tell Mom."

"Tell her what?" The aspirin left a bitter aftertaste on the back of his tongue, and he grimaced when he swallowed. He was bone-tired and starting to feel warm. He pushed back a handful of blanket and said, "You can't tell her. You got to promise."

"Noah," Sarah said but then stopped as a shaft of light crawled over the drawn bedroom shade. Noah's bedroom overlooked the end of the driveway, and now they both heard the rumble of tires over gravel, the sputter as someone killed the engine, the hard bang of a car door being slammed.

Sarah looked down at her brother. "I hope you know what you're doing."

Hannah Schroeder was a small, too-thin woman with the kind of dry, withered looks of a beautiful woman grown bitter by tragedy. Her brown hair was dull and brittle; the corners of her mouth hooked down in permanent disapproval; and her dark brown eyes had the furtive, darting, hunted quality of a stalked house wren.

First Isaiah, then Scott, and now Noah . . . "You lost track of *time*? You stay out until it's dark as pitch outside, come home after dark while I'm making calls and driving around town, sick with worry, and—"

Noah cut in. "I'm sorry. We were fooling around, that's all. Jeez, in summer, you don't get upset if I—"

"In summer, it stays light until nine o'clock. In summer, it's thirty C, not four degrees outside!"

"Mom," Noah said, "I'm sorry. I just . . . we got busy. We . . ." He moved his left shoulder in a half-shrug. "I'm sorry."

She was so angry she wanted to smack him. Slap his face good and hard. But she'd never hit her children because, with her Isaiah dead, she was frightened she might not stop. Instead, her restless fingers found a length of gold chain at her throat, and she worried it, sliding a gold medal of the Virgin back and forth. The metal over metal made a sound like a zipper. "You know how much I worry, Noah. You know—"

"I know, Mom." Noah was pale. His eyes were gray-green, like Isaiah's, and just as hooded. It hurt her to look at them. "Jesus, I said I was sorry."

"Don't blaspheme." She said it automatically, like a tic. Then: "You're sorry, you're so sorry, but not enough to come home, not sorry enough to keep me from worrying myself sick! The sheriff out looking for Joey, and you boys, you never . . ." Her fingers worked her necklace. Then she squinted as a new thought leaked in. "You were out with Scott, weren't you? You went to see him and that slut he's living with. I've told you to stay away from Scott. He's not good for you, and that little whore . . ."

She'd gone on like that for another five minutes, haranguing, berating—hating herself for what he made her do; hating her husband for dying; hating everything. Then, abruptly, she'd run down like an old wheezy grandfather's clock with rusty gears. "I'm tired. I can't worry about you any more right now." She turned, shuffled to the door, suddenly so weary her legs felt like water. "I need to sleep. I need to go to work tomorrow. Someone has to be responsible. Someone has to . . ."

She turned to look back at her son. Noah's face was very white beneath the cap of his wheat-colored hair, and he looked miserable. Well, let him suffer. What didn't destroy you made you stronger. Lord knows, she suffered.

Her voice was flat. "Don't think this is finished. I don't want you leaving this house Saturday. If I find out that you've even called Scott . . ." She left the sentence hanging. Her throat balled with tears, and she turned away, ashamed of her tears and angry all over again at the ingratitude and injustice of the world. Was this a trial, her cross to bear? None of this was fair, it wasn't *fair*! "You'd think that after everything that's happened, after your father and Scott, you'd think the least a boy could do is listen to his mother. No one will ever care for you as much as I do, Noah. No one."

She'd clicked off his light and closed the door and left him behind in the dark.

And that was Friday.

Saturday, 14 April 3136
0930 hours

Hot. He was burning up, and something drilled, bored into his head . . .

Noah cranked open his eyelids, blinked. Blinked again. His eyes were gummy, and his tongue was glued to the roof of his mouth. He could smell himself: sour with sweat and sickness. His right arm had settled to a constant dull throb. He tried an experimental swallow, grimaced at the bad taste in his mouth. His room was suffused with light filtering through his shades.

The scratching came again and resolved itself into a tapping at his door. "Yeah," he croaked.

The door opened a hair and Sarah stuck her head through. "You awake?"

"I am now." Noah pushed himself to a sit and instantly regretted it as the room spun. He gulped air, forcing his stomach to stay put.

"You don't look so good," Sarah said. She came to sit on his bed then put a hand against his forehead. "I think you have a fever."

"I'm cold." He was burning up and freezing at the same time. He shivered and pulled the blanket up to his chin. "Where's Mom?"

"Gone to work. I would've let you sleep but . . ."

The look on her face scared him. "What?"

Her face was solemn, her blue eyes bright with scrutiny. "Someone got killed last night. It's all over the news. A car went over the gorge near the landtrain trestle, and then it *exploded*. There was someone in the car, and he's dead, only now they're saying maybe he was murdered." When he didn't say anything, she said, "You have to tell what you saw, Noah. You have to tell somebody what happened."

A light flashed in Noah's brain, as if the events of the night before were a holomovie playing out on the black screen of his mind: the hum of a bullet splitting the air over his head; the *bang* of a shotgun, the way the big man jerked and crumpled like a discarded puppet. The flat *bap* as the old man killed him.

He looked up at his little sister. "No, I don't," he said.

7

Dawn had brought fog and the news people. By the time the sun burned off the chill, a clot of news vans and reporters clustered like agitated geese behind a hastily erected police line. Above, a pair of news VTOLs droned, circling like vultures. Ramsey had hung way back, made sure he turned away when the holocameras swept the crime scene people and police. He didn't hate news people the way other cops did. He viewed news people as opportunistic feeders, like Terran remoras, skimming under the belly of a shark and snapping up the leavings. It was just that he couldn't become the story.

So, instead, Ramsey spent his time eyeing Amanda. She'd ordered the body removed from the car, a process hampered by bits and pieces of the body flaking off, which then had to be gathered, bagged, and tagged. The mountain rescue people had rigged a traverse stretcher to haul up the body bag, but the going was slow, with the stretcher bumping against the wall, showering scree down the slope.

When the body was on level ground again, the ME crew climbed up. Ramsey watched as Amanda pulled her way up the side of the gorge. He liked the way she moved. She'd shucked the orange coverall to reveal jeans, a light denim shirt rolled up to the elbows, and a hunter-green insulated vest that highlighted her sable-colored hair. She had long legs, corded muscles in her forearms, and moved with the grace of a large cat. She caught him looking, flashed a quick smile, then moved to give instructions to the transport techs taking the body to the hospital morgue. She wasn't gorgeous, but she was very . . . handsome. Strong body matched by chiseled features. Early thirties, probably.

Someone called his name, and he turned. A deputy named John Boaz and an older jowly man who everyone else called Bobby and didn't seem to have a last name duckwalked over with a load of thermoses, cups, pastry boxes and white paper sacks spotted with grease. Ramsey helped them arrange everything on the trunk lid of one of the cruisers then drew a cup—black and strong—and started rooting around the bags.

"Ida heard what was going on, and she set her man back to the ovens," Boaz said. He had a laconic drawl, a lumpy face, and large ears. Each ear came to a curious point right at the top of each helix. He looked a little bit like an alien from a popular science fiction holo-drama, except his eyes were very small and gray, like lead pellets. "All these news people, she's tickled pink. Murder's good for business."

Ramsey was inspecting a bag of crullers. The crullers were still warm, and smelled of yeast and oily sugar. "Who said anything about murder?"

Boaz blinked. "Well, I did, I guess," he said around a doughnut. He chewed, swallowed, chased the doughnut with coffee then gave a slow, reluctant smile, the kind a dog makes when it's crapped on the carpet. "What I mean is, well, car blown to heck and back, guy with a bullet hole in his head, that's got to be a murder."

"Who's talking murder?" They turned as Ketchum strode up. His parka was open, his thumbs hooked in his belt loops. Boaz repeated his story, and Ramsey watched as color edged up the sheriff's grizzled neck. When Boaz was finished, Ketchum said, "Who heard you?"

Boaz thought. "Well, it was early yet, not a lot of

people in. So it was me and Bobby, Ida, her counter girl, a couple of fellas from Monk's place. I think that's it."

"Uh-huh." Ketchum did a slow simmer, his mouth working. "Okay, John, Bobby, here's how it goes. You boys keep a lid on this murder talk until I make a formal announcement. I'll do that once the body's out of here. But you go around dropping details that we might want to keep back, like that bullet hole, and you're going to make this harder than it already is. You understand?"

Coloring, Boaz gave a jerky nod. The other deputy, Bobby, simply said, "Okay, Hank," fished out a doughnut, bit, swiped jelly from his upper lip with his tongue.

Ramsey waited until Ketchum had drawn a cup and chosen a cinnamon roll, and then the two men stepped away. When they were out of earshot, Ramsey said, "Your people could be trouble."

"Yeah," said Ketchum. Scowling, he took a huge bite of roll, heaved a sigh, chewed. "Most of them are pretty good. Boaz, he's okay but kind of stupid."

"You're going to have to do some damage control with the press, too."

"I know it." Ketchum's scowl deepened. "Like a bunch of big black crows over roadkill."

"They have their place. Got to know how to play them is all."

Ketchum opened his mouth to say something else, but the mountain rescue people ambled over for coffee and got Ketchum involved in signing off on their time. Ramsey slowly edged away, stood at the lip of the gorge, looking down at orange suits still picking over rocks. The ambulance had pulled away, lights flashing but no siren. Ramsey looked up as Boaz sidled over. Ramsey nodded and Boaz said, "Sheriff had no call to say that."

"Yeah, he did. Murder investigations are easy to mess up. Three things you got to do." Ramsey ticked them off on his fingers. "Control your people. Control the press. Control the evidence. After that, everything else is luck and hard work."

"We work hard."

"I didn't say that you don't. But rumors'll kill you unless you're the one to plant them."

Boaz gave him a narrow look. "You do that?" And when Ramsey nodded, Boaz said, "That's *lying*."

"Sometimes. Sometimes not." Ramsey turned away to look in Amanda's general direction. Definitely a better view. "Sometimes you got to make things happen. So you put a bug in someone's ear."

Boaz said, "I can think of something else I'd like to put into someone, and it wouldn't be her *ear*." When Ramsey turned back, Boaz was smirking. "Know what I mean?"

"Yeah?" Ramsey said. He didn't mind cop talk. Part of the ritual, see who had bigger balls. But he didn't like talk that put down women.

Boaz was talking again. "Like I wouldn't mind me a piece of *that*." His tongue, pink and as pointed as his ears, flickered over his lower lip the way a snake tests the air. "I had me a wife once. Liked screwing fine until we had the kid, and then she let herself go. Just lay there. Like porking a Cartago bloodworm. Now, Amanda, she's standoffish, but in my experience, those brainy women, you screw 'em hard, peg 'em in the right place, you know, and they screw you right back."

The talk made him uncomfortable. "Listen, this makes me uncomfortable," Ramsey said. "Talking about women that way, it's really not my thing and, honestly, it just makes you sound like a hick-jackass." What he wanted to add was that a man like Boaz probably had a good right hand that saw a lot of action.

"Yeah?" Boaz wasn't smiling anymore, and for a minute, Ramsey wondered if the deputy was a mind reader. "So just what *is* your thing? Getting it on with guys like McFaine, *that* your kinda thing?"

"Look," Ramsey said but stopped when Ketchum wandered over with the arson specialist, Fletcher. Fletcher, a dry-looking man with steel-rimmed spectacles, carried a yellow and blue device about the size of a tool box.

"We've taken our samples with the sniffer," Fletcher said, primly adjusting his glasses. "We'll have some kind of answer in the next few days, say"—he did a mental calculation, his lips working—"Monday evening."

"Sniffer?" Ketchum asked.

Fletcher patted the box the way another man might a retriever. "A sniffer's a photo-ionization detector that registers volatile hydrocarbons."

"So that tells you what caused the fire?"

Fletcher's pencil-thin eyebrows arched. "Oh, it might tell us much more. Certain explosives and accelerants contain taggants, inert materials added to distinguish where something might've been manufactured. Industries add a taggant to aid in enforcement and investigation. But I think this is homegrown. The scene just doesn't have the feel of something very professional, or even military. This is farm country. Lots of fertilizer around, so your boy could've used ANFO, fuel oil mixed with fertilizer. Or the explosive might be commercial grade but untraceable."

"Then we're shit out of luck," Ramsey said.

Fletcher nodded. "Yes. I think you would be."

Fletcher and his team ran the news people gauntlet, were button-holed for fifteen minutes, and finally left. A little later, a knot of crime scene techs huffed up. One held up an evidence bag. "I got a wallet here. Found it about, oh, thirty meters to the right. Weird, actually, when you think about it. Shoulda been torched just like his clothes."

"Unless it wasn't in his pockets when the car went up," Ketchum observed.

"That might explain it." Still gloved, the tech carefully unfolded the wallet. The wallet was a bifold and must originally have been brown but was charred so the edges looked moth-eaten. There was a slot for an ID card but the card was a molten glob and unreadable. There were slots for photographs, all empty. "No money," the tech said.

Boaz grunted. "So you got someone who shoots the guy, then robs him, then torches his car. Nice guy."

"Is there anything else?" Ramsey asked.

"No," the tech said, "I think . . . wait a sec." He stopped, angled the wallet into the light. "There's something here."

The something turned out to be what looked like a business card of some kind, mostly black but a tan color where the fire had melted the plastic, which then stuck to the card. The tech said, "I can't make out much other than a word: *Industries*."

"Could be anything, anywhere," Ketchum said.

Ramsey pointed. "There are numbers. Looks like part of a sat-link code . . . a prefix and then a couple numbers." He recited the numbers, thought a minute, said, "I don't recognize that prefix code. You?"

Ketchum shook his head. "But give me a sec. Let me call dispatch."

While Ketchum was gone, Ramsey asked the tech, "You think your guys can separate the card from the plastic?"

The tech wrinkled his nose. "I dunno. That stuff's pretty hard. They can try separating it, but don't get your hopes up."

"Slovakia," Ketchum called, jogging back. "Dispatch says it's a number in Slovakia, some business called PolyTech Industries."

Ramsey blinked. "Slovakia? What would someone from Slovakia be doing way out here?"

Ketchum dug at the back of his neck in a vigorous scratch. "A lot of folks here, they got family come from back there. Call it the old country. Wrong season for tourists, otherwise."

"You could get someone to call the spaceport and see how many Slovakian citizens came through in the last two weeks. See if any rented cars. But if this guy's a Slovakian national, you're going to have to call this into the DBI."

"The Bureau?" Ketchum screwed up his face like he'd sucked a lemon. "The last time I talked with one of those special agents—this was a drug case a year or two back, local boy—he made me feel like I put my shorts on backwards and pissed out my ass."

"Maybe you'll be lucky. Maybe they'll just say attaboy and leave you alone. On the other hand, if this is someone important, they'll want to know."

"Or this might be just a lot of nothing," said Ketchum.

"But you have to cover your bases."

"I know it." Ketchum took off his hat and finger-combed his straw-colored hair. "Truth is I'm in over my head. Most we ever deal with is someone's tarise gets shot, or some fool goes out on the lake and gets in trouble, or hikers try to bushwhack to the river. Most of them split open their skulls on the rocks—that is, if they don't fall off and drown. These walls are wicked slippery, and the stone's rotten. Outside of a few drug things and a hunting accident couple years back that got a local killed, that's as crazy as it gets here."

"So what are you saying, Hank?"

"I'm *saying* that I could really use your help. Maybe run the show."

Ramsey felt his heart give a little kick, as if the muscle had jump-started. Still, he said, "I can't do that without approval, Hank. You need someone to cross jurisdictions, you got to call in a knight, maybe, especially if it turns out to be a nationality thing, or Count Kampephos, the planetary legate. Or talk to the governor."

But Ketchum was shaking his head. "I don't want a knight. Oh, I know we're supposed to kowtow to the nobility and all, but . . ." He shook his head again.

"Hank, that's the way things are," Ramsey said. He saw Amanda coming over, a cup of coffee in her hand and a smile on her face. Boaz leaned on his cruiser, thumbs hooked in his belt loops, his eyes tracking Amanda. When he caught Ramsey watching, the deputy threw him a wink and waggled his eyebrows.

Ramsey turned back as Ketchum was saying, "Things here go the way I say."

"You don't have that kind of discretion, Hank."

"The heck I don't," said Ketchum, looking almost fierce. "I don't want a knight. Take a look around. You think anyone's going to take to a knight snooping around?"

"He's got a point," Amanda said. She'd sidled between the men, though she stood just a little closer to Ramsey.

"And I'm a city cop with baggage. That's *not* a problem?" Ramsey asked.

There was a pause as Ramsey's words hung there, like a bad smell. Amanda looked at Ketchum. Ketchum cleared his throat, ran his hands around the brim of his sheriff's hat then settled the hat back into place.

"I'm sheriff," he said. "For right now, this is what I want. You let me make some calls, see what I can square up in terms of cooperation."

"Well . . ." But Ramsey's mind was already leaping five steps ahead. Pearl would be thrilled. Lending Ramsey would take care of a lot of headaches, the number one problem being visibility. "Your call, Hank."

"Yes, it is," Ketchum said and stalked off to make his calls.

Amanda sipped coffee. "Well," she said. "And don't you look like the cat that ate the canary?"

8

Walking to her truck, Amanda caught Boaz leering, a look that made Amanda want to pop out his eyeballs with her thumbs. Idiot. She'd looked for Ramsey but didn't spot him. So she left, feeling Boaz's eyes lasering her butt.

She headed east then swung south, the road edging the lake on her left. This was the time of morning she adored, with the sun, a Davion sunburst, hovering above water sparkling like sequins against cerulean velvet. She didn't see this often. Usually she was in surgery, her day starting at 5:30 a.m. She got so she knew spring was coming when sunrise caught up to *her*, the night sky giving way and the few lone stars that were left winking out before the advance of another day.

This morning, she felt good. Interesting case and Ramsey . . . very interesting guy. Her attitude about the case was, well, maybe a little sick. Murder was so *interesting*. She'd met MEs, cops who had this whole crusade thing going. But the really good cops were pretty weird. There was this detective on Towne, with whom she'd worked the Little Luthien killer. Now *that* cop was downright spooky, the way he talked about channeling the victim, stuff like that. But he was the only one who bought her argument about that government official. The rest of the killings were camouflage, so they should look at the official and work backward. No one liked that.

The legate got pissed when she ended up splashed all over the news. That got her booted out of the assistant ME's post, and smack-dab into Farway.

Farway was weird: a town inhabiting a pocket out of time. No 'Mechs, no hovers. Farm land and, in the summer, a fading tourist haunt. Religion was big: Old Romans and New Avalon Catholics, a feud that went back a ways, with the Slovakians clinging to the old ways. (Personally, she was a good Jewish girl and didn't care one way or t'other.)

But she was determined to make the best of it. As soon as she landed the job, she bought a farm. Point-three square klicks of grazing land, on the lake, and pretty much sight unseen. Now she had her house, her horses, her work. Being ME for the county wasn't really that bad, kind of a nifty second gig. A county coroner did the scut work, pronouncing at all the ninety-eight-year-old Aunt Bettie-Lous who keeled over from a heart attack, easy stuff like that. Anything else, they called her.

The one drawback: no men. Well, no eligible men for *her*. Men like Boaz just made her angry, and she had nothing in common with the rest.

Now Ramsey, he was a good-looking guy in a scary, dangerous way. All those scars made his face more interesting, not ugly, and she got a good look at his hands, too: big, capable. Muscled. The right ring finger looked like it had broken once and not been set right away. No ring on the left ring finger, but you never could tell with guys and now, come to think of it, wasn't he married, or had been? And what happened to McFaine? She'd do a search and . . .

"Whoa, Nellie," she said. "What are you thinking, girl?"

Our Lady of the Lake Hospital was small and based on threes: an emergency room with three bays; three floors; three wings; thirty beds; a nursery; and a three-bed ICU. (Someone said the three-thing was because of the Trinity. Whatever.) Highly complex cases were air-evaced to New Bonn by VTOL or tilt-wing from a helipad out front, though she'd only sent out three patients in the past four years. They had three PAs, one of whom did pediatrics, plus an intensivist, a pediatrician, two ob-gyns, a family practitioner and another surgeon. She held triple certification in surgery, internal medicine and forensic pathology. (So maybe there was something there with this three stuff.) There wasn't much they couldn't deal with.

The emergency room was on the hospital's north side, with its own breezeway, a bay for an ambulance, and a much-smaller, postage stamp of a parking lot where the doctors liked to park. She passed through a set of scrolling glass double doors into the ER lobby. Canned music silted through overhead speakers. There were four people in the waiting room: two regulars who slept off whatever they'd drunk the night before, and a harassed-looking brunette with a squalling two-year-old. (Amanda liked kids and had thought about becoming a pediatrician. Then she clerked in a pediatric ER. After two months of runny noses, projectile vomiting, diarrhea, a clientele whose repertoire of recounting symptoms was to cry or cry harder, and hysterical mothers, she decided that if she wanted patients who bit, kicked and howled—hell, she'd have been a vet.)

The nurses' station was behind the lobby, near admissions. When Amanda rolled in, she spotted two nurses—one with steely gray hair and a single brow—and a short man in green surgical scrubs and a surgical mask knotted loosely around his neck flipping through hard-copy patient charts and double-checking them against a noteputer.

"Hey, Craig," Amanda said. She dropped into a vacant chair and accessed the hospital computer to check on her day's admissions. "You're here early. Putting in some overtime?"

Craig Dickert said, "Hunh. They'd never pay overtime." His blue eyes were set a little too close together over a thin nose, a lantern-jaw and a thin wisp of a sand-colored mustache that covered a bad cleft lip repair. His voice was always a little nasal and wet because of the lip. "Getting a jump on this evening." *Thish evening.* "I heard it was kind of a mess out there." *Mesh.*

"Mmmm." Amanda squinted at her patient list. She'd have to hump it through her rounds plus move her late afternoon surgery—a gut reanastomosis—to the morning if she wanted to get to the cut on the corpse that afternoon. She dug out her noteputer, jotted down a few agenda changes then synced the information with the hospital computer. "Getting the body out of the car was hard—that and not falling off those rocks."

Another voice, male: "That'll teach you to be such a smart-ass know-it-all."

Amanda rolled her eyes as Fred Carruthers, the hospital's intensivist, blew in on a swirl of flapping white coat-tails. "As smart-ass as some fleas I know?"

Carruthers sniffed. He was reed-thin, with mussed dark brown hair and button-black eyes. Carruthers was smart, permanently harried, and his wife was expecting twins. The only drawback was they were separated. "You know, Manny, if you'd stop all that surgery crap and apply your talents to real medicine, we could get married."

"You've got a wife," the nurse with one brow said with a note of disapproval.

"Not for much longer." Carruthers was downright perky. "Four more weeks and then we are finito."

The two nurses and Dickert exchanged looks. "You're kidding," Amanda said.

"I kid you not. Good riddance, too."

"Mmmm." Amanda was uncomfortable. Getting a divorce was bad enough, but divorcing your pregnant wife? Talking about it in the ER? She changed the subject. "Fred, what're you doing here? You were just on. Get some sleep."

"But then I'd be far away from you, Manny," Carruthers said as he slid before a terminal and began calling up lab data. "Besides, I'm jacked. Drank a liter of coffee, so might as well work." He paused. "I heard Hank got a city cop."

"Jack Ramsey," Dickert said, wetly. "He's the one did McFaine."

"Whoa. *That* Jack Ramsey?" Now Carruthers was interested. "What's he like?"

"He's okay." Amanda shrugged then stood and tucked her noteputer into her hip pocket. She wandered to the coffeepot, studied the amoeboid scum oiling the surface, then poured a cup. "You know . . . just a cop."

"Listen to Miss La-Dee-Dah. Oh, just a cop. Just a bat-shit nutcase."

"Don't blaspheme," One-Brow said. "And can you blame the man? After his son . . . *Lord*." She shook her head. "Happened to me I'd've done the same thing."

"Well." Amanda sipped her coffee. The stuff tasted like it was brewed in the Terran early Paleozoic era. She dumped the cup in the trash. "He seems all right."

"Hey, Craig." Another nurse, not One-Brow, waved Dickert over. "My computer's messed up again."

"That's because you keep messing with it. Stop messing with it, it won't get messed up." Dickert sighed. "Nurses." *Nurtheth.*

One-Brow said, *"You're* a nurse."

"I'm a nurse *anesthetist*." Dickert had to work to get out the last word. He swiped at his bottom lip with the back of one hand. "There's a serious difference."

The nurse rolled her eyes. "Yeah, well, I'm getting old over here, Prince Charming."

As Dickert scuffed over, Carruthers leaned in. "Seriously, Manny, this Ramsey guy? Be careful."

"What?" Amanda didn't know whether to be offended, flattered, amused, or all three. "Why?"

"I was one of the guys who hired you, remember? I know all about this dark side thing you got going."

"I do not." She was getting mad now. "I just like my work."

"Correction, you *love* the work. It's okay. Look at *me*: work, work, work. The picture of mental health," he said, but the gaiety was forced now, like he'd been riding a high and coming crashing down. "This Ramsey, he might seem okay, but . . ."

"But what?"

Carruthers' button-black eyes locked on hers. "What he did to McFaine? I think this Ramsey guy liked it."

She held his gaze for another five seconds then blinked and said, "Okay. I . . . appreciate the concern." She backhanded a wave. "I gotta get ready for the cut."

As she left, she heard Dickert say to the nurse with the computer problem, "Jesus, not like *that*."

And One-Brow: "Don't blaspheme."

*   *   *

Hunh. Amanda cut a right out of the ER down a T-corridor. Well, now *that* was interesting. She puzzled over Carruthers as she passed radiology on her right, then hung a left and took the stairs to her basement-level office. (That was the only thing she hated about being ME. Morgues were always in the basement.)

She pushed Carruthers from her mind and focused on the case again. Autopsy probably would be succinct. Crispy critter. But that ring, and the necklace, now *that* was intriguing. She slid into a chair, swiveled, booted up her computer. Then she tweezed out her noteputer, tapped in a command and brought up an image file. She'd been so intrigued by the pendant she'd gotten a good holographic recording. She beamed the information to her work computer then accessed a VRML program. The program, a virtual reality modeling language, was used by forensic anthropologists for 3-D facial reconstructions. She wasn't qualified for that kind of work, but the program had many similarities to VRML programs she used in planning facial surgeries. If she tinkered with the parameters, she might be able to reconstruct the image on the medal. She might ask Craig Dickert to lend a hand; he was a geek computer guy. Yeah, if she could figure out a way that didn't sound like a come-on. Craig, she knew, was interested. A nice enough guy, but . . . She sighed. First, Carruthers, and now she worried about Dickert. On the other hand, Ramsey . . .

Just what are you thinking, girlfriend? You thinking about that there Ramsey?

Answer: *Well*, duh.

=== 9 ===

The news people took Ketchum about twenty minutes. The sheriff did pretty well, and if Ramsey hadn't known better, he could've sworn that Ketchum's aw-shucks drawl got a little thicker. Ramsey lurked in the background. A few reporters from New Bonn affiliates of the major Neurasian networks spotted him, and if anyone hadn't known who he was before—say, someone living under a rock—they knew now.

The news conference had just broken up when a deputy called over Ramsey and Ketchum. The deputy pointed at an orange suit struggling the last few meters up the hill. "Crime scene guys found something."

Blowing from the effort, the tech handed over a clear evidence bag. Inside the bag was a charred twist of metal, and the tech pointed out the series of numbers etched into the metal. "Probably part of a serial number. Must a blown clear."

Ramsey looked at Ketchum. "Now we're cooking. Even with a partial, you can get a probable ID on the car. Then we start backtracking to either an owner or rental agency." Then, another thought: "Anyone find a sat-link?"

"Haven't found one yet," said the tech. "We'll keep looking, but there might be nothing left. Fire heats up the batteries and then the things just explode."

*   *   *

As he and Ketchum headed back for Ketchum's car, Ramsey asked, "Hank, any possibility that this guy came from one of the islands? Or maybe took a ferry to one?"

"The only one we keep going as long as we can is to Cameron Island, that big island about three klicks off-shore, and that ferry opened up again last week. The island's got a winter population of about two hundred permanent residents. The ferry runs until there's too much ice, and then we open up an ice highway, or folks take ice sleds across. We have a ferry goes clear across the lake that runs mid-May to November. Why?"

"Just a thought. If he *was* a tourist, then maybe he went to Cameron Island. You could talk to the ferry people, see if anyone saw or spoke to him."

They dropped into Ketchum's patrol car, and Ramsey said, "So Pearl offer you money to adopt?"

"Not quite." Ketchum cranked the engine. "Just about."

"Okay. But in what capacity?"

Ketchum backed the car, did a three-point turn and settled into the straightaway back to town before answering. "Whatever you want. You can call all the shots, you can be chief of the task force, if you want."

"Hunh." Ramsey thought about it. "I like consultant better. You need to be out front, in full view. These are your people, and they're going to be watching. Or don't they elect sheriffs anymore?"

"They elect. I'm up again in a year and a half."

"So I'll do my thing, we work together, but you need to be the one to make assignments. Pick the people you want on this thing. Then we got to get moving if we want to crack this before the Bureau sweeps in if this guy turns out to be somebody."

"Suits me." Ketchum gave him a glance askance. "Got anything particular in mind to do next?"

"Yeah. Breakfast."

Breakfast was at Ida's, a combination bakery and diner that sat halfway down a boardwalk edging the harbor. The boardwalk fronted a jumble of eateries, knick-knack shops and empty slips for charter fishing rigs that advertised rates for a half or full day's excursion. Except for Ida's, the shops were all closed until the start of the tourist season.

Ida's smelled of coffee, cinnamon and fried eggs. Something retro played from a wheezy audiobox. Ketchum nodded to a trio of deputies—Ramsey saw the one named Bobby again and two fresh-faced, apple-pie twentysomethings—and he and Ketchum took chairs at a corner table overlooking the water. A formidable woman came with a pot of coffee and two white porcelain mugs.

"So, Hank," the woman said as she poured coffee. She had a whiskey burr that reminded Ramsey of a brief visit he'd made to Tikonov. "Who is this?"

"Ida, Jack Ramsey. Ramsey, meet Ida Kant, best cook and finest gossip in town."

"I do not gossip. I merely relate what I have heard." Kant did not smile. She had sharp coal-colored eyes set above a hatchet nose that lent her an imperious air. She had a stiff, formal way of speaking that Ramsey normally associated with nobles but might be because of the accent. She wore jeans, a black scooped-neck tee that showed the lines in her throat and a hint of gold. She turned her attention back to Ketchum. "With a deputy like Boaz, you do not need a gossip."

"Well, besides Boaz, you heard anything? Any strangers?"

"Do you mean besides all the reporters? No one except the regulars," Ida said, and then turned on her heel.

Ramsey looked after her. "Don't we get to order?"

Ketchum was stirring sugar into his coffee. "Nope. Ida decides what you get and that's what you get."

"What kind of restaurant is that?"

"Ida's," Ketchum said, and blew on his coffee.

Whatever Ida thought of Ramsey, her food was delicious: fried eggs, Javan warty sausages, flaky biscuits and sweet cream Maxwell tarise butter. "This is fabulous," Ramsey said when Ida came by with her coffeepot. "I haven't eaten this well in years."

"Yes." Ida gave Ramsey a hard look. "Cities are for barbarians."

When she was gone, Ramsey said, "I don't think she likes me."

Ketchum sucked at his teeth then hefted his mug. "That's just Ida. She's old country folk. Descended from one of the first settler families that came out of Slovakia. Ida still has a place way the heck out toward the mountains. She goes there every now and again, when she's had it with the rest of us."

They sipped coffee and swapped cop talk, sniffing around each other like dogs. Then Ramsey said, "On the way out, I saw farms, a lot of fields, tarises, Terran cows. But no AgroMechs. No hovers. Just trucks and cars and bicycles. You and your deputies only carry slugthrowers. I don't have anything against guns; I like them. But everything is so . . ."

"Backward?"

"Retro was the word I had in mind." *Actually*, prehistoric. "Your people against tech?"

"No. We could carry lasers same as city cops, but gun'll kill you just as dead, and I hate the smell of burned meat. Just because something's modern doesn't mean it's any better. Look at The Republic. Soon as those HPGs went down, whole thing fell apart."

"That's kind of harsh."

Ketchum's bushy eyebrows arched. "When was the last time you heard from or saw our beloved exarch, huh? Here's what matters"—he slapped the table—"stuff right in front of you. Here, you walk in a field, grub around, get some dirt under your nails and then take a good smell of something clean and natural. Keeps you rooted." A pause, and then Ketchum rubbed the back of his neck. "Listen to the old man jawing."

"It's okay. I never really think about things like that."

"You ought to," said Ketchum. "You might live longer."

"Yeah?" Ramsey said. "What's so good about that?"

Driving to the county courthouse, Ramsey said, "You mentioned something about a killing a few years back."

"Well," Ketchum drawled, "I *think* I said hunting accident, more like. They happen." A pause. "Truth is I hate thinking about it. If it hadn't happened, I wouldn't be sheriff."

"How's that?"

"Because the guy who died was the sheriff, Isaiah Schroeder. Practically a fixture in the community. Awful thing. Out hunting, tripped, rifle discharged . . ." Ketchum shook his head. "Heck of a thing."

"They're sure it was an accident?"

"Pretty sure. A darned shame, though. Born and raised in Clovis, about forty klicks south, and then came up here after he did his tour with the Planetary Militia. He wasn't one of those Triarii Protector poster boys or anything. Just a decent, God-fearing, larger than life kind of guy. Worst of it was that the whole thing was a dumb accident. Not the way Isaiah planned on going out. He'd been talking retirement soon."

"He was that old?"

"No, no, I just think he was sick of the politics, especially if it's got something to do with some darned noble playing tourist. Those nobles got sticks up their butts most the time. Usually, a bunch of us deputies and Isaiah, we'd hunt together. But Isaiah said he wanted to be alone, and he *had* been kind of down. I figured, you know, problems at home and such. Anyway, Isaiah got into his truck, stopped at Ida's for doughnuts, and that's the last anyone saw of him alive. When he didn't show by dark, Hannah—that's his wife—got worried, called it in. I got to be the one to find him." Ketchum paused. "Heck of a mess. Blast busted his face like a melon on ferrocrete."

"Jesus."

"Yeah. Now the two youngest—that's Noah and Sarah—they live at home. Isaiah had an older boy, Scott, from another marriage. Scott was a little wild, but Isaiah worked hard with the boy, go off hunting, just man to man. The boy started doing better, grades going up, looking happier. Then Isaiah died and Scott . . . you couldn't talk to the boy. Finally, Scott just up and left."

"Left his family?"

"Yup. Only came back about three months ago. Now he works a bar outside of town and lives with some girl he met. You can bet Hannah's not happy about that."

"Hunh." Ramsey paused then said casually, "So was Slade the ME? On Schroeder?"

"Amanda? Naw, she wasn't here yet. Old Doc Summers ruled the death an accident." Ketchum's eyes slid to Ramsey. "So you like our lady doctor, huh?"

"I was just asking . . ."

"Yeah, she's a fine-looking woman." Ketchum threw Ramsey a wink. "Fine-looking."

They pulled into a parking lot behind the county courthouse, a blocky three-story building of native Neurasian sandstone faced with arched windows accented with white stucco. As they clambered out of the patrol car, Ketchum said, "You know what everyone's thinking? They're thinking, maybe, the killer's one of us. Maybe he's my neighbor down the road, or that ornery farmer that my Aunt Gert picked a feud with years back, or maybe my wife, or maybe it's my husband."

Ramsey looked at Ketchum across the roof of the patrol car. "That's the hell of it, Hank. It probably is."

10

Hannah Schroeder left the house at nine-fifteen, though she'd been up all night, brooding. God was punishing her. First Isaiah keeping secrets, then Isaiah's death, then Scott's disappearance, and now Noah . . . Her vision blurred with tears. She was crying too much. Maybe she should see Old Doc Summers, or maybe Dr. Slade. Or maybe Father Gillis could help. Better yet, maybe call Father Gillis first then bring Noah in. Noah might talk to a man. Oh, why did Isaiah have to die?

She drove into Farway's downtown: seven blocks of brick and sandstone fronted buildings standing cheek by jowl, with the tumbledown look of a typical tourist town going to seed. Main cut the town east and west and Lake Drive was the north-south thoroughfare, edging the lake. There were three hotels (two closed); a swank bed and breakfast; a post office; a Comstar office (closed); a hardware store; an everything store selling, well, everything from women's clothing to pickling jars. Her chocolate and taffy shop, A Taste of Heaven, stood near dead center on the left and next door to a defunct gift shop. When she came on her shop, she pulled nose-in and then just sat there, her cheeks wet, the engine idling. Her eyes picked out every flaw: the sign's faded pink lettering, the sagging steps, the spatter of green-white bird droppings speckling the eaves over a bay window display she hadn't changed in four months.

Her purse nestled in the front passenger wheel well, and she leaned over, dug out a handkerchief, and blew her nose. She let the purse thud back to the well mat. Then she threw the car into reverse, backed out, cut left and drove. She passed the courthouse, a jumble of civilian and patrol cars; then the last bar and she was in open country, heading northwest.

Everything bad started with Isaiah. What she'd never told anyone, not even Father Gillis, was that months before he died, Isaiah had . . . changed. He'd become suspicious, morose. The night before Isaiah died, they had an awful fight, hurling words that cut like jagged glass. And then, the next day, Isaiah was dead.

She remembered Hank Ketchum, hat in hand, framed against the darkness beyond her kitchen door, yellow light puddling at his feet and glinting off his deputy's star. She and the children were clustered around the kitchen table, and she'd just brewed another pot of coffee when the flash of headlights caught her eye and she'd turned, seen the patrol car bouncing down the drive. No flashers. No siren. And . . . she just knew.

An accident. That's what Hank and Old Doc said. But there was more to it than that, she knew. But what?

About ten kilometers out, she came to a fork and continued northwest. In ten more klicks, she spied a small block of businesses: a gas station, a pizza place, and an auto chop shop on the right, and on the left, a fruit stand (closed for the season), a vacant storefront that had once been an ice cream place, and a two-story redbrick building housing a bar on the ground floor. The bar's holosign was black, but she knew the name well enough: *Good Time Charlie's*. She slowed, then swung around back into the bar's parking lot. She slid left of the bar's back door and killed the engine.

A black wrought iron fire escape led to another door on the building's second floor, and she craned her neck to scan the second-story windows. The shades were drawn.

The fire escape was steep, and gravity grabbed at her body and her purse—the weight of the world pulling her down. The door at the top of the stairs was black-painted metal. She listened, heard nothing, but the apartment beyond didn't feel empty. She rapped on the door.

More silence. She knocked again, and then heard something shambling up, the thunk of a bolt. The door squalled open, releasing a puff of air that smelled of cigarettes and stale beer.

The woman was about twenty-five, with tousled brown hair and murky brown eyes. She wore jeans and a too-tight, V-neck, short-sleeved tee that accentuated a pair of melon-like breasts. Her face was lean and hungry-looking, but she was a little thick around the middle. Her feet were bare. She pinched a lit cigarette between the index and second finger of her right hand. "Scott's not here," she said.

Hannah cleared her throat. "Do you know where I can find him?"

"No." The woman took a drag from her cigarette then jetted smoke out of the right corner of her mouth. "He didn't say where he was going."

"Was he here yesterday? Was he here last night?"

"Yeah, he was here. He worked the bar."

"What time did he get in?"

"Why?"

"Because I want to know. I'm his mother, Grace, and I should think . . ." Hannah let the sentence dangle.

Grace inhaled more smoke, her breasts swelling, held the smoke then let it go. "You should think what?" The words rode on puffs of smoke. "That Scotty ought to get Mommy's approval every time he goes out?"

"I have a right to know."

"No, you don't. You're his stepmother, not his wife."

"You're not his wife either."

"Maybe not." Grace hitched up a shoulder and let it fall. "But then again he's sleeping with me, not you."

Hannah's stomach iced with fury. "Why can't you leave? I'd give you money."

Grace's eyes were cool. "I don't suppose it matters that I love Scott."

"You *slut!*" Hannah raised the clenched fist of her right hand. Shook it in Grace's face. "You . . . you don't love my son! You think that getting pregnant, you own him? You're just using him, *blackmailing* him."

Grace snorted. "Oh, yeah, right. I got pregnant just so I could live in this dump. Relax, Mommy. Maybe I'll miscarry. Or maybe I'll get an abortion. Maybe—"

"Blasphemy!" Without thinking, Hannah smacked Grace's left cheek as hard as she could. Her hand stung with the blow and Grace staggered, grabbed for the door to keep from falling.

Then she was back on her feet, hurtling out of the apartment. Grace was fast and strong, and she shoved Hannah back against the fire escape. The wrought iron railing dug into Hannah's spine, and still Grace kept coming. For one, terrifying instant, Hannah saw blue sky as her back arched, knew she was going over the edge . . . and then Grace had her by the throat and jerked Hannah forward until they were eye to eye.

"You hit me again, I swear I'll kill you." Grace's face was blotchy with the imprint of Hannah's fingers. She still had the cigarette, and now she held the glowing tip at the corner of Hannah's left eye. "I'll burn your eyes out, one at a time. And then I'll burn you other places, Hannah, and I'll take a long, long time."

The cigarette was so close, Hannah heard the paper crackle and felt heat. Frantic, she tried jerking away but then Grace tightened her fingers, and Hannah's throat began to close off. Panicked, she choked, flailed, swung her fist again but Grace ducked.

"Don't." Grace's teeth bared in a feral grin. "Don't, or I'll kill you right now."

"Can't . . ." Hannah's lungs burned. "Can't . . . br . . . ee . . ."

Suddenly, Grace let go. Released, Hannah staggered, grappling for the railing to keep from falling down the stairs. When she could get her breath again, she sobbed, "I'll t-tell . . . wa-wait until Sc-Scott . . ."

"One word, Hannah, and you're dead." Grace's voice was flat. "You make one move to take away my Scott, and I'll kill you, Hannah. You won't even see me coming." She backed toward her door. "Or Scott will. You don't know your stepson, Hannah, but I do and I'll let you in on a little secret. Your sweet, innocent Scotty? He's not such a good little boy anymore."

"What do . . . what do you mean?" Hannah's throat convulsed. "What have you done to him?"

"No, no." Grace smiled, not nicely. "The question is what has *Scotty* done?"

11

When Sarah banged out of the house an hour later, Noah pushed out of bed. He was light-headed, and the room spun, but he made it to the bathroom. His skin crawled with sweat, and he felt oily. He was too freaked to check under the bandage.

Washing his teeth and taking a shower made him feel a little better, except he couldn't get warm. Shivering, he tugged on jeans, heavy socks, a button-up shirt because of his arm, and a bulky wool cardigan. He tottered downstairs, still feeling woozy. Debated about eating but didn't have an appetite.

He tried Joey on link, audio only. Joey's mom said he was out at soccer practice, and then when she started in about the night before, he told her he had to go, and clicked off. He debated about calling Troy. Troy's mother would be out because she was almost always "out," either out as a waitress at Ida's, out drinking, or—literally—out: dead drunk and sleeping it off.

No matter what, I gotta call Troy. We got to get his bike back.

Troy's mother *was* out—grocery shopping. Relieved, Noah switched to full vid and then got worried all over again. Troy's face was fish-belly white, with purple smudged under his eyes. He had on an old pair of glasses held together at the bridge with duct tape.

"You look crummy," Troy said.

"So do you. Did you get into trouble?"

Troy's mouth curled. "Mom was so worried, she didn't even notice that I wasn't home in time to eat. What about you?"

"I'm grounded, probably forever."

"How's your arm?"

"Hurts." Noah didn't want to get into it. "You heard about the car fire? You think it was the same guy?"

"Yeah." Troy's eyes were wide behind his glasses. "Even if it isn't, I got to go back and get my bike. If the guy who killed him comes looking . . ."

"I know. I'll come with you."

"But you're grounded."

"My mom works the shop today. She won't be back until after five. It's"—he squinted over at the wall chronometer—"almost ten-thirty. Plenty of time." Then he thought of something. "Uh-oh."

"What?"

"How are you going to *get* there? Your bike's out there, and I don't think I can steer so good with my arm racked up. Joey's at soccer, and he'll be gone all afternoon."

"Maybe we should just tell Joey's dad."

Noah shook his head. "Too late for that. Besides, Joey's the one who stole the cigarettes. He'll *really* get grounded for life."

"We don't have to tell about *that*."

"I'll bet they got ways of finding out. Besides, if his dad finds out we saw and didn't tell, then they get us for withholding evidence. My mom would kill me."

"Okay." The way he said it, Noah knew that Troy wasn't okay but would go along. Troy said, "I'll take my mom's bike. All I have to do is lower the seat a little bit."

"But then *her* bike will be gone," Noah pointed out. "That's no good."

"She'll never notice. Anyway, it's better than leaving mine, right? Besides, you got a better idea?"

Noah didn't. They agreed to meet at the cemetery in two hours, and then clicked off.

Time to kill.

He wished there was someone to talk to, even his

sister. But what he really wanted was an adult, someone who could tell him what to do and how not to be afraid. Maybe Scott . . . but if his mother found out he'd called or gone to see his stepbrother, she'd have a stroke.

He crawled back upstairs, his arm complaining with every step. Instead of going to his room, he turned left, went to the end of the hallway and stood before his parents'—no, his *mom's* room. A knotted string dangled from the ceiling, and now he grabbed that with his left hand and pulled down a panel with folding steps.

The attic was cold and smelled of dust, old cardboard and chilled steel. After his father died, his mother packed everything into boxes and stored them here. She even asked Sheriff Ketchum to get a few men together and move his father's gun safe into the attic. That had taken a whole day: unpacking all the guns and ammo, and then taking out the attic window and winching the safe up the side of the house. Noah had gone into the attic a few times over the past few years, usually when he really got to missing his dad, to huddle in the dark. But today, he sensed that something was . . . different and, after another moment, he knew what. One of the boxes was open.

Noah eased down, squatting by the cardboard container. He ran the tip of his left finger under a flap and levered the cardboard back. He frowned. These clothes were unfamiliar. When he riffled the stack, he heard the crinkle of pryolene pouches. He gently tugged a corner of one pouch, and his breath caught.

The shirt was military blue. Butter yellow rank insignia decorated the collar. Above the left breast pocket was a small embroidered insignia—a whorl of ten white stars cut by the tail of a comet set against a black background—and the name of a militia unit. Other pouches contained military trousers, a dress tunic, a pair of black boots with the outlines of his father's toes visible against the buffed leather. But it wasn't until Noah bent over to replace the pouches that he spied a square of pryolene wedged beneath a bottom flap. He teased out the pouch and held it to the light.

The medal was a burnished five-pointed gold star within a circlet of gold-veined, dark blue enameled oak leaves arranged in pairs, two between each of the star's five points. In the center of the star, also in gold, was a portrait in profile that Noah recognized immediately: Devlin Stone. The star dangled from a golden crossbar upon which the word GUARDIAN was cast. The entire medal hung from a length of sky-blue ribbon, with the ten stars, blue disc, and gray ribbon of the Republic embroidered above the point to which the star was attached.

Why did his father have a Republic medal? There hadn't been any action on Denebola that he knew about. And what did "guardian" mean? Guarding what?

Finally, he put all the clothes back, piece by piece. But he slipped the pouch with the medal into his hip pocket. He just wanted it.

He'd pushed up and was about to back down the attic stairs when his father's gun safe caught his eye. Odd. He'd have sworn the last time he snuck up here boxes were wedged up against the door. But now he tracked the entire door, all the way down to the seam along the bottom edge. When they'd moved the safe, his mother had to call a locksmith to come and open it because only his father knew the combination. She'd had the locksmith program in a new code, and now *she* was the only one who knew *that*. So—his mother? But why? She hated guns. Why she'd kept his dad's was a mystery.

This is getting a little weird.

The safe was solid twenty-centimeter steel two meters tall and one wide and painted the color of money. A rearing seven-point Morin odopudu was embossed in gold above a five-spoke gold-plated wheel. A combination digital lock was set at shoulder height left of the wheel. Enter the code, then twirl the handle to open the safe.

He didn't know the code. But . . . Noah reached out with his left hand, hesitated, then grasped the handle and jerked it counterclockwise, thinking the whole time: *It's locked, you watch, it's gonna be locked and . . .*

A perceptible *thunk*. The lock disengaged. He pulled, and the safe's door glided open on smoothly oiled, soundless hinges, releasing an odor of gun oil and steel.

The interior of the safe was carpeted in a deep, rich

green the same color as the safe itself. A door-mounted rack held shotguns and rifles, and his eyes skipped over his own Erral Colt that his mother had confiscated, his father's pump Winchester Astro, and more rifles but . . . Noah frowned. The rifles were out of order. He knew just how they ought to line up: from eldest to youngest. His father's Astro should've been on the far left. But the Astro had been moved and traded out for Scott's old Tharkad Griffin.

There were four carpeted shelves for gun cases and ammunition, and again Noah had the same sense of things being moved, replaced, taken away again, shifted. He chewed on his lower lip then flipped up the latches of a case he recognized at a glance. He lifted the lid, and a smell of oiled wood pillowed out. The case was lined with foam cut to the gun's contours. A soft beige chammy covered the gun, and when he lifted the cloth, he saw his father's service weapon, a stainless steel seven-shot revolver with walnut grips. He stared at the gun a long time, then carefully rewrapped it, thumbed the latches shut and was replacing the case when he noticed that another had been left open.

He knew what was in that case. He'd only seen it a couple of times, but he remembered: a .70 mm AE Skye Talon. A cannon—that was what Scott used to called it. A really, really big gun.

He also knew when he hefted the case that the gun was gone. The case was too light. But he looked anyway. Then he pawed open a box of ammo and stared at seven empty slots.

Seven shells missing. And the gun. From a safe for which no one had the combination.

Except his mother.

12

Saturday, 14 April 3136
1300 hours

"Maximilian Youssef," Boaz said, pronouncing the last name *YOU-cheff*. A holo of Boaz's face hovered in a tower of light over Ketchum's desk. The deputy had been assigned to run down the car's serial number. The serial number had bounced from the rental offices in Farway to New Bonn spaceport. "Rental place at New Bonn says Youssef picked the car up three days ago on a transport inbound from Slovakia. The agent there says he remembers the guy because he tried to talk him into a newer model Avanti hover on a promo deal. But Youssef wouldn't budge. Said he had to have a car-car. Thing is, when we ran Youssef's planetary ID, there's no background info at all."

"An alias?" Ketchum asked.

"Looks like it. And the other thing, Hank, this guy Youssef had a ticket outbound for day after tomorrow, first thing in the morning. No way that this guy would head west for the mountains. He'd never make it back in time."

After Boaz clicked off, Ketchum sat back with an irritable groan. He'd taken off his hat, and a ridge showed where the brim had squeezed his reddish-blond hair. "We're no better off than when we started."

"That's not true," Ramsey said. He leaned his right shoulder against a wall opposite Ketchum's desk and adjacent to a coffee maker squatting on a nicked side table. The carafe was half full of coffee that smelled like toxic waste. Typical cop coffee. "We know he came from Slovakia and was traveling under an alias. So either he was hiding from someone *here*, or running from someone *there*." Ramsey thought. "You said there were a bunch of people with ties to Slovakia, right? Anyone mention family coming recently?" When Ketchum shook his head, Ramsey said, "How about not so recently?"

Ketchum scratched chin stubble. "I could ask around. My wife's from Slovakia . . . well, her grandmother on her mom's side. But I don't think that's it."

The second and third calls came fifteen minutes later: deputies reporting in, their canvasses not turning up much. The fourth call came at 1:45 p.m.

Either the connection was better, or the Denebola Bureau of Investigation had excellent communications equipment. DBI Special Agent Garibaldi's holo was so crisp, he looked stenciled. He was like all government men: square, fit, impeccably dressed in a dark blue suit, white shirt, and red tie, and possessed of a supercilious air of superiority. When he spoke, he did so with the exaggerated concern of a schoolteacher lecturing a slow student. "The reason this request is so important is because it is so unusual."

"How's that?" Ketchum asked. His tone was polite, but he fidgeted. "Sounds just like a request for information to me."

Garibaldi allowed for a small, indulgent smile. "As I said, it happens that we had an inquiry about a missing person from a representative of the legate's office in the planetary capital of St. Cameron. This man's missing . . . no, he's not even due *back* to Slovakia until the day after tomorrow. But his family's worried, says he's been out of touch."

"Or he didn't check in," Ramsey suggested.

"In any event, Youssef is the name that's come up, and if it's an alias . . . well, we want to coordinate with our Slovakia office about whether to become formally involved."

"So what do you want us to do in the meantime?" Ketchum ground out. "Pick our teeth, or our noses, or what?"

"Continue with your investigation." Garibaldi moved to punch out. "We'll be in touch."

Ketchum was pissed. Ramsey let him rant then said, "Hank, I've dealt with the Bureau. They're not bad. They're just not cops. They do intelligence, and they *like* running all that computer stuff that'll just drive you buggy. If the Bureau's smart, they'll let you do your people."

"And if they're not?" Ketchum scowled. "They don't have to worry about elections."

"Deal with it when the time comes. Speaking of which . . ." Ramsey checked his watch. "We still got about four, five hours before anyone wakes up in Slovakia. So let's get moving, go see the cut. Then we start shaking a couple trees and see what falls out."

13

The tree clinched it.

Gabriel had disobeyed orders. He'd gone to work early, just to have something to do. Work didn't help as much as he thought it would. Once he was home again, he scrolled up the door to a modular shed behind the house, got his bicycle, and headed to the cemetery. Had to do it anyway, right? Anyway, the exercise would do his leg some good, keep it limber.

The cemetery was quiet. Always was. That's *wh*y his Handler had chosen this for the meet. After stashing his bike in a clump of evergreens, he checked the mausoleum. His guns, the plinker and 720, were still there. He wore a lightweight parka with extra-large pockets, so he checked the safeties, then zipped each weapon into a separate pocket. He left the walking stick. No graceful way to get that back to town.

As he slid the mausoleum's back panel into position, he was already planning. He had a number of stashes, places where he squirreled away supplies and weapons: a boat in a cove forty klicks west of the trestle; another on a small nubbin of island past Cameron, if he ran east.

His leg started to nag when he was halfway up the

hill. He pushed on, crested the hill and then turned back. Whoever had been here had an excellent view.

But they don't know it was me, otherwise the police would've come by now.

But who *were* they? There'd been too much movement for just one person, so who? Kids? Maybe—he'd tripped over a bike. So where would they hang out around there? Then, as soon as he turned his back on the cemetery and scanned the tall grass to the left, the grove of maples ahead to right, he remembered: the tree house. Of course. That damned tree house.

He let memory guide him, and eventually found the tree. But he also found something else: the bike, smeary with blood, a ribbon of ripped khaki cloth tangled in the biggest sprocket. *His* blood, his *trousers*. He reached to rip the cloth out of the sprocket then pulled back. Fingerprints. Couldn't touch the bike. Hell, he already *had*. What to do? Get the blood off, yeah, but he had to get it home. Even if he did, that didn't solve anything.

Parents don't like it when a kid loses his bike. They notice things like that.

If he only knew *whose* bike . . . Maybe a clue in the tree house. When he was a kid, he used to leave all sorts of junk up there.

The wooden steps were still nailed to the tree, but they looked old and dry. Some of the steps had wide fissures where the wood had split. He put his good foot on the first step, then gingerly let the step take his weight. He climbed, slowly, with cautious, circumspect movements. Even so, climbing was harder than he remembered, and his right leg throbbed. Six meters up, he heard that peculiar squeal that stressed wood makes and then the step shattered beneath his left foot. For a dizzying second, he flailed, slipped, snagged the palm of his right hand on a nail head. He came down hard on his right foot as the nail ripped his skin, said, "Shit," and then hugged the tree, waiting for his vertigo and a sudden lurch of nausea to go away. His right leg flared, and he had half a mind to give the thing up. But he kept going, saw the lip of the tree house coming up, grabbed a branch and boosted until he caught the edge with his stomach and then heaved himself the rest of the way.

"Son of a . . ." He was sweating like a Javan warty, and his *hand* . . . A ribbon of red bisected his lifeline. More problems; *more* bandages. He'd forgotten that tetanus shot, too. More things to do.

The floor of the tree house was strewn with detritus: candy wrappers, the petrified core of an apple; comic books; a greasy Black Knight Six playing card. He checked the date of a comic book. Last summer. So, maybe, whoever saw him wasn't in the house. The interior of the house was scarred with carvings, the graffiti of bygone ages incised by a thousand jackknives and mini-lasers over a score of years:

> *BT ♥ NS*
> *School sux*
> *Life sux*
> *Julie sucks*

A smile ghosted his mouth. Kids. Was the one *he'd* done . . . now where *was* that? He was scouring the wood when he heard something. He froze.

The rustle of grass. Voices. And one word, very distinct: "Troy."

14

"This guy's in pretty good shape, for a crispy critter," Amanda Slade said, peering through a pair of hexaglass eyeguards. Other than a pair of brown sertalene surgical gloves and the glasses, she was hospital baby blue from tip to toe: blue puffy cap for her hair, scrubs and booties. She stood over a steel autopsy table fitted with gutters. Although the table was long enough to accommodate an adult, the victim's body occupied a lipped metal tray about the size of schoolkid's desk. A mike hooked over her right ear and linked via infrared to a holorecorder suspended over the autopsy table.

She was midway through the autopsy and had already removed what was left of the breastplate as well as the heart and lungs *en bloc*. She'd flayed the heavily carbonized heart, and, in contrast to the coal black exterior, the tissue inside was a dull leathery brown and looked almost artificial, like a plastic cast.

Ketchum said, "Where's the necklace and that ring?"

"In back with the rest of his stuff," Amanda said. "I'll send everything down with the body when I'm done. You can look at them later if you want."

"Jesus," Ramsey said. "This looks like what happens

with a roast chicken if you forget to take out the heart and gizzard."

"That's exactly what it's like. Even if we didn't already know about the head shot, I'd say this guy was dead before the fire. There's no evidence of tracheal charring, nothing in the lungs, no soot anywhere along his bronchial tree."

"Here's what I don't figure." Ketchum scratched the back of his head. "Most fires like this get set to destroy evidence. But that's stupid here, right? I mean, it's kind of hard to miss that bullet hole."

"But what if the fire was set to destroy something else?" Amanda asked.

Ramsey and Ketchum looked at each other. "I never thought of that," Ramsey said.

Ketchum grunted. "Might be something to that. Question is . . ."

"Yeah," Ramsey said. "What was in the car?"

"It gets weirder than that. I think someone took a shot at him with another gun first." She retrieved another tray with the excised breastplate and waited until Ramsey and Ketchum crowded around. "See here?" Amanda used a long metal probe as a pointer. "On the sternum and the fourth and fifth left ribs. There's pitting in the bone."

"Meaning?" Ramsey asked.

"It looks like what you see when someone's hit with a shotgun. Except, here, there are no pellets, no buckshot. Might have been something else, though I don't know what. Sometimes people have pacemakers and the batteries explode, but the damage pattern isn't right and his heart's intact."

"A shotgun?" Ketchum frowned. "You hit someone with a shotgun in the chest, you're gonna pretty much kill 'im. Makes the shot to the head kind of irrelevant."

"Unless they wanted to direct our attention to the head shot. Maybe the killer figured *that* was so obvious we'd chalk up the chest to the fire."

"Any way to tell which came first, the shotgun or the head shot?" Ramsey asked. When Amanda shook her head, he looked at Ketchum. "Well, this leaves two possibilities. Either we've got one guy and the sequence of chest shot and then a covering head shot, or we've got two guys."

Ketchum made a face. "I don't like that."

"Which one?"

"Either. Toting two guns around is overkill. Like our boy likes the guns because he likes guns. Besides, why use a shotgun first and then have another guy follow up at close range with another gun? Youssef was probably on the ground already, either dying, or close to it. Head shot's over the top."

"Wait, wait," Amanda said. "I'm no expert on shotguns, but aren't those the kind of weapons used at a distance?"

"Depends," Ketchum said. "Why?"

"There's lots of fire damage here, no question. But not so much that I can't see the blast pattern. This pattern is stellate, star-shaped, as if there were explosive gases, like what you'd see with a shotgun blast that plowed into the sternum. The gases expand laterally, conducted under the tissues in a starburst pattern. So I think this person was close, except . . ." She paused.

"What?" Ramsey asked.

"There's also not *enough* damage. You hit someone with a shotgun blast to the chest, the lungs and heart ought to be shredded. There's some lung damage, sure, but it's not enough, and like I said, the heart just got cooked from the fire." She screwed up her face, like she'd just smelled something awful. "Still, I'd swear this looks like a contact wound. What's the range for a shotgun?"

"Maximum range for a conventional shotgun is about forty-five, fifty meters," Ketchum said. "But if you're aiming to take someone out at distance, you're going to use a sniper rifle not a shotgun. If he was ambushed while he was driving, then the shooter was going after a moving target. That's darned hard to do with a shotgun, and if you were going to use one, there'd sure as heck be pellets."

"He's right," Ramsey said. "Plus, to get that distribution, even if we assume that the guy was driving, you'd have to blast him through the windshield. But then we ought to see blast patterns in what's left of the face and neck, not his chest."

They all thought about that a moment. Then Amanda gasped. "What?" Ramsey asked.

"Oh, I am so stupid," she said. Stripping off her gloves, she crossed to a far aluminum counter and riffled through evidence pouches. "I can't believe it."

"What?" Ramsey asked again.

She came up with a pouch and hurried back. "Remember at the scene I said he was positioned kind of funny? He was angled with his feet in the passenger wheel well, like he was lying down. But how would the blast do that? Unless he was sleeping and someone popped the car door, or shot him straight through the glass, he'd be sitting *behind* the wheel." She held up the clear pouch. Inside were fragments of what looked like wood chips, or old dice. "This guy had to be killed outside his car."

"How do you know that?"

"Because of his fingers," she said. She opened the pouch and gently retrieved a spread of bones. "I haven't sorted these yet, but I know these are finger bones. But see here"—she tweezed up one fragment, then another—"these fingers were broken."

"How can you tell?"

"Torsion injuries. The fractures aren't clean breaks. Some are spiral and some are straight, greenstick breaks. The spiral breaks are torsion injuries. You only get those if you take the finger and actually twist it until it breaks. The greenstick breaks are from someone bending the fingers back until they broke."

"What about torture?" Ketchum asked.

"Maybe," Amanda said. "But couple this with the body's position, and I think this guy was already stiff from cadaveric spasm *before* whoever killed him put the body back in the car."

"I've seen that," Ramsey said. "You get to a scene and you swear the guy's been dead for hours. Only our ME says cadaveric spasm's rare."

Amanda shrugged. "Rare doesn't mean never. Usually, cadaveric spasm happens when the victim's in some kind of struggle. His muscles get oxygen-depleted, then he dies, and the normal rigor process is bypassed. For whatever reason, our guy went into cadaveric spasm, and his fingers were broken *after* he died. The only reason you do that . . ."

"Is to get at something he's got in his hand," Ramsey said.

"Something the killer worried might be used for identification," Amanda said. "Or a weapon. Find a weapon, and we'd know Youssef didn't come up for the scenery."

Ramsey said, "So Youssef's expecting trouble. Probably, he's got a weapon. But whatever happens, it happens outside the car—either at the scene, or someplace else. Then the killer rolls the car off the road and detonates a bomb to make sure the fire's hot enough to destroy the body, or whatever's in the car."

"You've still got a problem," Amanda said. "The killer drives out there, but how does he get away? He just torched the car. So either someone followed him in another vehicle, or he'd hidden one not too far away."

"We should get in touch with the crime scene people, have them expand their search radius," Ramsey said. "See if they can find tire tracks, bike or turbo treads, hover air-blast patterns, stuff like that."

"Worth a shot," Ketchum said.

Ketchum left to call the crime scene people, and Amanda started with the abdomen. "Stomach's still got food in it. I'd say he ate not more than an hour or two before he died. Not a large meal. More like a snack or something."

"Can you tell what he ate? Might give us a clue where he was before he died," Ramsey said.

"Well, it's hard to say. Everything's cooked, except . . ." She plucked something out that was small, shriveled and dark, about the size of a pea. "Voilà."

"Looks like a rat turd."

"Not unless he was desperate. It's a raisin. I can do a couple of other tests, see if there's gluten or something in there. That would tell us if he had bread or something like that." She dropped the raisin into a vial, sealed it. "Like the man said, worth a shot."

Ramsey never liked when MEs cracked a skull. Never got used to it, and it wasn't any better this time around even if Amanda didn't have much of Youssef's face to peel back. He looked away when she revved up the bone saw. The thing sounded like a dentist's pneumatic drill.

When she'd cut a bone cap, she removed the cap then lifted the brain out of the cranial vault. This brain wasn't runny or pink but like a very large, toasted walnut. After weighing the brain, Amanda flipped the organ over to get a good look at the frontal lobes, glancing now and again up at a shimmering green 3-D holograph of the brain in situ. "Okay, shot was close proximity, no exit wound—this is where your bullet entered the brain," she said, indicating a deep brown, puckered splotch that looked like very old clot. After a few minutes of gentle dissection, she dropped something that rattled against the sides of a molded aluminum basin. "And there's your bullet."

The bullet was scorched with heat and had blossomed, mushrooming into jagged petals. "Twenty-two hollow point," Ramsey said. He pinched the bullet between the index finger and thumb of his gloved right hand. "See, here's the mark from the firing pin, and you can see where it's grooved. Ballistics people ought to be able to track down the make, and match the bullet to the murder weapon, if we find it." Then he thought of something. "What are you going to do about DNA?"

Amanda blew out. "I'll take some from the organs and soak the bones to extract some DNA. I can use a phenol-chloroform solution for separating protein from the nucleic acid, then do a hot start PCR." At his mystified expression, she said, "The thing with bone is the calcium. Calcium messes up the DNA, so you have to separate the calcium first. Then, to make copies, you use hot start where you prevent Taq polymerase from working by heating . . ."

She'd lost him after two sentences, but her face was so animated, he just liked looking at her. He hadn't felt that in, well, a long time.

". . . And amplify only the region of DNA I need to make enough to run for an identification match. He'll have banked his DNA for identity and future medical purposes, and we'll know who he is for sure. But if that doesn't work, I can try mitochondrial DNA and . . . Detective? You with me?"

Ramsey nodded. "All the way."

"One more thing: Our guy's got a couple of dental anomalies that really might help." She called up an anterior to posterior, green glowing 3-D of Youssef's skull. "Look at the teeth. See, here, here, and . . . *here*."

Ramsey had seen enough dental 3-Ds to know how enamel, dentin and nerve root appeared on scan. But Youssef had what looked like long tent stakes driven into his gums in—he counted—seven teeth. "Is that something *inside* the teeth?"

"Dental posts for false teeth. I'm no forensic odontologist, but a post is made to order. The way a post is shaped can tell you where the dentist trained. Then you'll know who Youssef really is—or maybe what alias he used when he got the posts done."

"Can you take out one of these posts?"

"Well, that's specialty work, and I might damage something but . . ."

"What?"

"I was just thinking that the rest of this guy's bones, what's left of them, they look good. Old guys, they lose bone mass and density just like women do. *His* teeth don't look so good. Nothing as dramatic as the posts, but the densities vary and that's"—she shook her head—"that's kind of weird."

"So maybe he didn't drink his milk when he was a kid and that explains his teeth. Or maybe he ate a lot of candy."

"Then his long bones shouldn't be so good, and he ought to have fillings. Only his bones look fine, and he doesn't have fillings. And *this* tooth"—she pointed to a left rear molar—"it looks almost ready to fall out."

"Maybe it got damaged in the fire, or the blast."

"Mmmm." She was rooting around her instrument

tray then came up with a long, curved clamp without teeth. She caught his expression. "I just want to look."

"I thought you said you weren't a tooth doctor."

"Don't tell anyone," she said. She gently sectioned a bit of ligament, spread the mouth wider, then eased the clamp around the sooty tooth. "Don't want to rock on the other teeth and break them, got to pull straight . . . got it," she said, pulling out the clamp. A large, corrugated, pitted surface of a rear molar was held firmly in place. "No post," and then she turned the tooth over. "Oh, my God."

The fire had cooked the capsule hidden inside but not completely destroyed it. The gelatin was brown as melted sugar for caramel.

Ramsey said, "You know? This just keeps getting better and better."

15

1445

They found Troy's glasses and, a little farther on, Troy's bike smeared with dried blood, a scrap of khaki tangled in a sprocket. If Noah had any doubts about last night, he knew: this was for real.

He was sweating even though it wasn't that hot, and he felt water-weak. His arm was much worse. He'd taken down the dressing, right before he'd left his house. The wound was ugly: purplish edges and some kind of yellow, gooey crud in the center. The surrounding skin was warm, almost hot, and red. He did the peroxide the way Sarah had and the ointment, tears running down his cheeks by the end. On the way to the graveyard, he felt every bump and thump his bike made all the way into his teeth.

Troy was white as salt—from his diabetes or fear, or both, Noah didn't know. Troy said, "Maybe we ought to tell Joey's dad. You know? It might be evidence."

"Yeah, and then what?" Noah's head hurt, and his ears rang. "It's too late to do that. We just wash off the blood and that's that. Like it never happened."

"Yeah?" Troy bent, plucked something from the grass. He held up a brass shell case. "What about this? You going to tell me that there wasn't any guy shooting at us? Someone who shot *you*?"

"Could be anybody's brass," Noah said. It sounded dumb: *Anybody's brass*.

"Don't be dumb," Troy said. "They can match the brass. They do it all the time in cop shows. Maybe we should go down to the graveyard. There might be something there that we can show to Joey's dad."

"Are you nuts?" Noah's head was spinning. "We don't tell anybody. We don't *do* anything. We came to get the bike. We got it. So let's hide your mom's bike and get out of here."

"Then *he* gets away with it."

"And who cares? Look, we tell, and then what? What if they don't catch him? What if the blood doesn't tell them anything? What if he comes after *us*?"

"Maybe Joey's dad can send us away somewhere, or something," Troy said. He paused. "Something."

Pain and fever made Noah cruel. "Yeah, maybe that's okay for you. You don't like your home, or your mom. But I kind of like where I live." He was lying, of course, and he felt like a heel when Troy's eyes filled.

Troy swallowed, and when he spoke, his voice was watery. "Yeah? Well, at least *my* dad didn't kill himself."

The words were like a slap. Noah went cold all over. He didn't know whether to burst into tears, or hit Troy so hard that, maybe, he'd break something: Troy's nose, a tooth. Just to draw blood.

But before he could do anything, Troy's face crumpled. Tears rolled down his cheeks. "I'm sorry. I didn't mean—"

"Yes, you did," Noah said, but the moment was past, and he felt something in his chest loosen. "You meant it. That's okay because"—he swallowed past the lump in his throat—"I think he did, too."

They fell into a miserable silence, broken only by Troy's snuffling. Finally, Troy swiped a rope of clear mucus from his nose and rubbed his hand on his jeans. "This is what happens in movies. You know? People turning on each other when they get scared."

Noah felt as if it took all his strength just to nod his head. "Yeah. You know why, don't you?"

"Uh-huh." Troy's eyes were wide as saucers. "I got a

real good look at him, and you know who he looks like? *Walks* like? The *hair*?"

"Yeah. I do," Noah said. "He's one of *us*."

"Yeah, you're telling *me*?" Troy sounded small and scared and his voice came as a whisper. "He's *my* doctor."

= 16 =

1530 hours

Ramsey was exasperated. "Look, if you're so fired up, why don't you guys just assign an agent to work alongside this, this . . . what's her name again?"

"Kodza." The tiny shimmer that was Garibaldi's holo, projected from Amanda's office computer where the call had been routed, looked positively cheerful. "Dani Kodza."

"So why not assign one of your people to work with this Kodza woman and be done with it?"

"No, no." Garibaldi moved his head in an emphatic negative. "We can learn much more if you and Sheriff Ketchum's men front for us. Besides, *you*, Detective, are the best possible person for this job. A disgraced cop— no one's going to believe that you've got access to the john much less the Bureau."

"Well, gee, thanks a lot," Ramsey said, getting hot.

Ketchum broke in. "So what can you tell us about her?" Ramsey and Amanda had shown him the tooth when he'd gotten back after making his call to the crime scene techs. "She high up or what?"

"We're not quite sure. We do know that she was born off-world, on Dalkeith, and seems to have been all over the Prefecture." Garibaldi turned away a moment, and his hands extended out of sight, probably accessing data on a computer. "Now what's interesting is her travel. We have a couple of reports indicating that she traveled to . . . just give me a sec . . . here we go. Port Mosby, Xinyang, Itabiana, and, finally, Nykvarn."

"Is that important?" Ketchum asked.

"Maybe. Port Moseby is in Lyran space, right by House Kurita and the Ghost Bear Dominion border. Xinyang is the prefecture capital in the Benjamin Military District. Itabiana is a Clan Sea Fox clearinghouse world and part of Nova Cat's territories. And finally all of these are on a straight shot to Nykvarn, and from there, it's just another jump to the Periphery."

"So?" Ramsey was still ticked about the disgraced cop crap. "So what?"

"Detective Ramsey," Garibaldi began, though he might as well have said, *Now, now, little boy.* "Those planets are within the sway of Kuritan space. Now we *know* that House Kurita has moved to reclaim worlds ceded to The Republic. At this rate, Dieron will fall and they'll succeed. We hear that Katana Tormark is quite the warlord."

"So?"

"*So*, what did Kodza *do* out there? Some of those worlds are also Clan."

"But they're all different clans," Amanda said. "Call me slow, but so what?"

Garibaldi put a finger to his lips as if warning himself against being precipitous. He said, "It's no secret that with Prefecture X buttoned up, the various divisions of government here on Denebola might start making moves to shore up influence. Everyone's heard of the ghost knights, of course, and the Bureau believes the exarch has planted moles and agents in as many places as possible in the Inner Sphere."

Amanda and the two men glanced at one another. "So you're suggesting that this Kodza is a mole for the exarch?" Ramsey asked.

"Perhaps. Then again, perhaps not."

"Oh, well," Amanda said, "that was clear."

"All we know is that Kodza was obviously on some sort of mission."

"Even *I* can figure that," Ramsey said. "Do you know anything else?"

"She's never been married, doesn't have any children and no living relatives. Beyond that, we'd appreciate anything you can coax out of her."

"Now you want us to spy for you?" Ketchum asked.

"All you need to do is report on the progress of the investigation. Give us whatever Kodza tells you, let us crunch the data, and see what comes up. She'll probably have her own shadow or ghost agent, and that agent will likely be doing his own reconnaissance. It would be nice to know who he is."

Ketchum raised his hands like a cop stopping traffic. "Wait a minute, wait a minute. How are we supposed to figure out who the ghost agent is? You guys have all the intelligence data. We got nothing."

"Correction," Garibaldi said. "*You* will have *Kodza*. Wait for something to happen. Sometimes these ghost agents get themselves into trouble. But it's just as likely that the agent might be a sleeper already embedded in the community."

Ketchum and Ramsey glanced at one another. "Already here?" Ketchum asked.

Garibaldi explained the common practice of inserting operatives well before they were needed and integrating agents into a community. "Sometimes this sleeper agent thing runs in families. Then, all that's required is a contact to activate them, and they go to work."

"So just how does this help us?" Ramsey asked.

"Maybe no help at all. Maybe the agent's a sleeper, maybe not. But you and me and Ketchum, we're playing on the same team. It's the *legate's* office we don't trust. Spies are everywhere. Perfect time to take out the prefecture governments."

Amanda said, "I'm not so sure that wasn't the exarch's plan." When Ramsey and Ketchum turned to look at her, she said, "Think about it. Levin's pretty much left people to fend for themselves. But that has to mean that his resources are stretched. So he buttons up and hunkers down. He'll be back—but by then things will have shaken out, and he may have fewer personalities to deal with."

"She's got a point," Ramsey said.

Ketchum cleared his throat then pursed his lips, as if debating how to continue. "Okay, I want to ask a question here." He squinted narrowly at Garibaldi's image. "Do I get *any* kind of say about whether I want to cooperate with you fellas? I mean, seeing as how this is my jurisdiction and all."

"In a case of this magnitude, with a potential spy? I'm afraid not. You boys don't play ball, then we'll do it another way. And, Sheriff, you don't want to lose in the next election." Garibaldi showed a set of picture-perfect teeth in a humorless grin. "Do you?"

= 17 =

1530

The boys found two more shell cases, but not the fourth. Then they retrieved Troy's bike, hid another—a woman's bicycle—and left.

Gabriel waited. When he was sure they were gone, he backed out of the tree house, took the steps very carefully, his right leg complaining but not as badly as before. He spent fifteen minutes searching for that fourth piece of brass. He didn't find it.

He debated the wisdom of another call then decided he didn't have a choice. He hooked a bud to his right ear, tapped a channel.

And then the Handler was there against a background of voices and, he thought, music. "Yes?"

He kept it short but told the Handler everything. "Now they've got the bike with my blood on it and a piece of my trousers, and they've got brass from my gun."

"Yes, but they are scared, correct? So they will wash the blood away and no one will be the wiser. As for your casings, they have touched them. So there will not be useable prints and all they will be able to say is that someone fired at them."

"But I think I hit one of them."

"And nothing has come of it. So most likely you did not."

Gabriel remembered the third shot and a scream. "No, you're wrong." He had never contradicted the Handler before, and he waited for an explosion of anger. But none came. He said, "It's that they're too scared to go for help." Then, more boldly: "We need to talk."

"What is there to discuss?" The Handler's voice was like chipped ice. "When the one you hit comes to the hospital, you will take care of it. You will have to take care of all of it."

This, he really hadn't expected. Killing Limyanovich was the mission. But this . . . "You're asking me to kill a kid."

"No, no," the Handler said. "I am telling you to kill both of them."

18

"Frederic Limyanovich." The woman on the holovid
was fair-skinned, with an oval face framed with light
blond, almost white, hair that curled at the nape of her
neck and around her chin. Her eyes were almond-shaped
and a very light blue-silver. Her accent was noticeable
but not heavy, though her speech was a little stilted, as
if she were parsing her words just so. "He is . . . *was*
the brother of Vladimir Limyanovich, a very wealthy,
very influential businessman. His company, PolyTech,
primarily deals in biotechnology: medical advances,
things of this nature. He has no idea why his brother
would travel to Neurasia. They have no business inter-
ests in New Bonn that he is aware of. Surely, the condition of his brother's body suggests that Frederic
Limyanovich was not there for his health."

Amanda said, "Not so fast. We don't know if this is
Frederic Limyanovich."

"You have a body, yes? There are teeth? So we will
match the dental records. You could send the information now. Then you will see he is the same man."

Amanda frowned, and Ramsey tried another tack.
"Do you have any information about why Limyanovich

was killed? His brother doesn't know, but maybe they have business dealings . . . ?" He let the question dangle.

"We are mystified, and the family is shattered. I have been asked by the legate to assist you in your investigation. Of course, this has been cleared with the governor."

"Of course," Amanda said, arching her left eyebrow.

Kodza spared her a quick, measuring glance. Then she addressed Ramsey and Ketchum. "At all costs, the family wants the killers brought to justice."

"Killers?" Ramsey asked.

A smile flitted across Kodza's lips. "A figure of speech. I am confident that both you and the sheriff can understand that the family would like to reclaim the body and arrange for burial. I will arrive in Farway by tomorrow evening to assist in this."

"Ah," Ramsey said. "Great."

There was a small silence that Kodza filled. "What other evidence do you have pending?"

Ramsey listened as Ketchum and Amanda went through the list: the jewelry, the autopsy findings. But Amanda glossed over the teeth, didn't even mention them. Then Ketchum was talking about fibers and hair found by the crime scene people. "And what look like tread marks from a turbocycle," Ketchum said. "Found the marks in a briar patch about a quarter klick up the road. Our working hypothesis is he was killed somewhere else."

"And you found nothing else?"

"Was I supposed to?" Ketchum deadpanned.

"No, no, it is just odd that he should be in Farway and even odder that he is dead. One would think that if he *was* killed . . ."

"I think the bullet to the head is pretty conclusive," Ramsey said.

"Obviously. But one would think Limyanovich had something worth killing *for*."

After Kodza signed off, Ketchum looked at Ramsey. "You smell what I smell?"

"The cover-up, or the fishing expedition?"

"Both."

Ramsey nodded then washed his face with his hands and sighed. "I don't know what's worse: DBI, or the legate's office playing games." To Amanda: "You're awfully quiet." When Amanda raised that left eyebrow, he added, "You're pretty good at that."

"It's genetic," Amanda said, "and you guys are idiots, which might also be genetic. Didn't you hear it?"

Ketchum and Ramsey traded looks. Ramsey turned back to Amanda. "What?"

"Unbelievable. *God*." She huffed out in exasperation. "Kodza asked *specifically* for the dental information. She wanted the dental records sent right *now* and yet she's coming here, no matter *what* we find. But *we* already found the capsule, and *she* doesn't know that. Only a matter of time before the city lab people figure out what's in it, and I'm not releasing the body until a forensic odontologist gets his shot."

"May not be anything," Ketchum said.

"But may be," Amanda said. "You want to take bets that there's something else hidden away somewhere? So the question is, what is it about this guy that they don't want us to find? And why was it so important that he ended up dead?"

19

The only deputy with something new was Boaz. "Eric remembers running a guy out to Cameron Island last week. Remembers because the guy didn't look quite ready for the weather, you know?"

"Who's Eric?" Ramsey asked. They were grouped in the bullpen across from dispatch: the deputies slouching in chairs, Ketchum perched on a corner of vacant desk, and Ramsey holding up the wall next to a window.

Boaz's eyes skimmed past Ramsey to the floor and then Ketchum. "Eric runs the ferry. He said the guy wasn't really dressed for the occasion. This time of year, anyone going over to the island wears a hat, gloves, that kind of thing. But this guy wasn't even wearing a parka, just a sweater under some kind of black duster, and his boots were way too nice. Like expensive leather, the kind you wouldn't want to get wet. Description matches this Youssef, or Limyanovich, or whoever he is."

"Did he say what day?" Ramsey asked.

"This past Wednesday."

"Hunh." Ramsey eyed Ketchum. "What's on the island?"

"Nothing," Ketchum said. "Besides the permanent residents, that is. Used to be real popular a while back when we had a bunch more tourists. A lot of condos, vacation places but not so much anymore and sure as heck not this time of year. Hunting season comes around, we issue just enough licenses to thin the herd of Morin odopudu. The only other thing is the old sandstone quarry. Not a working one anymore, you understand. Tourists like to hike in, gawk. But that's it.''

And that *was* it. The meeting wound down. Ketchum handed out assignments for the next day, and fifteen minutes later, the deputies straggled out, with Boaz giving Ramsey a wide berth. Ketchum stared after the deputy's retreating back then said, "Something going on between you two?"

Ramsey was embarrassed. "We didn't see eye to eye on something. I almost lost my temper. Actually I pretty much told him I'd ream him a new asshole if he kept being one."

"Is there *anyone* you don't offend?"

"Have I offended you?" And when Ketchum shook his head, Ramsey said, "There you go."

Sighing, Ketchum screwed his sheriff's hat on his head. "I'm going home. I'm going to kiss my wife, have some supper, maybe talk to my boy. Then I'm going to sleep, and I sure as shooting ain't gonna be dreaming about you."

"And here I thought you cared."

"You want to come on over? Have something to eat?"

Ramsey shook his head. "Naw, you go be with your family. I'm going to stick around here awhile."

"What for?"

Ramsey hesitated. "What you said about the Schroeder case . . . that bothers me."

"Why?"

"Schroeder died on Cameron Island, right?"

"So?"

"So, maybe nothing. But it's the last big case around here and now Limyanovich goes to Cameron Island and *he's* dead."

"But Isaiah went hunting."

"Maybe," Ramsey said. "Only maybe he wasn't after any deer."

*　　*　　*

An hour later, Ramsey pushed up from Ketchum's computer, tossed back the last dregs of cold, rancid coffee, then lobbed the cup for a garbage can. The cup rimmed the can, teetered on the edge, fell in. Probably the only slam dunk he'd see for a long time.

Needed to move. Needed a break. He jammed his hands into the pockets of his jeans and paced. The Schroeder case bugged him, but he wasn't sure why. Something just a little . . . off.

Three years ago, give or take, Schroeder told his wife he was going hunting. He didn't say where, and his wife told Ketchum she assumed he was going west, into the foothills where the russet-tailed odopudu, a relative of the Morin variety, rutted. Schroeder left his house before dawn. He'd taken along a thermos of hot coffee and a packet of sandwiches. He kissed his wife goodbye, climbed into his truck and drove away. Ida Kant recalled Schroeder stopping by for breakfast and a sack of pastries. That was the last time anyone saw Isaiah Schroeder alive.

Three days later, after the Kendrake Mountain rangers reported that no vehicle license matching Schroeder's had passed into the mountain hunting preserve, Hank Ketchum went to Cameron Island on a hunch. He and three deputies found Schroeder's body along a spit of land overgrown by Denebola cypress on the opposite side of the island. Schroeder was facedown, sprawled across a tangle of cypress roots—or rather, what was left of his face was planted in a pool of half-frozen, coagulated blood, his rifle and right arm curled beneath his body. He wore the tattered remains of an orange-blaze pryolene parka, a red-and-black-checked flannel shirt, and blue jeans. He had no day pack but a fanny pack and inside was camo face paint, hand warmers, a pair of gutting gloves, a sat-link, a planetary ID, a hunting license, and a candy bar still in its wrapper. His thermos, half empty, was found ten meters down an incline.

Small animals had done a pretty good job. Big chunks of Schroeder's buttocks, thighs, and flanks were gone. His brains were gone, too, because the shotgun had blasted away the top of his skull, so all the animals had to do was slurp. Schroeder's left arm was severed at the shoulder and missing. His feet, still in their socks, were in his boots, but each boot had been gnawed away from the leg at the ankle.

The doctor of record was Ezekiel Summers. Summers did the autopsy and ruled the death accidental; he thought Schroeder tripped and died when the rifle discharged into the angle of his right jaw. The round tore through bone and exited below the left ear.

The rifle's magazine held ten rounds, and there were eight in the clip and one in the chamber. No box of ammo was found in Schroeder's truck or his home. The only prints found on the weapon were Schroeder's, and only his DNA was recovered at the scene. The bullets were clean, but the prints on the magazine were Schroeder's.

Hannah Schroeder thought her husband had been more irritable than depressed, but couldn't be specific. She had suggested counseling with their priest which her husband rejected. A check of the prisons showed no one released in the last six months with a grudge against the sheriff. Schroeder was buried; Ketchum was appointed sheriff in a special election that gave him the job for the next four years. And case closed.

Something wrong.

He ran through the report again. He read it twice before it hit him. Schroeder wasn't wearing a hat.

Cold enough for a parka and gloves, but no hat. If a guy's gonna stay outdoors in the cold for long, he brings a hat.

He reviewed the list of items in Schroeder's fanny pack. Gutting gloves but no knife and no rope. So how was Schroeder going to field-dress his game? And camo paint with a *bright orange* blaze parka, that didn't make sense. Ramsey did another search, nodded when he saw the results. Unlike Terran deer, odopudu could see red and orange hues. So why the camo paint when the parka was as good as taking out an ad?

But there was something else, something in the autopsy. Ramsey skimmed through the report, came to

Summers's report, read it, tabbed to the next section—then went back. Found the section that snagged his attention, read through it slowly.

A few minutes later, Ramsey threaded through the deputies' bullpen and stuck his head into the dispatch's office. "Can you give me the number for the hospital?"

"Sure," the dispatcher said. "You want me to put the call through for you?"

"That'd be great."

"Who should I ask for?"

"Dr. Slade."

"Okay," the dispatcher said. "I'll patch it to the sheriff's office."

Five minutes later, dispatch put the call through. The page operator told him to hold, and a few seconds after that, Amanda shimmered into view. "Yes?"

Ramsey explained. "So I had a couple questions. Can I meet you at the hospital?"

"Sure. I have someone to see in the emergency room, but that won't take long. Say, a half hour?"

"Great. Thanks."

"No problem," Amanda said, and disconnected.

Ramsey transferred a copy of the Schroeder report to his noteputer. Technically illegal, but screw it. Pearl said he should consult, so he was consulting with a consultant. It worked.

As he left, he stuck his head into the dispatcher's office again. "Thanks. I'm out of here."

"Okay," the dispatcher said. She had pencil-thin eyebrows and she did that left eyebrow trick Ramsey never could get. "Have a good time with our Dr. Slade."

"Uh . . . this . . . I'm . . . this is just business."

"Oh. Well, then." The eyebrow again. "Then make sure you two have a *really* good time."

$=$ 20 $=$

1830

The Handler was hunched over a mug of coffee and smoking when Gabriel came through a back door. "You were not seen?"

Gabriel shook his head then pointed at another man slouched in a chair to the Handler's right. The other man had a coffee mug in one hand, and a cigarette in the other. "I don't want him here."

The other man—older, a little jowly—stiffened. "I have a right to—"

The Handler silenced him with a look and said to Gabriel, "You are in no position to give orders. I asked him to come." His Handler knocked ash into an empty mug and waited until Gabriel drew a mug of coffee, splashed in cream and slid into the chair. Then the Handler said, "I am disappointed. These witnesses . . . this is not professional."

He was already mad, and that just made him madder. "Hell what you like. You weren't there." Gabriel blew on his coffee then sipped. The coffee was too hot. "Jesus."

"Watch your mouth, boy," the other man growled. He was still in his work clothes and picked lint from his trousers. "We're all at risk. This isn't a game."

Gabriel flared. "I know that, you sanctimonious—"

"Stop." The Handler glared at Gabriel and then the other man. "Both of you."

"I'm just saying," Gabriel began.

"I heard. Now, tell me again about last night."

Gabriel did. Fingering a linked gold chain, the Handler listened in silence, smoked, flicked ash. The other man simply scowled. Then the Handler said, "You are sure they cannot trace the bomb?"

"They might be able to figure out what I used, but I doubt it. It's a pretty unusual combination. Plus, I didn't use any commercial grade materials."

"Well, that's something," the other man said, grudgingly.

But the Handler's eyes slitted, both in thought and against the smoke. The Handler caressed a small oval medallion of gold, zipping the medal back and forth on its chain. "But how did you know the explosive would work? You had to test this, yes?"

This, Gabriel *hadn't* expected. He considered lying then thought better of it. "Yeah, I tested it. Just a small amount. I didn't want to attract attention."

"Where?"

He gnawed on the inside of his left cheek. "Cameron Island."

"The island?" The other man sat forward so quickly he sloshed coffee onto his pants. "You idiot, what if—"

"No one saw me." Gabriel kept his eyes on the Handler. If he didn't, he was likely to strangle the other man, and while that would give him a great deal of pleasure—would, indeed, make his day—they had to move past this. "I was careful."

The other man made a rude noise. "Like you were careful in the cemetery?"

Gabriel's voice was deadly. "I told you before. It was dark. They were downwind, so I didn't hear them, didn't think to look up the hill. We chose that spot because we *all* thought it would be deserted."

"Enough." The Handler held up a hand. "Mutual recrimination gets us nowhere. What is done is done. You said the boys had this bicycle, the one with your blood?"

Gabriel nodded. "I still might be able to get to it. But

that may not be necessary. Those kids are scared, and Troy's not going to want anyone to see the bike until it's cleaned up. I don't think—"

"I am not asking you to think. I am asking you to follow orders."

"But, for once, I agree with him." Screwing his cigarette in one corner of his mouth, the other man dabbed coffee from his trousers with a napkin. "Killing Limyanovich was necessary," he said. The cigarette bobbed. "These are just kids."

"This is necessary."

"They're *kids*."

"And we are at war. Regrettable, but these boys must be eliminated."

The other man shook his head. "But killing a kid, especially so *soon*—"

"Murders can be made to look like accidents, or even entirely natural happenings, yes? Whatever comes up, you will handle it. You will steer this as you have done before." Without waiting for the other man to respond, the Handler nodded at Gabriel. "And especially *this* boy, Troy, may be prone to accidents, yes? Diabetics frequently experience difficulties, do they not? So"—the Handler inhaled more smoke then blew out twin streams like a dragon—"you are in a unique position to make sure of it."

The other man chimed in again. "But what about Michael? I know he hasn't been as involved lately, but if he finds out . . ."

"We will not tell him." The Handler stood, signaling that the meeting was at an end. "We are very close. If we secure these last two crystals, then we have all three. But Michael must not find out. He will try to stop you, and if he finds out about the *other* matter, this Noah . . . you will have to eliminate Michael as well."

"I can do that," Gabriel said. "But that's a lot of dead people. Shouldn't we be making plans to move our operations?"

"If their deaths can be made to look like accidents, nothing else might be required. We could still move our operations, but rushing when there is no emergency? That is when mistakes are made."

"Okay." Gabriel checked the time and pushed to his feet. "I got to get to work. Give me some time to come up with something for the kids."

"You must also think of what we should do with Michael, just in case," the Handler said. "He knows too much and he is weak."

"Then we'd better make goddamn sure he doesn't find out," Gabriel said.

"Indeed. And, please," the Handler said, "do not blaspheme."

21

1900

Spring was as Scott Schroeder always remembered it: long in coming, with many false promises. Too cold still for frogs, and even the malgars—waterfowl with yellow webbed feet and vestigial upper arms reduced to a single claw—had waddled back to their nests, their sleepy *screeree* cries the very last sounds of anything living on that lake. Then the islands disappeared one by one as stars fanned across an inky dome until there was nothing but blackness and the slap of water on rock.

Cameron Island was the last to go, and Scott watched as it grayed out. He was a gaunt young man and very tall, so when he jammed his fists into the pockets of his jacket, the cuffs rode above his bony wrists. His sneakers were damp, his toes icy. His right ankle throbbed, and he still couldn't put all his weight on it. Grace was bound to notice.

He didn't make it back to the apartment until nearly time for him to work his shift at Charlie's. He threaded his car, a piece of crap junker that was all he could afford, into the back lot, nosing into the only available space, right next to the dumpster. The story of his life.

So many things had gone wrong. Still, he'd been relatively happy when his dad had been alive. Funny how it was the secrets that bound them together in ways that simple blood couldn't. Because they had a special mission that was more important than just about anything. Their mission was going to save the Inner Sphere.

And then you had to go and get yourself killed. Oh, Dad, I don't know if I can do this. I don't have the training. What am I supposed to do?

In the apartment, Grace was sprawled over the stained cushions of an old couch. She was reading under the too-weak glow of a light bar, a beer bottle in one hand and the gray rectangle of a noteputer in the other. The couch's frame was beige, but the cushions were a dirty liver color, scarred with cigarette burns and spilled coffee. The air vibrated with the surge of heavy bass from downstairs. She looked up. "Where have you been?"

"Out." Peeling his jacket, Scott headed for the bathroom, trying not to favor his right leg. He turned on the tap, splashing water into a chipped porcelain basin with yellow stains around the drain.

As he washed his face, Grace came to lean against the doorjamb. Her jeans were open at the waist, and she hadn't been able to work the zipper all the way over the swell in her abdomen. "You're late," she said. "Maass came up, threatened to kick us out if you weren't down there in twenty minutes. I was about ready to go down myself."

"Well, he can just throttle back," Scott said to her reflection. In the light of the bathroom, he could see that her left cheek was bruised. "What happened to your face?"

"I fell," she said, dismissively, as he squirted a rope of toothpaste onto a brush. "So where were you?"

"Out."

"Yeah, you said that."

"So, okay." He flicked on his toothbrush and foamed his teeth, saved from saying anything else for a little while more.

"Out," Grace said. "Like last night? I know you didn't work your whole shift."

He spat, rinsed. "I worked."

"No, you didn't. Maass told me. He said you came in late. So where were you?"

He shrugged by way of an answer then pushed past into the bedroom—forgetting, too late, about the limp.

"What happened to your leg?"

"I twisted my ankle." He palmed open a drawer and rooted around for a fresh pair of jeans and underwear, a T-shirt he could throw on.

She'd followed him into the bedroom, watching with her hawk's eyes as he sat on the edge of the unmade bed and shucked his jeans. "How?" When he didn't respond, she bent down, fingered his discarded jeans. "Your jeans are wet. Were you out to the island? I told you not to go out there. You'll spoil everything."

"More than things are ruined already?" He thrust his arms into the sleeves of his tee. The shirt was a black crew neck with a logo of a cave lion in silver and black.

"What did you do?"

"I just looked around." Scott dragged a comb through his shoulder-length hair that he then tugged into a ponytail. "It was my father who died, not yours. I can look around."

Grace opened her mouth as if to argue, seemed to think better of it and said, instead, "Hannah came by today. She wanted to see you."

This was a surprise. Scott stopped, socks in his hands. The floor needed sweeping. There was grit under the soles of his bare feet. "What did she want?"

"She offered me money if I'd leave."

Scott's chest was cold. "What did you say?"

"I told her she couldn't afford me. Then she hit me."

Scott felt sick. "Hannah *hit* you?"

"Don't worry about it. I told her I'd burn out her eyes. She stopped." Grace slid a packet of cigarettes off a broken-legged nightstand, knocked out a smoke, and jammed the cigarette into the corner of her mouth. Scratching a match to life, she touched it to the cigarette and sucked. The cigarette flared orange, and she shook out the match as smoke jetted from her nostrils. "So," she said, tossing the cigarettes back onto the nightstand and the match into a butt-filled ashtray, "you think she's still going to feel the same about her little Scotty once she finds out?"

"Don't threaten me, Grace." His lips shook. "Don't goddamn threaten me."

"I'll do anything I want." She gave a silent, taunting, dog's laugh. "And such language, it's blasphemy. Isn't that what dear, sweet Hannah's always saying? What will Hannah think if maybe I tell her all those dark little secrets she hasn't got a clue about dear old Isaiah? Then what, Scotty? Kill me? I don't think so. In fact—"

"*Damn* you!" Scott unfurled so quickly Grace didn't have time to duck. He caught her right cheek with his open palm. The smack was a loud crack, like an icicle breaking off. The blow knocked the cigarette out of her mouth, and she stumbled back on her heels then went down, banging her head against the edge of the nightstand.

"Oh, God." Hitting her knocked him off balance, and he'd come down hard on his right leg. Pain roared into his knee, and he thought he was going to burst with shame. "Oh, God, oh, Grace, I'm sorry, I didn't mean . . . I wasn't thinking . . ."

"Shut up." Her long hair fanned over her face, and she nudged a shank away with the back of her hand. Her right cheek was blotchy, the outlines of Scott's fingers tattooed in red welts. A trickle of blood inched from her mouth and when she spat, her saliva was foamy and red. She laughed, a little crazily. "Now I got a matching set. Who says you don't take after old Mom?"

Scott squeezed his hands into tight fists, felt his nails bite his palms. Nothing was working out; he was supposed to make things right and now look. He'd hit her, and he didn't hate Grace, he loved her. "Are you okay? Is the baby . . . is it . . . ?" His voice choked off when he saw her eyes.

"Screw the baby." Her teeth were orange with blood and her eyes bright as lasers. "And screw you. Now I want you to listen really good, Scotty-boy, okay? You listening?" When he nodded, she said, "Here's the deal. You touch me again, then you better not ever go to sleep. Because I'll kill you. I'll stab a knife through your fraccing heart. Then nothing gets settled. No one will pay. No one will ever know that your dad wasn't crazy. But we do things *my* way."

"All I care about is what happened to my dad. The rest of it, this stupid cause, Devlin Stone, the *future*"— and then his fury and regret got the better of him—"I don't *care!*"

"Care," she said. "Or you're dead."

22

1900

The ER receptionist told Ramsey that Dr. Slade was discussing a patient with Dr. Summers and to go on through. When he wandered back, he found Amanda arguing with an older, round-shouldered, reedy, sixty-something man with thick snow-white hair and eyebrows, and bright black eyes.

"No, no. If that appendix is hot, I take it," Summers was saying. His voice had the rounded vowels of a Slovakian native, and was a little raspy, the kind a smoker got over time. There were yellow nicotine stains on the thumb and first two fingers of his right hand. "Not so old I forgot where an appendix is. No, no," he said when Amanda started to object, "you go have a good time. Only you two best behave, or people will talk."

Ramsey was embarrassed but Amanda said, "More than they're talking already?"

"Can I help it if you feed the rumor mill?" Then Summers laughed and that should have been that. But as Amanda flipped through Ramsey's noteputer, Summers sidled up, limping a little as if favoring a bum knee. He glanced over her shoulder and then his keen black eyes slid to Ramsey's face. "You have a question about the Schroeder file?"

"Ah . . . not really." Ramsey wanted to get Amanda out of there, anywhere they could talk. "I just had a few questions. I thought since Amanda had the training . . ."

Summers puffed up. "I was doing autopsies for years before Dr. Slade arrived. No one ever questioned a single report."

"That's because the four homicides that happened before Dr. Slade arrived, you shipped those bodies down to New Bonn. That was the right thing to do."

Summers's bushy white eyebrows knit above the bridge of his nose. "Isaiah Schroeder wasn't a homicide."

Ramsey glanced around, aware that everyone in the station—even a janitor dragging a cart of mops and cleaning fluids that smelled of ammonia—was trying very hard to look as if they weren't listening to the conversation which, of course, they were. Ramsey shook his head, spread his hands in what he hoped looked like conciliation. "Honestly, it's really not worth bothering about."

"Not worth it?" Two spots of color dotted Doc's cheeks. "Then what was so gosh-darned important you needed to hike all the way down here to see Dr. Slade?"

"Doc." Amanda put her hand on Summers's arm. "I don't think Detective Ramsey's suggesting you did anything wrong."

"Mmmm." Summers reached for a patient file, shrugging his right shoulder as he did so, as if he had a touch of arthritis, and showed them his back.

Once in the hall, Ramsey said, "That was pleasant."

"He's right to be pissed," Amanda said. "No matter how you gussy it up, you're saying he's wrong. So, want to do this in my office?"

"I could use something to eat."

"Well, you don't want what's in the hospital cafeteria."

"So let's go somewhere."

"Okay. What do you like to eat?"

"I have choices?"

When that detective came in, Gabriel almost flinched. Almost. He'd heard of Jack Ramsey, that business with Quentin McFaine. Seeing him now, up close . . . a tickle of apprehension made the hackles on his neck stand. Ramsey looked tough, those scars on his face, and a lumpish blue-green bruise on his left cheek.

And now the report on Isaiah Schroeder. What did *that* mean? Maybe he should go down to Slade's office later on after the operation. Maybe he could figure out what was wrong, and . . .

He was so deep in thought that he flinched when an OR nurse tapped his right shoulder. The shoulder was sore from the tetanus shot he'd finally remembered.

"Sorry," the nurse said. "They're ready for you in Room Two."

"Sure." Gabriel shrugged his achy right shoulder to work out the kinks. "On my way."

23

Amanda suggested a place by the lake south of town. They took separate cars, Amanda in the lead and Ramsey following in an unmarked patrol car he had on loan. The loaner was handy because he could pop his Raptor into the glove box. Right at his fingertips, if he needed it, and he'd stash the weapon in his hotel room at night.

He'd expected a rickety place with sagging planked steps and squealing hinges on the door. Instead, the restaurant was opulent with a design that smacked of refined taste and a lot of money. The buildings were distinctly modernist, with Tharkad cedar-lapped shingles on peaked roofs. Off the main lobby was an art deco bar, with contemporary stained glass. They ordered martinis—Tharkad vodka, three olives, straight up—and Ramsey knew from the first icy sip that this was going to be one fantastic place.

The main dining room had glass walls, and they were shown to a table directly across from the kitchen, also glass-enclosed, and where they watched chefs in tall white hats and white aprons bustle around stoves and ovens. "You'd never expect a place like this in a place like Farway," Ramsey said.

"Mmmm." Amanda sipped at her drink. "The owner was originally from New Bonn. He used to come up here to hunt." She pointed to a variety of hunting trophies arrayed on a half wall of wood: Morin odopudu heads, a Terran elk, and a very large Kyotan armor bear pelt. Then she hooked a thumb toward the kitchen. "He's also the pastry chef, the one drizzling chocolate."

The waiter took their orders, and then the owner came out, still in his apron. When Ramsey commented on the Kyotan armor bear, the owner regaled him with the story of how he'd bagged the animal: "I'd been out all day, and it was still pretty cold, this being when the bears came out of hibernation. Hungry buggers, they'll come down the mountains a lot farther than usual. Anyway, I hadn't seen one all day and . . ."

Ramsey let his attention wander. Hunting left him cold. But he nodded at all the right places and when the owner said he had to get back, Ramsey waited until he was out of earshot then leaned in and said, "Is this what everyone talks about up here? Hunting?"

Amanda toyed with her swizzle stick. "Other than work, that's what people do up here for entertainment. That, or camping, fishing. I don't hunt, but I like guns."

"So what do *you* do? For fun, I mean."

"You mean, when I'm not working, which is most of the time?" She gave a small smile. "Work some more. Do a little research on the side. And I have horses."

"I thought you looked like a horsewoman."

"How does a horsewoman look?"

"Leggy, and you've got muscles in your forearms. I figure the only people like that either work a lot with their hands, or handle big animals." He paused. "Why'd you come to Farway?"

She told him about Towne. "I didn't do politics well. But facts are facts. They didn't like what I said about the Little Luthien killer, and they not so politely showed me the door. Maybe it was for the best."

Ramsey said, "What's the story on Summers? From the way you and Hank talked about him, I kept expecting this geezer on a heart-lung machine."

"He might still end up there if he doesn't quit smoking so much." Amanda sighed. "Doc hasn't been the same since Emma—that was his wife—died of cancer last year. Now he just works all the time. Actually, Doc reminds me of my dad in a way. Dad dropped dead one night on his way to the hospital. He was in his hover, and I think he knew he was going to die because he pulled over to the side of the road, called my mom, told her he loved her and to make sure I got all his old equipment and then he just . . . died." She looked sad. "He could've called for help. But instead he used his last moments to say good-bye to his wife. I hope someone loves me that much someday."

Amanda seemed to know a lot about wines. She ordered a bottle of Davion Syrah, a full-bodied, deep purple wine redolent with the aroma of spice. Ramsey took a sip, rolled wine around on his tongue, then swallowed. "What about the town?"

"Farway?" She swirled wine and studied how it flowed along the sides of her glass. "It's not as crazy as the city. Here, people leave their doors unlocked. Nothing really bad ever happens here." She paused then said, bemused, "I can't believe I just said that. There's a crisped, dead guy in my refrigerator."

"Do you miss the city?"

"I did at first. The first six months were hard."

"I'll bet. This place, it's like crossing into some kind of time warp. No 'Mechs, no hovers, the cops all carry guns, and the cars, there's not a fuel cell in sight. It's like the whole town's a throwback."

She sipped wine. "But it also grows on you. I mean, take a look around. I've got a fabulous old house, land for my horses. There's open space, mountains, the lake, and you can see the stars at night. When was the last time you saw stars in the city?"

An image shimmered in his mind's eye: of an orange glow obliterated by the lash of snow across his face. And he heard a child's scream . . . "I can't remember," he lied. "But you must miss some things."

"Oh, sure, I didn't say I didn't miss things. I miss all those great restaurants. I miss seeing the latest holos. Here, you have to wait a month for a download. I miss coffee shops where I can get something other than a straight black, milk, or sugar. And I miss the anonymity.

I used to walk out of my teeny-tiny little apartment and get lost. Here, everyone knows everybody else, and they hang together in their cliques."

"Is the religious thing part of that?"

"Yeah, you noticed that? The New Avalon Catholics versus the Old Romans—you can get consumed, you pay too much attention. I'm a good Jewish girl, so I don't really care. I just try to watch my language." Her full lips were stained faint purple from wine, and they curled in a grin. "That's hard. We surgeons got toilet mouths, especially in the OR when things are going shitty."

Ramsey laughed. "How do you cope?"

"I don't let things get shitty. I'm a malpractice lawyer's worst nightmare."

"And what about the rest of it? I mean, are you"—he searched for the right word—"do you take sides?"

"You mean do I believe in God?" She did the eyebrow thing again. "About as much as I believe in the second coming of Devlin Stone."

They had tangy salads sprinkled with sugar-glazed plownuts and rich, blue-veined Ganymede gorgonzola. Then the waiter brought their main courses: lake hippolepsis crusted in Stemson pecans for Amanda, and an Asbaroskis elk-steak with cabernet sauce for Ramsey.

"So what about you?" Amanda forked fish into her mouth. "You from Denebola?"

Ramsey sliced off a wedge of steak. The steak was done to perfection: a little charred with a juicy red interior. He chewed, swallowed, groaned with pleasure. The sauce was rich and complex, and did odd but not unpleasant things with the meat. "You got to taste this," he said, slicing another bite. "Give me your plate, I'll give you some. This is fantastic." But instead of handing over her plate, she took his fork and put the meat in her mouth. He was mildly taken aback and then decided he liked the way this felt, like they'd known each other a long time and certainly well enough to trade bites of food without getting finicky.

She rolled her eyes as she chewed. "I told you," she said, around steak. "Wait, wait, try this." Then she passed his fork back with the fish. She waited while he sampled and made appreciative noises then said, "So, stop stalling. Tell me about yourself."

"Not a lot to tell." This was, considering his history, a bit of a stretch. He saw from her expression that she didn't buy that either. So he told her about being a kid on Devil's Rock: "Hell of a place. I mean, it's really *like* hell. Hot most of the time and you can't breathe the air, so you're stuck in these domed cities." He told her about the three continents and then about vast volcanic fields on Ash. "You can walk for klicks and not see anything except black basalt. And, you know, the rock's hot because of the springs just underneath. You can hear the water hissing if you put your ear close to the rock and turn up the gain in your helmet. There's this desert, too, maybe two, three times as big as Terra's Sahara. The sun heats the rocks all day but then the temperature really drops off at night, and if you sit out there, you hear the rocks cooling down and making these big popping sound as they contract, like popcorn or gun shots. You get a whole of bunch of rocks going at once, like weapons' fire."

They ate, with him talking about his family, his father's business going bust. "The only way we were going to get any kind of education was the military. My two older brothers, they went for the Principes Guards. One's stationed on Alcor and the other's on remote assignment, I forget where. We're not that close."

"Why is that?"

"I'm a brawler," he said, easily. "They're clean behind the ears and I like—"

"Like breaking the rules?"

"I was going to say being inventive, but, yeah, I break rules. Anyway, the militia was the only way I could get past high school. Got my degree in criminal justice."

"Why not be a lawyer?"

"Please, I'm eating."

"That good?"

"The only difference between a lawyer and a crook is that the lawyer figures out how to screw you legally."

"Well, shrinks say that cops, crooks and lawyers are pretty much cut from the same cloth. It's just that cops and lawyers are more civilized." Her eyes drifted to his hands—the scars—and then she gave him a frank look. "Or, maybe, not. There are *some* good lawyers and even some innocent people behind bars . . ."

He cut her off. "No. Absolutely not. I know the guys I put in jail were guilty as sin. The rapists, the pedophiles, guys who figure they have a right to hurt other people just so they can get off and . . ." He sat back, shook his head. Thought: *Hoo-boy, don't go there.* Looked up and said, "Sorry. That's just a real sore point."

"I can see." She looked away, as if debating something, then turned back. "What would you do with them, then? The pedophiles, the child killers . . . what do you think would make it right?"

"I can't answer that," he said.

Her eyes on him, searching. "Why not?"

"Because once the child's gone, he's gone," he said. His throat knotted. "No way to bring him back. No way to make it right."

They didn't say much after that. They decided against dessert and coffee—despite the wounded protestations by the owner—gathered their coats and pushed outside. The air was cold but not as bad as that morning, and they were close enough to the lake to hear the light churning of water. Ramsey didn't feel depressed so much as *oppressed*, like a giant had grabbed his chest with both hands and squeezed. They walked in silence to their respective cars, and then Amanda said, "I'm sorry."

"Not your fault. I just . . . I'm just a little messed up."

A pause. "You want to talk about it?"

"I don't think it would help."

"Okay," she said. "But I don't want the evening to end like this. Let's go for a walk down by the lake. There's a path just off the restaurant's deck. Let's just walk."

"We'll probably start talking again."

"Is that so bad?"

He thought about that. "No."

And they did start talking again, tentatively, Amanda asking questions about his family. "So your brothers go off to brilliant military careers, and you studied criminal justice and then . . . ?"

"The militia, like I said. MP. Military police."

"Did you see a lot of action somewhere?"

He stopped and looked toward her. They were far enough south that the restaurant was just a dim glow and he couldn't read her expression. Her face was like the sun during an eclipse but without a corona. Just a sense of a shape. "Why do you ask?"

"Your hands, and your face. You've got some old scars and some new ones."

"I like to fight. When I was in the military, I boxed."

He felt her surprise. "Like, in a ring?"

"Yeah. All military outfits, they all have teams for basketball, football. I decided on boxing. Don't really know why, but maybe because I don't play so well with other kids, and I like to be in charge. So I boxed. Never got my nose broken boxing, though. Just a lot of other times. The first time was the worst. Broke it pitching little league. He slugged the ball, and I didn't duck fast enough. Second time, I flipped my bike. Third time was in basic. Some drunks hitting on this woman in a bar, and everyone just standing around, letting it happen. Anyway, they landed in the emergency room and then the stockade. The fourth time, I let a doctor do it. I got tired of having a nose that looked like a squashed tomato and I couldn't breathe."

"And all those scars are from boxing?"

"There aren't *that* many," he said, a little defensively.

"But that bruise on your left cheek, the cut, they're new."

"Yeah, well . . . I've had some free time lately. I was getting restless. Figured I'd go get a couple workouts. Before you know it, I'm at the gym seven, eight hours a day, lifting weights, working the bag, sparring. The cutman didn't do a good job, that's all."

She did not, as he expected, ask him what a cutman was or did. She was silent a moment and then, out of the darkness, he felt her fingers over his face. They were tentative, as if she were a blind woman reading his features. He stood and let her touch him, and then her fingers lingered over a moon-shaped divot just beneath his right cheek.

"That's not from boxing," she said. "It's different. How did you get it?"

She'd picked it right out. He felt something in his chest loosen, and he wanted to touch her—take her hands in his. But he stood absolutely motionless, aware of just how close she was. Aware, too, of a kind of hunger for much, much more.

"Teeth," he said.

24

Teeth?

Amanda was too keyed up to sleep. Pushing back in her chair, she tossed her noteputer onto her desk and turned to stare out the window of her study, but all she saw was her ghostly reflection floating in a rectangle of inky black.

Teeth. What had Ramsey meant? He hadn't said, and she hadn't pressed. After that, they'd walked in silence. But the silence had been comfortable. Like dinner—two people sharing a meal and conversation as if they'd been doing it for years.

Things were moving too fast. Her last relationship had been a disaster: a surgeon with bedroom eyes and a body to die for. Their affair lasted three months, and she was thinking marriage, kids. That is, until the surgeon's wife—a businesswoman who'd been off-world—gave her a jingle. Another reason she'd moved here.

She swiveled back to her computer, typed in a search, and ran it. The information was in the third news segment, a broadcast delivered by a breathless redhead:

"Jack Crawford Ramsey, a homicide detective with the New Bonn Police Department, was placed on indefinite administrative leave today, as an internal investigation continues regarding the detective's conduct in the case of Quentin Marc McFaine in December of last year. You may remember that McFaine was the serial pedophile

whose five-month spree claimed eleven victims, all young boys. The case reached its climax when McFaine abducted Ramsey's eight-year-old son . . ."

"Oh, my God," Amanda said. The report ended with a clip of an interview done in McFaine's hospital room. McFaine lay, inert, in a nest of tubes and wires. The combination of a bedside ventilator and trach made McFaine sound like a robot, though:

"I understand why Jack feels this way. Jack really is an acquired taste and I couldn't for the life of me figure out how to get him where we could . . ."

And then she remembered what Ramsey said: *Teeth.*

There was more, some about McFaine, but also about Ramsey. One psychiatrist observed, trenchantly: *"Oh, I think Jack Ramsey knew exactly what he was doing. Ramsey was a military man, a trained fighter. He knew precisely where to apply pressure. Completely understandable considering that his son . . ."*

"Oh, my God," she said again.

Jesus. *Teeth.* Why had he told her?

His hotel room smelled of soap and chlorine. Ramsey had taken a long shower, brushed his teeth and then switched out all the lights and tumbled, naked and still a little moist, on top of the quilt. His body was exhausted, but his mind was still going.

He was an idiot. What was he thinking? But it had been a long time since he'd liked *anyone.* And the counseling . . . what a disaster. He'd read Brannigan's horror at that moment when her eyes turned inward and he knew her thoughts: *Thank Christ, that didn't happen to my kid.* He'd read pity. Pity was the worst.

Easier to go beat up a bag and let others beat him because, deep down, he knew no punishment would ever be enough. Ever. Some things, you only got one chance. After that? Out of luck, buddy.

But, maybe, this was a roundabout way of . . . what? *Warning* her? Because Amanda would do a search, and then she'd figure how to keep her distance.

Better to think about Limyanovich, Schroeder's autopsy. He already knew what didn't make sense to him, but how did the two cases connect? Because he didn't buy coincidence. The town was too small for these cases not to be connected in some way.

"Because everyone knows everyone," he mumbled, and yawned again. He was beat. But his mind was going . . . McFaine, that damned McFaine . . . he was so . . .

The room's link screamed. He crawled back to consciousness, cold because he'd fallen asleep on the quilt. Groggy, he called for light, got pissed when nothing happened, then fumbled for the switch. Was about to punch in when he remembered that he was still naked and jabbed up audio instead. His mouth was gummy with sleep. "Yeah?"

"Jack? Jack, you okay?"

"Amanda? Yeah, uh, sure, I'm fine. I was asleep. What . . . ?"

She cut him off. "We have to talk. I think I found something."

"Limyanovich?"

"No." A pause. "Isaiah Schroeder. Jack, I think you're right. I think Isaiah Schroeder was murdered."

25

Sunday, 15 April 3136
0145 hours

After the appy, the hospital quieted down. The evening shift cleared out, the graveyard people came on, and the hospital ratcheted into low gear: nurses on their rounds, doing vitals, getting a pain med. But, mostly, the hospital slept.

Except Gabriel. His sneakers went *scree-scree* as he slipped along the basement corridor to the morgue. The hall was so silent the sound was like nails on blackboard and set his teeth on edge.

Things were not going well. First, the boys: they nagged like a bad toothache. Then the sheriff's people had backtracked the car and knew that Limyanovich was from Slovakia, that he'd been out to Cameron Island. On the other hand, the Handler said the car fire had worked. Someone had taken notice. The legate was sending a representative, maybe someone they could deal with.

But he hadn't found the crystal, or *crystals*, if Limyanovich had brought both as the coded message they'd sent said he should. So, maybe, he'd overlooked something with the body. If he could check Amanda's files . . .

Amanda's computer wasn't passcode protected and he

was in her files almost immediately. He scanned her autopsy findings and discovered two things. They knew who Youssef really was. But the autopsy wasn't complete yet. Excellent. That meant the body would still be available. What was she waiting on? He scrolled . . . ah. DNA and toxicology. But had she found anything *in* the body?

He almost missed it and when he found the detail, he read it twice. The remains of a capsule melted in a false tooth. *Hunh.* Gabriel sat, twisting his lower lip between his finger and thumb, thinking. Limyanovich had been prepared to kill himself.

"But you wouldn't do that unless you thought you might be captured, maybe tortured." His voice sounded unnaturally loud in the stillness. "So if you hid a poison capsule in a tooth, would you hide something else in the same place?"

He returned to the report. Amanda's report mentioned dental posts and at least seven false teeth, and her decision to let the New Bonn forensic odontologist examine the body. But if *he* could get to Limyanovich's teeth *first* . . .

His mind raced. He would have to study the 3-Ds, maybe make a full-scale holographic reconstruction of the skull so he'd know where to go first because there were no second chances. Then, if he found something, he'd have to alter the 3-Ds *and* Amanda's report. That was a lot to do and much to hide, but he had Sunday off. Monday, he could work on Limyanovich.

He thought briefly about switching out jobs: doing the one he'd set in his mind for tomorrow on Monday. Sundays at the hospital were usually slow, and Amanda wouldn't be in either. But, no, the longer he waited, the greater the chance one of those kids—or both—was going to talk. He had to move on at least one of the kids tomorrow.

"So let's start with you," he said, bringing up another hospital program, inputting a name. He read the information very carefully, and then—just as carefully—made a few changes. Nothing drastic. Just alter a date, save and then close.

He made copies of all the pertinent files on Amanda's

computer then dumped them to a remote, untraceable virtual address. Then he went out on Amanda's web, retrieved a program from his home computer and dumped the program into the guts of Amanda's desktop. He was proud of this program: custom-made, designed to lurk in the background, monitoring files, programs, or certain documents and intercept, if necessary. The program would detect when files were accessed, determine changes and then zip off a copy of the document and its modifications to a remote site. He'd stay on top of things. Whatever Amanda found, he'd know, and he could alter Amanda's final report—expunge certain evidence, insert a false lead if necessary—even though Amanda would believe she'd sent the report to the New Bonn medical examiner's office.

A few keystrokes, and he set the program to monitor the autopsy report and, in an afterthought, any file with *John Doe*, *Maximilian Youssef*, or *Frederic Limyanovich*.

He killed the computer then carefully wiped it down, thinking as he did so. Job one was to slow down Amanda, but how? The answer came a split second later: the DNA. That was the only test still outstanding that she did in-house: in her lab right next door.

The PCR machine was singularly unimpressive: a fancy-schmancy hot plate, really. The base of the machine contained all the programming hardware necessary to run discrete, pre-programmed steps. Along the base were two separate digital displays that counted off cycle, step, and time remaining. Below the displays were two sets of push-buttons: *Run, Stop, Prog, Data*. To the right were more push-buttons for numbers (zero-ten), a push-button that allowed for a decimal, and a button marked *Clr*.

The general principle behind PCR was simple because all a PCR machine did was run solutions at different temperatures. So if he bumped the temp a few times and buried the snafu, the DNA would be ruined. Amanda would start over, but she'd do controls to check the machine, and that would buy time for him to get at the body.

It took him a little under three minutes to ruin the

DNA. On an afterthought, he hit *Data* and wiped the accumulated data from the machine's memory.

His pager picked that moment to *brrr*. The sudden vibration jolted his heart like an electric shock. He checked the number, clicked off. Definitely out of time now.

Taking the stairs again, he thought about Schroeder. Gabriel had coddled the Schroeder case from start to finish, been careful to plant all the evidence just so. For crying out loud, *he* caught the coffee thing and poured out half the thermos. Maybe if he retrieved the Schroeder files from archives, he'd spot what this Ramsey had.

His pager vibrated again but he ignored it. Glancing toward the ER and seeing no one in the hall, he pivoted left, went past the entrance to the stairs and pushed his way through a door marked *Archives*. The room was empty, not a surprise. No one came here except to review scanned records that couldn't be accessed from an office computer, or a case in which all the records were hard copy. Accessing the computer, Gabriel found Schroeder's files, scanned them, and then cursed. Part of the record was available in the computer but another part containing the films—the X-rays though not the 3-Ds—were hard copy. Those films were stored in the next room.

His pager nagged again. What to do? Look at the films, or just dump these files to his remote site, retrieve them later and forget the films? The films were hard copy and couldn't be altered. Of course, he could just *take* the films. But, no, that was *too* coincidental: first, the DNA getting screwed up, then the films gone.

He heard the sound of sneakers scuffing tile and he turned as a nurse pushed through into the archives room. She looked up, startled. "Oh!" Her hand went to her chest and then she gave a little laugh. "You scared me."

He put on his most reassuring smile. "Sorry. I was just reviewing some files for a case."

"Oh. Is there another emergency?"

"No, this is for tomorrow."

The nurse frowned. "I thought you were off to-morrow."

"Oh." He feigned confusion. "Stupid me. Mind going. It's for Monday. Anyway, I was just prepping." His pager picked that moment to vibrate again, and this time, he looked down with relief. "Got to go," he said, moving to close the Schroeder file before she could see. "Never rains but it pours."

"No rest for the weary," the nurse said as Gabriel tapped keys. "Work yourself to an early grave, you're not careful."

"I was born old." He smiled again as he hit <exit>. Then he nodded goodnight, and in another minute, he was out the door, going back to work, heading for the ER.

And after that? The hospital pharmacy. For the other little job he had planned.

26

"**W**e'll catch him at church," Amanda had said. Ramsey had put her on visual as soon as he'd thrown on some clothes. "Hank always goes to ten o'clock Mass."

"Church?"

"Don't believe in God, Jack?"

"You kidding? I was raised New Avalon Catholic. You're talking to a defrocked altar boy."

"Altar boys can be defrocked?"

"When they drink the sacramental wine and throw up in the middle of Mass."

"Oh, God." She'd laughed. "Your parents must've just died."

"My mother, yeah. I think she went to confession *for* me. And the priest, she was apoplectic, practically banned me from the church. Religion never did it for me, anyway. The whole thing between New Avalons and the Old Romans, I never understood."

"Well, Lottie Ketchum's told me all about those heathen New Avalons. The way she said it, Cardinal Kinsey de Medici was a power-hungry, devil-worshipping heretic."

"I can see that. Think about it. About four hundred

years ago, Stefan Amaris storms the Vatican. The pope freaks out, transfers authority over the Church to the joint authority of the cardinals on the capital worlds of the Five Houses. Except Cardinal de Medici of New Avalon, he thinks the pope's transferring all authority to *him*. If he was any kind of guy who played nice with other children, he'd have double-checked."

"From what Lottie says, it sounds like de Medici changed everything: letting priests marry, women priests, abortion. The Old Romans still haven't gotten over it. Weren't the Vatican murders related? About two hundred, two hundred and fifty years after?"

"Two-fifty, yeah. During Hanse Davion's and Melissa Steiner's wedding, breakaway Swiss Guards tried to assassinate Cardinal Flynn." Then, recalling that he hadn't heard Ketchum curse even once: "Don't tell me Hank's into this whole religion thing."

"No. He's New Avalon, and they alternate: even-numbered days are Old Roman, odd New Avalon. No matter what he does, though, Lottie's parents won't come to the house. They didn't even go to the wedding even though it was Old Roman."

"That's a lot of bad blood."

"You can say that again. You don't know the half of it."

Now he was intrigued. "Oh? In what way?"

"Another time," she said. "Right now, we both need some sleep. Think you can find your way to the church?"

"Give me the address," he said, scribbling down the information on the back of a brochure for charter fishing trips. "Have breakfast with me." And when she'd shaken her head: "How about coffee?"

"I can't," she said.

"Okay," he said.

"It's not what you think."

"I don't think anything," he said, but he was hurt and he *was* thinking he'd probably freaked her out.

She sighed. "Honestly, Jack, not everything is about you."

"I didn't say it was."

"Don't be such a baby. I can't because I'll just have time to clean out my horses' stalls and feed them before

I meet you at the church. And no," she said, moving to disconnect, "you can't come help."

"I wasn't going to offer," he said, wishing she'd quit reading his mind. "I don't know horses. I'd just slow you down."

"Which is why you aren't invited."

"But I wasn't going to offer," he said again.

"Yes, you were," she said, and disconnected.

The church was, fittingly, on Church Street. St. Andrew the Apostle New Avalon Catholic Church was blue fieldstone, with a slate roof and three spires. The lot was full, but he spotted Amanda along the curb, standing on the running board of her truck.

"You're just in time," she said, and pointed. Across the lot, a neon yellow sports car with a convertible top of black canvas rumbled to a halt. The driver's side door opened, and Ketchum unfolded himself, then walked around to open the door for his wife.

"That's some car," Ramsey said to Amanda as she came up. She wore jeans, lightweight work boots, and a light blue denim blouse, and she looked fabulous.

She did the eyebrow. "Every boy needs his toys."

"I'm not even touching that," Ramsey said, and he fell into step beside her.

Ketchum saw them coming, said something to his wife, who tossed a scowl their way and then headed for the church where Ramsey saw a few deputies, including Boaz. "Nice car," Ramsey said to Ketchum. "Never pegged you for sports cars, Hank."

"You like it?" Ketchum wore a khaki-colored suit with a light blue shirt and a dark brown, braided leather bolo tie, with sterling tips and a polished agate set in a silver slide. He'd exchanged his sheriff's hat for a chocolate-brown Stetson. "Triumph TR-75 out of Highlander Industries on Northwind before Bannson Industries put them out of business." They talked cars for a minute, and then Ketchum asked, "So where's the fire?" Ketchum listened as Ramsey talked, his face growing glummer by the second. He looked worse when Amanda started in and when she paused, he reached behind to give the back of his head a good scratch. "You sure about this?" he asked. "Just those three little things?"

"They're not little. They're huge," Amanda said.

"Maybe Old Doc overlooked them."

"I don't think so. His exam was complete in every other way."

"So?"

"*So* the distribution of cranial fractures would indicate a low trajectory. The only way for that to happen is if the shot angled down."

"Or maybe we were wrong, and it was suicide."

"No. Then you aim up or straight back, but not down. And here's the clincher." She pulled out her noteputer and highlighted another section. "Right *here*."

In the end, Ketchum agreed, but he wasn't happy. "Then let's go talk to Summers," Ramsey said, but Ketchum was shaking his head. "Why not?"

"One, Doc always goes to Mass." Ketchum hooked a thumb over his shoulder. "Church of Peter the Apostle down the street. He won't be out until noon, and that's only if the church isn't having Sunday supper. Plus that Kodza woman comes in today."

Ramsey sighed. "I forgot about her. When's she due in New Bonn?"

"Round about four, five," Ketchum said, as his wife, who'd evidently tired of waiting, stalked back. "Boaz'll make the run."

"Oh, Boaz'll make a great first impression," Ramsey said then waved away Ketchum's bemused frown. "Never mind. This is getting to be a hell of a case, Hank."

Ketchum's wife pulled a face. She was a small woman with a beaky nose and snowy white hair. A gold religious medal and chain dangled around her neck and flashed in the sunlight. "We watch our language here, Mr. Ramsey." To Ketchum: "Time to go, Hank."

"Just a sec, Lottie." Then to Ramsey: "We'll see Doc after supper. Round about five. No damn point riling up folks more'n we have to."

"Hank," Ketchum's wife said, severely, as she tugged her husband toward the church. "Please, do not blaspheme."

27

"Well, that's just great," Ramsey said, as they made their way to Amanda's truck. "Six hours to kill and nothing's moving."

"But some things take time," Amanda said. A breath of wind plucked a stray lock of her hair across her eyes, and she reached to tuck it behind her ear. "Hank makes too much bad blood, then he's out of a job."

"Yeah, yeah," Ramsey said. He jammed his hands into his jacket pockets. "What about the DNA?"

"Ready this afternoon."

"Okay," Ramsey said. It wasn't. "This Schroeder thing bothers me."

"Me, too. You want to do something about it?"

"Such as?"

"How are you and boats?"

He drove his loaner, following her truck down to the harbor. They parked in a lot adjacent to the Farway yacht club, a three-story building of pale pink stucco with a red tile roof. Amanda chose a solar-powered, six-meter long console skiff with a two-fifty centimeter beam. The solar array, mounted on a diagonal lattice, attached at two points aft and astern, just behind a heavy duty rub rail. The skiff had a large forward casting deck and face-forward seats snugged against an open cockpit.

Amanda handed him an orange life jacket, then passed

him two plastic bottles of water and several plastic-wrapped muffins. "I'm pretty good, but that water's only a few degrees above freezing. If something happens, you'd be dead in less than five minutes."

"So how's a life jacket going to help?"

"Keeps you afloat *and* warm," she said. "The jacket's got pryolene pouches of various chemicals surrounded by compressed air in a buoyant shell. When the interior sensors detect a temperature drop, the air pouches rupture and the resultant chemical reaction creates iron oxide and—" She broke off when she saw his bemused expression. "*Rust.* The chemicals make rust, and making rust generates heat. Trust me on this."

The trip to Cameron Island took a good forty-five minutes. That was just fine with Ramsey who found the ride surprisingly relaxing. As they got nearer to the island's mainland shore, he saw strips of sand beach and individual piers but no boats. There were houses further up from the shoreline on ruddy red bluffs.

"Sandstone," Amanda said when he asked about the color. "There are quarries on most of the islands, but they went bust a long time ago."

Amanda circled to the far shore. This side was wilder and riddled with striated sandstone sea caves carved by wave action and repeated freeze/thaw cycles. They docked in a natural cove, beaching the boat on a tongue of sand bar, then clambered out. They stood, side by side, looking out over the lake. The water was blue as a sapphire and dotted with far-off islands rimmed bronze with red sand. Now and then, a solitary cloud scudded across the sky, and from somewhere, Ramsey heard the lonely cry of a seabird. The only other sounds were the faint rush of wind and the slap of water against sand.

"This is beautiful." Ramsey filled his lungs with air that smelled clean and wet. He looked over at Amanda. "You could spend a lot of time here and not even know it, or a lifetime and not care. All this"—he gestured toward the lake—"it might be enough."

"Actually," she said, "it almost is."

An hour hiking a rugged track inland took them where Isaiah Schroeder's body had been found over three years before. They lost the sound of the water when they were thirty meters from shore, and the terrain changed abruptly from the flat open expanse of red sand beach to a dense thatch of hardwoods whose branches were bare but studded with swollen buds. The terrain was rocky, with humps of rubble displaced by massive tree roots. The going was rough, and Ramsey stumbled enough to know that tripping and accidentally discharging a rifle wouldn't be a stretch. The track abruptly angled into a steep climb, and when they huffed to the top, they emerged on a rocky, forested plateau.

Ramsey stepped over to a tangle of exposed roots on the lip of a bowl-shaped depression to the right of the plateau. Pulling out his noteputer, he scrolled to a set of images taken of the scene then sidestepped down until he was ten meters from the lip. "Okay, the report says Schroeder probably tripped on his way down the hill. Rifle discharged, blew out his head and he landed with his head pointing . . . I'm all turned around. What direction is this?" He waved the noteputer to his left.

"South." Frowning, Amanda reached for Ramsey's noteputer. "Let me see that."

"What?"

"Now that I actually see this . . . Here, look at the pic and then look at the hill . . . you see it?"

"See what?"

"Isaiah's body is nearly perpendicular to the fall line. The head's actually *uphill*. Now you tell me: how do you trip downhill, presumably headfirst, and end up sideways with your head uphill?"

"Lemme see that." He took back his noteputer and compared the image with the hill, eyes clicking back and forth. "You're right, and I'll tell you something else. He's turned around. The rifle's under his chest on the right hand side, but his left side is closer to the top of the hill. So how did he fall, do a ninety-degree turn left, and shoot himself on the right? The blood spatter was concentrated *downhill*. Can't happen unless . . ."

"Unless he *was* facing the hill," Amanda said. "On his knees. With his hands tied behind his back."

*   *   *

Ramsey broke the silence first. "If you were Schroeder and you beached where we did and walked this track, where would you end up?"

She thought. "The old quarry, I think. Another half hour, give or take."

Ramsey tucked his noteputer into his right hip pocket. "Let's go."

The trail was steep, corkscrewing up the quarry's eastern rim. Ramsey had never seen a quarry before, but the hole reminded him of iron red craters gouged out by meteors on a desolate moon. The quarry was a bowl, roughly nine hundred meters in diameter, with sheer rock sides and random piles of rust red rubble like giant ant mounds. Far below, the rusted innards of an old ore car straddled a meandering rail track spooling from an arch blasted in the rock.

He touched Amanda's arm. "Are those doors blocking the mine entrance?"

Amanda shaded her eyes. "Could be. Probably to keep tourists out, but I don't know if you mine sandstone like other ores or minerals, or whatever. Might just be for storage. You wouldn't want to leave trucks and ore cars out in the rain."

The way down was treacherous and slippery with spoil. The two halves of the door were heavy timber strapped with iron on corroded hinges and secured with a rust-encrusted padlock bigger than Ramsey's fist. He yanked a few times but the lock didn't give. If he pulled on one door, a gap about a quarter meter opened up, but when Amanda pressed her face to the opening, she couldn't see anything.

"But I smell something." She gave Ramsey an odd look. "Cigarettes. In fact"—she turned, testing the air—"I smell something like chemicals only burnt. Don't you?"

"Yeah, I do. Someone's been around." He peered at the gravel strewn in front of one door and said, "Has it rained here? Say, within the past week or so."

Amanda shook her head. "Why?"

Ramsey pressed the pad of his index finger to the sandstone floor then held up the finger for Amanda. His skin was peppered with reddish-black flecks. "Rust," he said. Then he pushed up and inspected the lock. "Look, you can just see where some of the rust's been scraped off around the keyhole."

"Then someone's been here."

"That's right," Ramsey said. He bent down again, his eyes searching the ground. "And not very long ago. And here, there's this one pothole." He put his nose to the rock and sniffed. "That's the chemical smell. Like it's been blasted."

"Limyanovich?"

"I don't know. Boaz said he'd taken the ferry to the island. But you saw those shoe shanks. Why would a guy hoof all the way out here in expensive shoes unless he's coming to some sort of meet?" Ramsey paused, his eyes scouring the rubble. "Did they find a lighter on Limyanovich?"

"No. Why?"

He nudged bits of gravel aside then used two pieces of flat rock to tweeze something from the ground and showed her. Captured between the rocks was the crushed butt of a cigarette.

The padlock held. All Ramsey managed to break was a sweat and a rock he used to try and bash the lock free. Then they ran out of time and had to head back to meet Ketchum. They'd eaten muffins on the way in, and Ramsey used plastic wrap, wrong-side out, to carry the butt and rock samples from the tiny, chemical-smelling crater.

They didn't talk much on the boat ride back. Ramsey thought, guzzled the last of his water. He was sweating so much he felt basted. He'd have to shower before he met with Ketchum, and come to think of it, he had to find a laundry or get the hotel to wash his things. Between hiking and just plain living, he was running out of clean clothes.

Then, as Farway's waterfront swung into view, Amanda sighed. "And it started out to be such a pretty day."

28

Once on shore, Ramsey got dispatch to put him through to the crime scene people still working the car. Ramsey told a tech about the cigarette butt and the rocks, and the tech said, "Might be able to pull something off the butt. The rock, I don't know. Explosives are pretty volatile, dissipate fast. But, maybe."

They had a half hour before Ramsey met Ketchum at the courthouse. Amanda wanted in on their meeting with Summers and when Ramsey objected, she said, "I work with Doc. He'll take this better if it comes from another professional, not, you know . . ."

"From a cop?"

"Yes. From a cop. It'll sound like he's done something wrong."

"Well, he has."

"Yes, but it's not criminal. At the worst, it's negligence, and more likely, inexperience."

"*You* caught it."

"Because I was primed," Amanda said patiently. "You tell me to look at something, I figure there's something hinky."

"Hinky?"

"Yes." And now she looked a little defensive. "Hinky. That's what the cops on Towne said."

"No wonder they didn't catch that Kappa freak. You say hinky in New Bonn, they'll kick your ass to," he tried thinking of the armpit of the universe, decided there were several and finally said, "you know, somewhere like . . . Farway."

Now she did laugh. "Well, *you're* here."

They split up. He went to his hotel room, showered, changed for the second time that day, and decided that he'd either have to get stuff washed, or buy more clothes. He pulled on his last pair of clean jeans and a long-sleeved black shirt, then balled his dirty clothes, wadded them into a plastic bag, and humped the bag to the front desk.

He asked the desk attendant, "How much to do three pairs of socks, underwear, three shirts, three pairs of jeans?"

The attendant, a gum-chewing, anorectic-looking blonde with too-dark eyeliner showed him the price list. "You're kidding," he said.

"We have to send out. The manager's got this contract."

"Yeah, but"—he studied the price list again—"you could buy a house for less. Don't you just have a sonic washer somewhere? To do towels and sheets and stuff?"

"Can't do clothes in the laundry. Against the rules."

"Let me get this straight. You can't do laundry in a laundry?"

The attendant rolled her eyes toward the ceiling, thought about it, popped gum, then shook her head. "No."

Fuming, he hoofed out to his loaner, pitched the laundry bag in the backseat, and was late getting to the courthouse by about fifteen minutes.

Ketchum was waiting in his office. He'd changed back into his uniform and was nursing a mug of coffee from a pot on his bookshelf. Ramsey found a mug and helped himself. "I notice the news people left."

Ketchum made a sour face. "Vultures. I know gnats with a better attention span."

"Be happy." Ramsey dropped into a chair with a soft groan. His thighs ached from all that hiking. "No more bodies falling out of the sky, and they get tired showing the same holo of the same burned-out wreck. What's the story on Kodza?"

"Boaz called in about a half hour ago. They're running a little late. Some kind of snarl on the Slovakian end of things. Just as well, gives us time to run out to Doc's and back. I gave him a jingle, and he's expecting us. Speaking of which," he said, as Ramsey blew on his coffee and sipped, "Amanda called not five minutes ago. Imagine my surprise when she said she was going to be another fifteen minutes and not to leave without her." He peered down his nose at Ramsey. "Your idea to invite her along?"

"You know, this is pretty good coffee. Hey," Ramsey said in response to Ketchum's narrow look. "Really. Stuff we swill in New Bonn tastes like 'Mech coolant."

"All cop coffee tastes like 'Mech coolant." Ketchum's mouth twitched. "Thank the wife. Swears by egg shells. But you didn't answer the question."

"Ah . . . Amanda kind of invited herself. She thought Summers might take it better coming from her."

"Mmmm." Ketchum scratched at nonexistent stubble. "She said you found stuff out on Cameron Island."

"*Might* be stuff." He dug the wrapped butt and rocks out of his breast pocket. Ketchum fingered the packets as Ramsey talked about visiting the death scene and then the pit. When Ramsey was done, Ketchum said, "Pretty slim."

"Not when you consider that we *know* Limyanovich went to Cameron Island and that Schroeder's autopsy report is . . . questionable."

"Ten to one, you'd find more'n couple MEs agree with Doc. And maybe Limyanovich went to sightsee."

"With the wrong shoes? On the off season? And dare we forget the alias?"

"No one said the guy was intelligent. As for the alias, maybe he's got an angry wife somewhere."

Ramsey opened his mouth to reply, but the woman working dispatch knocked on the doorjamb. "Crime scene people just pulling up," she said, and then crossed to the pot. She poured, sipped. "Ah, you tried the egg shells." She turned to Ramsey. "I've been picking at this old coot for five months to listen to Lottie. Just about wore a hole in my stomach that stuff he was drinking and—"

"Sheila," Ketchum cut in. "Don't you have some emergency to attend to?"

"Actually, it's been kinda quiet and I—"

There was another knock on the sheriff's doorjamb, and then the crime scene tech brushed past Sheila, sniffed, said, "That fresh?" and went to pour a cup. He took an experimental sip. "Hey, that's not bad."

"Egg shells," Sheila said. "I was just saying, I've been picking at . . ."

Ketchum rolled his eyes. "Small towns."

His hands gloved, the tech pinched up the butt from the muffin wrapper and turned it in the light. "Doesn't look like it got wet," he said then brought the butt up to his nose. "Smells fresh. No stamp on the wrapper. Most brand names stamp the wrapper."

"So it's a knockoff brand?" Ramsey asked.

"Probably. Be pretty hard to narrow down distribution. One saving grace with the HPGs down is manufacturers aren't venturing far out of their prefectures. They can't coordinate shipments so well. So they stick to a certain preset route, where they've got JumpShip freighters hanging, waiting for the next pickup. As for DNA"— he shook out an evidence bag, dropped the butt inside and sealed the bag, then poked at a noteputer and wrote a number on the bag in indelible marker—"we might get something. The rocks, I don't know."

"Damn it," Ramsey said. "I was hoping we really had something."

Snapping off his gloves, the tech said, "That reminds me. New Bonn called right before I came over. That's why I was late. They have some results for you on that stuff we found in those brambles, and those tread marks." He closed out one program on his noteputer then opened another. "The treads are specific to a Bannson Hawk-Spirit turbocycle. Manufacturer's in Prefecture II. Pretty common, bread-and-butter turbo."

Ketchum nodded. "I can think of maybe fifty people off the top of my head."

"What about the fibers and that hair?" Ramsey asked.

"The fibers are cashmere," the tech said. "Made from a Nystera species of goat."

"Never heard of it."

"No reason you should've. Turns out that about the only people interested in Nystera were the Clans. Lessee," the tech said, checking his noteputer, "back a ways, the Ghost Bears owned the planet. Then the Diamond Sharks—"

"Who are the Diamond Sharks?"

"Better to ask who they are *now*. They renamed themselves Clan Sea Fox a while back. Anyway, the then–Diamond Sharks challenged the Ghost Bears, won and then lost the world the very next year after the Battle of Tukayyid."

"Who's active there now?"

"House Kurita, but that's about all we know. The Dracs aren't in the habit of providing updates to the database. But that might not help you much anyway because the blue dye's from Twycross, and that's Clan Sea Fox. But here's the kicker: Denebola never imported this type of cashmere. You can't legally buy it anywhere on the planet. There might be a black market, but I don't think people will risk jail time for a sweater."

"So where would you have to go to get this particular sweater?" Ramsey asked.

"*Had* to go," the tech corrected. "The manufacturer stopped production right before the Jihad. Only Clan Sea Fox, they're shills for just about anything. They'd sell their own Elementals to turn a profit. So Sea Fox might've stockpiled. Plus, the lab says the fibers are pretty brittle. The sweater's really old, like it belonged to someone's grandma. But there was no useful DNA they could find."

*Grandma—or grand*pa. "What about that white hair?"

"Ah, the *hair*. Some of the hair's from a wig. Most of it's human but treated with a synthetic for added durability. No word on the manufacturer, but New Bonn thinks they can extract the modacrylic synthetic and narrow down to manufacturers."

"Yeah, but distribution must be huge," Ketchum said.

The tech held up a finger. "But there's makeup on the fibers, commercial-grade, like what a woman might wear: foundation, crap like that."

"A woman?" Ramsey had assumed their killer was male, someone strong enough to hoist Limyanovich's rigid body *into* the car. Then Ramsey remembered Amanda's forearms and hands, all those muscles from baling hay and reining in horses.

Ketchum frowned. "Could we be looking at a team?"

"Doesn't feel right. Most teams have this erotic thing going, and this doesn't feel sexual." Ramsey looked back at the tech. "Anything else?"

"Yeah," the tech said. "Blood."

Ramsey felt a tingle on the back of his neck. "Like blowback?"

"*Exactly* like blowback. Only on the tips and not down the shaft, and the blood's not all from the same person. One type is O positive, the other's AB negative."

"Male or female?"

"Don't know yet," the tech said. "They're running the DNA."

"You said there were three things," Ketchum said.

"Right. That white hair? It's not all from a wig. Oh, it's real hair. It's just not human. *Felis domesticus Orestiana*" the tech said, with a flourish. "The hairs are from a cat."

29

1700 hours

All right, so what was that little huddle at the church?

Gabriel paced his kitchen like a caged Orestelian lynx. He was still in his Sunday best: dark blue jacket and trousers. Of all days to forget he'd volunteered to help with the church supper. The meal had dragged for hours, the minutes frittered away.

But what was that little powwow at the church? Obviously, something big. Anyone who wasn't inside the church, including Gabriel, saw the three of them, and soon the whole congregation was abuzz. He wouldn't be surprised if that was all over town by now. And it was probably about Schroeder.

He had to take action. Reaching into his hip pocket, he pulled out his wallet, unfolded it and riffled through bills. Had to use cash. No credit, no paper trail. He squared the wallet on the kitchen table then went to the refrigerator and dialed it open. (The keypad was a joke. When he was a kid, dear old Dad thought to keep him from that vodka in the freezer. Idiot. *He'd* cracked the code in an hour.) Then Gabriel reached in and retrieved three glass vials. He lined the vials up and stared at them for a long minute then crossed to his bedroom, his fingers already jerking at the knot of his tie.

Do this right, they'll have a hell of a lot more to worry about than Schroeder.

He would give them plenty.

Amanda showed up five minutes after the tech left. Her long hair was loose and damp around her shoulders, and she smelled of soap and, faintly, rose petals. "Sorry," she said as they hustled out for Ketchum's patrol car. "I was going to stop by the hospital, but I ran out of time."

Ketchum drove. Ramsey filled her in about the fibers, makeup and blood types then added, "We may need to rethink about whether there are two people involved."

Amanda was quiet a moment. "Do you think that Isaiah Schroeder was involved with something, I don't know, secret—and maybe the other people who knew the secret decided he couldn't keep it? And maybe that Limyanovich figured out the secret and then whoever killed Schroeder had to murder Limyanovich, too—or even"—she hesitated—"maybe Limyanovich was there *when* they killed Schroeder?"

"You know, you got to stop doing that," Ramsey said, shaking his head. "You're making me look bad. Anyway, how you figure that?"

Now Amanda looked almost apologetic. "If you assume one killer, why wear a disguise? The only reasons would be either you were afraid of being seen, *or* Limyanovich might have seen you before. *That* raises two possibilities. Either the killer used the disguise to keep Limyanovich from identifying him, or the disguise made Limyanovich relax because he knew *that* person wouldn't hurt him."

Ketchum grunted. "She's pretty darned good. We shoulda thought of that."

"Yeah," Ramsey said. "So maybe we're talking more than one or two people. Maybe we're talking a group—and now we're heading into Garibaldi-land." Ramsey looked over his shoulder at Amanda. "You got any other little bombshells?"

"You don't have to get pissy," she said.

Old Doc Summers's place was south and much further west, teetering on the very edge of town. The house was a rustic, black-and-white side-to-side split-level, facing north to south upon a rolling grade. A curl of driveway led to a two-car garage, and a footpath of white gravel wound from the driveway to disappear somewhere behind the house. A tired-looking navy blue sedan with a rust-speckled tailpipe was parked in the drive. To the left of the house and maybe eighteen meters back was a long, modular shed with a roll-down door.

"He live alone?" Ramsey asked as Ketchum pulled into the drive.

Ketchum nodded. "His boy Adam comes back off and on, sometimes for a couple weeks, sometimes longer. He's a little . . . off—you know what I mean?"

They'd rolled to a stop. Ketchum killed the engine, but Ramsey didn't unbuckle. "No, I don't know what you mean."

"He means psychiatric, Jack," Amanda said. She unbuckled. "He means like drugs and rehab and some prison time, and a kid who's a little bit crazy. Like that."

Summers was waiting for them on the porch. He was still in his Sunday best: dark blue trousers and a rumpled white shirt. No shoes, and a lit cigarette pinched between his fingers. Summers looked as rumpled as his shirt, and his thatch of silver-white hair was mussed. There were purple smudges under his eyes, which were bright and a little wary. They followed Summers through a front hall that smelled of coffee, cigarettes, old tomato sauce, sweaty feet, and cat piss.

"I just put on a pot," Summers ground out, his accent a little broader today. His voice was thick, and he cleared it with a phlegmy smoker's hack. "You want a cup, Hank? 'Manda?" He didn't ask Ramsey. When Ketchum and Amanda declined, Summers tipped more coffee into a chipped earthenware mug then unceremoniously dumped a white long-haired cat off a kitchen counter littered with a stack of dirty plates and cutlery. Summers leaned against the counter and knocked out another cigarette from a crumpled pack. "Okay," he said. He plucked his butt from his mouth, screwed in the unlit cigarette, touched it off with the butt and then

stubbed out the butt in an ashtray overflowing with crin-
kled stubs. He squinted past a column of new smoke.
"What's so darned important you had to call on a Sunday afternoon after I've been in the hospital all night
and church the whole blessed day?"

"You just got home?" Ketchum asked.

"That's right," Summers rapped. "Supper with Father
Gillis, and you can check with him to back me up on
that."

"Doc, we're not accusing you of anything."

"No?" Now, Summers rounded on Ramsey. "Well,
you're doing a fine job of not accusing me. Don't bother
denying it, Hank. Everyone saw you three at church, and
people can't stop wagging their fool tongues about it.
And then before that, *he*"—a jab of his cigarette at
Ramsey—"shows up at the hospital with questions about
a case I closed and you signed off on." Now he turned
a glare to Ramsey. "You don't think the nurses have
ears? The janitor? You don't think they weren't flapping
their gums?"

"Doc," Ketchum began.

Ramsey cut in. "You're getting pretty worked up over
a couple of theoreticals."

"You wouldn't?" Summers threw back.

"No, I wouldn't. If I was confident I was right, that
is." He paused to let Summers jump back in. When he
didn't, Ramsey said, "Look, I'm sorry I said something
in front of people. That was my error."

Summers snorted. "From what I heard about you, Detective, just one of many!"

Ramsey kept his temper. "But that doesn't change the
fact that there are discrepancies between your report
and Dr. Slade's impressions. So, yes, we're looking at
that again." He pulled out his noteputer. "Schroeder's
death is the only one of its kind in these parts in the
last decade, and I had questions."

"Such as? I know you went out to Cameron Island.
Eric down at the dock said you and Amanda rented a
boat, so I know you went."

Amanda jumped in. "Doc, please. I just had a couple
of questions about your findings, that's all. Your inter-

pretation of Schroeder's craniofacial trauma is a bit different from the radiologist. But that's certainly nothing criminal."

And, just like that, Summers visibly deflated. His shoulders hunched, and his chest caved in, and he looked, suddenly, extremely old. He swallowed and said, "You haven't been here as long as me. If word gets around that I've been negligent, you think anyone's going to see me? I guarantee, my practice will evaporate"—he snapped two shaky fingers together, flubbed it, and gave it up—"like that. It'll ruin me."

Ketchum said, "Doc, at this point, what's done is done. Right now, you can make it easier if you just look at the reports and see what you think."

"And that's all?"

"For now," Ramsey said.

Amanda shot him an angry look, and Summers stiffened. "Oh, yes, I forgot, Captain Republic," Summers said. "You ruin people as part of your job, is that it?"

"You want to talk about ruin?" Ramsey said. "Whenever somebody kills someone, people get hurt. I'm not just talking the obvious. I'm talking the community because all of you have to come to terms with the fact that, most likely, the killer's one of you and he's killed a lot more than just a man. He's killed trust. *He's* killed your town. Farway will never be the same again, but *I* haven't done that. The killer has."

Summers stared for a moment then took a drag from his cigarette and dropped the butt into his mug. The cigarette hissed, and died. Then, he held out his left hand for Ramsey's noteputer, and for the first time, Ramsey saw a small bandage crossing Doc's left palm.

"Let me see that goddamned thing," Doc said.

Summers read the report through three times, taking his time. Finally, he said, "I only see one thing, but I don't understand how it's a problem. The man was shot in the face with a rifle, for pity's sake."

"Doc." Amanda laid a hand on his arm. "You left out the wrists and you left out the part about the teeth."

"So?" Summers frowned. "The wrists were scraped. That could've happened when he fell, or from animals.

His front teeth were broken. He was shot in the face. Why is that a problem?"

"First, you're wrong about the wrists. Second, you didn't put either finding in the report. Third, they change the range of possible conclusions. Doc, I actually looked at the spot where Schroeder was found and the position of his body, and it doesn't add up. Plus, he had all those basilar skull fractures that you left out."

"So?"

"Doc," she said, gently, "Schroeder's walking up the hill. Or he's walking down it. Either way, if he trips and somehow ends up with the bore facing him, the blast will still have an upward trajectory. But he has *basal* fractures. His cerebellum is gone. That means the blast angled down and, most likely"—she paused—"the gun was in his mouth."

Summers didn't say anything for a moment. He lifted his nicotine-stained fingers to his mouth, seemed surprised there was no cigarette there and let the hand fall. "But it's possible it happened the way I said, isn't it? It's possible that—"

"No, Doc. It isn't."

"But," Summers stammered, "but he took a bullet in the *face*."

"And you put down all the other stuff that was broken, but not the front teeth," Ramsey said. "Why didn't you put the front teeth or the fractures into the record? Because it would've changed the interpretation, for one."

Whatever softness or hesitancy Summers had was gone. Flaring, his eyes blazing fire, he turned to Ketchum. "Hank, I have to protest—"

"Don't look at him. Look at me!" Ramsey snapped. He brought the flat of his hand down on the kitchen table hard enough to make crockery rattle and Summers flinch. "Look at *me*. The trajectory of the bullet couldn't have done the teeth. I've seen this before, and I caught it. Amanda's seen it before when she worked Towne, and that's why *she* caught it. Ketchum couldn't have known and wouldn't have questioned it because you've never had anyone murdered here before in quite this way."

"Murder," Summers said, numbly. "You're talking murder. You're saying—"

"Yes, I am. If you'd said you did it to protect Schroeder's widow from thinking that her husband killed himself, I almost would've believed you. But you didn't. And I *know* how teeth get broken like that." Ramsey leaned in. "Because someone forced the gun into Schroeder's mouth. They had him on his knees, and they'd tied his hands behind his back, and when he wouldn't open his mouth, they pushed that gun in hard enough to break his teeth. Then they pulled the trigger . . . and blew his head off."

No one said anything on the way to the car. Ramsey felt eyes, and when he looked back, the old man was watching from his porch, a cigarette scrolling smoke between his fingers and the white cat weaving in and out between his legs. Ramsey slid into the passenger's seat and pulled the door shut. The car rocked on its shocks as Amanda got into the back and Ketchum plopped into the driver's seat. "So what do you think?" Ramsey asked.

"I think that if this keeps up, I'm gonna be lucky they elect me dogcatcher." But Ketchum didn't sound angry. Just . . . depressed.

"That's what's really eating you?"

"No. *Hell*," Ketchum said, and he made it sound like a dirty word. "I sure hope we haven't wrecked a good man for nothing."

Ramsey craned his head back to look at Amanda. "You said the son and drugs, right? So what if Isaiah Schroeder was on to the drugs?" When Amanda only hunched a shoulder, he turned back to Ketchum. "You saw the cat."

"Yeah." Ketchum blew out, twisted the key, and threw the car into reverse. "I'm kind of glad that Kodza woman's due in. I could use the distraction."

"But you saw the cat," Ramsey persisted. "A white long-haired cat."

"Yeah, I saw the damn cat."

"There's something else, Jack." Amanda, from the backseat, her voice small and a little defeated. "You know why Doc works nights? Remember I told you about Emma, how she had cancer? Well, I remember Doc was talking to the nurses about the cost of live-in nurses, hospice, like that. Doc couldn't afford a nurse because he'd blown his money on rehabs for his son, Adam. So Doc worked nights while people from his church took turns with Emma, and he'd take care of her during the day. After she died, he never went back to days."

"Okay," Ramsey said, baffled. "But I don't get—"

"Shut up and listen, Jack." Not angry, not even pissed. Just matter-of-fact: *Pass the salt, Jack. Shut up and listen, Jack.* "Emma Summers had cancer. She had chemotherapy. She lost her hair. She wouldn't wear a turban or scarf because she said she didn't want to look like she had cancer." A pause. "So Doc bought wigs for Emma: a lot of very nice, very white wigs."

Ramsey waited a beat, then said, "You only need one. One wig and one white cat."

"Yeah," Ketchum said. "Now shut the fuck up."

30

They separated at the courthouse: Ketchum and Ramsey to meet Dani Kodza, and Amanda to wait at the hospital since Kodza would want to see the body. That suited Amanda since she had DNA to check. She left without a goodbye for Ramsey. Just couldn't do it, not right then. The way he'd handled Doc . . . she just couldn't do it. Instead, she'd headed for her truck, but not so quickly that she missed Boaz standing not ten meters away, leaning against his cruiser and leering. She wanted to smack him.

Pulling out of the courthouse lot, she turned right and drove south. The sunset off to her right was a spectacular burst of mauve splashed upon aqua, but she didn't really see it.

The way Ramsey treated Doc, so *harsh*. On the other hand, she'd worked with cops. A detective couldn't afford to get all gooey-eyed over a victim, or treat suspects with much humanity. But Ramsey was not a nice guy. He might be tender, compassionate, giving, tough as armor on a 'Mech—but not nice.

And she couldn't wait to see him again.

*　　*　　*

Amanda was so busy thinking about Jack Ramsey that when a turbocycle peeled out of a lay-by on her left and roared away in the opposite direction, she didn't notice.

Ramsey couldn't read Amanda's eyes, but when she said nothing and turned for her truck, he let her go. Then her head flicked left, and he saw Boaz, leaning against his cruiser, a wolfish grin splitting his lips from ear to pointy, protruding ear. Ramsey took a quick glance around: no one else in the lot, or on the street.

As Amanda's truck pulled away, Boaz looked up, saw Ramsey coming, and if he read anything in Ramsey's expression at all, didn't show it. If anything, his grin broadened, and Boaz actually ran his pink snake's tongue over his teeth.

"So," Boaz said, his drawl thicker than congealed molasses, "I heard you been seeing our lady doctor. Had dinner the other night, had a bottle of wine, a couple drinks. Real late, too. So tell me"—Boaz leaned in and dropped his voice to a confidential whisper—"she do it as good as she looks? I mean, you know, she get real enthusiastic like those brainy types do? Because once you're outta here and seeing as how she's all *primed* and *lubed*—"

And that's as far as Boaz got. Ramsey's left leg sliced air in a blur, arcing down and up before Boaz blinked or Ramsey had a chance to think about things like, oh, assault. (Later on, he could admit he *had* thought about it but didn't much care.) The blow clipped Boaz at his ankles. Boaz toppled, smacking his face at the angle made by the passenger's side door and the cruiser's roof with a loud *bam!* There was a distinct and very loud crackle and crunch, like splintery glass. Bright red blood sprayed from Boaz's nose in a geyser, spattering the passenger's side window. Boaz went down in a heap, his hands cupped over his ruined nose, road grease mingling with blood soaking his uniform jacket.

"Oh, Jesus, oh, Jesus, you broke my nose, you broke my nose!" Only Boaz couldn't breathe out of his nose now, only blubber and blow red bubbles, so it came out: *Ohsheeshush, ohsheeshush, ubwomunoth!*

"Aw, jeez, Boaz, be careful, man. I *told* you to watch

out for that oil there and now look." Ramsey put his left hand on Boaz's shoulder but kept his right cocked and ready, just in case. "Let me help you up. We got to get you some attention here." And then, dropping his voice: "You say one more word about Dr. Slade to *anyone*, you gonna be drinking steak through a fucking straw."

"I'm gonna press charges," Boaz grunted. Blood leaked through his fingers. "This is assault." *Dishishasshal.*

"You do that," Ramsey said. "And then you better grow some eyes out the back of your head."

By the time Ketchum came running, Boaz swayed to his feet, with Ramsey propping him up against Boaz's cruiser. The deputy was covered with bloody grit and oil smears from the parking lot, and looked like he'd barely survived assassination.

"The *hell* happened?" Ketchum said. "Boaz?"

"Shipped," Boaz bubbled.

"Yeah," Ramsey said, "I told him, Boaz, man, there's oil. But he wasn't looking, and he slipped and . . ." He shook his head. "Boom."

Boaz threw Ramsey a poisonous glare as the ambulance crew loaded him on a stretcher and whisked him to the hospital. When the ambulance's siren faded, Ketchum cleared his throat and said, "You got something to say?"

"He slipped," Ramsey said.

"Yeah?"

"Yeah."

Ketchum's dark blue eyes narrowed. "Well, I knew Boaz could be stupid, but I never pegged him as clumsy."

"People'll surprise you."

"Yes, they will." Ketchum paused. "Thing is, I was thinking about putting Boaz on surveillance, have him keep an eye on Doc. But now, with a busted nose, I can't do that. I guess I'll have to put Bobby on it." Another pause. "Amazing Boaz didn't lose a couple teeth, way he slipped and clocked hisself and all."

"Yeah. You know, he slips again, he might not be so lucky."

"Uh-huh. Well, let's hope he learned to watch his step."

"We live in hope," Ramsey said.

Summers chain-smoked, knocking ash into a mug. The cat was draped in his lap, its rumble the only sound other than the sizzle of burning paper and tobacco.

That thing with the teeth, the basal skull fractures, the *wrists . . .* why hadn't he foreseen the problems? He'd been so careful with that autopsy. He closed his eyes, bringing up a mental image of Schroeder's body on the autopsy table: his head a puddle of purple brains, clotted blood, caked mud, and blasted bone. Isaiah's mouth: the soft palate totally gone, the tissues pulped and rear molars ruined, but the hard palate relatively intact. Why hadn't he remembered about the fracture lines on the front teeth, why hadn't he seen the teeth coming?

Because you wanted to make it go away. Because Schroeder could've ruined you, but then he died, and you were safe and didn't want to ask too many questions.

Abruptly, Summers stood. The cat tumbled, righted then crouched, belly to the ground, and watched as the old man plucked up a bud, activated his link, and placed a call. When the link connected, he said, "I have to talk to you. Right now."

Gabriel heard the heavy tread of feet along the ceiling, and then the squeal of hinges, the slam of a door and, a second later, the crunch of gravel as someone rounded the gravel path. He opened the door before the man could knock. "What?"

The third man from Gabriel's meetings fidgeted. His features were pinched and gray, and he reeked of cigarettes. He swallowed hard and said, "We need to talk."

"About *what?*" Gabriel wasn't in the mood, and he didn't understand why the Handler insisted on keeping this *relic* involved. "I have to go."

"Just listen." The third man held up his hands, palms out, like an ordinary traffic cop. There was cigarette ash on his palms that bore a passing resemblance to stigmata, which, if Gabriel had been superstitious, might have given him pause. "There's talk. Not only the legate's office involved now but they're sniffing around Isaiah Schroeder. If we keep giving them things to look at—if you follow through on the boys right now—that won't be good for us. For the cause."

Gabriel bristled. *Always telling me what to do, where to go, how to act, while I take all the risk!* "It's *my* risk, *my* operation, while you sit on your fat ass."

"Watch your mouth, boy, watch it, you self-righteous little . . . !" The man swung, hard, cracking Gabriel's right cheek with his open palm hard enough to make Gabriel stagger and nearly fall. "I may not be young anymore, but I've been at this longer than you, taken more *risks* than you! This isn't like the old days when we could count on being protected. If they catch us, they will *crucify* us, *especially* if you kill the children. We might be able to expose Limyanovich, but the children are *innocents*!"

"The children are *casualties*." Gabriel spat a gobbet of rust-colored saliva. "This is *my* operation. *I* call the shots, not you."

The third man's face was purple with rage. He raised his hand again. "You'll follow *orders*—"

"No!" Gabriel caught the third man's wrist with his left hand then jabbed the man's stomach with his right. The man doubled over, backpedaled and nearly lost his footing, but Gabriel's hands shot out, grabbed the man by his throat and squeezed. "*Not* from you, never from you, never *again*!"

The man gawped like a fish, and his eyes bugged, his face blackening with trapped blood. At the last moment, Gabriel opened his hands and let the man fall. The third man sprawled, facedown on the gravel, his hands tearing at his shirt, his breath whistling in and out of his throat in thin shrieks.

"Touch me again," Gabriel said, "and I'll kill you. You got that . . . *Dad*?" Then Gabriel slammed the door on his father, and threw the lock.

31

Sunday, 15 April 3136
1930 hours

Even travel-worn, Dani Kodza was better-looking in person than she was on the holovid but smaller than Ramsey expected, barely topping a meter and a half. Her skin was not as pale but a little bronzed, perhaps with makeup, and her nails were square-cut and buffed to a gleam. A thin gold chain trickled along her collarbone before disappearing beneath an ivory camisole edged with lace.

When she looked at Limyanovich's remains, she didn't flinch. The color dribbled from her skin, but she didn't avert her face, not even when the smell—old charcoal left out during a frost—rolled out of the morgue refrigerator with the body. In fact, she barely blinked. Instead, as Amanda talked, pointing out the damage to the chest versus the skull and detailing the torsion fractures found in the fingers of Limyanovich's right hand, Kodza bent, her eyes raking the body the way a farmer sifted through chunky soil.

Amanda was saying, "So, as I said, not a lot left to identify."

"But there are the records, yes?" Kodza's eyes slid from the body to Amanda, and the smaller woman straightened. "The dental records are a precise match. The crowning touch, if you will pardon the pun"— Kodza's glossy pink lips curled to a half-moon—"is the dental post you extracted. The post is a match, and Limyanovich's blood type is O positive—very common but the blood is also a match. I would think that we will also find the DNA to be a match. Did you find anything else?"

Amanda didn't pause. "No. I've made arrangements for a forensic odontologist in New Bonn to consult."

"Why is this necessary? A DNA match would not be conclusive?"

"Well," Amanda hedged, "I like being thorough."

"Something I am sure his family will appreciate," Kodza said smoothly. "And his personal effects? They were recovered, yes? Certainly, they would be additional evidence."

If Amanda was a little surprised by the turn in the conversation, she didn't show it. Instead, she dragged out the evidence bags containing what they'd found on the body: the charred clothing, the wallet, the red diamond ring and, finally, the half-melted gold necklace. "This is the most interesting piece," Amanda said. She tapped the bag containing the gold chain. "It looks a lot like a religious medal, don't you think?"

"I would not know." Kodza held the bag to the light. "I am not so religious."

"What about Limyanovich?" Ramsey asked. He'd been standing back, watching Kodza. She wasn't strictly intelligence, he knew, because she hadn't flinched. Special agents flinched. Cops didn't.

Kodza said, "I could certainly ask, but I cannot see how this is germane to an autopsy." She looked over at Amanda. "Do you?"

"No, not really," Amanda said. "DNA would be definitive, not a necklace. I'm just curious. I'm crunching out a reconstruction. Then I'll cross-reference what I find."

"And this DNA?"

"Just about done."

"Very well." Kodza tossed the evidence bag back with

the others. "When will I be able to take possession of the body?"

"Well, now wait a minute," Ramsey said. "This is an ongoing investigation. We might find something later on that will make us look at the body again." When Kodza frowned, he said, "Do you know why Limyanovich was in Farway to begin with? Was it business?"

"No. Even if true, what is here to interest PolyTech? We do not know. Perhaps he met someone here."

"I can think of places a lot closer to New Bonn," Amanda said.

"Yeah, but not as low-tech," Ketchum said. "Farway's pretty invisible. That was one of the reasons people used to come here." He filled Kodza in on Limyanovich's trek to Cameron Island, though Ramsey noted that Ketchum omitted what he and Amanda had found. Ketchum finished with: "So maybe they met there, and then he killed Limyanovich later, and then left for the city. We know that Limyanovich was set to leave for Slovakia today."

"Possible." Kodza gave a slow, thoughtful nod. "In which case, the killer could be anywhere."

Ramsey said, "So let me get this straight. You're saying Limyanovich's just this businessman. He comes all the way out here for a meet of some kind, only we figure out he's carrying something—maybe a gun, maybe a noteputer—something someone wanted badly enough they broke Limyanovich's fingers to get it once Limyanovich was dead. Limyanovich gets capped with two different weapons and then his car blows up. And that's your story."

"Should there be another?"

"For starters, why kill Limyanovich so everyone notices? Why not just dump the body in the lake, or the middle of an island for that matter?"

"I am not a killer, Detective. Explaining all this is your job, not mine."

"Fair enough. So let's talk about your job. You're in the legate's office. You've got intelligence officers coming out your ears. So what is PolyTech up to? Legates don't get interested just because it's a businessman. Governors don't get excited unless there's a lot of money involved, or maybe someone's got the governor's nuts in a vise because he's in on the scheme, or both. So what about PolyTech?"

Kodza waited a beat when Ramsey stopped talking then said, "I think I am flattered that you believe the legate—or anyone in his office—knows so very much. I will be certain to let our PR department head know that she has done an excellent job. But I am so sorry to disappoint you, Detective. We simply do not know."

"Uh-huh." Ramsey turned to Ketchum, who just shrugged and shook his head. "Your call, man."

"I don't know." Ketchum palmed the back of his neck and moved his head from side to side to work out the kinks. "Can't very well let it go."

"What?" Kodza asked. "Let what go?"

"He's just trying to figure out how much more crap you're gonna spew," Ramsey said. "But I already know. You've been lying from the get-go." For the first time, Ramsey saw a suggestion of color stain Kodza's jaw. Thought: *Gotcha.*

"And why would I do that?" Kodza asked.

"Aw, man," Ramsey said, and he laughed. "You just keep putting your foot in it. There's so much crap coming out your mouth, you can't keep track."

Kodza pulled herself up, and for a small woman, she looked very impressive, almost majestic. "Then I suggest, Detective," she said, her accent razoring each word into individual syllables, "you stock up on toilet paper. Or consider something for that diarrhea you call speech, or the potty you fancy is your brain at work."

"Nice try," Ramsey said, unfazed. "But here's the thing. Most people, you accuse them of lying, they get pretty angry. But they don't ask you why you'd say that. Anyone who asks why is fishing to see if you've come up with the right reason. You didn't even get indignant, not until I kept going to get a rise out of you. Besides, the Bureau says you're a spy. So, are you a spy?"

Kodza's eyes slitted. "You want to have this conversation here?" She inclined her toward Amanda. "In front of *her?*"

"Why? Are you ashamed of being a spy?"

"Uhm, guys," Amanda said. "I'd say I'd be happy to leave, but this is my office."

Kodza cocked her head, as if Ramsey were a species of rare beetle. "Detective Ramsey, I am no more ashamed of who I am than a cop who might very well find himself either in jail, or without a job, or both."

Ramsey was impressed. "We can keep up this tit for tat, but let's trade instead. An information swap. That way, we both win."

Kodza smiled, like a carnivore sensing prey. "Very well. Who is your contact in the DBI?"

"No, no," Ramsey said. "We've done a lot of giving. You go first. Who is your ghost agent?"

"What is this . . . ghost agent? A clandestine operative, yes?" Kodza snorted. "You read too many spy thrillers, Detective."

"Oh, well then, since we cleared that up . . . I guess we're done talking. But I got to hand it to you. You're very good." Ramsey eyed Ketchum. "You remember what I asked her? The very first thing before we got sidetracked?"

"Yeah," Ketchum drawled. "I do."

"Well, thank God," Amanda said, "because I don't."

Things stalled. Kodza made noises about leaving, and Ketchum started herding her toward the door. "You coming?" the sheriff called. "Dinner?"

Ramsey waved him on. "Ten minutes."

"Better not be longer than that. The longer that sack of your unmentionables is in my patrol car, the more the stink . . ."

"Yeah, yeah. Go."

When they were alone, Amanda said, "What was all that about? The stink and his patrol car?"

"Uuuhhh." Ramsey was embarrassed. "It's, uh, it's nothing. Just got to find a place to do my laundry . . . jeez, I don't want to talk about my dirty underpants."

"That makes two of us," she said, coolly.

He thought there might be a touch of humor there but wasn't sure. "Listen, about this afternoon, about Doc . . ."

"Drop it," she said. "I was wrong. You were just doing your job."

"You sure?"

"Yeah." Then: "What happened to John Boaz? I heard he was pretty banged up. He was still upstairs until just awhile ago."

"Ahhh . . . Well, what did he say happened?"

"He said he slipped on a puddle of oil in the parking lot and bashed his face against his cruiser. He said you were right there and got help."

"Ah, yeah, well, yeah, that's what happened. So . . . how bad is he?"

"Banged up?" She mulled that one over. "Well, the smash won't improve his looks. He's awfully lucky he didn't lose a couple of teeth."

"You know, that's what I told him."

"Yes, he said that, too."

"Did he say anything else? About what I said?"

She shook her head. "But I can guess. Let me tell you a little secret, Detective. The next time you kick a guy's feet out from under him, think about the nasty bruise you're leaving. A good forensic pathologist picks that up right away."

"Ahhh, man . . ."

"Relax," she said, patting his arm. "Your secret is safe with me. That was a long time coming for Mr. Boaz, anyway. There's only one thing I wish."

"What's that?"

"I wish I was there to see it," she drawled. "Musta been real purty."

Amanda said, "I kind of like the way you and Ms. Kodza got at it."

"Yeah? Tell that to Kodza."

"Mmmm." Then: "You know, I can tell you why the legate might be in a lather about PolyTech."

He was startled. "You can?"

She nodded. "Did a little detecting on my own since you guys didn't. They have one very interesting division involved with biogenetics. Little things like giving parents a choice about whether a child has blue eyes or green."

"But eye color doesn't turn a profit."

"No, it doesn't. Most people—most parents—are interested in two things: sex determination and intelligence. Parents would pay a lot to make their kids smarter."

"Only problem is that it's illegal as all hell," Ramsey said.

"And with good reason. We'll forget the obvious: a population skewed toward men without enough women. But can you imagine a world where every child is a Kerensky, or another Htov Gbarleman? Society would collapse. Every society needs an undereducated, low intelligence undercaste to do the scut work."

"That's kind of harsh," Ramsey said.

"But true," Amanda said. "What do you think is under that bell curve, anyway?"

Then she added, "By the way, what was the question she didn't answer?"

"Ah. *That.* I asked her how come Limyanovich got killed so people would notice. Think about it. You kill somebody, you usually don't advertise unless Limyanovich was an example. You most certainly don't want the legate to sit up and take notice, or the Bureau. Blowing that car was like sending up a flare."

He thought of something. "Didn't you say you were going to check the DNA?"

"Yes. Gee, whiz." She made a disgusted sound. She started for her lab. "Between Doc and Boaz and now *her*, I got sidetracked."

Ramsey followed. "It won't be ruined, will it?"

"Shouldn't be." She was fiddling with a transparent plastic machine of some kind that held a clear gelatin-looking substance suspended between what Ramsey thought were two poles, one negative, and the other positive. "But I do want to get this report done and Limyanovich out of here. . . ."

"Yeah, I noticed you didn't say anything to Kodza about the other blood type, or that false tooth—or the capsule."

"Didn't want to give away the farm before I was ready," Amanda said, but she sounded distracted and a little puzzled. She'd pulled up 3-Ds on a computer: a series of what looked like radiographs, only the clear gel was now black streaked with white bands arranged in vertical ladderlike rungs.

"What is that?" Ramsey asked.

"Gel electrophoresis," she said, still studying the 3-Ds. "DNA's got a negative charge, and so you run specific sequences against controls in an electrical field through an acrylamide gel. Essentially, you're measuring speed. Larger pieces move more slowly. The number and position of segments in each lane form a DNA fingerprint."

"Okay," he said, but he wasn't sure he understood. "So is this okay, or what?"

She paused just long enough so he knew everything wasn't okay. "Every peak matches," she said, "except one." She pointed to a thin white band near the very bottom of the gel. "I don't know what that is."

"Is it, like, contamination?"

"Maybe."

He caught the tone. "But you don't think so."

"No," she said. "I don't think so."

"What do you want to do?" Ramsey asked.

She thought a second. "Well, I can't release the body, not without clearing up this discrepancy. So I'll run it again. I'll also run mDNA, mitochondrial DNA, see what I come up with."

"Mitochon . . . ?"

"Yeah. Mitochondrial DNA is specifically passed along the maternal line. Too complicated to explain right now, and you have to get going. Hank's waiting."

Ramsey didn't want to leave. But he sidled to the door, said, "You want to, I don't know, maybe have a drink or something later on?"

"Sure. We can go to Good Time Charlie's."

"It an okay place?"

"No, it's a dive. But if you want to drink on a Sunday, that's where you go." She drew a quick map. "Ask the page operator to beep me, and I'll meet you."

"Great." Ramsey turned to go then came back. "We got so hung up on the DNA, I forgot. Can you pull up blood types from the hospital database?"

"Why? You want to know if Doc's got AB blood?" When Ramsey nodded, she said, "The hospital can't release that information without a warrant—you know that."

"If I get a warrant?"

"Then you take it to admin and they'll do it."

"Fair enough." He paused. "Ah, listen, about tonight. You're not worried? That people . . . ?" He trailed off.

"You mean am I worried that people will see me with the same man two nights in a row and wonder maybe, I don't know, if I'm sleeping with him?"

"Hey, wait, I didn't—"

"Are you saying that you're not interested in going to bed with me?"

"No." Now Ramsey was alarmed. "Hey, no. Jesus, I didn't say that."

"So, Jack?" She slipped her arms around his waist, and because she was so tall, looked him in the eye. She smelled like roses. "Would you like to go to bed with me?"

He said, "Is this one of those multiple choice questions, or true-false?"

"Yes," she said.

32

2030

The encounter with his father left him sweaty and feeling vaguely filthy, like he'd been contaminated. He'd showered in water as hot as he could stand. Now, naked, moisture wicking away from his skin and his cat rumbling against his bare thighs, Gabriel sat before his computer, watching as Limyanovich's revised files popped up on his screen. Ah, and so what had Amanda found . . . oh, this was interesting. The DNA was being repeated, just as he'd hoped but—he frowned—something was wrong. Something was definitely wrong.

He reread the files twice then sat back in his chair as he worried the information. Amanda had taken the amplified DNA from PCR and run a gel. But if he'd really ruined the PCR ahead of time, she'd have noticed. But Limyanovich's DNA looked as if it had survived the temperatures to which he'd exposed it. If he was reading this right, there was an anomalous peak: DNA that didn't correspond to anything. Then it hit him.

Something hidden in Limyanovich . . . in more than one place.

He picked up his sat-link, said the number and waited for the connection.

"Yes?" said the Handler.

"It just hit me," he said. "Limyanovich's cover was PolyTech, right? So what if this data isn't in a crystal at all? What if it's encoded in Limyanovich's *DNA*?"

"Explain to me this PCR." The Handler was silent as he rattled off the information. When he was done, the Handler said, "And you are saying that additional DNA . . ."

"Might interfere with the primers, yes. There's some anomaly, some difference in Limyanovich's DNA that Slade doesn't understand." When the Handler didn't respond, he added, "You have to admit, that would be right in keeping with their mentality."

"Yes, I agree. The problem is the deviation from pattern. All previous information transfers were via data crystal. On the other hand, couriering information in DNA would be like taking out an advertisement, yes? Doing so would alert anyone who managed to capture one of their operatives exactly where to look. For all we know, this is precisely what they wish us to think."

"But we could be wrong. We've been so focused on getting the three crystals that we've overlooked the fact that the enemy might have adapted."

"True. Even if you are right, what do you propose?"

"We have two choices: steal some DNA ourselves, or let Slade do the heavy lifting. You can bet she'll sequence this stuff. When she does, I'll have it and then I can apply the information to what we have from the crystals."

"And if the DNA is nothing but garbage?"

"It won't be. It's something."

"We shall see. So what are your plans? With the boys?" The scratch of a match and then a quick inhale as the Handler lit up. "Although now anything you do is more complicated. There is this new person in town, someone from the legate's office."

"Yes. You think they're . . . ?"

"Trying to ferret us out? I would say that is an excellent surmise. We will have to wait and see if this operative initiates contact."

"Mmmm." Gabriel nibbled on his lower lip. Destroying Limyanovich's car in such a spectacular fashion had been a calculated risk designed to attract attention, and that seemed to have worked because, now, there was this woman from the legate's office, this Dani Kodza. "One kid dying, I can make that go away. The other one, Noah . . . he'll be harder. We want the police to go away, not stick around. If Troy dies, I can make that look like an accident. Noah, I can't."

"Agreed," the Handler said. "Just so long as this spy Kodza does not walk away with our prize. I am certain this is why she is so intent upon reclaiming the body."

"Then I'll have to get moving on that. Tomorrow night. First, I do the kid. Slade is redoing the test, so I've got time." Then he had a thought. "What if Slade finds the crystal first?"

The Handler laughed then: a rattling, phlegmy, smoker's hack. "You really need to ask?"

33

They ate at the restaurant Amanda had taken Ramsey to the evening before. Phil Pearl called during dinner, with dispatch tagging Ramsey through Ketchum's sat-link. At the mention of Pearl's name, Kodza's eyebrows rode toward her hairline, and she might've started in if the owner hadn't chosen that moment to wander by. Ramsey excused himself, dragged his jacket out of coat check and headed outside.

The night was brisk without the bone-numbing cold of early Saturday morning, and the stars were out again. Ramsey leaned against Ketchum's cruiser, plugged in his earbud, got dispatch and then there was Pearl. Ramsey said, "Checking up?"

"Actually, yes. Some jerk-off from DBI talked my ear off this afternoon."

"Garibaldi."

"That's him. He said you weren't that cooperative. Said you were supposed to report in after you met with this legate person, what's his name?"

"*Her* name. Dani Kodza."

"Whatever. Garibaldi strongly implied that if you didn't cooperate, he wouldn't see this as an example of patriotic macho, or some crap like that."

"He's just pissed that I'm not signing up to play secret agent."

"Yeah, well, now he's pissing on me. Threatened to go to the mayor and then the governor if I didn't cooperate. Chewed me a new asshole. Imagine my surprise when I sat down for a crap."

That made Ramsey laugh. "Did you tell him what to do with his opposable thumb?"

"Very handy device if inserted and spun upon properly." There was a pause. "IA's going to present their recommendations sometime Monday, Tuesday at the latest."

"Okay." Funny, how tight his stomach squeezed. "You got a read?"

"I've got someone on the inside says it's an even split. There's a lot of sympathy for you, and not just because of Kevin. You got rid of a monster, and I hope this line is bugged because McFaine deserved what he got."

"But that's not why they hired me. Can't have those rogue, vigilante cops."

"No. Final decision's the chief's, of course."

"Meaning the mayor, or maybe the governor."

"Meaning I don't know. I know what *I* think, and I know what I'm going to say."

"But they'll want you to get rid of me. Then you show everybody the police can police the police." Saying the words made his stomach get cold, and he closed his eyes, feeling a little sick. "You want me to resign, Phil?"

"No." Then, stronger: "No. You don't do a damn thing, Jack. You submit your resignation I'll use it for toilet paper."

"Well," Ramsey said, "now that you got that new asshole . . ."

They talked about the case, and before he disconnected, Pearl said, "Call Garibaldi. That'll be one less headache."

So Ramsey got dispatch and, in thirty seconds, he was patched through to a secure line on Garibaldi's end. "It's Jack Ramsey."

"Ah, Ramsey." Cool, like he'd been buffing his nails. "About time."

"I was busy. You know, doing cop things."

Garibaldi ignored the sarcasm. "So what do you have?"

Ramsey went over Dani Kodza, what happened at the hospital, and her shutting down any discussion on motive. When he got to the DNA, he said, "So, I was wondering if there was some kind of connection."

"Might be. Hang on." Garibaldi's voice got faint as if he'd moved away from his sat, and then he heard Garibaldi giving commands to his computer. A few moments later, Garibaldi was back. "There's one little bit. Poly-Tech's been quite busy, flying executives toward the periphery. The worlds involved border very close to Clan worlds. We all know the Clans aren't shy about genetic manipulation."

"How would the legate's office be involved?"

"I'm not sure. Maybe Kodza's real mission is to uncover Clan influence."

"So you think *she's* thinking that Limyanovich comes out all this way to barter for information to trade back to a Clanner? Or that there are maybe Clan sympathizers here, in the civilian population? Clandestine Clan groups? That's . . ." He'd been about to tell Garibaldi how nuts that was but then he remembered something. "Didn't you say that Kodza traveled a lot on missions that are straight shots to Nykvarn, and Nykvarn's on the periphery, right?"

"Yes, I did."

"Well, I'm not an agent, but you've got Kodza on known Clan worlds. You got her going to a planet that's about as far out in the Inner Sphere as you can get. What if there are factions within the Clans we don't know about that are involved in some kind of espionage?"

"That doesn't sound very Clanlike," Garibaldi said. "Clans aren't exactly subtle, and they're not big in the espionage business, not like the Kuritans, or Capellans."

"But what if these clansmen have been entrenched so long, they've morphed to be more like us? What if Kodza's investigating that kind of threat?" Then he had a new thought. "Hell, what if *she's* the threat? Using an entrenched megabusiness like PolyTech might be the cover Clanners would use to set down roots, maybe even distribute small cells all over the Inner Sphere." The more he thought about this, the more Ramsey thought he might be on to something. "The best way to insinuate yourself into a society is to become part of its fabric and bide your time. So maybe Kodza isn't investigating so much as keeping tabs on all her people, or simply reporting in."

In the silence that followed, Ramsey could practically hear the gears turning in Garibaldi's head. Then: "You might be right. Maybe Kodza does know what's what, so she's anxious to know how her operation—whatever this is—has been compromised, or even if PolyTech has sold them out somehow. Maybe Limyanovich was killed because he either knew something, or was a threat in some other way."

"Or maybe," Ramsey said, "Kodza is damage control."

34

Dinner was lousy, just some leftovers thrown together, but Noah wasn't hungry anyway. He pushed food around, and every now and again, he saw Sarah out of corner of his eye, the way she skipped looks at his face and then away. She hadn't liked the look of the thing on his arm and wanted to tell Mom. But she hadn't because his mother would have been all over Noah like a bad case of tartanfleas. When he pushed back from the table, his chair scraped the floor loudly enough to make his mother's head swivel like it was on ball bearings. One glance at those red eyes of hers snapping to his plate and then his face, and he knew he was a goner.

"Why aren't you eating?" she asked. Her voice was raspy, like she'd swallowed sand. "Aren't you hungry?" Then before he could flinch away, she had him by the wrist with one hand and her other clapped to his forehead. "You're burning up. And you're sweating. Are you getting chills? Maybe you have the flu."

That ploy hadn't occurred to him. It also helped that he *was* getting chills: small at first, just tremors, but now bone-rattling quakes that made him want to wrap about eighteen thousand blankets around his body. "Well," he said, "the flu's going around." (That sounded good.) "Maybe I caught it."

"Well, you hop right into bed, young man. Honestly, just one more thing to worry about," she said, trailing in his wake as he mounted the stairs. "I'm going to draw you a nice hot bath, and then I'll bring you some hot soup . . ."

He protested but she was firm. "And if you're still not feeling well by morning, then we're going to see Dr. Slade."

"No!" Noah cried, too vehemently, and then, when his mother stared, he stammered, "I-it's just the flu, Mom."

She stood there, a bath towel clutched in her hands, her eyes searching his. "Are you in some kind of trouble?" she said. "Have you gotten yourself into something?"

Somehow he was able to convince her that he wasn't. But he could tell by the set in her mouth that she wasn't sold on his story.

His arm was bad. The wound was clogged with putrid yellow and green pus that stank like a forgotten sandwich in an old lunchbox. Red streaks ran to his armpit. When he washed the wound with peroxide and water, the pain made him woozy and his stomach convulsed. He made it just in the nick of time to the toilet, grateful that the sound of running bathwater covered the sound of his vomiting. When his stomach was empty, he hugged the cool porcelain of the bowl and felt like, maybe, he was dying.

Maybe got to tell somebody. Maybe tomorrow. Maybe got to tell . . .

That night, Noah fell into a restless, fevered sleep and dreamt of fire and raving skeletons with guns and wild, white hair.

35

By the time Ramsey got back to the table, the owner was regaling Kodza with the story of his great bear hunt. Ramsey listened with half an ear, his mind busy, mulling over his conversation with Garibaldi.

Damage control fit. It explained Kodza's hurry to whisk away the body; her insistence that there was nothing to look at in PolyTech; her general uncooperativeness. Or, maybe, she'd put up PolyTech as a red herring, something to divert their attention. From sleeper cells? Denebola was certainly prime real estate: a planet where animosities ran deep. (And no matter how the Republic liked to gussy that up and paint this lovely, friendly, all-inclusive picture, Neurasians didn't like Zadiposians, and Zadiposians didn't like Slovakians, and Slovakians hated everybody. Just wasn't something you talked about.)

So he heard but didn't quite comprehend when the owner said, "I was so close, I had less than a second to decide whether to knock that Kyotan armor bear in the snout with my Winchester 88, or jam him with a bang stick."

Ramsey had heard the story and almost tuned out

when the owner said: "The problem with a bang stick is you can ruin the pelt, so you only use it as a last resort."

Then Kodza asked, "What is this, bang stick? I do not know about hunting."

And the owner said, "A bang stick is, well, a stick with a cartridge at the end, a shotgun shell. Divers use it sometimes for marsharks off the coast of Zadipos, and I know some people use them for those butt-ugly paelleocrocs in the Weslan Swamps on Slovakia. I use them for emergencies, like if I'm too close."

Then Kodza said, "Are these bang sticks, they are difficult to make?"

And the owner said, "Hell, no. Very easy to make. Then just jam the business end into your target and pull the trigger, usually something easy, like a thumb depress."

Then Ketchum jumped in: "So would you use pellets? Like a regular shotgun?"

And the owner said: "Depends on what you're after. You want to kill something, you'd use pellets. You want to stun a critter, maybe just damage the soft tissues but preserve the hide as best you could, you'd go for something without pellets."

Then Kodza looked from the owner to Ketchum, then to Ramsey and said, "This bang stick . . . this is important?"

"Ahhhh . . . could we get the check, please?" Ramsey said.

"So you are not going to tell me why this, ah, bang stick is so important?" Kodza's breath steamed. "But if this is related to Frederic Limyanovich, then you must divulge the information, yes?"

"I must divulge the information, no," Ramsey said. They were still in the parking lot. Once they'd paid the tab and gotten out of the restaurant, Kodza peppered Ramsey and Ketchum with questions. Now Ramsey leaned against the front fender of his loaner and let Kodza see the grin. "People share their information. You tell me something, I tell you something. But so far we've done all the telling."

Kodza made a rude sound. "You ask stupid questions. A ghost agent. This is preposterous."

"Yeah, and ghost knights are figments of my fevered imagination. Look, Limyanovich could've been a total sleaze. Maybe he deserved what he got. But that's why there are judges and juries. My job is to catch the guy who killed him."

There was just enough light from the restaurant to catch the hard glint in Kodza's eyes. "Well, here is my position. You want to know how much I care, personally, about Limyanovich? I do not care. I do not care about his family. I do not particularly care about the killer. But I care about Denebola."

"I can respect that, but here's the problem. Suppose, if this ghost agent is already here, or has followed you, and I find out that some stranger's been nosing around. Then I waste time because I'm looking at your guy as a suspect instead of someone else. So you save me time if you let us know who your guy is." It was on the tip of his tongue to mention what Amanda had found and Garibaldi had said—about her secret little jaunts to the periphery of the Inner Sphere—but playing that card might be useful later.

Kodza was silent a good ten seconds. Then she said, "Let me make some calls."

They dropped off Kodza at her hotel. Once she was inside, Ketchum said, "The bang stick idea means we could be back to looking at just one guy."

"Yeah." Through a square of lighted window, Ramsey saw Kodza stop at the front desk, say something to the clerk, nod and then cross left and out of sight. He looked over at Ketchum. "You and I know that. I'll bet Amanda will agree that the injury pattern's consistent with a bang stick."

Ketchum racked the cruiser into reverse. "Doesn't prove it."

"We may not need proof," Ramsey said as the cruiser slid north toward the courthouse. "The point is *Kodza* doesn't know that. You can just bet she's making calls right now, trying to figure out how many butts she's got to cover."

In the courthouse parking lot, he unbuckled and hauled himself out of Ketchum's cruiser, then turned around and bent down. "We ought to interview Summers again. Maybe even get ourselves a warrant to search the place, and I may want to get one for the hospital database. And I think Summers knows where his boy is."

"How you figure?"

"Just a feeling. But his kid's the only one out of the people we've thought about with priors, *and* he's nuts."

"You really think Limyanovich was killed for drugs, or his cash?"

"No. But we have to look."

Ketchum sighed. "I suppose. I hate opening this up for Doc, though. I'll talk to the judge tomorrow about a warrant. Meet you round about eight tomorrow morning. And one other thing: Get your damn stinking underwear the hell out of my patrol car, or I'll boot your butt into next week."

"Hank," Ramsey said, "your *mouth*."

36

Good Time Charlie's was the only place within spitting distance that a person could both dance and legally get drunk on a Sunday. The place was also a dump: working-class bar basically decorated with beer posters so old they curled at the corners. By nine, the air was thick enough with smoke you could just inhale and save your money. Tonight, there was an all-boy band playing bad country rock so bass-heavy the walls thumped like a heart.

Gabriel made his way to a corner table, far right and within a stone's throw of the toilets. This particular seat was not his favorite. The wall between him and the men's room was thin, so he heard every tinkle, burp, grunt, and splash. He even knew which patrons washed their hands (answer: not many). But the seat was good because he saw most everyone in the place while he sat in a half-wedge of shadow.

When Gabriel first arrived, there'd been another bartender earlier, a young, gawky kid Gabriel didn't know well. But, an hour later, Michael walked past the bouncer at the front door, ambled behind the bar, clapped the kid on the shoulder, and took over.

Michael saw him coming, nodded, said, "Haven't seen you around for a while."

"Been busy." Gabriel asked for a bottle brand that promised to taste great and be less filling.

Michael popped the cap and tacked a napkin to the bar with the bottle. "On the house."

"No, no." Gabriel shook his head, dug out a half-century and slapped it on the bar. Michael shrugged and made change which Gabriel tossed into Michael's tip jar. Gabriel read the questions in Michael's eyes but turned his back and headed for his table.

That was the extent of their conversation, but it had the desired effect. Gabriel caught Michael casting furtive glances his way, and thought that Michael probably would arrange a meet. That was good because then Gabriel could figure out just how much Michael knew. Michael might—a very big might—try to kill Gabriel first. But Gabriel thought he could take Michael and probably enjoy it.

The near-miss with his father had done something to him. In that moment when he realized he held his father's life on a knife edge . . . it was like something had snapped. No, no, not snapped. Come undone, like a leash. Now he felt the urge to kill like a hungry claw ripping at his gut.

Gabriel sat, listened to very bad music, watched people wander in and out, and sipped beer that neither tasted good nor left him wanting more. The beer did make him have to pee though, and so he left his bottle, tipped the chair and went to do his business.

Three men huddled in a knot a few meters from the men's room. One was bald while the other had greasy blond hair pulled into a tail. The third man, also bald, smoked and slouched against the wall opposite the men's room. Gabriel avoided eye contact, letting his gaze slide left. Bikers, and likely a drug buy. None of his business.

The men's room reeked: an eye-watering stink of ammonia, feces, and regurgitated beer. There was wet toilet paper on the floor, and a puddle of something, chunky and rancid that Gabriel minced around. Standing in front of a urinal, Gabriel unzipped, aimed, peed, and stared blankly at the wall. Finished with his business, he rinsed his hands under cold water, dried his hands on his jeans, and shouldered open the door.

The blond man was gone, though Gabriel spotted the two bald ones at the bar. Gabriel dropped into his chair, checked his watch. She should've been here by now. Unless she'd turned over a new leaf. But, small town, he'd have heard if she'd gone on the wagon. On the other hand, it was getting close to last call. Not much time . . .

Then he had another thought. Maybe she'd come in while he was in the john. Or maybe she was already home, somebody else with her. He might risk a trip out to her place. After all, he had his father's car, and no one would give it a moment's thought.

Just about the time he talked himself into believing he'd lost his chance, he saw the front door open. The bouncer's head turned—and Sandra Underhill wobbled in.

Sandra Underhill wasn't quite drunk enough. This past year, she'd noticed it took a lot more booze to get to the place where she didn't have to think too hard about what came next. She'd once been pretty. Her husband—gone now, the bum, leaving her with a mortgage, Troy and his diabetes, and a mountain of bills— he'd liked her body, her looks. Told her she had blue eyes he could drown in, and he loved the honey blond of her hair. Her own hair, too, not a color she borrowed from a bottle. When she was sober—and that was too damned often—she knew she wasn't half bad. The drinking hadn't quite caught up. Getting there, though.

Jostling her way to the bar, her gaze bounced around, ticking off faces. She knew most of the men here, though she spotted a few new boys. Always an interesting moment, this: new or old? An old face, she knew what he wanted, and if she played things right, she could score maybe two or three before getting around to a good long fourth. So, old faces then: she slid in between a muscled mechanic in red flannel and a man in cowboy denim. She gave each man just enough butt and boob contact—a little encouragement.

Cowboy looked down, licked his teeth, and smiled. "Buy you a drink, darlin'?"

* * *

Gabriel watched Sandra Underhill work her way between what looked like a farmhand in a flannel checked shirt, jeans, and work boots to her left, and a guy in cowboy denim. Cowboy looked like he'd been in a fight, and he also looked a little . . . familiar. Where? The light was bad and Gabriel couldn't place him but he saw Cowboy's hand ease down to cup her right buttock.

Time to make his move. Picking up his beer, Gabriel scraped back his chair when he happened to glance left—and locked eyes with Amanda Slade.

Wouldn't you know, the one night in a dog's age she goes to a bar, and the place is jammed. . . . Then Amanda spotted a couple pushing up from a table about as big around as a manhole cover off to her left. Just as she made it to the table, her pager vibrated. She pushed aside the previous patrons' empties, thumbed her pager, checked the number. The hospital, *again* . . . She plugged in her bud, told the link where to call and as she waited for the hospital operator to punch in, her eyes bounced over faces—and stopped. Was that . . . ?

The link clicked. "Emergency room."

"Yes. It's Dr. Slade. You paged me?" Plugging her right ear with her pinky, Amanda hitched her body around to face the wall and forgot all about who she'd seen—until much later, when it was too late.

Oh, hell. Gabriel saw Amanda's quizzical look, and then she turned away, talking into her bud. Time to get out, but Sandra . . . He threw a quick glance at the bar. Sandra was gone. So was Cowboy.

He had to get out. Amanda didn't strike him as a woman who went to a bar for a pickup. So she was meeting someone, probably Ramsey. And now Sandra Underhill was gone and his chance to get at Troy. But maybe he could catch her out on the sidewalk. He moved toward the door. Amanda was still talking, still had her back to him. Good. Had to get out before she registered who he was.

The night air slapped his face, and the door clapped shut, cutting the rope of sound in two. He smelled like an ashtray, the cigarette reek rising from his clothes like heat shimmers off sunbaked asphalt. Behind, through the closed door, he heard the dull thump of the bass. But then, off to his left, he caught the sound of someone stumbling, followed by a man's curse. A woman's giggle.

And then . . . a groan.

37

Dispatch put Amanda through just as Ramsey pulled out of the courthouse parking lot. He heard music and voices in the background. "You getting a head start?"

"Yes. I'd forgotten how busy this place gets on Sunday night."

"That's because no one wants to go to work on Monday."

"Mmmm. Tell that to those of us who work Sundays. I've already gotten paged four times."

"You have to go back in?"

"I don't think so. Just get here, okay?"

A hodgepodge of cars and cycles littered the street in front of Charlie's and a quick pull-through tour of the back lot revealed several cars with fogged-up windows and no empty slots. Ramsey pulled back out to the main road, turned left and slowly rolled north. He had to continue on a good hundred meters before he came to bare shoulder. He swung the patrol car around in a U-turn then eased in behind a trio of turbo squatting on the gravel shoulder.

The front door to Charlie's opened when Ramsey was still some thirty meters away, and a man stepped out on a cloud of tinny music and the strong, astringent scent of cigarette smoke. He stood a moment in a puddle of yellow from a light above the bar door, looking first right and then left toward Ramsey. Ramsey saw a Stetson, white bandage and knew: Boaz. Ramsey slowed, but Boaz didn't appear to have noticed Ramsey. Boaz started forward then pivoted right and cocked his head as if listening to something. The deputy went right, out of the light, turned the corner to the back parking lot and was gone.

Ramsey pulled open the door, slid past the bouncer and stood, waiting for his eyes to adjust. Couples gyrated on the dance floor while a very bad male singer sang off-key about broken hearts, backed by a band that sounded like three cats stuck with a dog in a burlap bag. Then he spotted Amanda, waving him down to his right. The waitress appeared as he slid into a seat. He ordered a beer, got another white wine for Amanda then looked around. "Pretty popular place," he said. He had to lean in until his lips were practically in her hair. "I saw our boy Boaz."

Amanda did the eyebrow. "Yeah," she shouted back, "I was hoping he'd leave before you got here. Didn't really feel like patching him back up."

"Hey, he slipped. He see you?"

She nodded. "Didn't look very happy about it."

"Well, look at this way. If he got embarrassed, he won't hit on you again."

She made a face. "I doubt that. As soon as you leave town, he'll be back. But he's like that. A guy has to talk about it all the time, he's probably made best friends with his right hand."

"Mmmm." Ramsey massaged his chin and pretended to think. He leaned over and shouted, "But what if he's a lefty?"

The band played another five minutes then took a break. Ramsey's ears were ringing, and he thought maybe a couple of his fillings had jostled loose.

"Anyway, I'm glad you're here," Amanda said. "Those two guys at the bar have been gawking for . . . oh, for crying out loud, don't turn around and *look*."

But Ramsey did look. Both were bald, with bullet-shaped heads and muscles like melons, and wore basic biker black. They didn't look away, and Ramsey gave them a hard look for a long five seconds then turned back. "Nice class of guys you attract."

"Present company included?" She didn't smile. Instead, she sipped wine, made a face, said, "Ugh," and then asked, "So what happened at dinner?"

With the buzz of conversation all around and since he could lower his voice, he told her. She listened without comment, asked him to repeat the part about bang sticks, said, "Hmmm."

"Hmmm, what?" he asked.

"Hmmm, I think it's worth looking into." She lowered her voice another notch and switched gears. "I don't suppose she's telling the truth? That she doesn't have a ghost agent?"

"No, she's lying, and I think that somebody's already here. So does Garibaldi. We wait her out. Meanwhile, there's always Summers."

"I can't see Doc as involved. He's just not that kind of man."

"People will surprise you."

"Yes, but not Doc. I know, I know," she said as he opened his mouth. "There's the cat and Emma's wigs. But why dress that way? Doc's already got the hair."

"Maybe the killer dressed up as a woman. What's so scary about a little old lady?"

"You obviously haven't met some of my patients," she said.

The band played no better than before, but the dance floor snarled up again with sweating couples. Leaning in, Ramsey said, "I heard from my captain back in New Bonn. He says IA's going to make its recommendations."

"What does he want you to do?"

"Stick it out. I offered to resign, but he refused."

"He sounds like a good man. He sounds—" And then she jumped as if she'd been scalded and began fumbling with her belt.

"What?" he asked.

"Pager." She held up a thin, wafer-sized device with

a winking, angry red light. She read what scrolled past on the illuminated display and then fished for her bud again. "Honestly, with this SatNav, it's one of these you can't run, you can't hide kind of things."

"We got those, only they're smaller, like a wristwatch. Uniforms have to wear them on duty. Once you make the jump to detective, the theory is you got to be reachable day or night. I got one of those."

"So where . . ." she began, then said, "Hospital" into her bud, and then looked back at Ramsey. "So where is it?"

"Home. Probably under my socks."

"Speaking of socks," she said, and then held up a finger, turned away, and listened, stoppered her right ear with her pinky, said, "Say that again?" a couple of times and then shouted, "Hang on" twice. She turned back to Ramsey. "I'm going outside just to take this. Either it's the noise or maybe a crummy connection, but I can't hear myself think in here. And my brain's turning to oatmeal listening to that band. Tell you what, bring your dirty socks back to my place, and we'll throw them in the wash, and I'll find us something decent to drink."

He put a hand on her elbow as she stood. "I'll pay the tab and meet you outside."

She nodded, mouthed "Okay," grabbed her purse and jacket and hurried out. Ramsey got the check from the waitress, dug around for change, paid the bill and stood. The beer picked that instant to remind him that he was, after all, only renting, and he figured Amanda would be a few more minutes.

After the men's room and as he came out of the short corridor, he heard the bartender announce last call. The bar was on his right, and he glanced that way. A reflex action. Wasn't thinking too hard about it, or even looking at anything in particular. But something off-kilter snagged his attention, and he stopped, looked again, puzzled over what was wrong for a good five seconds. And then he knew.

The bikers were gone.

38

Troy was sitting at the kitchen table when his mother's car rattled down the drive. Waiting for his mother was always scary because while he knew exactly what she'd be like when she stumbled in, he was never certain who she'd bring home. Once, she brought home his principal. That had been embarrassing, as much for him as the principal whose daughter was in Troy's grade.

He'd scrubbed his bike. Jimmying free the scrap of khaki fabric had taken some doing, and his fingers were black with sprocket grease before he worked the strip out. He studied the bit of cloth for a few seconds and he remembered the sound of bullets cleaving air, and then Noah's scream. Remembered the man coming for them. Jamming the scrap into his jeans pocket, he wheeled his bike into the shed.

After, he was wobbly from fatigue, emotion, and lack of food. In the kitchen, he checked his sugar. His sugar was low, big surprise, and so he downed a glass of orange juice, then another and waited until the shakes went away. They did, and his knees stopped feeling like water. When he returned the carton to the fridge, he saw that he was down to his last vial of insulin for his pump. The vial would last him a week, and he usually changed out on Sundays. Had to remember to bug his mom about the script.

He pulled up his shirt. The pump was about the size of a deck of playing cards, dark blue with a digital read-out, and clipped to his belt. He wore the pump pretty much around the clock, detaching it from a clear plastic cannula attached to a catheter inserted through the skin of his abdomen when he took a shower or bath. The rest of the time, insulin was delivered in pre-programmed infusions which Troy controlled himself. Now, he checked the level in his pump, reasoned he had enough for several more hours before he had to change out to his last vial, and made himself a fried egg sandwich on toast with lots of butter. Then he got a book and waited up for his mother.

The hall chrono had just called out the half hour when he heard the crunch of gravel beneath tires. A wedge of yellow light slid along the far wall as headlights brightened a set of fraying lace curtains in the kitchen window. Troy closed his book, slid from the table and peeked between slats of a vertical blind that hung over a square of six-paned glass in the kitchen door. He recognized his mother's car and, then, with a jolt of surprise, realized that the car that had slid in behind was a sheriff's patrol car. Oh, my God, had his mother gotten herself into trouble? He waited, his nerves tingling.

His mother slid into the pool of light from the side door. Her hair was tumbling down around her shoulders, and she was having a hard time negotiating the steps. An instant later, another figure emerged from the darkness, came up behind his mother, grabbed her arm and spun her around. They pressed up close to one another, his mother swaying, grinding her hips against the guy's front. When his mother pulled away and tripped up the stairs, light skimmed the guy's face and Troy's stomach knotted.

Oh, no, not him . . .

The rattle of a knob, and then his mother's giddy laughter sloshed across the threshold, dragging with it the smell of cheap beer and men's sweat. "Sweetheart!" She wrapped him in a bear hug and planted a woozy, wet smack on his forehead like he was, maybe, three. "I brought a friend home."

His mother must be the most popular person on the planet. "Hi."

"Hey." The guy stared at Troy a long second, and then his eyes slid to Troy's mother. "Where to?"

"I'm going upstairs." Troy's cheeks flamed. He flashed on punching the guy in the face, maybe bashing in his nose or mouth more than it was already mashed in—for all the good that would do. And he needed his insulin. Should've taken that last vial when he was thinking about it. But no way he was doing that now, just no way. Now he'd have to stay awake and listen, and there were some sounds he just didn't want to hear.

As bad as this was, the worst part was yet to come. Tomorrow morning, his mother wouldn't remember coming home, or who she'd brought. That was worse.

His last view of his mother was of her butt sticking in the air as she rooted around the fridge. "You want beer or wine? I got wine and I also got . . ."

Troy scooted up the stairs, fast as he could, his hands over his ears and the burn of tears on his cheeks.

39

Ramsey elbowed his way through a crush of patrons pressing toward the bar for last call. There were exclamations and one guy took a swat at him but went wide and ended up smacking a woman to his left. Then she hit the guy, and then more pushing and now Ramsey was wading through a wave of curious onlookers and the bouncer banging his way through, yelling, "Hey, hey, *hey*!"

Ramsey squirted through, burst out the door and onto a narrow strip of sidewalk in front of the bar. No Amanda, but he caught the glint of something metallic a few meters away. Amanda's earbud.

Where was she? He remembered the turbos he'd passed up the road. They could have taken her away already. But then another thought occurred to him.

What if these are Kodza's ghost agents? What if this is to shut me down?

She'd put up a fight. He was counting on that, because if she fought, he could . . .

Then he heard a scream. He wasn't even sure it was a woman's but it was very short, abortive, terrified: "*Gah!*"

Parking lot. Instantly, he was moving, crouching low, wanting to run and knowing he couldn't because he didn't know if there were only two or where they were, or whether he had cover. He ran out of sidewalk fast and then ducked into a long inky peel of black shadow at the left side of the building. Too late he remembered the Raptor in his loaner, debated a half second then kept moving. Faster now, keeping his head down. What seemed like an ocean of vehicles in the lot, but there was enough of a glow from the light above the bar's rear door and another at the very top of a fire escape that he could pick out some details. He hunkered down, leaned against the right rear wheel of a vehicle that smelled of oil, gasoline and road dust, then eased round.

He caught movement out of the corner of his left eye, looked that way, and then he saw them. One biker, his back turned, his jeans sagging around his knees, his buttocks a dull glabrous gleam, his hands fumbling at Amanda's waist. The other, standing behind Amanda, his beefy biceps clamped around her neck in a stranglehold and the other wrapped around her arms. And Amanda, struggling, rearing back, her mouth open but making no sound because she couldn't get air, and the one with his pants down muttering, "Come on, man, keep her still. Keep the bi—"

"YAAAHHHH!" Ramsey exploded with the fury of a pent-up volcano. Still screaming, he charged, head down, legs pistoning, pounding asphalt. He hit the biker with his pants down—literally—and just as the man half-turned. They collided, hard, and the biker flew back, Ramsey still with him, on top. They landed, the biker on his back and Ramsey astride. The biker's head hit the asphalt with a solid and audible *thunk*, like the sound of a full plastic milk jug breaking on tile. The biker went *uhhhhhhh*, a cross between a moan and the slowly deflating wheeze of an accordion, and then he flailed with one arm, took a drunken swat: "Nooooo . . . fuhhhh . . ."

Ramsey's hands were scrubbed raw and already bloody from asphalt, but he clamped the biker's head on either side and slammed the biker's head once, twice, three times against the blacktop, would have done it more, was going for blood even though the biker was unconscious after the first slam. But then, from behind, Amanda's ragged, gasping shriek sliced through: "*Jaaaaahhhh! NIIIIII . . . !*"

Knife! In a flash, he was up, pivoting right, shifting his weight, left foot whipping and then coming down and bouncing up onto his toes into a classical stance: knees slightly bent, right foot back, left foot in the lead and turned slightly in, balled fists held high and level with his chin.

Knife, knife, where's the knife? A fraction of a second to find the knife—*where where where?* A glint of reflected light . . . There! Right hand, coming around fast, and now the biker lumbering in, feinting clumsily with his left, dropping his hands, screaming, "*Motherfu . . . !*"

Quick as lightning, Ramsey danced in, his left fist shooting out, banging against the biker's right forearm and knocking him off-balance. The biker staggered to Ramsey's left, and Ramsey closed now, his eyes on the knife and then his balled right fist jackhammering fast *bambambam!* His hand exploded with pain, streaking like hot lava all the way to his shoulder. There was a crunching sound like crackly cellophane, and for an instant, Ramsey thought he'd broken his hand. Then he looked and saw the dent in the biker's face. Blood bubbled through a mass of pulped flesh and bone that had been the man's nose and upper jaw. But he was still roaring, staggering back, shaking his head like a groggy bull. And he hadn't dropped the knife.

"Maaahhffuhhhh, maaahhhffffuhhhh!" The biker wheezed. Blood streamed down his face. "Cuuuulllll ooooo! *CUUULLLLOOOO!*"

But before Ramsey could make a move, Amanda was there, her hair flying, her face contorted into a Medusa's mask of naked rage. "Fucker!" she screamed, and her booted foot connected with the biker's back, right between his shoulder blades.

All the biker's breath came out in a whooshing, bloody spray: *HUNH!* His arms flew apart, and his back arched like he'd been shot. His fingers opened, and the knife skittered away, spinning across black asphalt. He stumbled, tried to keep to his feet, couldn't, and sprawled facedown.

Amanda, still on him, her boot swiping a low arc that clocked the biker on the side of the head. "Fuck, you fuck, you *fuck!*"

The biker coughed out a scream, but she kept at him, kicking his chest, his belly, his face. She was still kicking and screaming when Ramsey hauled her off, and she kept on screaming until Ramsey wrapped her in his arms. And then she buried her face in his shirt, but she didn't cry.

That pretty much emptied out the bar. Four deputies whose names Ramsey couldn't recall were first on the scene, followed by Ketchum who tumbled out of his car looking rumpled and fit to be tied. The deputies pushed back gawkers. But Ramsey still felt eyes, and he craned his neck up, and saw a figure at the top of the fire escape.

He turned back as the ambulance whooped once, twice, and then pulled away with a wail of siren, speeding for the hospital where a med-evac tilt-wing, already en route, was on its way from New Bonn to whisk the men to a hospital where the needed reconstructive surgery could be done on the one biker's face, and the other monitored until he awoke. As luck would have it, Ramsey had not cracked the man's skull, but the biker had a nasty gash that had split the scalp and over which the med-tech had slapped a coag bandage. The med tech had done a quick check of Ramsey's hand, told him he should get it 3-D'ed first thing, wrapped the hand in bio-ice, and gave Ramsey a pain med to chew, which Ramsey promptly dropped in his pocket. Aside from scratches and a necklace of bruises around her neck, Amanda was physically okay.

Ketchum gave them both a one-eyed once-over. "Amanda, you gonna press charges, right?"

Amanda, her face white and eyes dark, glistening and huge: "Yes." She wore a scrub top that the med-tech had given her. Her blouse was in tatters, and she held it now, wadded in her right hand. "They need to be off the street."

"Oh, I can guarantee you that whether you charge them or not. But I also guarantee they'll find themselves some pie-eyed public defender to protect their sorry backsides—and *you*"—he jabbed Ramsey in the chest with the point of a finger—"you're already in trouble."

"Yeah, yeah." Ramsey had his arm around Amanda's shoulders. She was shivering like she was catching her death. "They had it coming and you know it."

"Probably. But it's not your place to say how much and when. That's why we got courts so justice gets done."

"No," Ramsey said, and hugged Amanda harder. "That's why we have me."

40

Sandra Underhill passed out from a combination of too much beer and the amnestics he'd dissolved in her bottle when she went to the john. She lay on the couch, left arm flung back over her head, mouth unhinged. A snail's track of drool glistened on her right cheek. A low-heeled black pump dangled from the toes of her right foot.

Pig. Gabriel wanted to scald his mouth against the taste of her sour, beer-flavored tongue. Now when he thought back to what he'd been forced to do, and what he'd let her do to *him* . . . he felt physically ill.

Kill her. She was a whore, going to hell anyway. Yet as much as he yearned to throttle the life out of her, he needed her alive. One dead Underhill was all he was allowed.

He found Troy's insulin easily enough. Flicking out a pocket knife, he pried away the metal seal. Nothing left to chance: Troy would have no choice. Then he pulled out the doctored vials from his back pocket, wiped all five vials with a kitchen towel then replaced the vials in the fridge and wiped the handle.

He went back into the living room. He'd been very careful to avoid having a drink or using a glass but, of course, he'd touched *her* and she'd touched *him*. No way to avoid it. He stood for several seconds, thinking. Things hadn't escalated to actual, well, sex, a relief because he'd leave even less of himself behind. The beauty of the amnestic was she wouldn't recall anything from two hours preceding unconsciousness. She'd never remember him—and if, by some remote chance, she *did*, the last thing Sandra Underhill would want was for everyone to know she was whoring around while her kid died in his sleep.

Troy flinched awake at the sound of a car's engine revving. He'd fallen asleep at his desk. He fingered apart his blinds and watched the car's brake lights flare as the car slowed before making a left.

"Hunh," Troy whispered to no one. "Betcha you ain't gonna sound your old siren about this, are ya, ya asshole?"

From the top of his stairs, he heard his mother snoring: a loud, nasal, snorting noise. Once in the kitchen, he opened the fridge, and frowned. Four new vials, about a month's supply. He dragged out a vial and inspected it. The vial was warm, but it was his insulin all right. A good thing, because his last vial was ruined. He tried to remember if the seal had been broken before, and couldn't. But his mother *had* remembered him after all.

Once he'd changed out his insulin and thrown away the ruined vial, he went to stand over his mother. He removed the black pump that dangled from her toes.

"I hate you," he whispered, tucking a crocheted comforter under her chin. Hot tears rolled down his cheeks. "I hate you, I hate you, I hate you."

At the end of the Underhills' drive, Gabriel turned left. The car's high beams swept a wide, very bright swath, cutting the night in two like a gleaming scimitar, and Gabriel watched, without really seeing, a blur of images winking in and out: a length of wire fence, the dip of a culvert, and now, a patrol car on the shoulder . . .

What? Gabriel jerked to full alertness, his eyes wide, white-knuckling the wheel. Holy God, what was a patrol car doing out here? What could he . . . ?

Slow down, just slow down, boy. You just might get out of this.

He was in a patrol car, too. That was good. But he had a problem. He couldn't stop or afford to be recognized. Easing his right hand off the wheel, he tapped in the code for the glove box—thankful now that he'd insisted, just in case—and the glove box sighed open. Clicking off the safety, he laid the gun—his cannon—on the seat. There was a round already jacked in the chamber because he liked to be prepared.

Then he realized something else. His headlights were on, but the other patrol car's were not. *Why* not? Maybe the car wasn't there in an official capacity. But *he* could get a good look at the driver while whoever was in there couldn't see him.

Rolling closer, closer . . . And he saw who it was.

Tension drained from his limbs like water. The other man was already ducking his head, trying to keep his face out of sight because he *wouldn't* want to be seen.

"But I see you," Gabriel whispered, "I see you."

The other man, even though he didn't know it yet—he was dead.

41

They'd finished their statements at the courthouse. Amanda had walked out ahead, but Ramsey hung back, turned to Ketchum and said, "I know this is a bad time to mention this, but with the med-evac and me involved, the news people might show up again. That'll create complications. Maybe best if I left town."

Ketchum was already shaking his head. "No, then it'd look like you'd done something we're ashamed of. Now it *would* be better if you didn't go rearranging people's faces, but those guys didn't deserve any better. Besides, Limyanovich got killed on my watch. That makes me mad, and I want to get the son of a bitch who did it." Ketchum jerked his head. "So go on, get out of here. Get some sleep."

Ramsey left. There was an awkward moment in the parking lot, with Amanda looking waiflike in her too-large scrub top and Ramsey's jacket, and Ramsey, his right hand still wrapped in lukewarm bio-ice, freezing his ass off but not wanting to leave. He was desperately tired, feeling the pain in his hand now. He knew better than to bare-knuckle fight like that. It had also dawned on him that maybe, this time he'd scored a KO on his career. McFaine was a monster. But this was different.

Too much to think about.

Amanda said, "Well . . ." Her breath steamed, and the word hung like a balloon.

"I'm so tired I can barely see straight. But I really don't want to leave. I mean, leave you *alone*."

"I know what you meant." She tucked a shank of her long hair behind her ear: an oddly touching, almost girlish gesture. "So, don't leave me alone."

"Uhhh . . . well, I only got the one bed at the hotel. Maybe they got a roll-out—"

"I have a guest bedroom with its own shower. Besides, I have your jacket, and I'm not taking it off until I get home."

She had a point. "Okay."

"Good." Her lips wobbled into an imitation of a smile. "Don't forget your socks."

She led, and he followed in his loaner. Amanda's place was south of the hospital, and at her drive, they turned left, heading east for the lake. The drive curled in an elongated *S*, and a smear of light appeared, resolving into the overhead light of a wraparound porch with white balustrades and wood railing. A wood swing, big enough for three, dangled on linked chain to the left of a wide bay window. Two verdigris fan-back rockers stood by a low end table to the right and just off a double window edged in white. He pulled to the front of the house while Amanda continued to the right and disappeared into an attached garage. Lights winked on; the front door opened, and she was waving him inside.

She took his laundry, disappeared, and in two minutes, he heard the hum of a sonic washer. Then she reappeared, clutching an insulated satchel, and led him through a two-story foyer with hardwood floors and into a sitting room. A deep, overstuffed couch, bracketed at acute angles by two upholstered wood-slat recliners, stood before a freestanding, gray and slate blue fieldstone fireplace. The far wall was shrouded with floor-to-ceiling beige draperies.

He said, "You know, I'm dog-tired, but I'm too

cranked to sleep. I need to come down. If you want to show me where the bedroom is, I'll—"

"No, that's all right." She placed the insulated bag on a low knotty pine coffee table and then eased herself into a recliner. "Just turn on the fire before you sit down—that little switch at the base of the hearth."

He flipped the switch, and instantly, orange-yellow and blue flames bloomed around a stack of artfully arranged ceramic logs. She sighed, said, "That's better," and hunkered into Ramsey's jacket. She gestured at the satchel. "Bio-ice for your hand."

"Thanks." Ramsey slid onto the couch, dug out a packet, massaged it to start the chemical cooling then laid the bio-ice over his hand. The knuckles were puffy and turning purple, and he was having trouble bending his fingers.

They were silent a moment then Amanda said, "I never thanked you."

Ramsey looked at her. The bruise under her left eye was livid and a high collar of blue-black thumb- and finger-shaped bruises ringed her neck. "You don't need to. I'm just sorry I couldn't let you kill the bastard."

Her skin, where she wasn't bruised, was very pale. "I wanted to kill him. I've never been that angry before. What I wasn't prepared for was this moment of total shock, and then I felt real, *personal* fear for the first time in my life. But then I went ballistic." She paused, looked at the fire. "I understand now."

"Understand what?"

She looked him in the eye. "I read about what you did to McFaine. My first reaction was . . . revulsion."

"You don't have . . ."

"No, no, let me finish. On an intellectual level, I understood. Who wouldn't? But, emotionally, I thought you were some kind of sadist and maybe worse than McFaine because *his* victims died. You made sure that wouldn't happen for him."

The words hit him harder than he expected. In his own mind, he'd accepted that he had acted with a clear-eyed, pitiless certainty because he knew exactly what would happen. Had known the moment right *before* it happened: when McFaine was down, stunned, and he'd straddled McFaine's back, felt the space between McFaine's fourth and fifth cervical vertebrae with his thumbs—and bore down.

She was watching his face. "Would you do it again?"

"McFaine?"

"Yes."

"Yes, I would," he said.

She nodded. Then she got up, slid onto the couch, gently draped his left arm over her shoulders and laid her head against his chest.

"I hear your heart," she said.

42

Her link shrilled them awake. Ramsey jumped, had a disorienting moment, then realized he was still slouched on the couch, the room toasty from the fire. Bright sunlight diffused through the drawn curtains. His neck was stiff, the fingers of his left hand were cold, his arm was numb, and Amanda had slumped over sometime while they slept, her long sable-brown hair spilling over his lap. At the link's second scream, she jerked, nearly clocked his chin scrambling to get up, said, "Sorry," and then staggered to a hall link that promptly stopped screaming when she told it to shut the hell up.

Ramsey stood, working out the kinks in his back, scrubbing eye-grit with the heel of his left hand. What time was it? He checked his watch. After *nine*? They'd been out for maybe four hours, though he felt as if he'd slept for fifteen minutes. His brain felt the way half-coagulated gelatin looked, and lack of sleep reared up as a headache trying to bleed out of his ears.

Amanda came back. Her skin was pale, her hair disheveled, the bruises on her neck and cheek a bright purple, and there were blue-black smudges under her eyes. "We have to go to the hospital," she said, finger-combing hair from her eyes. "Hank will meet us there. The ambulance crew just brought in Noah Schroeder."

"Isaiah's kid?"

"That's the one."

"What happened?"

"All I know is that when the nurses were putting a call to Carruthers, Sarah Schroeder became kind of, well, hysterical."

"Why?"

"Apparently, her brother not only needs a doctor," she said, hurrying down a near hall. "He needs the police."

Hammering the accelerator, Ramsey made the trip in three minutes thirty. He came to a rolling stop just long enough for Amanda to jump out, and then he continued around the breezeway, nosed the loaner into a parking spot, and pushed out. He spotted Ketchum's cruiser pulling in, and they jogged across the parking lot and breezeway into the emergency room. Ketchum's stubble was gone, and he smelled like aftershave, but his blue eyes were sunken and fatigue had carved deep hollows under his cheekbones.

The lobby was empty except for a strained, anguished-looking woman sitting along the far wall to the right, and a young girl with mussed blond hair and puffy eyes. The woman started up when she saw Ketchum, but the receptionist waved them down.

"Dr. Slade said you should come on back." The receptionist's eyes were so wide her iris looked like a piece of coal in a snowbank. "She said you'd better hurry."

In the back bay, there was that sense of barely controlled chaos Ramsey knew from experience meant that things were just this side of totally out of control: shoes scuffing linoleum, the clatter of metal trays bouncing on casters, and from behind a yellow gauze curtain, a gabble of urgent voices, and Amanda's, barking out orders.

They ducked behind the curtain. A cluster of nurses were gathered around a metal gurney festooned with two IV poles and bags of intravenous fluids with snakes of clear tubing. Amanda stood with her back to him and left of the gurney. A medical scanner hung suspended from the ceiling and off to Amanda's left. All he could see of the boy on the gurney were a pair of tennis shoes attached to feet jutting from jeans.

A nurse spotted them, said something, and Amanda craned her neck around. She waved them over with a heavy pair of surgical scissors. "It's pretty terrible," she said, as another nurse dropped back and Ramsey squeezed in, Ketchum at his left elbow.

The boy, Noah, lay on his back, his eyes closed, face shiny with sweat. Besides the jeans, he wore a crew-cut light gray sweatshirt with blotchy sweat stains around the neck and under his armpits. The boy gave off a gassy smell, like half-boiled garbage. A light green, two-pronged nasal cannula delivered additional oxygen, but his skin was white as salt, his lips and nail beds were blue, and the black circles under his eyes looked painted on. IVs dripped fluid into veins along either wrist, and he could see and hear from the scanner that Noah's heart rate was hectic, rapid and irregular. Noah's temperature was elevated—40° C—and Ramsey knew that was bad. A red digital readout with a capitalized *BP* showed a set of numbers, both low, meaning shock.

"Why's he dropping his pressure? Is he bleeding?" he asked, and then added, "And what's that smell? It's like . . . Jesus, it's like rotted meat."

"We don't know," Amanda said. "We were just going to cut off his clothes." They did that, Amanda and three nurses, their scissors flashing, and then Amanda stared. "What the . . . ?"

A gauze bandage covered half Noah's right biceps. The coag-gauze might have been white once, but now the bandage was sodden and colored a greenish-yellow. The bandage was secured with surgical tape, and as Amanda teased that off, the rotten-meat smell got worse. Then Amanda peeled away the bandage. "Oh, God," she said.

The wound was putrid: a fist-sized crater of viscous green-yellow pus, blackened dead skin at the margins edged with inflamed, still-living flesh and a spidery filamentous web of red streaks running into his armpit.

"This is bad," Amanda said. "This is worse than bad." She was already irrigating the wound with huge syringes filled with sterile saline. A gloved tech held a basin beneath Noah's shoulder, and the fluid that ran into it was sludgy and greenish-gray. "It's definitely infected, and the infection's dissecting along the soft tissues, might even be in the bone. If it's in the bone or seeded the brain, then we might lose him. He's septic, but maybe we've got it in time. Maybe this is the worst . . ."

The shriek of an alarm told the lie because things went, suddenly, to hell.

"It's his BP, he's crashing," Amanda said urgently. "Open up his IVs. Craig, intubate him now. Sheryl, get me a CVP tray. With that wound there, I'm going to have go for a right internal jugular stick. And somebody page Dr. Carruthers from ICU, I need another set of hands down here pronto. I want an initial bolus of eight hundred mills of saline, and I'm going to draw off blood for cultures. Let's go, let's go, people, now!"

Then Amanda turned, ripping off her soiled gloves and plucking up another packet. "Sorry," she said, snapping on first her left glove and then her right. She moved to a tray of instruments a nurse wheeled over and began sloshing a brown antiseptic rinse over Noah's neck. "We'll get pretty busy here, Jack, Hank. Better wait outside."

They ducked out without saying anything, just trying to keep out of everyone's way. But Ramsey turned back in time to catch a glimpse of Amanda jabbing a needle on a massive syringe into Noah's neck.

Noah's mother and sister were where they'd left them. Noah's mother fisted a wadded tissue to her mouth. "How is he, Hank?"

"Noah's bad, Hannah. Dr. Slade says there's shock because he has an infection. Up here." Ketchum touched his right biceps. "Infection's poisoned the blood."

"An infection? But how?" Hannah Schroeder's eyes ticked from Ketchum to Ramsey and back again, jittering like a terrified bird. "He hasn't been anywhere since Friday afternoon after school! You remember, that day he came in so late, and I got so worried. But he never said *anything*!"

"The way I heard it, Sarah here pitched a fit when

the ER people wanted to call Dr. Carruthers. You want to tell us what that's about, Sarah?"

The girl spoke through sobs in little hiccups. "He-he showed m-me on Friday. This was while you were still ou-out," she said as Hannah turned an astonished look on her daughter. "He got hurt on-only he did . . . didn't want anyone to kn-know."

"Know about what?" Ramsey asked.

"That he'd been shot," she said.

43

Before they left, a nurse ducked out and said that Noah had gone into surgery. "Doctor says she'll try to save the arm," the nurse said.

"Will he make it?" Ketchum asked.

"That will depend on how extensive the infection is, whether it's seeded his brain. If his brain is involved, there could be neurological problems. It's just too early to tell."

"Tell her that we think Noah was hit with some kind of bullet," Ramsey said. "We're going to go check it out now."

"I'll tell her." The nurse shook her head. "Such a shame, that family, first Isaiah, then Scott and now Noah. Some families are just born for heartache."

Outside the ER, in the parking lot, Ketchum said, "I should call Kodza. If Sarah's right, then the man who shot Noah probably killed Limyanovich."

"You could call her," Ramsey said.

Ketchum gave him a one-eyed squint. "But you wouldn't?"

"It's *your* kid. Do you want to?"

Ketchum's lips pursed, and then he scuffed the pavement with the toe of his boot. "No. I want to talk to my boy."

Ramsey nodded. "Then let's go talk to your boy."

Ketchum led and Ramsey followed: a thirty-kilometer trek northwest out of town to the school that served Farway and two other rural townships. Ketchum had called ahead, and when they pulled in, the school principal, a rotund man with oily hair, was waiting. Ramsey sat in his loaner while Ketchum got out, conferred a moment with the principal, and then disappeared into the building. Ketchum re-emerged ten minutes later, his jaw set, his look thunderous, and his left hand firmly clamped on a young boy's shoulder.

Up close, Ramsey saw the resemblance. The boy had Ketchum's jaw and cheekbones but dark brown hair and the wild-eyed look of a kid terrified out of his wits.

"This is Joey." Ketchum's face was a rock. "Most of what Joey and I have to discuss, we're going to do in private. But, for now, Joey's got something to show us."

"Right there." Joey pointed up a steep, leaf-strewn slope. "By the stone angel."

Facing the rise, Ramsey looked left and spotted the angel, sword in one hand and scales in the other. "And you boys didn't see anyone before that?"

Joey shook his head. "The only reason we saw anything was we heard the car. I bet *he* wouldn't have seen us if the sun wasn't going down."

"Why?"

"That rise looks west. Troy wears glasses and the sun got the glasses," Joey said, simply. He thought a minute then added, "I remember walking close to the edge of the rise when we got here, and we didn't see anything."

Ramsey looked at Ketchum. "Two possibilities: either the killer came in on a bike, like the boys, or he was dropped off because he figured on having Limyanovich's car."

The lettering on the grave marker was worn and stained with lichen and mineral tracks left by rainwater. Ramsey traced the inscription with the fingers of his left hand. "Can't make out a date, or who's buried here.

But I'll bet the church in town has records about who's buried where."

"Maybe," Ketchum said. "But there hasn't been a burial *here* since the end of the Jihad. This is deconsecrated ground. There was a lot of trouble here during the Jihad, you know, between the Old Romans and the New Avalons."

Ramsey thought back to Sunday morning. Was that only yesterday? Seemed like a year ago, so much had happened. "Yeah, Amanda said there was a lot of bad blood."

"That'd be an understatement. I was a kid at the time, over in Clovis and just out of diapers, when the Jihad really got going. In Farway, the New Avalons and Old Romans started accusing each other of being in league with the Blakists. There was talk about a break-away faction of Blakists scattered all through the lake islands."

"Anyone implicated?"

"As far as I know, no one ever proved anything about anybody. A bunch of families run out of town, though. One family got wiped out, right here in this cemetery. Old Romans had come to pray, but the rumor started in on how they really were meeting with Blakists. Before you know it, people bore down and butchered those people. The cemetery hasn't been used since. When Isaiah died—he was Old Roman—they buried him in a smaller cemetery outside of town."

"How many Old Romans left in town?"

"Not too many. I'd say round about fifty families, all told."

"And Doc Summers," Ramsey said. Out of the corner of his eye, he saw Joey wince. "What?"

Joey fidgeted. "Well, one thing about the guy we saw, I mean . . . we all kind of thought, with his hair, you know . . ."

"No, I *don't* know," Ketchum said. "What are you saying, son?"

"Well, the guy looked kind of old, and his hair was"— Joey swallowed—"white. And he had a lot of it, kind of wild, and—"

"Old Doc," Ketchum cut in. He closed his eyes. "Lord help us. They saw Doc."

44

The operating room was chill and smelled of antiseptic, coagulating blood, and rotted meat. Noah Schroeder's blood pressure had dropped twice during the operation, and once he'd almost arrested. Three hours later, and Amanda had excavated a double handful of dead and dying flesh.

Finally, Amanda looked up and signaled the circulating nurse. "Call ICU. Tell them he's on his way." As the nurse hip-butted the door into post-op, she said, "We'll have to leave the wound open to granulate in, and we'll load him with antibiotics. But I really don't like his blood pressure. It's been in the basement too many times."

Gabriel stripped off his gloves. "I'd keep him on a pressor. Once the anesthetic wears off and we have a chance to settle him down in the ICU, his blood pressure will probably read closer to true. His urine output's bad, so he's still pretty vasodilated. I'd keep him on a vaso-pressor, make sure his kidneys get blood. I'll keep a real close eye on him while he's in ICU. That way—"

"That way, we don't get renal failure on top of whatever infection might be cooking." Amanda nodded. "Sounds like a plan. By the way, I didn't get a chance to thank you for this morning. When his blood pressure crashed, I needed all the hands I could get."

"Don't mention it," Gabriel said. "Just doing my job."

His job.

Five minutes after the ambulance call went out that morning for Noah Schroeder, Gabriel was on his turbo, heading for the hospital. Everyone knew he pulled extra duty, came in on his off-hours, and practically lived in the hospital, so no one gave a second thought when he barreled into the emergency room.

Noah was an incredible piece of good luck. He'd had a nervous moment when Ketchum and that detective showed, but a few minutes of listening in relieved his anxiety. They didn't know. They didn't have a clue. If not for Noah's sister, the meddling brat, they might have remained in the dark even longer. But now he might be able to kill two birds, not with one stone but in fairly short order.

Now, he sat in the ICU, poking numbers into a chartputer, just doing the job, monitoring his patient—and it was like his mind worked on two divergent streams: the routine rituals, and then this wilder, more turbulent river churning through his mind.

He was starting to feel a little . . . unhinged? Was that the word? He wasn't sure. So much had happened between Friday night and now. He and the Handler hadn't spoken since, when, Saturday? Sunday? He couldn't remember. He was running on not enough sleep and too much left to do.

The problem was every time he got closer to what he saw as a solution, something else popped up. Like the deputy staking out Underhill's house: who'd have guessed? He was reasonably certain that the deputy had not seen Underhill after Gabriel had left. Even if he had, what was there to see? A woman, dead drunk and passed out on her sofa, and her son upstairs, tucked out of sight. Nothing to see.

But now they knew Noah had been shot. Only a matter of time before they tied Noah to Troy—and if Troy Underhill died soon, they'd start looking closer at the hospital. The personnel.

On the other hand, so what? He'd given Underhill the

amnestic. She wouldn't remember him. If the other deputy had gone up to the house—and by some miracle, roused Underhill—she'd more than likely remember *him*. Gabriel had wiped everything he'd touched. The doctored vials were the only incriminating evidence, and they might be chalked up to pharmacy or manufacturer's error. But the prescription was valid, and Sandra Underhill's signature card was on file (he knew because he'd methodically forged her name to the refill request).

What was more, Gabriel would bet money, Sandra Underhill would lie her head off. Who wanted to be known as the mom who bedded a guy for money while her kid slipped into a diabetic coma?

Got to keep going. Got to keep my eye on the prize.

Another unexpected windfall: with all this business about Noah, Amanda Slade hadn't had a chance to go to the bathroom much less wrap up an autopsy. At last check, Limyanovich was still a guest of the ETU: Eternal Care Unit. Aka the morgue.

Because if there was a capsule in one tooth, maybe in another . . .

He met Amanda in the hall, going the opposite direction. This, he interpreted, as a good sign. If Amanda was in the ICU with Noah, while *he* was in the morgue . . .

Amanda stopped. "How's he doing?" She carefully listened, asked a few questions, then nodded. "Okay. Thanks again for coming in, especially since I know you had a late night."

Charlie's. He'd completely forgotten. She'd seen him there. Judging from her appearance—the bruises around her neck and a liver-colored welt on her left cheek—it looked like he'd missed something. He'd picked up the police call, of course, but only found out about Amanda from the nurses that morning. "Yeah, well, you know . . ."

Amanda seemed to take this as meaning something because she nodded as if she understood. "I was kind of surprised. Didn't peg you for a Charlie's person."

"I don't go there often." This much was true. "It's not really my style."

"Mine either. Why didn't you stop and say hello before you left?"

"Oh, well, I didn't want to intrude. You and this detective boyfriend of yours . . ." He trailed off when she began to blush, furiously. "Sorry, but you look pretty banged up. You've got to be more careful. Can't afford to lose you."

"Yeah, I'd be kind of sad to see me go, too," Amanda quipped and then touched his arm. "It's fine. Thanks for being concerned, and the help. You're a real angel, you know that?"

"Yeah," Gabriel said. "That's what all the girls say."

He had, he calculated, about thirty minutes before Amanda might be done puttering with Noah. Thirty minutes.

The morgue was next door to Amanda's basement office and was a large square room with buffed linoleum floors, overhead fluorescent light bars, and teal-blue tile walls. Three morgue refrigerators occupied one entire wall and faced long metal counters and sinks along the opposite wall. A neat queue of six metal gurneys with scalloped body trays were racked in two rows along the near wall closest to the entrance. The morgue was, trading on a bad pun, dead quiet.

Gabriel studied the refrigerators. Each refrigerated, stainless steel bay held six corpses in a conveyor tray system, three to a side. A body was placed on a body tray mounted on a gurney, then rolled end on to the open door. The conveyor tray system was designed such that the body tray rolled in or out of the cooler using the conveyor mechanism. According to Amanda's records, Limyanovich lay in refrigerator #2, berth #2. Gabriel reached for the locking handle to Limyanovich's berth—and paused.

Next to the handle was a dataset lock. For a crystal-key. Which he didn't have.

He spent thirty precious seconds cursing, his hoarse whispers filling the morgue with a sound like rats' feet on glass. He didn't know, hadn't stopped to think! Amanda had to have a key, but where? Would she carry a passkey all the time?

In her office, now, pulling open drawers, thanking whatever angel was watching over him that, at least,

Amanda didn't lock her desk drawers. (And why should she? No one here but us dead guys, *ha-yuck, ha-yuck.*) He shuffled papers, various pens and pencils, a makeup kit, a pair of old running shoes. My God, women were pack rats. . . .

He found the crystalkey tucked in an envelope in the bottom right-hand drawer. The crystalkey was hexagonal and pale pink, and fit the lock perfectly. Gabriel inserted the crystalkey, twisted counterclockwise while pulling down on the locking handle and presto! The refrigerator puffed open, releasing a ball of air that smelled of damply cold chemicals. Gabriel could make out a lumpy black body bag on a body tray. Pulling the tray out a third of the way, he unzipped the bag. The smell inside the bag was worse than outside: a stink of wet charcoal and rubberized chemicals. But he was working quickly now, using his gloved hands to pry open Limyanovich's jaws and the tip of a curved metal clamp to count out the teeth.

He'd studied his holoreconstructions thoroughly and completely. There were a total of five remaining candidates, not counting the teeth Amanda had already examined: one that contained a legitimate dental post, and the hollow rear molar with the remains of that capsule.

The first tooth he tried, the upper left second bicuspid, didn't so much as budge. The second, a lower right first molar, came away with only minimal tugging and revealed a steel post. The third, the right lower third molar, resisted though he thought he detected a tiny amount of give. He stepped back to move out of the light. The pitted crannies of the tooth looked a little off-center, like a table with one leg shorter than the others. He reached in with his clamp and gave the tooth another nudge, but couldn't move it.

Time, time! He checked his watch. Thirteen minutes since he entered the morgue, four since he started with the teeth. Three teeth left: one he couldn't budge, one he hadn't tried and this off-center molar.

He tried the first tooth again. The clamp bit against the tooth's enamel with a faint yet perceptible click. He twisted his hand right and then left. No dice.

Break it. By the time anyone knows anything, you'll be long gone.

He sucked in a breath, gave the clamp a violent twist counterclockwise, and jerked the clamp straight up. The tooth gave with a loud snap! Another post.

He released his breath in a sigh of frustration. Did a watch check. Five more minutes and then he had to leave. Two teeth left.

All right, smart ass, where is it? Think, think, think! There's something I'm missing, but I'm smarter than this, this has to be something staring me right in the face.

Smart ass. Thinking that sent a little frisson tripping up his spine. Something about smart—and then he knew.

He'd studied the holoreconstructions of Limyanovich's teeth and jaw many times over, cross-referencing with dental texts. The mature adult has thirty-two teeth, counting all four third molars, the wisdom teeth. But Limyanovich had twenty-nine teeth. Limyanovich was missing three of his wisdom teeth

"But not the fourth," Gabriel said. He stared down at Limyanovich and then at that stubborn back molar, a sooty peg canted like one of those ancient cemetery grave stones. "You smart ass, you've only got one wisdom tooth."

This time, he didn't hesitate. He slid the clamp around the tooth, held on and then levered the tooth back and forth, back and forth, rocking it the way he might rock a car stuck in the snow. Sweat trickled down his temples, and when he ran his tongue over his upper lip, he tasted salty bristle. The tooth wouldn't budge.

"Come on," he muttered, "come on, come on!"

The tooth gave, suddenly. The clamp jerked free, the tooth clenched in its jaws, and he saw something arc away in a bright twinkle to *tick-tick-tick* over the floor.

A crystal. A very minute, very red data crystal.

In three minutes, Limyanovich was back on ice. Thirty seconds later, Amanda's key was back in her bottom right-hand desk drawer. And in six minutes, he was gone.

Now, on his turbo zipping along and the wind whistling past his cheeks, he felt buoyant. He was untethered, nearly a free agent. He hadn't included the Handler in his plans, just thought them up and told the Handler what he was going to do—and then did it. For all the danger, he was enjoying the hell out of this.

When he got the Handler over his earbud, he said, "I got it." He explained about the tooth then added, "I'm on my way home now to run it on my decryption program."

"That is excellent." The Handler's smoky burr vibrated with triumph. "This is superb. You have done very well, extremely well. Only there are still problems, yes?"

"I'll take care of them," Gabriel said, suddenly irritated. Spoiling it for him.

"You are not concerned about the proximity?"

"It's too late for that." He explained about the Underhill boy. "With Noah unconscious," he didn't say *dead* because he had to figure out how he'd pull that off, "and the Underhill boy eliminated, that ought to do it. They'll never tie them to me."

"What about the crime scene evidence?"

"Don't worry. They'll get themselves tied up in knots trying to figure that."

After they disconnected, Gabriel was vaguely annoyed. Hadn't he proven himself? Bringing up the kids; he knew what he was doing! Well, he'd show the Handler a thing or two about taking care of problems, little and big ones.

Like his father.

45

They found a bike in a stand of nearby juniper. Twenty meters closer in, Ramsey spotted blotches of rust-colored dirt arranged in a rough semicircle, and then a short distance away, dime-sized blotches speckling the gravel in a halo.

"Blood spatter," he said, backing up toward Ketchum. "We need to be careful where we walk. Treat the whole place like a crime scene and get the county people up here and go over this place a centimeter at a time. But those are two distinct patterns."

"He was shot twice," Joey said. "Noah said he heard a shotgun, and then we all saw the other gun go off."

"You actually *see* a shotgun?" Ramsey asked.

"No." And now Joey looked uncertain. "What we saw was, well, like a cane or something. You know, Old Doc's got that bum knee, only he got close to the other guy, the one with the mustache and long hair, and then Old Doc whipped the stick around and jammed it into the guy's chest. BOOM! Just like that."

"Bang stick," Ketchum said. "Then he shot at you, son?" When Joey nodded, he said, "Show us."

*   *   *

The hill was slick with leaves, and Ramsey slipped a couple of times, staining the knees of his jeans a muddy green. Ramsey was in reasonable shape, but he and Ketchum were huffing by the time they made it to the top. Arming sweat from his forehead, Ramsey said to Joey, "So you guys huddle here at the edge, hear a bang, see the big guy with the mustache go down, and then the other guy shoots him with another gun while he's on the ground. That's when Troy screamed?"

"Right. We were here." Joey indicated a swatch of trammeled grass and then pointed east toward a field of taller meadow grass. "Then, you know, we started to run to get to our bikes, only we got all turned around. We were pretty scared. Anyway, we had to double back. We got our bikes and then . . ." He faltered.

They waited a moment, then Ketchum said, "Then?"

Joey's eyes slid to a spot in front of his toes. "I, uh, I'm not exactly sure what happened next."

"Why not?" Ketchum ground out.

"Because," Joey gulped air and then looked up, "because I got on my bike, and I took off. I told Noah and Troy to come on, but Troy'd lost his glasses and couldn't get his bike up and . . ."

"And *what*?"

Joey's Adam's apple bobbled. "Noah wouldn't leave without Troy. That's why he got shot. I heard the shots, but I didn't see anything."

"How many shots?" Ramsey said, as much to forestall Ketchum as nail things down.

"Four. Three close together and then nothing, then one more time. I think it was when he fell."

Ketchum and Ramsey looked at one another. "Brass," Ketchum said. "Think he came back and picked them up?"

"*I* would." To Joey: "What happened to Troy's bike?"

"Troy said he'd go back Saturday and get it." Joey flicked a quick look at his father. "I was grounded, so I don't know if he did or not. I bet he did but he'd have to find a way to get here."

"That could explain the other bike in those junipers," Ketchum said. "Noah was shot up and probably couldn't handle getting Troy here."

"We need to talk to this kid, this Troy Underhill." Ramsey touched Joey's shoulder. "You've done good. Now show me this tree house."

There were swollen rust-colored buds sprinkled along the maple's limbs: only a day or two before the tree finally shed its dead leaves, like shaking off a layer of dandruff. Ramsey surveyed the broad, rough stem and arc of branches then inspected the wood slats nailed to the trunk. "This third slat, the one right here"—he pointed—"that break looks fresh. Was that broken the last time you were here?"

Joey's face pruned in thought. "I don't think so."

Ramsey was up on tiptoe. "There's blood on that fifth slat smeared around where that nail is crooked. Looks like someone got tagged."

Ketchum looked unhappy. "Did you get a look at the bandage on Old Doc's left hand?"

There was more blood and crushed grass where the killer had gotten tangled in Troy's bike and then a short distance away, a woman's bike: the killer's or Troy's, they didn't know, but there was no blood.

After the men sent Joey to wait in the patrol car, Ketchum said, "I don't see this. That hill is a climb. An old guy like Doc taking that at a run, with a bum knee, much less having anything left over when he gets up top . . . I just don't see it."

"I was kind of thinking the same thing because here's what really bothers me," Ramsey said. "Why would an old guy who has white hair get himself a white wig? And then there's the makeup. Crime lab says it's women's makeup. But Joey knew the killer was a guy, so the killer must've done the wig to look like a guy's hair, or just got a man's wig. But the makeup suggests that our guy is young and used makeup to *look* old. Everything points to Summers: the limp, the hair, the bandage on his hand. But it's too perfect."

Ketchum was grim. "Unless it *is* Doc. He's smart enough to plant enough evidence so we think it's too obvious and dismiss him. But how about two people? Still might be Old Doc, and somebody else."

Ramsey chewed the inside of his cheek. "If that's true and that person wasn't here, then we've got at least two people and maybe more, if Kodza's right. We got to talk to Troy, and maybe the techs can pull something from those bikes. Speaking of Kodza, she's probably chewing titanium right now wondering where we are. I would've expected dispatch to call by now."

Ketchum look both embarrassed and defiant. "I told dispatch not to put Kodza through. I mean, hang it, it's my department. If I wanted to be at someone's beck and call, I'd work for the government."

"You *do* work for the government."

"Don't get mean," Ketchum said. "Tell you what, I'll give you a deputy—"

"Not Boaz."

"*Not* Boaz, and that way, the deputy can go with you to see Troy and his mom. Troy'll be home from school by now, and his mom will feel better with one of us around. She ought to be . . ." He stopped.

Ramsey waited. "What?"

Ketchum scrubbed his lips with the fingers of one hand. "I was gonna say she oughta be sobered up by now."

"She that bad?"

"Worse."

"Well, that doesn't sound good," Ramsey said.

"It never is," Ketchum said.

46

They had their first inkling something was up right before they left the cemetery. Joey sat in his father's patrol car, and Ramsey and Ketchum were outside, talking damage control with Kodza when Ramsey heard a familiar but totally out of character sound—at least, for Farway. The sound was a distant *whopwhopwhopwhopwhop*. He knew right away. "You hear that?"

"I do." Ketchum turned a complete circle. "Sounds like they're going north."

"Toward Farway. Hank, this is about those two guys from last night. Reporters covering the police must've picked up the story. This kind of scrutiny we don't need, not with a potentially very pissed-off legate rep."

Ketchum started for the driver's side. "What's done is done. Only thing to do now is go see just how pissed-off she is."

Very pissed off.

"I was to have complete access." Kodza was stiff with anger. Her hands twitched in such a way that Ramsey was grateful she wasn't near anything loaded. Or sharp. Today she wore a black pinstripe suit with a high neck that made her look like an armor-plated BattleMech, and stiletto heels that could take out an eye. "Instead, I awaken to the wonderful news that Detective Ramsey has mauled two men, one of whom is even now in intensive care. And what about *those*?" She jabbed a finger at Ketchum's window. There was a crowd of news hovers, reporters, holomen, and two VTOLS stitching a lazy crisscross pattern across blue sky.

"Reporters," Ramsey said. Running the gauntlet of reporters had left him cranky. "You know, guys who make up the news."

"I *know* who they are! But what are they doing here? I will tell you why: because of *you*." She took aim with a well-manicured index finger. "Bad enough what is happening even now in New Bonn, but you have contaminated this investigation . . ."

They let her run on for a good ten minutes. Finally, as she was winding down, Ramsey said, "So did you talk to your people last night?"

"Yes." She was sweating, and blotting her upper lip with the back of her hand. "I have checked with all the relevant authorities, and they have checked with their superiors. I am assured there is no ghost agent, and I do not care what your DBI tells you."

"You have any idea why the Bureau would lie?"

"I would suspect that the allure of intrigue is far greater than its reality."

"Okay." Ramsey wanted to believe her. Catching the bad guys was hard enough. "I want to believe you. You're probably lying, but I just don't have the energy or time to fight you about it. I don't really care about you, your ghost agent, or your secret missions. They're all bullshit."

Ketchum, who'd barricaded himself behind his desk, just rolled his eyes. Kodza said, "Ah. So. Cracking open skulls, this is not bullshit?"

"If you were half as concerned about justice as you are about whatever little secrets you're playing around with, you'd see it's not. Ask yourself that question the next time some woman gets her face cut up and half her bones broken because she said no to a guy. Ask yourself if it's a load of crap when you go to an apartment and find some kid, all skin and bones, lying in a puddle of feces in its crib because his parents are more concerned with what they put up their noses or in their arms."

"You are being melodramatic."

"Hell I am," Ramsey snapped. "There's a boy who might die because some asshole shot him. Don't tell me I'm being melodramatic when there are people dying. Don't give me that shit."

Kodza let that hang a few seconds. "You are finished? Yes? Fine." She paused, inhaled a deep breath and blew out. "Let us start again. If you would be so kind as to tell me where you two have been and what you have found, I would be grateful."

Squinting, Ketchum stretched his neck like a turtle coming out of a shell. "You actually *care* who killed Limyanovich?"

"Let us say," Kodza said, delicately, "that the legate and family have taken a renewed interest. That was also something we discussed last night. The, ah, potential for unfavorable publicity has made the legate quite, ah . . . anxious. In addition"—and now she gave Ramsey a frank look—"it seems that you still have advocates, Detective."

"What?" Ramsey was confused.

"Someone has put pressure on your behalf on the governor, who has put pressure on the legate, and who is now pressuring *me*. So, Sheriff, Detective, please, I would like very much to know what is up."

Ramsey thought about that while Ketchum filled her in. Someone had acted on his behalf? Pearl?

Kodza was saying, "So you believe, perhaps, that this doctor is the killer? Why not arrest him?"

"Because there're some things we can't square. Oh, we'll question him again, get a warrant to search his house, and I'm going to post a deputy to keep an eye on him."

"Why not tap into his link, or computer?"

"He can't do that," Ramsey said. "We'd have to convince someone that Doc's a serious candidate, and then hope a judge authorizes the tap. But before we do that, we need to get an assistant district attorney or DA involved. If you look at this from a lawyer's perspective, they'll poke holes through this thing faster than . . ."

Ramsey searched for a metaphor, couldn't find one, said, "They'll do it fast. What we got is the word of one boy who saw somebody shoot Limyanovich, but it was getting dark, the shooter was far away, wore a wig and makeup, and the kid was scared out of his wits. What we really don't have is motive. Why would Summers kill Limyanovich? For that matter, why would *anyone*?"

Kodza held up an admonishing finger. "You have forgotten. What if this killing is somehow related to this, ah, enmity between your various religious groups? Perhaps then, *where* Limyanovich was killed is quite important."

"We thought of that." Then Ramsey looked away, unfocused, thought, then said, "What if this has something to do only with *Blakists*?"

"Blakists?" Kodza asked. Ketchum told her the graveyard's history, and when he was done, Kodza pulled her eyebrows together in a frown. "The Blakists were wiped out, or assimilated back into the existing culture."

Ramsey said, "I don't buy that. Religion's important. Ethnicity's important, especially here on Denebola. The Neurasians and Zadiposians fought for how long? Years? Needed the Hegemony to step in before they wiped each other out? Some regions in Slovakia, they still speak in dialect. Look at the Sphere and how fast factions like Dragon's Fury have grown once the HPGs went down. Cultural memory counts."

Another mental pop: the pendant. Something religious? Amanda thought so: *Like what Catholics wear.* A heart, maybe, with a sword or cross. But that snake, if it was a snake . . . what was *that* about?

Familiar, somehow, like I've seen it before, only a very long time ago . . .

But instead of saying anything about the pendant, he said, "It's a theory. Now all we need is proof."

Things went better after that. Kodza seemed interested and wanted to come along when Ramsey talked to the Underhill boy that evening.

That triggered another thought. "Hank, we should post a deputy to watch over Noah Schroeder, and his mother might want to restrict visitors. If the killer's local, he might try to finish what he started. We took Joey out of class, too, and I'll bet the story's all over town. You'll maybe want someone with him, too."

"For how long? If the killer is local, he can bide his time, wait for things to die down," Ketchum said.

"I don't think so," Ramsey said. "Things are happening. We have a witness, we have a location. If we can find something tying someone here with Limyanovich, or PolyTech, then this could end soon."

Ketchum grunted. "From your mouth to God's ear."

"Yeah," Ramsey said, "if God's listening."

Then, another break:

Ten minutes later, after Ketchum had pulled deputies to watch Noah at the hospital, and his son at home, Fletcher, the arson specialist, patched in from New Bonn.

"Got something I think you're *really* gonna like." The arson investigator looked and sounded positively perky, his thin eyebrows bobbing up and down with excitement. "Remember how worried I was that maybe this was ANFO? It's not. It's good old nitroglycerine, with some mannite thrown in. Our boy, he's got guts."

"Why's that?" Ramsey asked.

" 'Cause nitro's hard as hell to keep from going off so you don't end up splattered all over the inside of your garage. Your boy rigged nitroglycerin powder it to mix with alcohol. He probably used some kind of booster to spark the explosion, or take out whatever was keeping the powder and alcohol apart. That wouldn't have to be anything more complicated than a partition rigged with a cap, and that's when you use mannite."

"What's mannite?"

"A sugar. Used in laxatives or for cutting other drugs. But if you *nitrate* mannite, you've got a blasting cap. Here's the kicker: you can get nitro and mannite only through a medical supply place, or pharmacy."

"Like maybe in a hospital?" Ketchum asked.

"Absolutely. Theft's like background music in a hospital. Controlled substances disappear all the time. But nitro and mannite aren't controlled substances. So either our boy has access to someone who has access to a pharmacy, or he forged a couple of prescriptions and stock-piled. Anyway you cut it, this narrows things down a bit."

"Oh," Ketchum said, dryly, and with a glance at Ramsey, "I think that's an understatement."

"Things are starting to pop," Ramsey said after Fletcher punched out. He had this sense of a mental break in the clouds, the way he always did when a case started to move.

"Like popcorn," Kodza said, who also looked pleased, an uncharacteristic expression Ramsey would remember later. "Enough heat and first one kernel goes, then another: pop, pop. Yes?"

More news, another pop:

Dispatch snagged Ramsey just as he and Kodza threaded through the cop bullpen for the door. "It's Dr. Slade." The dispatcher's eyes bounced off Kodza and back to Ramsey. "It sounded a little, ah, *personal*. Maybe you'd like to take this . . . ?"

Ramsey caught on. "Sure." To Kodza: "Let me take this, and then we'll get going." Without waiting for her approval, he ducked back to Ketchum's office.

Ketchum looked up, surprised. "Didn't you just leave?"

Pulling the door shut, Ramsey explained then said, "She must've told your dispatch she wanted to talk in private. She'd never do that unless she had something."

The bruise on Amanda's cheek was liver-colored, and the holo shimmer couldn't disguise her fatigue. "Sorry, guys," she said, forking hair from her face with her fingers. "There's either something wrong with my technique, or something wrong with my PCR machine, or my gels. Except when I run a few controls, they come out okay."

"What are you talking about?" Ketchum asked.

She explained what had happened with the DNA to Ketchum, then added, "So I'm still getting that anomalous peak when I run my gel. The easiest way to think about it is to compare DNA to fingerprints. You have a set of ten fingerprints and you match prints at a scene with what you have on record. But what if your guy has eleven fingers and you didn't know that? All of a sudden, you've got ten prints that say he's the right guy, and an eleventh that says he isn't. That's what this is like. I have a DNA print from someone with eleven fingers."

"So what's the eleventh finger?"

"I won't know until I sequence it. But the down and dirty is that Limyanovich has weird DNA. Limyanovich works for PolyTech. PolyTech does biogenetics. So maybe what I'm looking at is what either PolyTech or Kodza doesn't want us to find because there's something else."

"There's more?" Ramsey asked.

She nodded. "Remember I told you I was gonna run some mitochondrial DNA? Just to double-check and make sure we were talking about the same guy or at least someone in the same family?"

Ramsey nodded. "I remember. That stuff only comes from the mother."

"Exactly. So mDNA helps us differentiate everything from, say, prehistoric migration patterns of early man on Terra to teasing out whether a person's from Buckminster, or Styk, or Sorunda, and even subpopulations within those worlds. But there's one mDNA marker that no one in the Inner Sphere has except one group."

"Who?" Ramsey asked.

"Where's the better question," Amanda said.

"All right, then," Ketchum said, "where?"

"Kittery," Amanda said. She waited with an air of expectancy, but when Ketchum and Ramsey said nothing, she amplified, impatiently, "Kittery, as in the showcase Blakist reeducation camp. Kittery, as in Devlin Stone."

That rang a bell. "Wait a minute," Ramsey said. "Wasn't the resistance involved in something on Terra, right around the election for exarch? I remember that Levin's office tried to keep that all very hushed-up, but then the story leaked and . . ." A bulb flashed in Ramsey's mind. "Uh-oh."

"What?" Ketchum and Amanda asked, simultaneously.

"The medal on that necklace. We thought maybe that

was maybe a sword, right? Well, the Blakists used a sword on their logo."

And Ketchum said, "Add to that a murder in a town where maybe Blakist factions were hanging out, and that now this fellow Limyanovich, or someone on his mom's side came from *Kittery* . . ."

"And that the Blakists were heavily concentrated on Kittery, only the Blakists are supposed to be extinct. So there's only one explanation," Amanda said. "Don't look now, guys, but I think we just found ourselves a dinosaur."

47

1600

The cat motored, its purr a deep basso rumble that vibrated into Gabriel's thighs. The cat was happy, but Gabriel was pissed, his buoyant mood deflated like a blown tire.

Something wrong. He stared at the garbage his computer had spit out. *They changed the encryption code. Either that, or there's something I'm missing.*

Just when things had been going so well! Frustrated, he abruptly pushed back, startling the cat, hacking its purr in mid-rumble. Dumping the cat, he stood, snatched up his sat-link and punched in. When the Handler clicked in, he said, without preamble, "Something's wrong."

"I cannot talk now." The Handler didn't sound surprised, or even upset. Gabriel heard the usual background chatter. "You know better than—"

"Shut the fuck up." He was in no mood for a reprimand. "Just shut up and listen. Jesus H. Christ, I'm the one who's really at risk here, remember? They put together a few more pieces, I'm toast. So back off and listen for a change."

"All right, all right," the Handler said, as if dealing

with a fractious two-year-old. "I will shut the fuck up. This is about the crystal?"

"Yeah. This is some privileged code where I need the key to crack it. Unless this is doubly encrypted, the third crystal must contain the key."

"Is it possible that the key is *not* a crystal at all? This DNA you talked about?"

"Maybe. But if it's a crystal and it's on the body, I'm screwed. There's no way I can go back now without attracting a lot of notice. I got the night off for coming in this morning and . . ." He'd been about to say that he had certain *plans*, but instead added, "I won't get a crack until tomorrow."

"What about the Underhill boy?"

"That could go at any time. I just hope it's not too soon. Schroeder . . . I think I can make something happen, but I have to do it soon. The better he looks, the more things are going to look suspicious if he dies."

"Mmmm. And if the code really is in Limyanovich's DNA?"

"Then we might be okay. Anything Amanda puts in the official record, I'm gonna see. The thing is, these guys always do things in threes. *Always* threes. So I think we need that third crystal. Give me a sec, let me check Amanda's files." A few commands later, and he said, "I got it. She ran another gel and some controls, and she got that garbage peak again. No doubt now that she'll sequence it."

The Handler said, "Ah. So, one woman's garbage may be another's treasure."

Much later, Gabriel would remember he hadn't checked up on that mDNA.

That was a mistake.

48

Things kept popping.

Ramsey told Amanda what Fletcher, the arson specialist, said about the explosive, then asked, "You have nitroglycerine and mannite in your hospital formulary?"

Amanda had already turned aside and was busy telling her computer which files to access. "Yup."

"Any way of figuring out if any's gone missing?"

Amanda's smooth forehead furrowed. "Well, sure, but the pharmacy's pretty good about keeping track. The last time the hospital had any problem was a few years ago. Some narcotics went missing."

Ketchum said, "I don't remember the hospital coming to me with anything."

"They wouldn't. Pretty bad publicity if word gets out that the guy with the scalpel might be high."

"Did they catch anyone?"

"Not that I heard. The pilfering just stopped after the hospital instituted some kind of heightened surveillance system, and there's a record of all transactions in the hospital's database. Of course, that wouldn't stop someone from either forging a prescription, or writing a legit prescription but stockpiling over months and months."

"Any way to access that surveillance?"

"You'd have to talk to administration about that."

"We should do that. Ask them to cull through their records, focus on who's been giving out nitroglycerin tablets and see if they catch any scripts that look suspect. Just giving us a list of who's been prescribing would be a start. But this is good." Ramsey grinned. "Like the lady said: pop, pop."

Ketchum left to make assignments and contact the hospital administrator. Ramsey was about to sign off when Amanda said, "Jack, are you going to get into trouble because of me?"

"Because of you? What are you talking about?"

"*Jack*." Exasperation in her voice now. "I mean, because of last *night*. I heard the reporters . . ."

He cut her off right there. "Stop that. Stop that shit. You didn't do a damn thing. If I get into trouble, it will be because of *me*. But I'd do it again." He was going to say something else then thought, maybe, he didn't want to scare her. So instead, he said, "I'd do it again."

Ramsey tried Garibaldi, but another agent answered, said that Garibaldi had stepped out and offered to relay a message. Ramsey left word that he'd check in later that evening, and disconnected. He glanced out Ketchum's window, saw that the clot of reporters hadn't dissolved, and went to Ketchum with the problem. Ketchum agreed to an impromptu press conference as a diversion while Ramsey and Kodza ducked out the back. Five minutes later, Ketchum was surrounded by reporters who sounded like tar-eyed Makepeace grackles quarreling over a single worm, and Ramsey and Kodza were on their way.

Their driver was a deputy named Brett. Brett was older and jowly, with a smoker's hack. Brett had run through three different sheriffs, and he knew Sandra Underhill. "In high school. Not real well, I was a year ahead. She wasn't very good-looking, but she was smart. Talked about being a doctor, or maybe a big animal vet."

"So what happened?" Ramsey was sitting next to Brett, while Kodza was in the back. "I heard she's a bit of a drinker."

Brett grunted. "She's a *lot* of a drinker. What happened was Vern Underhill. Vern worked the chop shop north out of town, near Charlie's. A dropout but an okay guy, good for a couple of beers, game of pool. Way I heard it, Vern took Sandy out as a dare. Like, you know, for money. I guess Sandy was so grateful, she let Vern pork . . . ah"—Brett shifted gears—"she got pregnant, and they got married mainly because Vern's family was Old Roman. Trouble started right away, and with Troy's medical problems, just got worse. Vern left a couple of years back, but Sandy was already drinking and fuh . . . ah, dispensing *favors*."

Kodza leaned forward. "Tell me something. In a small town, everyone knows that this woman drinks, yes? And that she will, ah, sell her body? So why not help?"

A crimson band edged up the back of Brett's neck. "Old Doc, he got Sandy into rehab a coupla times, and the hospital takes care of all Troy's medical expenses. Church had a fundraiser, bought that insulin pump for him. But every time Sandy got dried out, she wasn't sober more'n eight months or so."

Kodza's lips thinned. "So you mean to say that the poor woman returns to the same town, the same house, the same bills, and the same job that forces her to dispense *favors*. Tell me, did any of the men in town say that *they* should stop? I think the answer is no. I know women like this, and drinking numbs the mind, so a woman does not have to confront the ashes of her life. A pity, no one declines to offer her the match."

The Underhill house was a depressing two-story gray-on-white farmhouse with paint peels like carrot shavings. There were no lights except one bare bulb by a side porch. The unmarked crunched to a stop, and they all piled out, Brett in the lead. Brett leaned on the buzzer next to the front door. When no one answered by the third buzz and several knocks, Brett said, "Must not be home."

Ramsey stepped back, surveyed the front. The house

didn't feel empty, just . . . asleep. There were a pair of windows to either side of the front door, but the curtains were drawn. He stepped to one window, cupped his hands around his eyes, and peered through the crack. "Looks like a living room." Then: "Uh-oh."

"What?" Kodza asked.

He straightened. "Someone's on the couch. I see a foot. Brett, get your dispatcher to try the Underhills' link. If no one answers, we'll break down the door."

Brett did. A few seconds later, they heard the characteristic shrill of a link. That went on for a few seconds, and then there was a sense of movement in the house, a *bang* as something fell over. Brett knocked again. "Sandy? Open up. It's Brett. Just want to talk to you a couple minutes."

The link was still screaming, but they heard someone stumble. A muffled "Aw, mother . . ." Then more clearly, a woman's voice, cranky: "Yeah, yeah." A rattle at the door, and then the door opened.

Sandra Underhill was a wreck. She wore a rumpled, low-cut black pullover and black pants pickled with wrinkles. She was barefoot, her honey blond hair was in disarray, and a crusted track of saliva tracked the angle of her left jaw. Her skin was ruddy with a network of broken capillaries, the whites of her eyes were the color of boiled egg yolk, and she smelled: old sex, cheap booze, wet ashes.

"What?" Sandra's eyes were red-rimmed and her mascara smudged into black half-moons like a Terran raccoon. "I didn't do anything."

The link was still squalling. Brett edged in and said, loudly, "This is Detective Ramsey and Ms. . . ."

"Kodza." Kodza stepped from behind Ramsey. "Dani Kodza, from the legate's office in Slovakia. May we come in, Ms. Underhill?"

"Is this about Troy?" Sandra's features puckered into an approximation of motherly concern. "Did he . . . is he in trouble?"

"Can we come in?" Ramsey pressed.

Sandra glanced at her clothes, seeming to become aware for the first time of what she must look like. She put a hand to her hair. "I . . . I'm not dressed for visitors."

"That is all right," Kodza said. "We should have called first. But we are here and I am a little cold and cannot hear well with your link. Perhaps you should answer?"

"Oh. Sure. Sorry." Sandra pulled the door open, and they stepped into the front foyer as she ducked down the hall and disappeared into what must be a kitchen. The link stopped in mid-scream, and Sandra was back a few seconds later. "Please, ah, come in. Would you like tea? I . . . I can make tea. Or coffee, would you like coffee?"

"We're fine," Ramsey said. "Actually, we came to speak with Troy."

"Troy?" Sandra's hand went to her throat, and her fingers played with a length of chain. Her nails were coated with chipped paint, like the house, only red instead of white, and the cuticles were ragged. "Has he . . . did he get into trouble at school?"

"No, no. We just wanted to talk to him about last Friday. You know that we're investigating that car fire out by the landtrain trestle."

"That's all they talk about at Ida's. What does that have to do with Troy?"

"We think that Troy might have seen something. Has he mentioned this to you?"

"No, but"—more fidgeting with the necklace—"we haven't spent much time together this weekend, and I only got home a few hours ago. I'd have to wake him up."

"Wake him up? Does he always go to bed this early?" Ramsey asked.

"Early?" Sandra gave a crooked half-smile, and her bleary eyes flicked to the window. Her brows squirmed as if she were just now registering the fading light. "That's funny, I could've sworn . . ."

Uh-oh. Ramsey had a sudden awful premonition. "Ms. Underhill, what day do you think this is?"

"*Think* it is? Why, it's Sunday. Sunday afternoon."

Kodza said, "It is Monday. Around"—she checked a fingerwatch—"six."

"What?" Sandra looked startled, like a flushed quail.

"I just got home from work or . . ." Sudden confusion swirled across her features. "I could've sworn . . ."

"Where's your son, Ms. Underhill?" Ramsey grated.

"What? Why?"

"Because Noah Schroeder was shot on Friday evening and we think the boys were witnesses to a murder."

"Witnesses?" Sandra echoed. Her voice was shrill. "Shot?"

But Ramsey was already looking past her, moving from the front foyer. "Where's Troy's bedroom? Where is it?"

"Upstairs, on the left," Sandra said, panic in her eyes. She rushed past Ramsey and pounded up the stairs. "I'll get him, you'll see this is nothing, you'll see. . . ."

Ramsey charged after, Brett and Kodza in his wake. Sandra hurried left of the landing then rapped rapid-fire on a door at the end of the hall. "Troy? *Troy?*"

She pushed open the door. A few seconds later, she screamed.

49

They ran hot all the way to the hospital: Ramsey and Brett in front; Kodza and Sandra crowded into the unmarked's backseat; and Troy—unconscious, sweaty, and panting like a winded animal—draped across the women's laps. As Brett roared into the hospital access road, Ramsey spotted Amanda, another doctor, and two ER orderlies waiting in the light of the emergency room breezeway. Brett slammed on the brakes, popped the unmarked's back door and the techs had Troy on a gurney and were whisking him through the double doors before Ramsey had even gotten out.

Ramsey fell into a trot beside Amanda. "Where's Summers?"

"Either not home, or not answering," Amanda said. "Hank's on his way in."

"Got to stop him. We don't need the press, and *he* needs to think about Joey now. Any place I can get in touch with him?"

"Reception." Then, at the back bay, she turned, put a hand on his chest. "Wait outside. I called Carruthers back in, and he's the best. I'll let you know soonest."

Just as Ramsey rounded toward reception, the sliding glass doors parted and Ketchum burst through on a gust of nippy April evening air, with Brett trailing a half step behind. "Reporters?" Ramsey asked.

"Left after I talked with them. Haven't seen them since," Ketchum said. "What's the story?"

Ramsey quickly filled him in then said, "Hank, this is getting out of control. First Noah, now Troy. You got to keep Joey close, maybe out of town until this is over."

The color had slowly leeched from Ketchum's face until his stubble looked inked on. "Lottie's got a sister in Clovis. Let me go make some calls."

"Let's go," Ramsey said to Brett. They found Sandra Underhill perched on the edge of a chair in the lobby, and Kodza in an adjoining chair to her right. Sandra was rocking back and forth, a tissue knotted through the fingers of her right hand as Kodza hung on to her left.

Sandra looked up as they walked over, and said, "How is he?"

"We don't know yet. No one could reach Dr. Summers, but Dr. Slade said she asked another doctor to take care of your boy," Ramsey said.

"That'd be Dr. Carruthers," Sandra quavered. "He's a good doctor."

"Ms. Underhill, I don't want to embarrass you, but I have to know what happened on Sunday night. Have you, ah, ever slept through an entire day before?"

"You mean have I ever been drunk enough?" Sandra's eyes bounced over Brett, standing behind Ramsey's left shoulder, and then to Ramsey. "No. At my worst, I'll sleep maybe until eleven the next morning because I have to be in at Ida's by one. Troy knows when I've had too much to drink, and he doesn't bother me. Just takes himself off to school." The tears started again, welling over the lip of her lower eyelids and trickling to her chin. "He never makes any trouble, and I've been such a horrible mother that—"

Ramsey cut her off. "I'm sorry, but we don't have time for that." Time was, it seemed, their enemy now, and the killer a few steps ahead.

But still here. Has to be because no one's made a play for Joey. Noah was a lucky shot, but the only way he could've known about Troy was if he'd seen him.

Then he remembered the tree house and that broken step. The blood in the grass and on the tree. That the killer might've been there when Troy and Noah came back for Troy's bike. That might also mean the killer didn't know about Joey—not yet.

He said to Sandra, "It's possible you've had contact with the killer. Did you bring anyone home with you Sunday night?"

The tip of Sandra's nose glowed pink, and her cheeks flamed. "Yes, I did. I . . . I had a few drinks at the bar, and then I . . . we . . . I took him home. We might have stopped off somewhere else beforehand. I really don't remember."

"Okay," Ramsey said. "Did you know him?"

"I'm pretty sure I did."

"What does that mean?"

"I mean, I have the feeling that I did."

"But you don't remember who, exactly?" When she shook her head, he said, "Okay. Can you describe him?"

"Just . . ." Her brows knit in concentration. "Bits and pieces. I don't know why this should be so hard . . . I remember that I came home from Charlie's—"

"You were at Charlie's?" When she nodded, he said, "What time?"

"I don't remember. Round about eleven, I think. Maybe a little earlier. Anyway, I'm pretty sure he came home with me from Charlie's."

"Did he ride in your car?" If so, they could sweep for evidence. Probably do that anyway.

"No, that I *do* remember. I remember thinking that his car was a little strange."

"Strange how?"

"Different. I . . ." She pressed her fingers to her eyebrows. "I just don't remember. We had something to drink, and then we went into the . . . to the couch . . ." Her face worked as she remembered some detail.

"What?" Ramsey asked.

"Nothing. I keep thinking . . . *white*."

Ramsey was confused. "White? White what?"

"Something about his face . . ." She gave it up. "I don't know. But that's the last thing I remember. White, and then drinking beer and then, you know, the couch."

"Maybe he put something in your drink to knock you out. I'd like to get a sample of your blood and see if there's anything there."

"Sure," Sandra said, and her lips trembled. "Take as much as what you want. Take it all."

Ketchum returned, having made arrangements for Joey, and Amanda appeared a short time later. She looked beyond exhaustion, the purple of her bruise competing with the smudges under her eyes. "I won't kid you, Ms. Underhill. Troy's blood sugar is sky-high and he's acidotic, like having battery acid in his blood. But neither Dr. Carruthers nor I understand how this happened. His insulin pump is working fine, and the insulin is fresh because you refilled his prescription Saturday."

Sandra looked bewildered. "No, I didn't."

A frown lightly touched Amanda's forehead. "The pharmacy records show you came around three o'clock. We have your signature."

"Three? I was at Ida's. There's no way I could've come here."

Ramsey said, "Maybe you don't remember."

But Sandra was adamant. "I remember that we were busy because Ida was serving ham and sweet potatoes and we're always packed when there's ham."

They all thought about that a minute, and then Kodza said, "No drug can be that selective. If she remembers the menu but not coming here, that is likely accurate."

Ramsey agreed. "Ms. Underhill, who orders Troy's insulin?"

"Why," Sandra said, "Doc Summers."

Ramsey said, "Ms. Underhill, when I asked you about the guy's car, you said it was strange. What did you mean?"

"I mean, *strange*." Sandra made a helpless gesture. "At Charlie's . . ."

"Charlie's?" Amanda blurted, and they all looked at her. "I remember seeing a patrol car way down the road, and *I* thought that maybe there'd been trouble. But there was nothing."

Sandra said, "That's it! The patrol car, *that's* what was so strange. He was driving one of your cars, Hank."

"And something white on his face, like a bandage," Amanda said. "John Boaz."

50

John Boaz sprawled in his boxers on an overstuffed recliner. A can of beer balanced on his stomach and two slices of cold pizza and rinds lay in a cardboard box on a side table.

Damn Jack Ramsey. Boaz took a pull off his beer. And Amanda, she needed straightening out. He should've taken her around back of Charlie's and done her until her eyes crossed. If Ramsey hadn't shown up, he'd have done that, too. He should've done it before that Underhill bitch. Underhill had been like a giggly rag doll, just a quickie in the alley. But then after he'd hitched his pants and gone back in, Ramsey was there. So he left and went out to Underhill's place. Underhill hadn't cared about the bandage, either at the bar or later, at her house. Hell, at the house, she'd barely been conscious. Just kind of snorted and slept through the whole thing. He'd almost left. And that other patrol car . . .

"Bobby," he said, out loud. He'd never have figured Bobby for a guy who'd pork anyone, let alone Sandra Underhill. Bobby was just . . . there. A gray guy with a hound-dog face and a couple belly rolls lipping his belt. But he'd recognized the number as the car rolled past.

That was Bobby all right: had the hat squared on and everything and . . .

The angry hornet's buzz at his door made him slop beer onto his belly. Cursing, he sat up, jiggled to shake off the beer and glanced at the time scrolling along the bottom of the holo. Almost a quarter to eleven. Who the . . . ?

Beer can still in hand, he padded to the door. He lived in an end unit townhouse with a tiny patch of front lawn he didn't give two fracs about and no neighbors in the next unit over. As he neared the front door, he noticed something a little off. The porch light was out. Odd. The light was on a timer, and he thought he remembered the light clicking on because he remembered the pizza delivery boy digging in his back pocket, counting out change. Now he'd have to change a stupid bulb.

"Well, fuck me," he said, and then as the buzzer buzzed again: "Yeah, yeah." There were decorative waterglass sidelights mulled to either side of his front door, and a corner street lamp threw just enough light for him to make out the blurry silhouette of an officer's hat. Ketchum? "Yeah?"

A voice, muffled by the door: "It's Bobby. Want to talk 'bout last night."

"Yeah?" Grinning now, Boaz tapped numbers on a pad next to his door, keying out his lock. The lock snicked back, and he pulled open the door. Said: "I'll *bet* you want to talk about last night, you son—"

And froze when he saw the broad round *O* of a gun muzzle pointing at a spot between his eyes.

"Well, maybe not," Gabriel said, and pulled the trigger.

51

"I feel like my head's gonna explode." Ramsey was pacing, cranked on caffeine, just about zero sleep, and sugar. They'd appropriated a conference room on the hospital's second floor. Amanda got coffee and everyone—excluding Brett who'd volunteered to escort Joey and his mother to an aunt's home out of town—doped up on caffeine. A few minutes later, one of the ER techs showed with a tray of yesterday's muffins and pastries filched from the cafeteria. "Too much going on at once and it's got to be connected, but I don't see Boaz being this organized, or this sneaky. Just because he was at Charlie's doesn't prove anything other than he was in the same place at the same time as Sandra Underhill, and her memory's not *that* reliable."

"There are two things that bother me," Kodza said. Pensive, she fingered the rim of her coffee cup. "Noah and Troy seem to have happened in very short order, yes? But why has nothing happened to Joey?"

Ketchum said, slowly, "Well, Joey took us out this afternoon . . . I mean, yesterday. Monday. That's when we found the blood and broken step at the tree house, and that blood where Limyanovich was killed. But

Troy's bike was already gone. Joey wasn't involved with that because he was grounded Saturday and Sunday."

"So the killer may not know about Joey. If he was in the tree house as Detective Ramsey suspects, he was too focused on Troy's bicycle. But a deputy would think about leaving behind evidence, especially DNA, and yet there is blood on a nail, on the ground where Limyanovich was killed, on the grass up the hill." Kodza shook her head. "I cannot see a policeman making that mistake."

"So that means the killer has limited knowledge and expertise," Amanda said. "Troy was planned, but Noah was a lucky break."

"And now we're back to whodunit." Ramsey picked up his cup, swirled dregs, put it down without tasting. "Joey says Doc Summers, but there's that hill. So we're back to a younger guy, in a wig and makeup. Or *two* killers. Or a woman."

"Well, *someone* knows medicine," Amanda said. She gestured to a computer pop-up screen where a ream of laboratory data still shimmered in emerald green. "The lab says the stuff in Troy's pump is sterile saline. Whoever switched out the vials had access to the pharmacy, knew how to manipulate records, steal the right vials, forge Sandra's signature. . . . Can you see Boaz doing that? Because I sure can't—not all that *and* filling vials with *sterile* saline.

"What's so important about the saline?" Ketchum asked. "That it's sterile?"

"If you're going to inject something, it better be sterile. But only a medically trained person would care. It's like a reflex. But I can't wrap my head around Doc, and Doc and Boaz together? There's just no way. They'd kill each other. Boaz is mean, and he's stupid. Does that strike you as the kind of person Doc would hang his life on?"

"No." Ketchum screwed up his nose. "He sure doesn't. But we can't just toss the idea."

"Which still brings us back to motive because if we knew *that*," Ramsey said, and now he locked eyes with Kodza, "we'd know how to look at it. All this pop-pop-pop is tied to Limyanovich, and *you've* been much more"—he considered the word—"*tractable* since speaking with your superiors. Whether that's because you're on our side, or you're just angling for information, I don't know if I care. But I'm asking you again. Help us."

Kodza's face was an absolute blank. "I believe that is what I have been doing."

"The hell you have!" Ramsey grabbed hold of an armrest on Kodza's swivel chair and swung the woman around until their faces were no more than twelve centimeters apart. "These are *kids* we're talking about. This maniac shot Noah, and if we hadn't gone to the Underhill's house, Troy'd be dead right now. So don't give me this crap. You keep messing around, I'm going to blow this up. I'll contact every news organization on the planet and tell them how the legate's not interested in a guy who goes around killing kids, and I'm sure I'll let slip something about Blakists."

Two high spots of color blossomed on Kodza's cheeks. "What is this Blakist nonsense? The Blakists were wiped out."

Ramsey barked a laugh. "That's crap. The Kittery Resistance is all over the news. Maybe that's why you wanted the body so quickly, to get rid of all that inconvenient evidence. But now we know, and I'll bury the legate before I'm through."

"You?" Kodza's eyes were as dead and flat as the eyes as a Hel cobra. "You do not have the power."

"Try me. I think you'll be surprised. I'm not like Hank. I don't have to worry about getting elected. Personally, I don't care if people like me. I'm in enough trouble now where going public would end my career. But I'll do it."

There was a short silence and then Ketchum cleared his throat. "Ramsey talks to the news people, I'm right there at his side, star or no star. Because, lady, you don't give a damn about my people—and I *sure* as hell don't give a damn about you."

Finally, Kodza said, "First, you must tell me this. You say that Limyanovich is a Blakist or—at the very least—part of the Kittery Resistance. So I ask you, Detective. How do you know?"

"His DNA," Ramsey said. "Amanda found DNA evidence that his mother or his relatives came from Kittery. Limyanovich was murdered in a cemetery where the townspeople butchered a lot of people they believed were Blakist sympathizers. Add to that local legend that Farway—and especially, the islands—were Blakist hideouts back in the Jihad. Noah Schroeder's dad was the sheriff before Hank, and he was murdered on Cameron Island and we know that Limyanovich went to Cameron Island two days before he died, and I think our killer went out there to test his explosive. So they're all connected somehow. It's too much coincidence."

Kodza nodded, silent, her face pensive now. "I see." Then a hint of a smile touched the corners of her mouth. "Well, are you going to tower over me like a Kyotan bear, or will you sit? Frankly, you are making me nervous."

Without a word, Ramsey backed up but stayed on his feet. "Talk."

"The stakes are much higher than you realize. Yes, we had suspicions that Limyanovich was a Blakist. But rumors are not proof. For that matter, we are concerned about the Clans," Kodza said.

"How?" Ramsey asked. Thinking: *That odd DNA Amanda found. Hmmm.*

"We are not sure. To say that Clanners have infiltrated the Inner Sphere is patently obvious. Clanners have associated with certain houses, etcetera, etcetera. But Clanners actually *interfering* is more disturbing. I have been investigating rumors that several Clans have banded together to make a push for Prefecture X."

"You mean, like the Jade Falcon invasion?"

She waved that idea away. "No, no, nothing so obvious as an all-out assault. This is something quite different, very novel for the Clans. We do not even know if the rumors are true, or part of a disinformation campaign to make us look away from what is actually happening. We have managed to intercept a few messages, some a year or so before the HPGs collapsed, and many more within the last few years as things have become so much more unstable: about a shadowy cabal, a *triumvi-*

rate. But we don't know what that is. For that matter, it might be nothing more than a new term coined to describe a clan leader."

Amanda said, "Triumvirate implies three. But three what?"

"We do not know. We have no direct proof that the Blakists have regrouped, or that they are related in any way to one clan, or three, or none at all."

"So how is PolyTech involved?" Ramsey asked.

"Because of their genetics work," Kodza said. "Who else would be so interested in genetic advances except Clanners? Again, we have no proof."

Ketchum frowned. "But you've got ideas about Clanners on one hand and ideas about Blakists on the other, and nothing to tie them. I know everyone in Farway and you're saying some people might be Clanners? Descendants of Clanners? I can't see it. My God," he said, shaking his head, "I don't want to think about word getting out about this. Talk about a witch hunt."

"Yes, so you can see, precisely, why we . . . *I* have not been at liberty to share so many things. You must understand the need for absolute secrecy." Kodza paused, put a finger to her lips in thought then said, "Of the available theories, we do not believe that there is a clan group on Denebola per se, or a Blakist cell in the sense of Jihad. But Kittery Resistance on Denebola, in Neurasia? Perhaps. Our best guess is that Limyanovich was lured here, and that is what we are even more interested in." She eyed Ketchum. "Part of your town's mythology revolves around homegrown vigilante cells that were actively tracking down Blakists during the Jihad, yes? Well, I tell you now: this is no myth. There *were* such cells. After the Jihad was over, Devlin Stone allowed these cells to continue—to track down Blakists and turn them over to a war crimes tribunal."

The other three stared at each other. Amanda said. "Devlin Stone?"

Kodza showed a thin smile. "There is much one does not know about Devlin Stone. To the best of our knowledge, these cells ceased operations when they ran out of Blakists to hunt. To the best of our knowledge."

Ramsey got there a split second before everyone else.

"Rogue cells. Sleeper cells. You're saying that there're still some out there. So, now with the HPGs down, the land grabs going on between people like Katana Tormark and Bannson, the Capellans pushing in, and add to that the fact that Prefecture X gets sealed off, these people must be going nuts. They've got to be seeing enemies everywhere."

"Exactly." Kodza paused. "This cell, they are good. They see themselves as The Republic's guardian angels, I believe. That they stumbled on Limyanovich was accidental. We had our eye on Limyanovich for some time because of his extensive travels, PolyTech, and his background. But we could not prove anything."

"But why lure in Limyanovich? What did they think he had?"

"That is the mystery," Kodza said, without irony. "Perhaps they felt Limyanovich had additional information about a secret conclave of Blakists. This cell, their core belief revolves around Blakists, hop-skipping from world to world. There have been other incidents on other planets: suspicious murders without resolution. The only clues we have are rumors of a confiscated data crystal."

"What's on it?" Ramsey asked.

Kodza shrugged. "Intelligence indicates that these people have a map of some kind, but that it is incomplete. Our best guess is that the information is an itinerary: worlds where this triumvirate is active, recorded as jump points."

"But you don't know, really, if *any* of this is true," Ramsey said, his voice clogged with sudden fury. "In the meantime, kids are getting shot. They're getting killed. *This*," he jabbed the table with an index finger, "is reality. This is all I care about: this planet, these kids, my home. Go look at Troy, and tell me this other stuff matters. Take a hard look at evil, and then try to wash the blood from your hands, or the stink of death out of your clothes. Live *my* life for a change, and then tell me how any of this crap means a good goddamn—because it *doesn't*. It never can, and it never will."

Kodza didn't reply at first. Then she said, very quietly, "You are right to be angry, Detective, and though you may not believe, I have known death, very well." She pulled in a deep breath, released it. "I do indeed have a ghost agent I have not wished to compromise. I assure you, this agent has had absolutely nothing to do with Limyanovich's death, or what has been happening to your people, Sheriff Ketchum. In fact, this agent has been working very hard to find out just exactly who did." Another pause. "I have two ghosts, actually."

"Kinda overkill," Ketchum drawled.

"An interesting turn of a phrase, Sheriff, because one agent you knew very well. He was Isaiah Schroeder."

Ketchum's face crumpled. Not into tears but as a slow draining of animation into a look of utter shock. "Isaiah? He worked for you? He was—?"

"Was murdered, yes. So there is every reason to suspect your Doctor Summers."

"What about Boaz?" Ketchum asked. He was getting angry; Ramsey heard the energy crackle under Ketchum's words, like lightening in an advancing storm.

"Not out of the question."

"You said two agents," Ramsey interjected. "Who's the other one, the one you lost contact with? Is he dead, too?"

"I believe," Kodza said, "not quite yet."

52

Tuesday, 17 April 3136
0345 hours

They agreed on only one thing: sleep. The case was taking weird twists and turns, and they were beat. Come morning, they'd meet with Kodza's agent, whoever he was. Privately, Ramsey thought Kodza wanted time to brief her agent. Nothing to do about it.

Troy and Noah were in ICU, with deputies standing guard, and probably as safe as they were going to be. Ketchum checked the duty roster and found that Boaz had clocked out late, at twenty-one hundred, because he'd had paper to catch up on.

"So, as far as we know, both men are still in town. But if this keeps up, I can't make it work," Ketchum said. "Either we get on the horn to New Bonn or DBI and get some extra people, or something's got to break, and soon."

"Give it twenty-four hours. Things really *are* starting to pop." Ramsey reached for the nearly-empty coffeepot, thought better of it, and leaned back in his chair. Kodza was gone, shuttled back to her hotel by a deputy, and Amanda was rearranging her schedule for the next morning. "Our guy's going to try for Troy again, and probably Noah. Either that or he goes underground and bides his time." Ramsey hooked a thumb toward Kod-za's empty chair. "What'd you think?"

"Of her sudden candor, or that semicontradictory load of tarise crap?"

"Both."

Ketchum shrugged kinks from his neck. "I don't know. Parts about the Blakists almost make sense. But I have a hard time with the Clans. Yeah, yeah, Limya-novich's got some strange stuff in his DNA, that doesn't mean there's Clan involved."

"I agree. But what about Isaiah Schroeder?"

Ketchum made an inarticulate sound, something be-tween a groan and an *mmmm*. Said: "Isaiah was a good man. So could he have worked for the government, maybe volunteered or got himself killed trying to do the right thing? I can believe that."

"What about Doc? Boaz?"

"Heck, I don't know." Ketchum scrubbed his face with his hands. "I just don't know. Whatever, I'm gonna get Bobby on the horn, have him watch Doc, then maybe we can see Doc round about noon after we meet our secret agent. When you getting Kodza?"

"Around nine," Ramsey said. "We'll go to Ida's and meet you there."

Ramsey found Amanda in admissions. She'd pinned up her hair, but it was coming down, giving her a frayed look. "Hi," she said, and yawned, stood, and stretched like a cat. "You know, between our bumps and bruises, people are gonna start talking about just what goes on when we get together." While he was figuring out how to reply to that, she said, "I'm so tired, I'm thinking of crashing in an on-call room. So, how's the hand?"

"It's okay. Sore."

"Mmmm." She sauntered over, slid her arms around his waist, tilted up her chin and said, "Wanna sack out in an on-call room? Maybe . . . show me your gun?"

"Why . . . *Doctor*."

In the end, he didn't stay. He needed sleep, and he needed a car. So he said good-night, chastely kissed her forehead and left to meet Ketchum in the ER lobby.

Ketchum was waiting on dispatch to put him through to a last call. "I'm getting old. Muscles feel like banjo strings," he said, palming the back of his neck. "Just one more, and we're gone and . . . he . . . hello, Bobby? Hank Ketchum. Sorry to roust you at this hour but something's come up and . . ."

". . . absolutely no problem. But one thing, Hank: let Doc go to noon Mass. If you don't let him get his praying in . . . yeah . . . yeah, I thought you'd see it that way . . . Now get some sleep, Hank, and don't you worry," Gabriel said, and smiled. "I'll take care of everything."

53

Tuesday, 17 April 3136
0900 hours

Change of shift was at seven, and by nine, Hannah Schroeder smelled warm scrambled eggs and fresh coffee wafting through the ICU doors as an orderly clattered by with a cart loaded with breakfast trays for patients down the hall.

Noah was still unconscious, tubes and needles sticking in and out every which way, and monitors going, the hiss of the ventilator a weird counterpoint to the high-pitched beep-beep-beep that was Noah's heart. Dr. Slade said that Noah was young and this was in his favor. But one look at Noah's poor, ravaged face and her chest clenched with a bad, black feeling, like the fingers of an icy fist, the same feeling she'd gotten the night Isaiah hadn't come home.

Scott. If only he'd come home instead of shacking up with that *slut*, none of this would've happened. Grace was the real problem. If Grace would just go away, then Scott would come home, and there would be a man around the house. If only Grace would just go *away*.

Hannah stood, bent and picked up her handbag: so light, suddenly, as if the weight had transferred to her heart. Then, a slight touch at her elbow, and Hannah flinched, whipped round, her eyes wide.

"Oh!" A nurse: young, blond, and taken aback. "I didn't mean to startle you. It's just that . . . wouldn't you like to lie down? Or maybe something to eat, you haven't eaten anything since yesterday morning."

The woman's kindness made Hannah's eyes fill. "No, no, I'm all right. I just remembered. There's something I have to do."

She didn't remember leaving the hospital, but suddenly she was outside. Heat splashed her face but did nothing to thaw the ice in her chest. She was numb all over as if she'd pushed into a blackness darker than night: black upon black.

She urged her car north along a road that the sun transformed into a gleaming silver-black ribbon. She slowed as she went through town. The familiar storefronts slid past the way she remembered those painted scenes on a merry-go-round spooled by, there and gone. She saw everything clearly. People out now, neighbors and folks she knew, and every one a stranger.

Then she was through the town, heading north, the road opening out like vast, black space void of stars. The town receded the way a planet shrinks beneath a ship hurtling at escape velocity—and then the town was gone, and she was free.

Like the release of gravity and with it, all the rules.

Ketchum walked into Ida's as Kodza ate breakfast and Ramsey sucked down coffee. Sighing, Ketchum dropped into a chair, raised a finger to signal for coffee, and palmed his sheriff's hat from his head. He waited until the waitress—a new girl—splashed coffee into his mug, gave Ramsey and Kodza refills, and then walked away before he said, "Talked to Lottie this morning. They're all just fine. Brett was up the whole night, said it was quiet."

"You send up another deputy?" Ramsey asked.

"Yeah," Ketchum replied. He raised his mug to his lips, blew on his coffee, swallowed back a mouthful. "I already fielded three calls from a couple of parents worried about their kids in school, and one call from Doc's priest, Father Gillis.''

"Don't tell me Summers went to confession."

Ketchum gave Ramsey a bleary look. "I'm sure he did. Gillis was calling because he was concerned. Says Doc's under a lot of stress and pretty angry. They sat together most of yesterday and half the night, talking.''

"At least, we know Summers is still around, and he's pissed.''

"And how is that good?" Ketchum rasped.

Ramsey stared at Ketchum for a long moment. Finally, he said, "Hank, how much investigative work have you really done?"

Ketchum sat back and hooked his thumbs into his belt loops. "Some. Not much. After Isaiah"—his blue eyes flicked to Kodza and then back to Ramsey—"not hardly any. Some drug cases, that's about it.''

"Then try not to take this the wrong way. The more stress you put on a system—town, person, whatever— the better your chance of getting something to crack. People get stressed, they make mistakes, and then you've got them.''

"Okay," Ketchum said. "But here's the thing. When this is over and you're gone, who picks up the pieces of all those things that didn't need fixing in the first place?"

They took Ramsey's unmarked, figuring there was no need to advertise. Then Kodza told them where they were going, and the two men did a double-take.

"You're kidding," Ramsey said.

"Of course not." Kodza wore pants: no-nonsense black trousers and a tapered black jacket with a creamy white shell. "Where better to pick up gossip?"

On the way, Ramsey punched up Garibaldi's private channel. The agent was not pleased. "Damn it, Ramsey. The Bureau *knew* something wasn't right with the legate's office and now this! Blakists. Clans!"

"They're just theories, Garibaldi. Not everything hangs together."

"It's *my* job to decide that, not yours. If the legate's

involved, this is treason and that's *our* jurisdiction. I can't authorize you and Ketchum to continue."

"Oh, cut the crap," Ramsey said. "I'm investigating a murder, and two other attempted murders, and probably a third. If not for us, you wouldn't have this much."

"Well . . . at the very least, I should send up some agents."

It was on the tip of Ramsey's tongue to observe that Bureau-types knew dick about homicide investigation, but he said, instead, "Sure. We could use help with surveillance."

"I can have agents in place by the end of the day. Until then, you're to do nothing. As for Kodza, you're to hold her. Don't let that woman out of your sight."

"Okay." Ramsey punched out then craned his head over his shoulder. "I'm not supposed to let you out of my sight."

Kodza was bland. "Better not blink."

"Mmmm." To Ketchum: "You'll be happy to know we're not supposed to do anything until the cavalry comes to rescue our collective asses."

"Yeah, I'll keep that in mind," Ketchum said, then angled his chin left. "Here's Charlie's."

The bar was closed. There were two cars in the back lot: a junker of indeterminate lineage, and another that Ramsey could've sworn he'd seen before. "I know that car," he said, as they got out.

"Hannah Schroeder." Ketchum put his hand on the hood. "Still pretty warm. Hannah must've just got here."

Kodza looked up at Ramsey. "If she is here, this is not good."

"Why not?" Ramsey asked. But Kodza was already moving, heading for the fire escape, and then Ramsey saw why she wore the jacket because Kodza reached around to the small of her back and pulled a laser-pistol from its holster.

"Hank, go after her!" Ramsey raced back to the unmarked, popped the glove box, grabbed his Raptor, jacked a shell into the chamber, and flipped off .the safety.

Kodza was on the fire escape now, threading her way

to the third floor landing. "Hold it, hold up!" Ramsey hissed, racing up the steps two at a time. He crowded in just as Ketchum grabbed Kodza's elbow six steps shy of the landing. "What's going . . . ?" But now he heard voices: angry shouts behind the closed door. And then the roaring *BOOM* of a very big gun.

"Oh, shit." Ramsey and Ketchum pushed past Kodza then flattened against the wall, Ramsey left and Ketchum peeling off right, with Kodza bringing up the rear.

Ketchum shouted, "Hannah? Scott? It's Hank Ketchum. Open up the door, Scott, we just want to talk, son."

Silence. Ketchum jerked his head toward the door, and Ramsey held up three fingers, counted down then whirled around, cop-kicked the door: once, twice. The door deformed on the first kick, banged open on the second, and then Ramsey was through the door, his Raptor sweeping the room, with Ketchum a step behind, and Kodza bringing up the rear.

The air was thick with the smell of burnt cordite, cigarette ash, and fresh blood. Hannah Schroeder sat at a rickety card table, her hands cradling a blocky gun. Milk drizzled from an overturned carton, pooling along the body of a woman: on her back, eyes wide open; a bloody crater in her belly. The milk began to turn a sludgy pink where it mixed with blood.

"Oh, my Lord," Ketchum said. He eased the gun from Hannah's nerveless fingers. "Where's Scott, Hannah?"

"Gone," Hannah said. Her face was dry, and her eyes vacant. "She's gone now, Hank, she's gone."

"Mrs. Schroeder," Ramsey pressed, "where's your *son*?"

"Gone," Hannah repeated. "Just gone."

Ramsey turned as Kodza, expressionless, hunkered beside the dead woman. "That yours?" he asked.

Kodza looked up. "She *was*."

54

Tuesday, 17 April 3136
1430 hours

Father Gillis said Summers should go home because it was a blessedly fine day and God would see all this trouble as so much water under the bridge. The priest was so chipper, Doc Summers wanted to yank out the man's tongue by the roots. Oh, Summers was grateful, but the world was grinding him down, and God seemed a little deaf, or maybe just didn't give a damn.

He wanted a drink. He wanted a smoke, maybe a whole pack. Maybe he could just smoke himself to death. Be a sight more pleasant than the rumors killing him.

Gillis said to tell Ketchum everything. But Summers couldn't. That would ruin him. But if he didn't tell, all they had to do was check the hospital pharmacy records. After that, they'd never trust him again, and no matter what happened with whatever homicidal maniac was out there, people would always wonder.

"Oh, Emma." Tears leaked from the corners of his eyes. Things had been bad in the past, what with always having to worry about Adam. As long as he had Emma and his work, he'd pulled through. Now he didn't have anything.

He spotted the patrol car in his driveway and lights on in his house. Fear lurched in his chest. Oh, God, had they . . . had *Adam* . . . ? He had an insane moment when he thought maybe he'd just keep going, heading south, and then hook a right and go west toward open county. But he was too old to run.

He knew there was something very wrong as soon as he walked into the house. The cat didn't meet him at the door, and the house felt empty. But he smelled fresh coffee. Strange. He'd emptied the pot before he left early yesterday morning. Put out food and water for the cat, and left. So what . . . ?

It was then that he smelled something else. A bad, rotted smell, like maybe the toilet had stopped up, or the garbage had tipped over. He crossed into the kitchen, caught something—a man?—out of the corner of his right eye, turned—and froze, dead in his tracks.

There was a neat round red hole drilled above the bridge of the deputy's nose, like a third eye. A ribbon of coagulated blood was glued along the right side of the deputy's nose, as if Bobby's new eye had cried fat blood tears. Bobby's eyes were open and buggy but clouding because Bobby had been dead a long time. Still, as horrified as he was, Bobby wasn't what make Doc Summers begin to cry.

What made him cry was his cat. His cat lay on its side in a pool of green-and-black vomit and overturned milk. The cat's eyes bulged and its darkly purple tongue lolled like a fat worm. The cat's bowels and bladder emptied as it died, leaving feces and cat pee mingling with dried milk splattered over the cabinetry

Stunned, weeping uncontrollably, Summers dropped to his knees. "Why?" He pressed the heels of his hands to his streaming eyes. "What kind of monster does this?"

A man's voice, one he recognized: "That's what they're gonna say."

Summers wheeled round on his heels then gawked in disbelief. "What are you doing here? *Why* did you do this?"

"You know, that's *just* what people are gonna say. Why'd Doc do that? They'll figure you went nuts.

They'll say Old Doc didn't see there was any way out, so he killed that deputy and then killed his cat and then . . ." The man shrugged and waggled the gun in his hand. "Whaddaya say we have a nice, hot cup of coffee, Doc, and talk it over?"

And then Gabriel's lips parted in a beatific smile: one suited to an angel that was fallen.

55

Scott Schroeder was gone.

"He and Mom had a fight," Sarah said. Her eyes were so puffy from weeping they'd narrowed to blue slits. Her aunt, a stocky woman who'd arrived the day before, hugged her closer.

"Where would your mom get a gun?" Ramsey asked. "Did your father have a couple?"

"More than a couple," Sarah said.

Fifteen minutes later, Ramsey, Ketchum, and Kodza—along with Sarah and her aunt—were in the attic. Ramsey squatted next to the only open box, marked *Militia* in black marker, and used a pen to ease aside a flap. "Was this full?" he asked Sarah.

"Sure. Mom packed everything right up to the top."

"Did your mom keep a list of things she put away?"

"Probably. She's kind of that way, a place for everything and . . ." Sarah's lips wobbled as fat tears rolled down her cheeks. "When I can see my mom?"

The ER doc had taken one look at Hannah Schroeder and arranged for a med-evac to New Bonn. Ketchum said, "She's shook up pretty bad, Sarah. For now we got to find Scott. You know where he is?"

Sarah didn't know, and she let her aunt take her back

downstairs. Ramsey stepped over to the gun safe. "Digital lock, but I think it's already open." He shrugged his jacket over his hand then cranked down on the handle. Ramsey whistled. "Ho-boy, he liked guns." He found the empty Raptor case, half-filled ammo box, and then, another case, its hasps open. "Empty."

Ketchum sidled in, looked at the cut foam. "Might be Isaiah's service weapon." He squinted at Kodza. "Scott was part of this cell?"

"Not completely," Kodza said. She'd been relatively quiet since Charlie's. "Isaiah felt that the boy would be a good cover. If he brought his son in, the others would trust him. After his father's death, Scott disappeared. We eventually tracked him and asked for his help."

"He just sign right on up?" Ramsey grated.

"No. We worked on him."

"You mean, sex."

"I mean, whatever was necessary." Kodza was unmoved. "Someone must do this work, and I do not apologize for our tactics. So. My agent was to establish who the members of the cell were. I do not know if she succeeded because she has been out of touch. But now Scott is in danger, and he has important information, perhaps more so than he realizes."

Ramsey thought of something. "Oh, Christ, Amanda saw Boaz at Charlie's, and Scott tended bar Sunday night. If Boaz is involved, and *Scott's* involved . . ."

"Well, goddamn it, then," Ketchum said. "Let's go talk to Boaz."

Ketchum reported in then asked dispatch to patch him through to Doc Summers' place. The dispatcher came back, said there was no answer but that Bobby had called in earlier and told Ketchum to call Father Gillis.

Gillis, an older man judging from his voice, said that Summers had spent the better part of yesterday, the night, and most of that day at the rectory before going home around two that afternoon. "He's taking these suspicions of that loose autocannon, that Jack Ramsey, pretty hard. Doc's a proud man, Hank. Almost nothing worse than destroying his reputation. He'd rather die."

"He use those words?" Ramsey asked.

"Who's that?" Gillis asked.

"The loose autocannon," Ketchum said.

"Oh. Well, Detective, I think what you're doing is shameful."

"I don't have time to argue with you about it," Ramsey said. "But we have to know: Did Doc Summers actually say he'd rather die? Because I'm Catholic . . ."

"New Avalon?" Gillis asked. He said *New Avalon* the way someone else might say *horse turd*. "Or Old Roman?"

"New Avalon. Lapsed, if that makes you feel better. But New Avalons believe suicide is a sin."

"Hmmm." Gillis was annoyed now, as if Ramsey had trumped him. "Well, no, actually, Bobby called in maybe a half hour later and he said that Doc was pretty upset and talking about how he'd rather die that see his reputation smeared."

"You know something that Summers thinks is worth dying for?"

A pause, as if Gillis were debating something. Then: "Yes. But it's privileged, told in the confessional, so don't ask. But I can tell you that you're going to want to hear him out. Doc just can't stand the guilt he's carrying. I told Bobby that, and he said he had the same impression. Said he was going to try and talk Doc into turning himself in."

Ramsey blinked. Ketchum said, "Turn himself in?"

"Yup. So go easy, Hank. Doc's a proud man brought low."

And then Bobby *did* call. About thirty seconds after Ketchum punched out from the priest, dispatch was back, and said that Bobby had talked Doc into coming to the station house. "Round about eight. Bobby said that Doc had some things he needed to take care of but he'd bring him on down. Right around eight."

As Ketchum turned the cruiser into Boaz's street, Ramsey said, "Hunh." He looked over at Ketchum. "What do you think?"

"Bobby's been around a long time, and he knows everyone. He and Doc are Old Romans. So, if Bobby says Doc's coming in, Doc's coming in."

Boaz's townhouse looked quiet and the curtains were drawn. "Didn't pick up his paper," Ramsey said as they climbed out and started for the walk. This time, Ramsey clipped his holster to his belt because you never could tell.

"Maybe he's waiting until dark so no one can see how nicely you rearranged his nose." Then Ketchum's expression darkened. "Be real interesting to hear what Mr. Boaz has to say."

Kodza, bringing up the rear, said, "With Boaz, and now this Doc, things are going pop, pop, yes?"

"Yeah, yeah," Ramsey began, and stopped when he saw, through the sidelight waterglass, the fragmented but quite distinctive shape of a man's naked foot.

Ramsey kicked in the door—and things didn't just pop. Things exploded.

Boaz was in his boxers, a beer can in one hand and his brains splattered along the floor, banister, and front hall. Weapons drawn, Ramsey and Ketchum did a fast walk-through while Kodza backed out, leaned over the railing and puked her guts out.

By five-thirty, Amanda had come from the scene at Charlie's to the townhouse. Ketchum sent Kodza to sit in one of two patrol cars that had arrived when Ketchum called in the murder on his command frequency.

"Well, beyond the obvious that he's dead, he was killed with one big bullet," Amanda said. She was gloved, kneeling by the body, and now directed the tech where she wanted close-ups. "Judging from the rectal temperature, condition of the body and the extent of rigor, I'd say he was killed sometime last night."

Ramsey looked at that beer can in what could now legitimately be called a death grip. "He clocked out of the station around twenty-one hundred yesterday. There was a pizza box in the other room where the holo's still going. We checked with the pizza place, and they delivered at eight-thirty, and looks like he pretty much ate it. Only one piece left."

"Unless you have a hungry killer," Amanda said, dryly.

When she was done and they'd gone outside, Ramsey nodded toward Ketchum who was inside his patrol car, talking animatedly, gesturing with his hands. "Hank's going nuts."

"Wouldn't you? You really think Scott Schroeder did this?"

"I don't know. It sort of fits, but the thing is I can't see how Scott could've known about Boaz being a suspect unless Scott was part of the operation to begin with. But then he'd have known about Noah way beforehand, and I think he'd have done something about it. Was Scott at the hospital when Troy came in?"

"I don't remember. Let me ask the ICU nurses," Amanda said, punching up her sat-link. Two minutes later, she punched out and said, "Scott visited the ICU, fought about something with his mother and then stormed out before Troy arrived. Unless he saw Boaz leave with Sandra, he couldn't have made the connection."

Ramsey nodded. Thought: *But I can think of someone who did.*

Amanda forked her hair from her face. "Well, I'd better get Boaz packed up. I swear, you're keeping me so busy, I don't have time to see my *living* patients. This keeps up I'll have to close my practice."

"Things will wind down soon. I've got this feeling. Then I'll be gone, and things will get back to normal."

She edged closer, took his lapel in one hand, leaned in, and kissed him on the lips. "That's what I'm afraid of," she said. "The time when you'll be gone."

56

Gabriel stood under a stinging hot shower, washing away all the sweat and grime and blood of the day. He felt wonderful, like he was being re-born. The worst had been the boys, but he'd prevailed. He'd even handled the Handler. *Shut the fuck up and listen.* He said it out loud now, standing in the shower. Felt good to say it. Felt the power.

He'd used the big gun, the 720, on Boaz. He shuddered deliciously as he remembered Boaz's face the split second before: the dumb amazement. And then POW!

After he'd toweled off, he inspected his leg: healing nicely. Then, as he scrubbed his teeth, his mind bounced back to the police. He'd been monitoring the command frequency all afternoon, and so he knew they'd found Boaz. But no one had come, so he had to assume the Bobby ploy had worked. Dispatch had called in once, requesting that Bobby reconfirm, and he had because *he* had Bobby's ID-link. Now *that* had been downright brilliant. The ID-link's audio wasn't that good, and bursts of jargon could fool anyone. Anyone using the ID-link had to enter a code, a kind of fail-safe—and Gabriel had been insistent Bobby tell him the code, just in case. He'd bought himself, maybe, an hour. Once they found Doc, Ketchum would know.

But he'd beat them, *had* beaten them already. He'd listened as dispatch relayed Ketchum's APB on Scott Schroeder, and then the general comchatter on the command frequency. People running around not knowing shit from shinola.

The Handler had been pleased. "I must confess. You are resourceful."

"I told you I could handle it. Now we wait for Amanda to sequence that DNA, and we're set. If I have enough time after the Schroeder kid, I'll dump in another spy program to take pictures of her entire system every time she makes a change. That way, I can stay on top of anything she comes up with, under any file."

"Do not become greedy. Your primary objective is to eliminate the witnesses. Then you will proceed to the rendezvous point. You are prepared?"

"I'm ready. I've already been out and put in a series of belays to get down the gorge fast and into the boat. They'll be covering the roads and maybe the lake, but they'll never think of the river, and even if they do, they won't know which branch I'll take. I'll get out and be at the rendezvous in three days."

In his bedroom now, pulling on his clothes. His cat was asleep on his pillow. His only regret was the cat, but he didn't have a choice. So he'd hit upon a plan and thought it'd work. Once he was gone, only a creep would take things out on a defenseless cat.

Hefting his knapsack and feeling hungry, he headed for the kitchen. Had he boiled up the last of his eggs? An egg salad sandwich was all he had time for. He couldn't be late to work. Until the end, he had to be the person everyone else thought he was, and *that* person was never late.

So he was thinking about mayonnaise and bread and lettuce when he turned into his kitchen—and stopped dead.

Scott Schroeder looked terrible, and there were crimson tracks gouged along his left cheek where someone had tried to scratch off his face. But his blue eyes were glittery and bright with hate.

Gabriel's heart kicked up several notches, but his mind was working. He debated for a half second, decided on a strategy and broke silence first. "Michael, Jesus, man, put down the gun, man! What the hell? What are you doing?"

Scott's face twisted. "Stop calling me that. I'm Scott. I'm *Scott*, you bastard!"

"Okay, okay!" Hands up, palms out, shaking, and no faking there. "Easy, man, easy, just calm down!"

"What the hell for?" The cords on Scott's neck bulged. "My father's dead, my brother might die, and you're telling me to calm down?"

"I'm sorry, look, I'm sorry, man, but Jesus, Mi . . . Scott, you're making me nervous, man. You don't have to drop it, but just aim somewhere else!"

"No!" Scott's hand floated to the scratches on his face. "Grace, I made her, I made her tell me, *really* tell me about my brother. About my *dad!*"

"Tell you what? Christ, she *scratched* you? Tell you what?" *Good, good, lots of questions, a blizzard of nervous patter, that's what a man who's about to crap his pants does.* At the same time, Gabriel was keenly aware of the knapsack slung over the hump of his right shoulder. *Scott's left-handed, gun's in his left hand.* "What, she thinks *I* had something to do with your brother? Come on. We can talk, whatever you—"

"You want to talk?" Scott jabbed the gun at Gabriel. "Then talk about what really happened to my father, and what you did to Noah!"

"Noah? Your dad? What, you think I killed your dad?" Gauging the distance to the knives, the heft of his sack. "That's what Grace told you? Man, Scott, I've known you for years. I *told* you what happened."

"Bullshit!" Scott was crying now. "You told me that he'd been ambushed by those Blakists! You said he wouldn't listen to you or anyone about having someone with him. But it was you, you and Bobby—"

"Bobby?" Eyes wide with incredulity. "Bobby couldn't find his asshole if you gave him a mirror and a flashlight. Is Grace handing you this crap? Let me talk to her. She'll change her tune." Good, that was just indignant enough. Turn the tables, confuse him. "I told you, man. They ambushed him. By the time we figured out what was going on, they already had him. I got there as fast as I could, but there were too many of them. I didn't stand a chance."

"Yeah, *yeah*? You're so good with a gun, why didn't you shoot?" Scott wasn't crying anymore—a bad sign because that meant he was angrier than sad and angry men killed you faster. "If there were so many, why aren't *you* dead?"

"I . . ." Gabriel forced his eyes to slide away from Scott—from the gun—as if embarrassed. "Because I ran."

"You ran?" Clearly, not what Scott had expected and when Gabriel looked back, he saw Scott's mouth had dropped open. More important, his left hand unconsciously mimicked the gesture, and the gun barrel slewed down and left. "You *ran*?"

"Yeah. I guess I freaked out, man. I was terrified. I . . . I was so scared, I just ran, and I guess the noise, they started after me." He felt his eyes water. Jesus, he was good. He let his shoulders slump and felt the strap slip to midbiceps. *Just a little more.* "I'm so, so sorry, I'm so . . . damn it, I was so ashamed, I . . ." Smearing away tears with his left hand. "Man, look what you made do . . . aw, God . . ."

"Why didn't you say anything?" Scott sounded uncertain, even a little concerned.

"I dunno." He judged they were no more than five meters apart. "I didn't want anyone to find out, and—" And then he saw that Scott's gun pointed at the floor.

Now, now, go go go!

Gabriel sprang. He roared, a loud guttural *hiyahhhh!* Scott flinched, backed up a step, but Gabriel was moving, going fast, the strap of his knapsack in his hand now, the weight dragging at his palm, and he swung his right arm, put his weight behind it, used the heavy sack like a bolo. Scott, off-balance, surprised, saw the sack coming and tried bringing the gun to bear a fraction of a second too late. The sack smashed into Scott's left shoulder and arm, a blow Gabriel felt as a bone-shudder rippling through his arm and into his shoulder.

Bang! The gun went off, a deafening sound in such a

small space that left Gabriel's ears ringing. A searing pain striped along his left side—*I'm shot, I'm shot*—and he was falling now, letting go of the sack as Scott crumpled and they hit the floor together. The gun roared again, and this time Gabriel saw the muzzle flash, felt the bullet whiz by his eye. *That was too damn close!* He outweighed Scott by a good ten kilos, and had the advantage because he was on top. Stretching now, reaching for Scott's gun hand and Gabriel was talking, too, not aware until he heard the words spilling out like water roaring over a dam: *motherfucker, you motherfucker, you fucker* . . .

Scott held on. He bucked and heaved, and Gabriel rode him the way a ranch-hand broke a wild horse. Scott was cursing, too, spittle flying: "Killed my dad, you killed my dad, you *killed* him!" So close, Gabriel felt Scott's breath caress his cheek like a lover.

So Gabriel bit him. He clamped down on Scott's left cheek, felt his teeth break through skin. Scott screamed, a sound that spiked Gabriel's left ear. But he bit down harder, grinding his jaws, and now he tasted blood—salty and warm—and Scott was shrieking, trying to twist free, and Gabriel felt the flesh giving way, tearing . . .

And Scott dropped the gun.

Quick as a snake, Gabriel uncoiled, lunged, swept up the gun with his right hand, rolled. His back slammed against a kitchen cupboard, and the pain in his side roared to life, but now Gabriel was up, the gun in his hand.

Scott's scream choked off to a dribbling repetitive moan: "Aw, Jesus, aw Jesus, aw Jesus!" Bright red blood sheeted his fingers. "Aw God God . . . !"

"You *fuck*!" Gabriel spat a mouthful of Scott's blood and a chunk of flesh. "You want to know what happened, you want to know what happened? You want to know what your big hero dad did when I got him to his knees? He crapped his pants. He peed all over himself, and he started to cry."

"No, no, that's not true!" Scott screamed, his spit mingling with the blood soaking his collar. "Not true!"

"Yes," Gabriel said, suddenly tired of the argument. "It is. And I killed him. Just. Like. This."

He thrust the gun at Scott Schroeder's bloodstained face, and pulled the trigger.

57

1930 hours

Kodza was out of the loop.

"If Scott killed Boaz, then Grace told him," Ramsey argued. At last word, Kodza was in her hotel room, a deputy at her door, under protective custody, a euphemism that sounded better than *shut down*. "Isaiah was an agent, and he's dead. Grace was one of Kodza's agents, and now Grace is dead, Boaz is dead, and Scott's missing. She's out."

"So did we make a mistake?" Ketchum asked. "Listening to her?"

"Man, I don't know." Ramsey blew out. "There are so many actors, I can't keep track."

"Yeah, well," Ketchum said, "not at this rate."

The press was in full gear. The air thrummed with the *whop-whop-whop* of a news VTOL, its spotlight playing over a milling crowd of reporters as if they were celebrities. Ketchum confirmed Boaz's death then no-commented everything else.

Even though Bobby called in at seven and was given instructions to come in cold, no sirens, no light bar, he didn't show at eight. At eight-oh-two, dispatch tried raising Bobby and couldn't. They wasted about five minutes, dispatch fussing with various channels, and eight-oh-eight, they'd cranked up Ramsey's unmarked, pulled out of the back lot while a deputy appeared on the steps as a diversion. Once out of visual, Ramsey dropped the accelerator.

Doc's place was lit up like a Christmas tree. Then the car's headlamps picked out one of the reflective decals of Bobby's cruiser, and Ramsey said, "Uh-oh."

"I'll be damned, I'll be *goddamned*," Ketchum said, and he popped his door while Ramsey was still rolling, Ramsey yelling, "Easy, Hank, easy!" But Ketchum, weapon drawn, was already bounding up the steps when Ramsey slammed on the brakes and was out of the car, his hand automatically going for his Raptor: "Hank, Hank, Jesus, wait!"

Once through the door, Ramsey knew: The house was dead. And there was a smell: metal mixed with feces. He followed his nose, and Ketchum, and when he made it into the kitchen, said, "Aw, Jesus."

The deputy had been dead for at least a day and was starting to bloat. But Doc hadn't been dead long. Vomit as grainy and dark as coffee caked his throat and the front of his shirt and smelled like scorched iron. Doc sprawled in a slurry of excrement and urine, his legs tangled in his overturned chair. Doc's eyes were wide, and his mouth hung open. Doc's right hand was wrapped around the deputy's service weapon. There was no note.

Ramsey squatted, touched the back of an index finger to Doc's left wrist. "Still warm. Maybe dead six hours. So he died not too long after he left the rectory."

Ketchum looked shell-shocked. "First Boaz, now Bobby and now we know Bobby couldn't have talked Doc into anything. But Doc wouldn't kill a man, and he loved that damn cat. He'd never kill it, never."

"Hunh." One constant about suicides: If a person killed a child or animal first, that was done out of love and seen as a mercy, a way to relieve future suffering. Ramsey looked at the stiff, vomit-splattered animal. No doubt about that: The animal had suffered, and it wouldn't have if Doc had just shot it. But he didn't, and he didn't use the gun on himself. One thing was certain, though: Dispatch hadn't been talking to Bobby.

He said as much to Ketchum then added, "I don't think it's Scott, either. Probably, the reason there's no forced entry at Boaz's is because Boaz either knew the guy, or saw a patrol car at the curb and figured there wasn't any threat. Then the killer goes to Doc's place using the deputy's patrol car, poisons the cat, calls Father Gillis to plant stuff about Doc's frame of mind, and then waits for Doc. This guy's killed four people, maybe more, and he's going to make a run at the boys. So, think, Hank. You *know* everybody. Who'd be able to do all this *and* have a chance at taking out two boys *in* a hospital?"

Ketchum squinted, thinking, and then Ramsey saw the light flare behind Ketchum's eyes.

"Holy God," Ketchum said. "It's Craig Dickert."

58

2130

Even if that hoity-toity Hannah Schroeder wouldn't get off her damned high horse and say a civil word or two—and oh, how the mighty have fallen, how the mighty are fallen—the nurses were kind. Still, Sandra Underhill heard the undercurrent of disdain. That's why she kept the gauzy yellow curtain drawn around Troy's bed: to hide from the eyes. She was done in this town. Everything said behind her back would be said to her face, and she deserved it.

I'm going to rot in hell. She hugged her arms, chafing them as if they were cold—and she was cold and *so* lonely and so *alone*—and began to rock. *This is judgment, this is God's punishment, bringing me low, and I'm going straight to hell. . . .*

She heard shoes scuffing linoleum then the rasp of metal against metal as someone pulled aside the curtain around Noah's bed. A nurse, probably, doing checks. She heard a few muted beeps, then a click, and then the metallic rattle of Noah's curtain being pulled back into place. Straightening, she palmed tears from her face and wiped her nose on her sleeve. She'd be damned if she'd give anyone the satisfaction.

The curtain twitched aside. She looked up—and then

she, literally, froze, her lips trapped in a smile halfway to being.

The man scuffled in. He wore a hospital scrub top and blue jeans. They locked eyes—his were very blue—and then his slid away. He glanced at various readouts, stabbed a noteputer as Sandra Underhill stared . . .

As she saw in her mind's eye images that fell into place, haltingly clicking in one by one, like the rusty tumblers of an ancient lock. Then the vault of her memory swung open, and she knew.

The face of the man who'd poisoned her son.

2145

Ketchum slammed a portable flasher and siren on the unmarked's roof as Ramsey hammered the accelerator and held it there, roaring through turns, going so fast everything was a blur. Ketchum was yelling at dispatch: "He's got Bobby's ID-link! Get everyone to switch over from command frequency! If we're lucky, he's not going to understand the code! This is an eleven-ninety-nine! I repeat, eleven-ninety-nine! All available units within spitting distance at the hospital, and I mean *now*!"

They flashed by the cutoff for Amanda's farm, and then Ketchum shouted at Ramsey, "Hold it, hold it, take the right, the *right!*"

"Hang on!" Ramsey cut the car hard, felt the rear fishtail, heard the high squeal of tires.

"Watch it!" Ketchum, bracing himself on the dash. "Watch it, *watch it*!"

"I got it, I got it!" Ramsey wrestled the car straight and punched the gas. The car leapt forward, like a fighter kicking on afterburners. "How far?"

"Three minutes!" Ketchum shouted over the siren's wail. "We'll probably get there first! But the deputies on duty, they'll know when dispatch tells them to switch channels! They'll know!"

And Ramsey thought: *And if he's listening in, so might Dickert.*

*   *   *

Time was his enemy now. Time was running out, and Craig Dickert—Gabriel—hurt like a son of a bitch. The bullet from Scott's gun had zipped a deep trough in the space between his fifth and sixth rib and banged bone along the way. He cleaned the wound then used coags and a pressure bandage, gritting his teeth the whole time.

Scott's blood smeared across his mouth in a grotesque circus clown's too-red grin, and there was more blood in crescents beneath his nails. He washed his face, scrubbed his fingers, brushed his teeth twice. He'd have liked a shower; he could smell the adrenalin stink saturating his pores. But no time. He had to get to the hospital, and it *had* to be tonight. They'd find his father, and a dead man with half a skull in *his* kitchen.

Before he left, he tucked his cannon into his waistband at the small of his back and stashed Scott's gun in a leather fanny sack. The fanny sack held money, too, as well as the two crystals he already had—and a little vac-pac for one more: because there was something he'd just figured out and hadn't told the Handler.

Threes. The agents had always done things in threes. He'd read back over Amanda's autopsy and he now *knew* where the third crystal was.

Then I'll have it all, every piece of the puzzle. The DNA isn't the key. The DNA's something, but not the key.

An hour late but rounding, now. Doing his work, not hurrying. Moving hurt, and he was sweating again. But no one noticed—because everyone knew that Craig Dickert was quiet, had a lisp and was a bit of a geek.

When he turned the corner and spotted the two deputies at the ICU, he almost lost it. One read something on a noteputer: a magazine, probably. The other held up the wall and looked bored. They glanced up as he approached. He plastered a smile on his face, said, "Hey," as he came up . . .

Keep going, move!

. . . And passed them into the ICU. He tensed, waiting for the shout, the clap of hands on his shoulders. But nothing came.

He glanced at the nurses' station, gave the charge nurse his usual half-wave. She flashed an automatic smile and forgot about him in less than a second.

It took him twenty seconds to silence the alarms and reset the pumps to deliver the maximum lethal dose into Noah's body in the shortest period of time. Then he jabbed garbage into a chartputer—*beep, bop, boop*—counted to ten, and backed out. Just another busy nurse anesthetist, making his rounds.

He fingered open the curtain around Troy's bed, stepped through, looked left—and that's when his stomach bottomed out. But he didn't lose it. Sweat beaded along his upper lip. Every nerve ending sang an alarm, and his brain was screaming: *Get out, get out now before she screams, before she says something, before she realizes! Run!*

Instead, he jabbed nonsense into a chartputer, his pulse banging away like something living in his throat. The Underhill woman was standing now, her eyes wild.

Time to go, time to move, go, go.

He fingered open the curtain and walked out, eyes facing front. *Not too fast, not too slow, steady, steady, and now left, go left, there are the stairs, there are . . .*

Suddenly, the air split with the shrill of the deputies' links at the same moment that Sandra Underhill screamed.

Go!

He banged through the doors like a rocket. He heard a shout: "Hey, *hey* . . . !" But he was through the doors and pelting down stairs, taking them at a near-run. There was a ripping sensation in his side, and the pain made him gasp. But he kept going, past the first floor, wheeling around, nearly losing his footing, slipping. The damn scrub booties. He paused to rip them off, and then he ran full-out, his side hitching.

Can't use the turbo. I need a car, and I need something to buy me enough time so I can get away, and I need that crystal!

Down the last flight of stairs now, basement coming up fast, and as he cut left, straight-arming the door, he reached around for his gun, dragging it free of his waistband.

*   *   *

Amanda was talking to her computer when she heard the *thwap-bang* of a door connecting with cinderblock. She looked up, dumbfounded, as someone smashed her door open so hard, the impact sent a picture crashing to the floor.

"Craig?" She was half-out of her seat now, a quizzical smile playing over her lips. "Craig, what's wrong?"

Then she spotted the gun and, well, she was pretty much up to speed.

59

Dickert beat them by ten minutes. They'd slewed into the ER breezeway, nearly colliding with deputies and hospital personnel. As they jumped out, Ramsey heard sirens converging on the hospital and then, very distinctly, the thumping *whop-whop-whop* of a VTOL, and knew the press was onto the story. Then they told him about Amanda.

Now five minutes later, the page operator said, "I've located her pager. It's receiving. She's just not answering."

"She probably can't. But the pager has a SatNav, right?" Ramsey said, impatiently. He and Ketchum stood behind the operator. "Something so you can always find her, that's what she said."

"It's not that sophisticated. It's more of a general locator." The page operator's fingers clattered over her keyboard. "I can't tell you what street she's on but I *can* pinpoint . . . hang on, just hang on. . . . Got it. Heading west toward the mountains."

"Hank, how much time to get on the straightaway west of here?" Ramsey asked.

"Fifteen minutes, and that'd be taking it fast. He's got a good jump, but I'll bet he sure as heck wouldn't want to get Amanda so rattled she cracks up. So probably closer to twenty minutes.''

"So he's got at least a half hour lead. The landtrain trestle's forty-five minutes away. But he has to expect we'd think of that first. Besides, the crime scene people have been crawling all over that place, so he's got to be headed further out. Where can he go from there?''

"To the mountains, or down the river," Ketchum said. "River's more dangerous, but Emerald River branches into three before the trestle. Once he's on the water, he could go anywhere. But trying those rocks at night . . . he'd have to be crazy.''

"Hank." Ramsey was already moving for the door. "Does he strike you as a guy who's operating on all thrusters?''

The hospital parking lot looked like a circus ring minus the tents and the clowns. Behind a police barricade, the press gabbled like eager spectators waiting to see if the trapeze artist was going to break his neck, or not. The VTOL hovered overhead, its rotors slapping air, the harsh ball of its spotlight turning Ramsey's skin light blue.

He dodged deputies, running for the car, digging for the keys. Time was working against them. Dickert had a head start, he was crazy and he had Amanda either as insurance, or maybe just for her car. The *pager* was alive, but Amanda might already be dead. Or maybe Dickert would remember the pager, ditch it, and continue on. If Dickert was part of a group, he must have confederates, and they might be waiting for him.

He fumbled the keys, dropped them. *Whoa, whoa, going too fast, hold on, hold on.* He felt his mind tilting off its axis, veering into panic. He was so keyed with anxiety and adrenalin, his head felt like a geyser, ready to blow. The last time he'd felt like this was McFaine and, God, no, that had ended in . . .

Stop this shit. You know how to do this. Just do the job.

He reached the unmarked, aimed the remote and vaulted around the open door—and paused as the pool of the VTOL's glare white light washed past like a wave.

The *VTOL*.

Whirling round, Ramsey sprinted back. "Hank, *Hank!*"

Well, she hadn't stabbed him with a scalpel, screamed her head off, or kicked his nuts so hard he had to blow them out of his nose. So this all pretty much sucked the big one.

Pitch black. Foamy clouds had moved in during the afternoon, so there weren't any stars, either. She'd mashed the accelerator and now they were going so fast, she felt as if they were skating over frictionless black ice.

Craig Dickert: in the backseat, the muzzle of a gun pressed just below her right ear. When her gaze flicked to her rear view, she saw his eyes. Glittery, intent. Insane.

She was shivering now, uncontrollably, and fear coated her mouth with a metallic, sharp taste. Her abdomen cramped, and the bubble of a scream pushed the back of her throat. But she was also getting a little pissed off, and that was probably good.

She'd acted like a numb nut: getting Limyanovich's personal effects, then picking out the evidence bag with that red diamond ring—and how did Dickert even *know* about the ring? The newspeople? No, they'd held back the ring, necklace and bang stick from the press. But Dickert *knew*. From whom? Kodza?

"You scared?"

Amanda blinked back to attention. "What?"

"I asked if you were scared," Dickert said. "You think you're gonna die?"

"Well, *duh*," she said, and decided, yeah, honesty was best. This *was* Dickert, after all. She had worked with him for a couple of years, and that had to count for something. She wasn't sure that calculus panned out but, right now, she didn't much care.

And if I can get him talking, maybe I can distract him long enough to throttle back, give whoever's after us— because Hank's got to know by now, Jack's got to know—time to catch up.

She said, "Of course, I'm scared, and I'd rather not

die. How about we talk? It's better than me pissing my pants."

Dickert's voice turned suspicious. "What's there to talk about?"

"Well, gee, let me think," Amanda said. "How about what the hell is this all about? Why'd you kill Limyanovich? Was he a Blakist? Kittery Resistance? What?"

A pause. Then: "Where'd you get all that?"

"Around. I found something in Limyanovich's DNA."

Another silence. "You people, you think you're so smart. But you've got no idea. You're clueless."

"Okay. So clue me in."

"It's all right there, hiding in plain sight. I mean, what happens after the HPGs go down? The Republic falls apart; the Houses make land grabs; the exarch seals off Prefecture X; there are probably dozens of civil wars."

"So?"

"You don't think this was engineered? That whoever did this didn't *know* that nothing had really changed?"

"I'm not sure I see it," Amanda said, easing off her speed a little. *Not too much, keep him talking, buy time.* "Who do you think engineered it?"

"Blakists, of course: just biding their time. You really believe all that crap about getting rid of them?"

"Actually, no, not entirely. The Inner Sphere's big."

"So what do you think the Blakists have been doing all this time? I'll tell you what they've been doing." He was talking faster now, the words tumbling out like the jackpot from a one-armed bandit. "They've been planning, they've been building alliances, and now they're spreading like a cancer all through the Inner Sphere. What about those Kittery Resistance cells, like the one that showed up on Terra? And who wouldn't mind seeing all the Houses fall, and The Republic, too?"

"Wait a minute, wait a minute. Just because all those dots exist doesn't mean they connect."

"Oh, they connect. We've got their data crystals. It's the Clans, that's what."

"Clans?" *There it is again. Clans, and Kodza, at the periphery.* "Which ones?"

His tone was petulant now, a little sulky. "If we knew

that, then we could come forward. Tell people. All we know is it's Clanners, probably way the hell out on the periphery, and you can bet your bottom century *they've* got HPGs and they're in league with the Blakists. You religious?"

The shift threw her. "Uh," she said, not certain what the right answer was, then risked it. "No. Why?"

"Because these guys, they *always* do things in *threes*. They've got this whole new trinity: Clanners, Blakists and God. Only God ain't Jesus. It's *Devlin . . . Stone*."

She almost laughed. The idea was insane. "How do you guys figure?" Bleeding a bit more speed. "What's the logic?"

"Stone appears the first time, saves the Inner Sphere with The Republic, then disappears with the promise that he'll come if we *need him*," Dickert said. He made quotation marks with the fingers of his left hand. "When the time is right." More quotes. "That remind you of anything in particular?"

She was silent. Because he was right. She was a good Jewish girl, but she knew Dickert was right.

Trinity? Or . . . Triumvirate?

But Stone would have to be, well, pretty old. Pushing a hundred and maybe more, and no one could live much longer than a hundred ten—not and have any marbles left. No one.

And then she remembered what she'd said: *Boys, we got ourselves a dinosaur.*

She was still thinking when Dickert said, "Right."

She was confused. For a fleeting second, she thought he'd read her mind. "Right?"

"Yeah. *Right.* As in pull over. Right *here*." This time, he punctuated the word with a tap of the gun on her ear. "End of the line."

60

"**H**ow much longer?" Ramsey shouted over the jack-hammer thud of rotors. He'd forgotten how loud VTOLs were, even with headsets.

"Five minutes, max!" The news VTOL pilot's voice crackled with static. "The hospital said she's stationary, has been for forty minutes. So she's stopped along here."

They'd passed the lighted expanse of the landtrain trestle ten minutes ago, and from then on, there was nothing but black. The only other lights were the distant twinkles of a snake's tail of patrol cars, forty klicks back. The VTOL was running black, and other than the pilot's instrument panel, the cabin was dark. But Dickert would still *hear* them coming.

Ramsey felt a tap on his left shoulder, craned his head round, pulled the headset away from his left ear. "What?"

"Don't forget we got a deal!" Ramsey and the pilot had to shout, but the reporter was screaming. No headset. She was classic reporter material: leggy, blond, perfect teeth, and a good wardrobe. "I get an exclusive with Dickert, and I get the doctor!"

"Yeah, yeah, I won't forget." Ramsey faced forward

again before he could say something else. Then he saw something bright, off to the right. A pinprick of light. He pointed: minus forty degrees off horizontal and to the right. "You see that?"

The pilot leaned forward, nodded. "That him?"

The light winked out. "Yeah," Ramsey said. "Hit the spot."

The pilot pushed the VTOL out over the river then shed altitude, a sensation like going down an express elevator. The brilliant spear of the VTOL's spot slid over crumbly gray-black rock and scree, scrub . . . and then Ramsey's chest unclenched.

Amanda was in the lead, with Dickert just behind. Both Amanda and Dickert looked up, and then Dickert was raising his fist, pointing.

"Gun!" Ramsey shouted. *"Gun!"*

Dickert wasted five minutes searching the edge with a flashlight and cursing. "What is it?" Amanda asked. Her breath steamed, and she could feel gooseflesh.

"My *ropes*." Dickert bit the words. "They were all here; I had this *planned*!" Fuming, he turned and shoved the gun in her face and the flashlight into her hand. "Let's go. *You* lead."

"Craig, I can't do it," she said. She heard the panic, couldn't control it and didn't care. The drop-off scared the heck out of her, all that yawning blackness and, in the distance, the muted roar of water. "I'll fall."

"In that case," Dickert said, "don't forget to give me the flashlight before you go."

They made achingly slow progress. The rocks were scalpel-sharp, and slick with tongues of pea-sized rubble and scree. Within ten minutes she'd slipped twice and ripped open her left palm and right elbow. She was bloody and coated with an oily sheen of grit mingling with sweat. Dickert stayed right behind, that stupid gun aimed at her head.

"Just make sure you've got the safety on that." She was twisted like a corkscrew, her blood-slicked left hand clutching rock, her right searching with the flashlight ahead and slightly below her right foot. "All I need is for you to trip and that damn thing goes . . ." She stopped talking. What was that? A sound, like a tennis ball hitting wood. She looked up, felt the air thrumming, and then the spot caught them, and she knew.

But so, evidently, did Dickert. Because he began to fire.

"Gun, *gun!*" Ramsey shouted.

Two spurts—sparkles, really—and then the reporter was screaming and the pilot was swearing and the VTOL was sliding right and pushing high over open space.

"I'm not doing that again, man!" The pilot was freaked out. "He's got a goddamn gun! This ain't no military, and I sure as shit don't have no armor!"

"Just get me down!" Ramsey was already fumbling with his harness. "Pull ahead of the car about two hundred meters then let me out right on the road. Then get on the horn, tell Ketchum where we are and get yourself some altitude, and keep the light on *them*, you understand? Light *me* up, I'm *dead*. You got that?"

The road whizzed by as the VTOL skimmed beyond Amanda's car, then dropped, bounced on the road, and Ramsey hopped out, ducking beneath the main rotor. Instantly, the VTOL was sailing up, and then slid off the gorge and hung, like a one-eyed dragonfly. The spotlight jabbed the dark, the cone of light skewering Dickert and Amanda against the rocks. Dickert raised his fist again; a spark, and then the report, a sharp clap that bounced and echoed against stone. This time, the VTOL hung steady.

All *right*. Ramsey got rid of his jacket, screwed in his earbud, checked the safety on his pistol. As long as Dickert was paying attention to the VTOL, he was in business. Ketchum was coming, too; he heard the sirens clearly now and saw the flash of light bars. They'd outnumber Dickert, and then Dickert would either surrender or panic.

All right, go, go! But then Ramsey looked down again—and watched in horror as Dickert grabbed Amanda by the hair and shoved his gun in her face.

*   *   *

Dickert was screaming. "I'll fucking kill her, right now, right now, *right now*, you understand? Get the light off, get it off, *GET IT OFF GET IT OFF*!"

He'd snagged her hair just behind the crown of her head, and when he jerked back, he nearly took her off her feet. She screamed, and then something brighter than the light flashed and then the gun was in her face. She lost it. She started shrieking, throwing up her arms to shield her face. "No, no *no*!" Her screams rebounded off stone. "No, nononono!"

"Craig!" An amplified voice, gravelly with age and weirdly mechanical with a resonant thrum. "This is Hank Ketchum. Come on, son, you can't get down there. Just stay where you are so we can get someone to help."

"No!" Dickert screamed back. "I'm getting out of here, and I'm taking her with me! Now get that light off me, or I'll put a bullet in her ear, I swear to God!"

A pause. Then Ketchum's voice with steel in it: "You do that, Craig—and I'll kill you for sure."

But the VTOL's light cut out.

Ramsey crouched a few meters down the rocky wall, facing east so his right cheek lay against moist, cool rock. He'd had only the briefest time to scan the terrain and now he concentrated, trying to recall the landscape. The wall was steep but not sheer. He remembered a jagged series of natural but irregular switchbacks and heaped boulders from landslides. Plus, he had a mental picture of where Dickert and Amanda were: about two, two-fifty meters ahead now and maybe a hundred below, moving in a rough diagonal toward him. Far below, he made out a dull glimmer of a ribbon of water, and in the glow of headlights from the patrol cars he saw the crisp silhouettes of men and even the shimmering fog of their breaths.

He inhaled and began to move.

"Go," Dickert hissed. He butted Amanda's head with the gun. He'd released her hair but now had a fistful of her shirt. "Move!"

Amanda didn't argue. She concentrated, instead, on

taking one cautious step at a time. Hunched over until she was nearly doubled, she crabbed along, groping with her free hand and the toes of her boots. They kept on like that for a while, even though Hank kept yelling at Dickert. Dickert didn't yell back, though, and eventually, Hank stopped.

Giving up? Please, God, no. Her legs wobbled, and her arms felt like shivery jelly. The burst of adrenaline that had fueled her was long gone, and left her feeling depleted, drained. Running on empty.

Dickert was right behind. She could hear his ragged breathing and stumbles as they crept across slimy rock. Every once in a while he jabbed her in the ribs with the damn gun and hissed at her to move.

She wasn't sure when she became aware of something else. But, all of a sudden, she, well, heard something different. This new sound was crisp. Then, she heard it again: the crunch of rock under a shoe. Boot?

Someone else on the rocks. But where? In front of us? Yes, in front and above. Maybe somebody trying to cut them off, moving down another grade not far away and then she heard the faint, low murmur of a voice— or was it her imagination? She listened hard.

No. It wasn't.

Got to get closer. Ramsey took another hesitant step, then another. Stopped. Listened for movement. Caught the slip-slide of rocks almost dead ahead. Maybe twenty meters, or fifteen.

He was caught at a crappy angle. His gun hand was jammed against the slope, and he wasn't sure he could both shoot and get to Amanda in time.

Have to risk it eventually. No other way.

He tapped his earbud, whispered. "Hank?"

"Here. Where are you?"

"On the rocks. This is what I want you to do." He quickly sketched it out, heard no reply then whispered, "Hank?"

"Yeah." Pause. "You're not a southpaw."

"I know that. On my mark." Easing out his pistol with his right hand, Ramsey thumbed off the safety then transferred the weapon to his left. The stippled grip felt odd. He crept forward with painstaking slowness, hardly daring to breathe. A half meter, a meter, three meters. Heard the scrabble of Dickert and Amanda, but getting closer. The darkness ahead had a sort of shape to it, as if the night were gathering itself into some recognizable form. Then he heard Dickert, very distinctly, swear, and Amanda's gasp of pain.

Dead ahead.

"Now!" Ramsey hissed.

Light from the VTOL and high-intensity torches from the cruisers above splashed the rocks. Dickert and Amanda and Ramsey lit up as if they'd suddenly leapt through a trapdoor. But Dickert, anticipating this with an eerie sixth sense, was yanking Amanda up by her hair, using her as a shield, even as Ramsey was pulling down with his left.

Ramsey swore, broke at his elbow. "Hank, Hank, hold up, hold up, don't fire!"

"Jack!" Amanda screamed. "No, Jack, no, no!"

"You!" Dickert reared up behind, rising like some demon from the rock, and his pistol was out, stabbing at Ramsey. "You! *YOU!*"

"No!" Amanda shouted. "No, I won't let you!" Then she was whirling round, her long hair like a whip, and she heaved back, twisting right, her right arm sweeping like a scimitar. She caught Dickert's wrist with the flashlight just as the gun went off with an earsplitting *boom!*

An orange tongue of muzzle flash and then the high zing of a bullet clipping rock someplace far above Ramsey's head. Then everything slowed, balancing on the knife edge between past and present. Dickert, still screaming, was off-balance, and as he peeled away from the rock, his left hand flew out and snagged Amanda's hair.

"No!" Ramsey shouted. They were five meters apart. He scrambled frantically, trying to reach her in time. No time, no time, no *time!* *"Amanda!"*

Amanda shrieked a loud, long wailing ribbon of despair: *"Jaaaaaaack!"*

Then Dickert pulled Amanda off the rock.

"No!" Ramsey lunged, missed, bounced off rock with a sickening thud that blew the air out of his lungs, and then he was rolling. His Raptor spun away end over end,

as Ramsey banged over stone and then flipped to his stomach. He scrambled for a handhold, but then his left foot snagged on something. Suddenly, he was slewing sideways, careening in a perpendicular to the fall line like a powerboarder totally out of control. The flesh of his palms tore, and his fingers slicked with blood. He risked a look down the mountain, saw rock rushing for his face then screamed and tucked himself into a roll as his back crashed against an outcropping of jagged gray rock.

He stopped falling. For a moment, he lay there, still curled, blood from his hands seeping into his hair. His stomach and left side and back flamed with pain. His breath came in great, ragged gasps, and then as his heart slowed down, he heard men shouting from above and pebbles sluicing over rock with a sound like water.

Water. He listened, caught the gush of the river. How far had he fallen? What about Amanda? He uncurled, hitching his body around onto his shrieking back and then his right side. He grabbed rock and craned around to look. His breath left him in a moan of mingled pain, relief, and horror. "Oh, my God, oh my God."

There, not fifteen meters away, Amanda clung with both hands to the edge of a rocky ledge no more than a meter across. Her body was jackknifed over the side, folded at the waist, her bloodied arms outstretched, her fingers clutching rock. Ramsey was so close he saw the cords bulging in her forearms as she fought to hang on— a task that was doubly difficult because Dickert clung to *her*, his left hand hooked over the waistband of her jeans and his right wrapped around her right thigh. Dickert was scrabbling, trying to climb up and over Amanda to safety.

"Help!" Dickert's voice was stuttery, panicked. "P-p-plee—p-p-please, please, I don't want to d-d-die, I don't want . . . !"

"Dickert, stop moving. Stop!" Ramsey heaved himself around until he got his rear seated against the rock. Ketchum and his men, too far away, no time, no time! He started scuttling like a crab, moving as fast as he dared and knowing he wouldn't be fast enough. "Dickert, stop! You'll pull her off!"

"Jaaaacck?" Amanda's voice rose like a question, and then he saw her face glistening with tears, and read the strain in her face, the muscles of her neck, her grimace of fear and desperation. "Jack?"

"*Jack!*" Ketchum, far above, too far. "*Jack, get her, get her!*"

"Jack!" Amanda cried, her voice cracking now with exhaustion. "Jack, I can't hold on! I'm slipping, I'm . . . !"

"Heeeellllppp!" Dickert wailed. "Please!"

"Jack!"

"Hold on, baby," Ramsey shouted, "hold on, I'm almost there!" And he was: ten meters, nine, come on, *come on*! He would not let this woman die; he could not because if he did, he might as well fling himself after because there would be nothing left for him afterward, nothing. Do it, do it, *do it*, come on! Dragging in a breath, he launched himself right, pivoting around the long axis of his body until he felt his left hand slap rock. Then he lowered himself down the wall, like a human spider. Almost there, almost there! Not two meters away, and now he could see her eyes, white all around, and now the tears slicking her cheeks. "I'm here, baby, I'm—!"

Then she gasped, a crescendo scream, and her fingers crimped then fumbled—and then he simply stopped thinking. Ramsey dropped his right foot, felt it hit the ledge, and then he was twisting, hanging on with his right hand while his left shot out. He felt flesh, her fingers, and then his palm clamped down around her wrist just as her strength failed. Her fingers slid over his wrist, and then he felt her grab hold, trying to help. He heaved back, roaring with the effort and pain that blossomed in his left shoulder like a fireball. "I've got you, baby, I've got you! I'll get you up, just hold on!"

But he was lying. He could not possibly pull both Amanda and Dickert to the ledge. Even as he strained with all his might, they were, all three, slipping centimeter by inexorable centimeter.

Then, out of the blackness below and ahead, Ramsey heard the whip-crack of a shot. Spotted a sudden flare, there and gone and so fast, he wasn't sure he'd seen it.

But Dickert screamed. Then he let go and fell away.

"JACK!" Amanda shrieked. The sudden movement had jostled her, and she was slipping away. *"JACK!"*

"No, God! *No!*" Ramsey made a frantic grab, snagged her, reeled her in. But they were rolling now, off the ledge and onto a drop-off not quite sixty degrees from true. Ramsey had a sense of something black and huge, and he twisted, clutching Amanda with his left hand and taking the blow with his right shoulder with a stunning, sickening jolt.

And they stopped.

Someone was screaming: Dickert, hurtling through darkness, dragging a keening shriek that stretched and thinned to a single line of sound as sharply etched as a white line on black paper. A scream he sketched on his way down the abyss.

Amanda's voice was shuddery. "Jack, who saved us? Who saved us?"

"I don't know, baby," Ramsey said. He hugged her against his chest, her weight along the length of his body and though he couldn't hear her heart, he felt the wild gallop of her pulse. His arms tightened round. "I don't know."

Dickert fell, bouncing against rock. Blood filled his mouth, and when his left leg snapped, he gurgled in agony. Somehow he was still alive when he slid off the wall: when he was, briefly, airborne without wings, or grace.

He was still alive when he hit the water, a hard slap that shattered his ribs and smashed his spine and drove bone into his right lung. Somehow, he floated even as he drowned in his own blood. His world began to collapse, constricting the way an iris closes down against sudden light.

Then a shadow. Someone? Yes, now there were hands reeling him in from the water. Fingers crawling like spider's legs over his waist, stripping his pack.

"H . . . heh . . . heh . . ." He struggled for breath. "Heeehhhlllppp . . ."

"Of course." A voice that was, oddly, familiar. Then metal on his forehead. The snick of a hammer being cocked.

But, even before the shot, Dickert's world was slipping away, the iris closing to a pinprick and then . . .

Black.

Epilogue

Wednesday, 18 April 3136
1130 hours

The morning dawned bright. The clouds were gone. So was Dani Kodza.

Garibaldi was apoplectic. "Bad enough Limyanovich might've been a Blakist or Kittery Resistance, you got more dead bodies in three, four days than most city blocks in a week, my friend, and some old vigilante cell and God knows who else running around, and now we're talking conspiracy, my friend, and—"

Ketchum cut in, his eyes cop-flat. "Let's get some things real straight, okay? First thing, I'm not your friend. Second, one of those dead bodies wasn't more'n a boy, and the other *was* my friend. Third, don't give me any crap about Kodza. I'm out after a crazy killer, and some baron—"

"Count," Garibaldi interjected.

"Whoever." Ketchum swiped the distinction aside. "Some legate who's probably got his own personal ass wiper, some damned count orders Kodza's release while I'm kinda preoccupied, you're going to chew *my* ass because *your* legate gets *his* spy out of *my* town? Well, let me tell you something, Mr. Garibaldi. I do not rise every day to greet the sun so I can think about how I'm gonna be pleasing you.''

It went on like that until Garibaldi's face got purple as a Denebolan plum, but Ketchum didn't give a centimeter. When it was over and Garibaldi winked out, Ketchum sighed, leaned back, laced his fingers over his middle, and squinted up at Ramsey who stood in his usual place: by the coffeepot, holding up the wall. "That was kinda fun.''

"Not if you end up as the personal servant to the count's ass-wiper.''

"Here's what I don't understand," Amanda said. She shifted in her chair, and winced. There were new bruises on her face and neck, a long gash along her left cheek, and more bruising along her torso and legs but hidden beneath clothing. "Kodza's a spy of some kind, right? Blakist, Kittery Resistance.''

"Clan," Ramsey said.

"Or some other faction we don't know about. She comes all this way because she wants Limyanovich's body, right? But then she disappears, and Limyanovich is *still* here. Dickert took some of Limyanovich's jewelry and I still don't get that.'' She punctuated with a shrug. "I don't get it.''

"Only *one* thing you don't get?'' Ramsey asked. He was marginally better off than Amanda, but that was only because he was pretty beat up to begin with. He went to tuck his hands into his back pockets then winced when the bandages snagged. Carruthers said he didn't need a hand specialist, gave him pain meds, commented on how Ramsey had so much scar tissue and callous from boxing that his skin was already like tanned leather, and then threw in stitches: ten on the left, and eight on the right. The right hand, his gun hand worried him a little. "I'm still trying to digest the idea that there's been this whacked-out, vigilante religious cell of anti-Blakists who still go around tracking down and executing people. And this trinity, Triumvirate, whatever: I mean, talk about overheated imaginations.''

"Well," Ketchum said, "I can see it. Besides, what Kodza said about Isaiah rings true.''

Amanda was solemn. "What's worse is that Doc covered up Isaiah's murder for the wrong reasons." They had discovered from Gillis and the hospital surveillance what Summers wanted to confess. Desperate to secure some peace for his dying wife, Summers had stolen narcotics for his son: a bribe to keep Adam Summers out of their lives. "We might've been able to stop all this."

Ketchum looked glum. "A lot of that was my fault. There was stuff I just didn't see because I didn't want to believe Isaiah could be anything more than an accident. If I'd just *seen* it, I might've been able to help Doc *and* do justice to Isaiah, all at the same time. But this way"—he shrugged—"I got nothing but graves."

Amanda said, "Dickert mentioned data crystals, and Kodza said the same thing. But now Dickert's gone and whatever *he* had is gone and Kodza's gone."

"And what did he want to see again?"

"The jewelry. He took the red diamond." Then she and Ramsey looked at one another, and she said, "Oh, my God."

"What?" Ketchum asked. "What about the diamond?"

"That's just it," Amanda said. "It wasn't a diamond."

"How are the boys?" Ketchum asked.

"Better," Amanda said. "I checked on them after Carruthers let me out of the ER."

"Let you out," Ramsey grunted. "I could hear you yelling all the way down the hall. Let you out."

She ignored him. "As soon as the ICU nurses figured out what was what—about five seconds after Sandra Underhill recognized Dickert—they dialed back Noah's IVs. Carruthers was talking about taking him off the ventilator tonight."

"So he'll be okay."

Amanda's lips curled halfway between a smile and a frown. "Okay? His father is dead, his brother is dead, his mother's in a psychiatric wing, and *he's* lost a chunk of his arm and will need bone grafts. I don't think he's going to be okay, Hank. What I *think* is he'll *live*—probably with his aunt and sister, and not in Farway. He won't be okay for a long time."

"What about Troy?" Ramsey asked.

"He can probably go home tomorrow morning. What happens next is really up to Sandra, but she might leave town, and I'm not sure I blame her." Amanda's eyes held Ketchum. "Small towns don't forgive and forget."

Amanda and Ramsey were just leaving when Amanda turned back and pulled something from her hip pocket. "I almost forgot. Carruthers gave me this when he turned me loose. The nurses said they found it in Noah's pockets. In all the excitement, Carruthers forgot to give it to Hannah, and now, well"—she handed the item over—"he thought I should let you see it."

The two men stared at the gold medal, that blue ribbon for a few seconds, Ketchum turning it this way and that. The sheriff looked a mute question at Ramsey who shook his head and shrugged.

"Guardian?" Ketchum said, finally. "Guardian of *what*?"

Thursday, 19 April 3136

That afternoon, Dickert washed up fifteen klicks downstream: his body bloated and his eyes and lips and nose nibbled away by hungry fish overjoyed at an early season feed. Much later, when Amanda did the cut, she would find Dickert had an assortment of broken bones, a macerated liver, a collapsed lung, and a depressed skull fracture.

She would also find that Dickert had two bullet holes: one in his left flank and the other drilled right between his eyes. The hole in his flank, the one that Ramsey knew came from a rifle because he'd heard the shot, was a 7mm Magnum load of a make Ramsey had never seen or heard of. The second bullet, the one between the eyes, was a .357 Mag of a fairly rare vintage—like, essentially extinct.

The thing was, none of Ketchum's marksmen—and he'd hauled out two—carried 7mm Mags. As for the .357, Ketchum would swear up and down that only one man he knew who'd *ever* owned a handgun that used a bullet that big was Isaiah Schroeder. But a search of Schroeder's gun safe and residence failed to locate the weapon.

Friday, 20 April 3136

After lunch and a bottle of wine, in front of the fire:

Ramsey was drifting off when Amanda said, "In all the excitement, I almost forgot. You remember that weird peak? In Limyanovich's DNA?"

"Mmmm?" Ramsey was warm and a little dozy from good food and wine on top of pain pills. Amanda's head rested on his chest, and Ramsey cupped her head in his left hand. Amanda's hair smelled clean and sweet and a little bit like warm baby powder. "What about it?"

"I finally figured out what that stuff was. It's fish DNA."

"Fish? As in hook and worm?"

"Yup. A Tharkad species that can survive in very extreme, very cold conditions. Essentially, its blood acts as a kind of anti-freeze and they stay alive under the ice for a very, very long time."

"How cold?"

"Cold." She pushed up to stare at him. The bruise and cut along her cheek had swollen her left eye halfway shut, but she still took his breath away. "As in frigid."

"How frigid?"

"Think deep freeze. Think." And now she took a deep breath as if unwilling to finish. But she did. "Think cryohibernation."

The only sound for several seconds was the crackle of the artificial fire and the tick of her antique mantle clock. That and the rumble of Dickert's cat who drowsed on a throw rug at Amanda's feet: a long story.

Finally, Ramsey said, "Cryohibernation. As in keeping someone asleep and *alive* and in deep freeze for a really, really long time?"

Amanda bobbed her head. "Until, maybe, it's time for him to wake up."

Ramsey was silent.

Amanda opened her mouth, shut it. Said: "You remember that medal—Limyanovich's, not Isaiah's—that gold one on the chain? I ran it through the database. It doesn't really match up to anything, but there are two or three symbols that are similar."

"Like?"

She ticked them off on her fingers. "The sword: we know that's World of Blake. But that red heart, it's not a heart. I think it's a teardrop, a red teardrop, or maybe some sort of sun-disk. The only thing that fits is the symbol of this old, isolationist Clan that died out years and years ago. They were called Clan Blood Spirit, and get this. The only name I could find in the database references a *nonexclusive* Bloodname: Zadok." She spelled it, then said, "*Kodza.* It's an anagram."

"For Zadok. Oh, my God," Ramsey said. "You mean, Kodza is *Clan*?"

"It gets even better. In Old Testament times, Zadok was the last true Levitical high priest before the Temple fell, and New Testament prophecy says that when the Messiah comes, the priesthood of Zadok will be reinstituted."

"Jesus Christ."

"No, not Jesus," Amanda said. "Devlin Stone."

Amanda said, "Jack, if we find something more . . . if Kodza, or Zadok or whatever her name is, if even some of what she told us is true, what do we do about it?"

"We hand over the information, that's for damn sure. Then it's not our problem."

"But there might be other people in this cell . . . why are you shaking your head?"

"Kodza got what she came for. Why else would she drop hints and then leave? She knows that there's nothing left of any value or importance here. She gave us a lot of information, only we don't know how much is true, do we? And now she's gone. *They're* gone," he said, and then repeated, "*They're gone.*"

Her face worked, and her eyes were watery-bright. "But this is my town," she whispered. "You said it. We live here. It's our *planet.*"

"I know," Ramsey said. "But it's their Sphere."

That night, Ramsey jerked awake. Amanda's bedroom was dark, and Amanda slept on her side, facing away. He thought he'd heard something but realized after a moment that, no, he'd been dreaming. He stared into the blackness above the bed, trying to recapture what he'd seen in the dream. Something about sunlight, the sun?

Then he knew. Kodza and Zadok and anagrams and double meanings. Threes, and a Triumvirate. And, finally, *Guardian*—and the sun-disk on that medal.

A play on something? Not sun—but Son?

"Wrong question, Hank," he whispered. "It's not guardian of what. It's guardian of *whom*."

Saturday, 21 April 3136
0730 hours

A gray day in the Kendrakes, misty and cool. She had done quite a bit of traveling, mainly to accommodate the Handler who could not afford to draw immediate attention, and so this had eaten time. But time? She had time.

Now Dani Kodza tramped up a mountain path to a cabin nestled in a grove of evergreens. The forest floor was carpeted with fallen needles, and to her right, Kodza heard the splash of water gurgling over rocks. A square of yellow light from one of the cabin's windows played over dead pine needles, and a streamer of blue smoke rose straight up from the chimney because there was no wind.

The front door was unlocked. Inside, she was greeted with the aroma of fresh coffee, cigarette smoke and sweet yeasty bread. A globe threw out a warm, golden, welcoming light, and a lively fire crackled and spit. Kodza inhaled gratefully. "That smells good."

The Handler smiled. "They do say that. Far behind?"

"At last report, I do believe the Bureau was looking toward Zadipos."

The Handler exhaled a snort of smoke. Her chain, with its minutely engraved pendant, shimmered like golden water. "I think I will stay here for a time." Gesturing with a cigarette tweezed between two fingers. "I have everything a person needs: fresh air, trees, solitude."

"And cigarettes."

"True. No need to go back, of course. We have recovered our property, and my work here is done. As I said, I simply needed to stay on for appearances"—a jet of smoke—"and the funerals."

"Mmmm." Kodza inclined her head at a paper sack squared on the table. "Those for me?"

"Yes, very good sweet rolls with pecans that I baked fresh this morning in that very nice wood stove there. Just with three of the rolls? Watch where you bite."

"Excellent. What is it, they say?" Kodza reached for the paper bag. "All good things come in threes?"

"They do." Then Kodza's third and best ghost—the Handler—smiled because all good things did indeed come in threes. "Have a nice trip," Ida Kant said.

1000

The link screamed. Swathed in sheets, Amanda moaned, rolled over, croaked, "ID, audio." When the link told her who was calling, she came alert, said, "Privacy," then plucked up an earbud from her nightstand. She sat up, sheets puddling around her naked, still-bruised middle and poked a hummock of sheet on her right. "I know you're up. You want to take this, or shall I tell dispatch to tell Captain Pearl that you need your beauty sleep?"

Groaning, Ramsey pulled the sheet from his head. "How many people in town *don't* know about us?"

"Life in a small town." Eyes serious, she held out the earbud. "Jack, you better take this. I think it's about McFaine."

"Oh, God." Now Ramsey rolled over, very, very slowly. Amanda was a big bruise, but he was a big bruise plus a whole lot of ache. (All that made for some fairly creative love-making.) Amanda plumped up a pillow, and he pushed to a sit, took the earbud—but didn't screw it in right away.

McFaine. With all that had happened he'd forgotten

about that. If this was bad news, what would he do next? Could he live without his life back there in the city? Without the adrenaline rush that came with putting monsters down? Without the job?

Then he thought back to everything that had happened over one short week, and thought there were plenty of monsters, some in the most unexpected places.

His eyes roved the bedroom, the view of the lake shimmering through glass, the face of the woman who even now simply watched and waited—and he thought back to what she'd said: *I hear your heart.*

It had been so long since anyone had bothered to listen.

"Come here," he said, lifting his left arm. "Snuggle up." And as she slid alongside, he put the bud into his ear and said, "Yeah, it's me. Go ahead. I'm listening."

About the Author

Ilsa J. Bick is a writer as well as a recovering child and forensic psychiatrist. She is the author of prizewinning stories, such as "A Ribbon for Rosie," *Star Trek: Strange New Worlds II*; "Shadows, in the Dark," *Strange New Worlds IV*; and "The Quality of Wetness," *Writers of the Future, Volume XVI*. She's written for BattleCorps.com devoted to the Classic BattleTech universe, including "Memories of Fire and Ice at the Edge of the World" and "Surkai." Her novella, "Break-Away" was the first installment of the *Proliferation Anthology*. She is currently at work on several more Classic BattleTech stories, including "A Mystery Before Dying," part of the anthology *The Wedding Album*.

Other work has appeared in *SCIFICTION*, *Challenging Destiny*, *Talebones*, *Beyond the Last Star*, and *Star Trek: New Frontier: No Limits*, among many others. Her *Star Trek: Starfleet Corps of Engineers* e-book *Lost Time* was released in April 2005 and the SCE two-part e-book *Wounds* appeared in August and September 2005. Also forthcoming is "Bottomless" in the *Star Trek: Voyager* anniversary anthology *Distant Shores*.

Her first published novel, *Star Trek: The Lost Era: Well of Souls*, cracked the 2003 Barnes & Noble Bestseller List. She is the author of *Daughter of the Dragon*, a MWDA novel chronicling the rise of Katana Tormark. She is currently at work on a sequel, *Dragon Rising*, slated for release in 2006.

When she isn't working, she enjoys long bike rides, obsessive exercise, martinis—and the occasional breakdown.